SMOULDER

LAURELL K. HAMILTON

SMOULDER

HEADLINE

First published in the USA in 2023 by
BERKLEY
An imprint of Penguin Random House LLC

First published in Great Britain in 2023 by
HEADLINE PUBLISHING GROUP

1

Cataloguing in Publication Data is available from the British Library

Hardback ISBN 978 1 4722 8538 6
Trade Paperback ISBN 978 1 4722 8539 3

Offset in 11.25/16.25pt Janson Text LT Std by Jouve (UK), Milton Keynes

Printed and bound in Great Britain by Clays Ltd, Elcograf S.p.A.

Headline's policy is to use papers that are natural, renewable and recyclable
products and made from wood grown in well-managed forests and other
controlled sources. The logging and manufacturing processes are expected
to conform to the environmental regulations of the country of origin.

HEADLINE PUBLISHING GROUP
An Hachette UK Company
Carmelite House
50 Victoria Embankment
London EC4Y 0DZ

www.headline.co.uk
www.hachette.co.uk

This book is dedicated to everyone who has had the courage to face their personal demons and fight.

SMOULDER

1

EDWARD STOOD IN front of the half circle of mirrors getting fitted for the wedding clothes he'd be wearing as best man in my wedding. I'd been his best man/person less than a year ago, so turnabout was fair play. He was even hating the clothes almost as much as I hated the formal-length dress that his bride had forced me to wear at the last moment when I thought I'd get away with a tux like the men. Now it was his turn to think he'd get to wear a tux and find out he was half right. Since I was marrying someone who either designed or helped design most of his own clothes, Jean-Claude had ideas for spicing up the traditional boring clothes that most modern men wore. Normally his fashion sense wouldn't have bothered Edward, who had a very traditional style, but now as he glared at himself in the mirror he was bothered, very bothered.

"You have got to be kidding me," he said. His blue eyes were already starting to turn pale like winter skies, which usually meant he was about to kill something, or that he wanted to kill something.

Peter, his very grown-up son, and I sat in little chairs that were usually reserved for mothers of the bride, or other members of the female side of the wedding, because men didn't have to come to the designer wedding couture side—ever. Edward was my bestest friend, but I grinned at him, because I was enjoying the men getting outfitted in something they hated so much more than any normal tux.

"You look great," I said, smiling, and that at least was true, unlike me in every bridesmaid dress I'd ever been forced to wear.

He looked to Peter for a different opinion. "This is ridiculous." He spread his arms out to his sides so that Peter could get the full effect of the black leather and cloth tailcoat with its high, stiff collar that framed about half of Edward's head. His blond hair looked brighter yellow than I'd ever seen it, maybe it was the black leather framing it? Or maybe it was his desert tan, which wasn't tanned by most standards, but it was the most color I'd ever seen on Edward's skin.

"Except for the collar, the jacket looks great on you, and the collar isn't bad, it's just"—Peter made a waffling motion with his hand—"it's odd, like it shouldn't be there, but I really like the leather over the shoulders, and the scalloped leather over the forearm looks like a leather bracer from armor. It's really cool, Ted." Peter's desert tan was a lot darker than Edward's; technically they were stepson and stepfather, but for them it wasn't about genetics, it was about love.

Edward's glare softened a little and turned back to the mirrors. He took a visible deep breath and let it out slowly as if he were counting to ten. He pulled on the edges of the jacket as if it needed to be settled in place, but it fit him perfectly; the little bump of the tails on the coat actually drew the eyes to his ass, and since we had never ever been anything but friends I didn't usually notice Edward's body like that. I'd thought of tailcoats as old-fashioned until I saw the first of our wedding party in them and realized that they actually accentuated everyone's booty a lot more than modern jackets did.

"Why do I hate this so much, besides the stand-up collar?" he asked.

"Maybe it's just so different from your usual cowboy–U.S. Marshal aesthetic?" Peter suggested.

I looked at Edward, and finally said, "It's the most fitted thing

I've seen you in since you slimmed down for your wedding. You look slender, more . . . delicate almost, and in all the years we've been friends, *delicate* has never been a word I used for you."

He nodded at himself in the mirror. "That's what it is, I look smaller even to me."

"You're in the fiercest shape I've ever seen you in, unless you've put on weight since I saw you at the pool during the wedding trip. You're all muscle. Hell, Ed"—and I had to stop and force myself to say, "Ted, I didn't even know you had a six-pack under there until that weekend."

"I hadn't. Not since I was in the military twenty years ago, so never since you've known me."

"All the moms and most of the daughters at martial arts class think I have the hottest dad and that includes the male instructors." Peter said it with a touch of pride, unlike some twenty-year-old sons who would have felt competitive with their fathers. Of course, Edward had never been competitive with Peter either.

"High praise, I take it, since I haven't seen your instructors," I said.

Peter grinned. "Yep."

"Since you're one of the instructors now, very high praise," Edward said, and he smiled at his son with a pride that I never thought I'd ever see in his eyes for anyone. When we first met, Edward and I had both been so alone, and neither of us had ever expected that to change. Now here we were, both of us happier than I'd ever seen us. Sometimes life was good.

Peter looked embarrassed but pleased.

"Why didn't you tell me you'd made instructor, Peter? Congratulations."

"It's just part-time."

"But you're still in college, so part-time is all you can really do," I said.

"There's really not a lot of money in owning a good martial arts school, and instructors make less. You have to be a belt factory or offer kickboxing as a fitness class or something sell-out like that to earn enough money to pay full-time staff, full-time wages," Peter said.

"You talked to Bill like I suggested," Edward said.

"Bill owns the school," Peter explained to me, "and yes, I talked to him. I'd need another job that paid better if I wanted to be full-time at the dojo." He made quote marks with his fingers when he said *full-time*.

"How's the double major going?" I asked.

"I'm really enjoying Preternatural Primates this semester. I never knew how many species of trolls there were, and did you hear new DNA testing split the Yeti into three species instead of just the two?"

"Really? I hadn't heard about that."

"I can send you the link to the article our prof shared with us."

"Please," I said.

"But now I want to see some of the trolls we have in this country in person."

"I've seen the Lesser Smoky Mountain Trolls." I almost added that I knew someone who had their doctorate on the trolls, but the person in question was my ex, Richard Zeeman, and the last time Peter had seen him, someone we both knew had died. Today was a good day; we didn't need to rake up horrible memories and ruin it.

"Really, when?"

"They're indigenous to the area of Tennessee where one of my mentors lives. I don't remember if I've talked to you about Marianne."

"The witch who helped you learn to control your magic, right?"

"Yeah, I guess I did talk about her."

He shook his head. "Nathaniel told me after the trip when he went with you and Micah to try and learn how the magical energy worked between the three of you."

I knew that Nathaniel talked to Peter even more than I did, and

Marianne was out of the broom closet as a witch, so I guess it was okay that Nathaniel shared. Besides . . . I looked at his eager face so happy in college, learning new things that he'd call up to share, and realized that I trusted Peter. He knew how to keep secret whatever needed kept.

"Your face went all serious, Anita, what are you thinking about?" he asked.

I smiled. "My first thought was that what Nathaniel had shared could get Marianne in trouble, and then I realized that I trusted you. Trusted your judgment, trusted you to keep secret what needs keeping."

He smiled at me like I'd said something wonderful; maybe I had, but it was one of the best smiles I'd seen on his face since he got to watch his parents walk down the aisle together. "Thanks, Anita, that means a lot."

"You've earned it, Peter."

"He's starting to like his biology classes better than his criminal justice ones," Edward said, still tugging at the perfectly tailored coat.

"Are you still fast-tracked for preternatural law enforcement, or did the trolls lure you to the biology side?"

"I still want to be a preternatural marshal like you and Ted, but I failed my blood test for lycanthropy so they're letting me stay in the program, but they aren't sure about my future in it."

"I'm sorry, Peter, really," I said, and patted his arm.

"It's not your fault, Anita."

"You got hurt protecting me."

"If I hadn't been there the weretiger would have killed you. I don't regret what I did, and you shouldn't either."

I looked at that calm, wise face, and thought, *When did he get so grown-up?* "I'll do my best to be all healthy and therapy-evolved, but I am sorry that you popping hot on the test is keeping you out of the military and law enforcement."

"I don't shift, and my test is undetermined just like Ted's."

"And it's my fault both times."

"I'm still a marshal, and that you and I got to keep our badges sets a good precedent for Peter to get into law enforcement."

"True, but if it's my blood getting all up in your wounds when we were both cut up by wereanimals, why don't both of you show full-blown Therianthropy at least on the test? I mean I don't change form either, but my test always comes back listing every type of Therianthropy I have inside me."

"The doctors don't know," Ted said.

"They were interested in the fact that both Ted and I test the same because we were father and son and they thought they had a theory, until they found out we're not genetically related."

"I went in with Peter last time so the doctors could talk to us together."

"And draw more blood," Peter said.

Edward nodded. "And draw more blood."

"Dr. Lillian wants to draw more blood tomorrow from both of you and from me so she can compare it. Sorry."

"No, we came here to figure out what's happening to us," Edward said, then tugged on the jacket as if it didn't fit right, but I'd never seen him in a piece of clothing that fit him better and that included the tux he'd worn for his own wedding.

"And to try on beautiful wedding clothes," I said, smiling.

The seamstress rejoined us then; she had the pants that were supposed to go with the jacket instead of the temporary ones that she'd forced Edward into so she could see how the jacket fit. The pants were black leather.

"You are so going to owe me for this," Edward said.

"One, I've seen you wear leather for undercover work before. Two, I wore a formal-length dress on a beach with bedazzled flip-flops for your wedding."

"That was not this bad," he said, motioning at the pants that the patient woman was holding up for him.

"I tried on dresses that were so low that I flashed an entire bridal store when I tripped over the hem."

He grinned, then shook his head. "Okay, that's fair."

"If I said I'm sorry I missed you trying on dresses, would you be mad?" Peter asked.

"Yes," I said firmly.

He and Edward both laughed. I tried to hold out, but I finally gave in, and we laughed until Edward had to go into the changing room and get into the freshly hemmed leather pants.

2

PETER AND I were still sitting in the chairs listening to Edward curse as he wiggled into the pants when my phone rang. It was my dad's ringtone; my stomach dropped into my shoes with dread, but I answered it.

"Hey, Dad, what's up?"

"You're going through with this wedding no matter what I say, aren't you?"

I stood up and said, "Jesus, Dad, yes, I am marrying Jean-Claude no matter what you say."

Peter startled in his chair and stared up at me like he couldn't believe it either. Who could? My father just kept talking all the hate about the man I loved. "He's a vampire, Anita; in the eyes of the Church he's a suicide at best, and at worst he's a demon-possessed corpse."

"We've discussed the Catholic Church's view on vampires for a few weeks now, Dad. Tell me something new."

"I know the wedding is a big event, but can't you just live with each other without getting married?"

"I can't believe you're encouraging me to live in sin with a vampire. I thought that was one of the things you hated about all the people in my life?"

"If it's a choice of cohabitating with one of them or marrying one, then I know which is my preference for my daughter."

"I am not canceling the wedding, Dad, and the fact that you keep asking is really starting to piss me off."

"No need to use language like that, Anita."

"The hell there isn't. You're the one who's insulting me and Jean-Claude. You wouldn't even come to St. Louis and meet him in person before passing judgment on him."

"He's a vampire, Anita, I don't have to meet him."

"Fine, then if that's your last word I guess I'll find someone else to give me away, or walk my own damn self down the aisle."

"I'm coming to St. Louis to meet your fiancé."

"What?"

"I'm coming to meet him and I'm coming to get fitted in the wedding clothes. I don't understand why there will be multiple fittings for a tuxedo, but you told me if I don't come now for the first fitting I can't be in the wedding at all."

"So, you're going to be in the wedding, just like that?"

"No, I'm coming for the fitting so that I have the option to be in the wedding. I need to meet this . . . your fiancé. I can't believe you're going to marry him, but I want to meet him before you do. I want to try and have a more open mind about it."

I just stood there holding the phone, not sure what to say. My face must have looked more shocked than I felt, because Peter stood up and hovered near me as if he wasn't sure how I'd take a hug, but he was thinking about risking it.

"I'm sorry that my beliefs are making your wedding difficult, Anita. I want to walk you down the aisle, I just don't know if I can hand you over to a . . . vampire."

"I know, Dad. You raised me to believe they were monsters, inhuman, so it wasn't murder to kill them. If you had raised me differently I would never have become a vampire executioner and never met Jean-Claude."

"The irony is not lost on me, Anita."

"Good, when are you coming into town?"

"I'm working on arranging for someone to cover my practice here, so next week, if it's not too late. We'll stay at a hotel since I know you already have guests at your house who are going to be in the wedding."

"Okay, wow, that's quick, you surprised me, Dad."

"In a good way, I hope."

"Yeah, good, but I honestly had given up on you even meeting Jean-Claude, let alone entertaining the idea of giving me away."

"I still haven't decided on that, but Judith showed me that article you sent about vampires not going brain-dead, which means that they don't technically die. If medical technology can prove that vampires aren't the walking dead, then the Church needs to know about the new studies."

"That's great, Dad, thank Judith for me."

"You can thank her yourself when we get there."

"Great, I'll do that. Text me your flight details and I'll have someone meet you at the airport."

"Someone, not you?"

I took a deep breath and let it out while I counted slowly. The guilt-tripping had already begun, and he wasn't even here yet. "Dad, I'm in the middle of planning a wedding bigger than the last royal one, or that's how it feels, plus I'm still working, and I've got friends here from out of town for the wedding. My schedule is a little smashed, but I or someone will meet your plane."

"Fine, is there a hotel that you'd recommend for us?"

"We've got some hotel rooms reserved for out-of-town guests; when you know your exact dates let me know and I'm sure we can arrange rooms since it's this far ahead of the wedding. I'll text you with the information."

"Text Judith or Josh, I'm not a big one for texting."

"Will do. Wait, is Josh coming, too? I need to know how many rooms we'll need."

"Four rooms, but I'll pay for our rooms. I don't want to take hospitality from . . . your fiancé."

"Wait, four rooms? You and Judith get one, Josh is two, is Andria coming?"

"Yes."

"You aren't going to make her and Kevin sleep in separate rooms at the hotel while they're here, are you? They've been living together for years, Dad."

"No, I'm not going to make Andria and her fiancé sleep separately on the trip."

"So, Andria and Kevin are the third room; who needs a fourth room, Dad?"

"We'll see you next week."

"If you hang up on me without telling me who the fourth room is for, then don't bother coming."

"You don't mean that, Anita."

"The fuck I don't."

"We did not raise you to use language like that."

"Fuck it, Dad, I am not playing these passive-aggressive games with you anymore. You tell me who the fourth room is for right now."

"I don't take well to demands, Anita, especially from my children."

"I'm thirty-two, Dad, I'm not a child, and as one adult to another and your hostess, I deserve to know who is coming to visit me."

"Your grandmother wants to help convince you . . ."

"No, fuck no, hell no!"

"Anita, please don't keep using language like that."

"Language? Dad, that woman verbally and emotionally abused me as a child."

"'Abuse' is a strong word, Anita."

"Motherfucking son of a bitch!" I realized I was yelling when

Edward asked what was wrong through the door. I heard Milligan and Craven, tonight's bodyguards, keeping people out of the changing rooms. Milligan poked his head in; I waved him away and Peter tried to explain to Edward.

"Anita Katerine Blake, we raised you to be a lady."

"You raised me to be a lot of things, Dad."

"Your grandmother is worried about your immortal soul, and so am I."

"Dad, if you bring Grandma Blake then you aren't coming with an open mind about me marrying Jean-Claude, because she will close your mind to anything but her hatred and prejudice against anything supernatural."

"Momma is a good old-school Catholic, there's nothing wrong with that."

"She burned me when I was fourteen, so I'd know what hell felt like, Dad. She thought it would encourage me to stop using my powers to raise the dead."

"What? You told me that was an accident."

"No, Dad, she told you it was an accident."

"Why didn't you tell me?"

"You hadn't believed me about anything else, why bother?"

"That was a second-degree burn, Anita."

"I know, Dad, trust me, I remember."

"You should have told me."

"Told you that your beloved saint of a mother pinned my arm and forced a candle flame against my skin?"

"She said you were playing with the candle, and it fell."

"You don't get second-degree burns from a falling candle if you can move out of the way, Dad."

He was quiet on the other end of the phone. I just let the silence build because I didn't know what else to say. It had taken me months of therapy to own the memory, and not try to find some explanation for what happened that would exonerate my father for not protecting me. Nothing would ever exonerate my grandmother. She could rot in the hell she was so fond of for all I cared.

I heard him talking to someone on his end. "She says you hit her."

"She was burning my arm with an open flame."

"She had a bruise on her face, said she fell when you burned yourself. Did you hit your grandmother?"

"You taught me to fight, Dad, what else was it for except to protect myself?"

"You punched your grandmother in the face?"

I yelled, "She was burning my arm, telling me that I'd burn like that all over my body forever if I didn't give up my evil ways. I protected myself, used what you taught me and saved myself from a third-degree burn or worse."

"I can't believe this happened the way you're telling it, Anita."

"You always believed her." I wasn't yelling now, I wasn't even angry, I was tired, so tired.

"You both had marks on you, I might have believed you."

"Might, might?" The anger was back, the anger I'd always believed had been from my mother's death, but therapy had helped me pull memories from childhood that explained my rage. It wasn't like I'd forgotten what happened, more like my family repeated their version so often that I just accepted it. My family loved me, even my grandmother loved me, they wouldn't hurt me like that on purpose, right? Right? Wrong, so fucking wrong.

"Anita, I'm sorry."

"Sorry for what, Dad?" My voice was calm, too calm. It wasn't the right reaction to this much emotion; I knew now that it was both a protective mechanism and a destructive one. Protective because it helped me get through the moment, but destructive because the stuffed emotions that I should have been experiencing just got buried and resurfaced all over my life for years.

"I'm sorry you were hurt. I'm sorry you felt you had to strike your grandmother."

"She plays the martyr to perfection, Dad, she always did."

"Anita, please."

"Please what, Dad?"

"I love you both."

"If you say so, Dad."

"I love you, Anita."

"I love you, too, Dad. Thanks for teaching me how to box, because she never laid a hand on me after that. I guess I really did have a mean right hook, just like you said."

"I don't know what to say."

"Then let's hang up, because I don't know what to say either."

"I love you," he said.

"Yeah, I love you, too, Dad." My voice was still even and unemotional, the way you'd say *I love you* if you didn't mean it at all, but that wasn't it. I did love my dad, I just wished like hell I didn't, because if I didn't then I could have told him to go to hell and never darken my door again. If I didn't love my family, I could have been done with them and just been happy in the life I'd built, but I did love them and there is always that fragile part of you, that inner-child part, that wants your family to love you, to protect you even if they didn't. Part of us wants them to say sorry and make it up to us. We want our Hallmark movie moment that almost never really happens outside of the movies. I was a U.S. Marshal with the highest number of executions in the service, I knew better than to hope like that, but hope is a lying bitch that strings you along with just enough promise that you don't want to give up. Damn it, damn it!

Peter stood beside me not saying anything; he started to try and hug me, which would have been a mistake, but then he held out his hand to me. I didn't take it, but he just left it there open and waiting if I wanted to hold on to something. I didn't need to hold on to anything or anyone, and the moment I thought it I realized why I had isolated myself for so long: because that was safer. If I didn't depend on anyone but myself, then nobody got close enough to hurt me again. I'd lived like that, protected myself like that, and been miserable and terribly alone.

Peter's hand was just there if I wanted to take it, no demands, no force, no presumption. He was pretty damned smart for twenty. I hadn't been that smart at twenty. Hell, I wasn't sure I was that smart now. I took his hand, and he slowly wrapped his fingers around mine, but he didn't try for more, he waited for me. My chest hurt; brokenhearted in books and movies is reserved for romantic love, but all kinds of love can break your heart. My eyes burned, my throat was tight like I was choking; what the hell was wrong with me?

"It's okay, Anita," he said, voice low and soft the way you talk jumpers off ledges, "whatever you're feeling is okay."

I tried to say *I'm all right*, or something else sensible, but what came out was a sob and what came next was another. I collapsed against Peter, and he caught me the way I'd caught him once when he was small and bad things had happened. I cried into his chest like a freaking child because bad things had happened, and no one had protected me. I had saved myself; I was still saving myself and everyone else, but in that moment I let Peter save a little piece of me, a piece that was still fourteen and hadn't realized that my grandmother hated me more than she loved me, and that I hated her right back.

3

THE CRYING HAD almost stopped. I was just standing there with my arms around Peter's waist while he held me in place, and I leaned against him. I felt light and airy, and quiet inside like the world after a storm wiped it clean. It didn't feel much like me.

Peter hugged me carefully and said, "I've always wanted to hold you in my arms, but this wasn't how I pictured it."

It made me laugh, just a little. "Didn't meet expectations, huh?" I said, sighing with my head still resting on his chest.

"In some ways, no." He stroked his hand down the back of my hair.

I raised my head up and away from the touch. It was borderline between comfort and more.

"But in other ways, totally exceeded expectations." He smiled down at me, and it was a good smile full of all the years we'd known each other, all the things we'd been through together, how much we'd both grown, though mine had been more internal instead of gaining ten inches of height like he had. "Thank you for trusting me," he said, and just like that I knew he understood how much it had cost me to fall apart and how much I had to trust anyone to let them catch me while I did it.

"Thanks for being trustworthy," I said.

"Oh, when a woman calls you trustworthy you're so in the friend-zone." He made a dramatic face to go with the comment. It made me laugh and start to push away as the far curtain opened and a vampire and a werehyena came through. Asher, the vampire, was tall with long golden hair that he wore loose to hide half his face. The half that showed looked almost artificial in its beauty. Kane, the werehyena, was tall, dark, and sullenly handsome. The vampire said, "Anita, what's wrong?" The hyena said, "Found another man to fuck, I don't know how you find the time."

I wanted to punch Kane in the face, but I debated whether the comment was enough to justify it, or just my anger with my family talking. Peter beat me to it, moving faster than I'd ever seen him move. One second we were holding each other, the next he was across the room punching Kane in the solar plexus with his right hand, so hard it doubled him over, then bringing his left elbow into the side of Kane's face. Kane tried to stand up, swung at him, and Peter raised his left arm to block the blow just in case, but he was already coming up under Kane's chin with as pretty an undercut as I'd seen in a while. Kane fell over backward, and the fight was over.

"I've never seen you move that fast, Peter," Edward said from behind us in the door of the dressing room.

"Or hit that hard," I said.

Peter was staring at his hands like he couldn't quite believe what he'd just done. Apparently, he hadn't seen himself move like that before either.

Asher looked at his fallen lover and then at Peter and then back to Kane. "I apologize for what Kane said, it was inexcusably rude, but could we begin with verbal insults before resorting to violence next time?"

Milligan was back through the curtains with Craven at his heels. Milligan had his pale hair newly military cut. He kept trying to grow it out since testing positive for lycanthropy had gotten him a medical discharge from the Navy, but he hated it touching his ears.

Craven was so newly discharged that his black hair was still in its original high and tight. It seemed weird to have Milligan on duty without his usual partner, Custer, but we'd divided all the more experienced military security among the newer guys who were still transitioning from career military to civilian security. It was a good idea, but I still missed Custer, and Milligan was a lot less chatty and comfortable to be around with the newbie.

Milligan said, "Blake, if you're going to pick fights with shapeshifters I'm going to have to stay on this side of the curtain."

"If Kane's involved it might be for the best," I said.

Craven knelt and checked for the pulse in Kane's neck.

"He's a werehyena, I didn't hit him that hard," Peter said, but his voice held a note of panic.

"He's alive," Asher said, but not with the emotion you'd expect about the news. Kane's cruel streak had started to wear thin on everyone.

"He's got a pulse," Craven said.

I heard Peter let out a breath, his shoulders slumping with relief.

"And that's the other reason we're here," Edward said.

"Can you move like that now, too?" I asked.

He shook his head. "Neither of us has ever moved like that. We're stronger and faster, but not like that."

Peter backed far enough away from Kane so he might have some warning if the werehyena came to and wanted to have a rematch. He backed up until he was standing by Edward. Peter looked pale. "I don't know what happened."

"You cleaned his clock," I said.

"You lost control of your temper," Edward said.

Peter just nodded. "Worse than I have in a long time."

"I taught you to fight, and you've learned more at the dojo, but with those skills comes responsibility and judgment about when to use them and how hard to go at it. Today was not the moment to go this hard, Peter," Edward said.

"I know that, I really do, but he said what he said after Anita had talked to her dad on the phone and it was . . . I lost control. I don't have an excuse for it, but I'm sorry."

"You didn't lose control," I said, "that was very controlled, very precise."

"I wanted to hurt him, Anita, that's not okay. I'm too big and too strong, and now it's even worse. I have to control my emotions as much as I do the physical stuff, or someone will get hurt and I could end up arrested."

"Well, if you hit a human this hard someone could get dead," Craven said.

"I don't want to kill someone by accident," Peter said. He suddenly looked scared, the shadow of the boy I'd first met on his face. I didn't blame him.

"You're here to work out with us, right?" Milligan said.

Peter nodded.

"We'll teach you how to manage your new strength and speed, and how to hide it."

"Yeah, that, too. I mean, if I moved like that in the dojo they'd all know."

"You were fast, kid, but not as fast as we are," Craven said.

Peter looked at him. "Are you serious?"

Craven smiled that smile that big, athletic men have been smiling since the first one realized he was bigger and stronger than everyone else.

"They are serious," Asher said, "and please remember that when Kane comes to, he will take this as a grave insult."

"Is that a threat?" Edward asked.

"No, it is a warning. As I become healthier and less prone to being what Anita calls a shit stirrer, Kane is getting worse. He's only here today for my fitting because he didn't trust me out of his sight."

"The jealousy issues are that much worse?" I asked.

"I fear so."

"How much worse, since we're supposed to be keeping everyone safe?" Craven asked.

Milligan answered, "You haven't been around Kane much, but he'll probably try and tear the kid up next time he sees him."

Asher lowered his head, putting his hands in front of his face like he might weep or didn't want to see Kane lying on the floor. He shoved his hands back through his hair so it pulled back completely, exposing the scars on the left side of his face. It let me know how upset he was, because he would never have done that in front of so many people if he'd been thinking about it.

Peter gasped.

Asher froze and then very slowly moved his hands so his hair would fall back like a dark golden curtain to hide behind again. He spoke with his face still hidden. "If Kane wakes and the young man is still here, he will attack him. He can take such an insult to his honor from Anita and others at the apex of our power structure, but he is too insecure to take it from anyone he perceives as less able." He never moved his head at all while he spoke, so his hair was all we could see of his face. He didn't even show us the unmarked side of his face, which meant all his issues had been hit hard by that one small sound.

"If everyone is okay with it, we'll just send Kane to the medical area at the Circus of the Damned so he can wake up there," Milligan said.

"Fine with me," I said.

"Yes," Asher said, still unmoving as if he was afraid to give Peter a second look at his face.

I walked over to Asher as Milligan picked Kane up like a sack of potatoes, putting him in a fireman's carry over one of his shoulders.

"What if he has a spinal injury?" Peter asked.

"Kid, if his spine was injured he'd either be dead or it'll heal no matter what," Milligan said, and then he walked out while Craven held the curtain for him.

He hesitated in the doorway and said, "We're not supposed to leave you without someone to watch your back."

"We've got her back," Edward said. I was a little uncomfortable with Peter being part of that *we*, but he had earned the right to be included.

Milligan yelled back, "If Forrester says he has her, he has her. Now let's get the werehyena to medical before he comes to."

Craven almost saluted, remembered in time, and hurried to catch up with Milligan.

I tried to stand in front of Asher, but he moved just enough so that his hair was between me and seeing any of his face. I hadn't seen him this insecure in maybe ever. Damn it. I reached up to touch his hair, but he moved just out of reach, so I dropped my hand to his arm. Which he let me hold, but he was immobile under my touch like he was trying not to be there.

"Asher, please," I said.

"I'm sorry," Peter said.

"Your reaction was honest, don't be sorry for that," Asher said, but his voice held bitterness that made the words a lie.

"It wasn't for the reason you think."

"Now you will tell me that I don't know my own mind. You do have the arrogance of youth and beauty."

"I'm young but I'm not beautiful, not compared to you," Peter said.

Asher made a sound that was too bitter to be a laugh, but I didn't have another word for it. He pulled away from my hand and I didn't fight him over it. I had my own issues to work today, I didn't have enough energy left over to deal with one of Asher's famous fits. He was gorgeous, but eventually beauty and great sex aren't enough.

Peter said, "You're so good at hiding the scars with your hair that I forget they are there."

"Good that you can forget that I am ruined."

"All you let me see is the perfect parts of you physically. Nicky lets me see the scars where he lost his eye now, so it's part of him, but you never seem to treat your scars that way."

"Oh, they are very much a part of me, a part that I can never forget. I have wished often that vampires had no reflections like in movies, because then it would not be a constant reminder of what I have lost."

"If that is how you feel, Asher, then why don't you go back to consult with the plastic surgeon? He was hopeful about helping you," I said.

He just shook his head hard enough that his hair moved but never showed any of his face. Peter was right, Asher had spent centuries using his hair to shield his face. He always seemed to know where every shadow or patch of light would hit him and what it would show. He used all of it to keep his scars hidden. The scars didn't cover that much of his face because he could keep the hair over it while looking at someone with both eyes and most of his face, but it wasn't my face, it wasn't me who had gone from the kind of beauty that would make people gasp in wonder, to scars that made people gasp like Peter had.

I felt Jean-Claude like a distant dream down the metaphysical connection between us. He was being subtle because if Asher sensed his presence then he would say that I didn't want him except through Jean-Claude's eyes. Since I was beginning to agree with that, it was hard to argue. I'd only been in an off-again, on-again relationship with Asher for a few years; Jean-Claude had been trying for centuries. That breath of power asked me in emotions to please try. Jean-Claude could have simply spoken in my mind, but that much power between us and Asher would have sensed it happening.

I reached for his hand. He startled, his hand tensing under my touch. He darted a glance at me, a flash of those ice-blue eyes through the wilderness of his golden hair. "Why would you want to touch me when you have unblemished youth before you?"

I settled my hand more securely in his; Jean-Claude was gone from the part of me where I could feel it, because touching made all our powers stronger. If Asher realized that it hadn't been just my idea to hold his hand, then it would have made things worse. "You know that Peter and I aren't an item."

"Only a lover will defend someone's honor so swiftly and so decisively."

"Any suggestions, Ted?" Peter asked.

"You made the mess, you clean it up, that's the rule; besides, this isn't the part of Anita's life that I help out with, and I'm good with the division of labor."

Peter took a few steps toward us and my hand in Asher's kept him from moving away. Peter took the hint, though, and stopped where he was, giving the vampire the space he seemed to need. "Somewhere in all that talking, did you imply that you're jealous of me?" Peter asked, *so* not what I thought he would lead with.

Asher laughed, and it was so bitter it felt like broken glass in my ears just to hear it.

"No vampire mind tricks," Edward said, "or I will join in, and you don't want that."

"No," Asher said, "I do not. My apologies, for losing control for a moment."

"You didn't go off your meds, did you?" I asked, because this was the moody Asher of old, not the one who had taken his therapy so seriously that they'd found meds that worked on a vampire, which hadn't been easy. The doctor was writing a paper on it because it was a first. Finding meds that evened out Asher's brain chemistry had made an amazing difference. He was healthier than he'd ever been, and we were all happier for it, except for Kane, apparently.

"No, I did not go off my meds, but I can understand why you asked." He squeezed my hand gently.

"If the meds are still working, then what's wrong?" I asked.

"The medicine clears my head and helps my heart be less tempestuous, but now the true work of therapy begins. I am finding that working on internal issues is far more challenging than I had imagined."

I squeezed his hand back and said, "I'm proud of you for working your issues, instead of letting them work you."

"It's so hard to do the work in therapy; I'm sorry that I made it worse," Peter said.

"You are young, you don't know any better."

"Let me try to do better; first can I say something without you taking it as flirting, because I don't like men, so I don't mean it that way, but I want to try and explain."

Asher laughed again and it was bitter, but it didn't hurt to hear it. He was trying, too. "You are safe from my advances. I would not want to be with anyone who reacts to me as you did."

"It's not the scars, it's the fact that you have one of the most beautiful faces I've ever seen. I think that every time I see you, but this is the first time you've ever let me see your whole face."

"I'm sorry you found it revolting."

"No, that's not it," Peter said, reaching out as if he were trying to pull the words from the air. "I knew you were scarred by holy water and I knew that it burns like acid on vampire skin, but theory is different from seeing it."

"So much worse than you imagined," Asher said, and tried to pull his hand away from me; when I didn't let him go he let me keep holding him, but it was like his hand was only there for politeness' sake. I had to breathe through the anger that started to boil up inside me. I really didn't have the emotional spoons left for Asher today, but for Jean-Claude's sake I kept trying.

"Damn it," Peter said, "I'm not saying this right, but the scars aren't that bad, it just surprised me, and it was shitty of me to react like that. I'm sorry."

"Apology accepted," Asher said, but his voice said plainly that he didn't mean it.

"Asher, what does he have to do to make this better?" I asked, shaking his hand, trying to get him to look at me.

"How did you word it, that I was unblemished youth?" Peter

pulled the hem of his T-shirt up with one hand, exposing the scars on his upper stomach that traced over one side of his chest. I knew they went up onto one shoulder, but the shirt would have to come off to see them. The scars looked like what they were, claw marks. It had been a weretiger that meant to kill me; both Peter and I almost died, but I'd had enough magic to heal completely, and he hadn't.

Asher turned with his hair swinging to hide the scarred side of his face, but he gave the full perfection of the other side of his profile so he could look at the scars that traced Peter's body. "I am a fool, please forgive me for forgetting that I am not the only one who has suffered."

Peter let his shirt fall back into place. "I don't let people see me without a shirt much, even the girls who say they don't mind, how can they not? The girls who like the scars seem to like them more than the rest of me, and that's creepy for a different reason."

Peter had never mentioned any of this to me, but he was sharing with Asher and the rest of us, because he was trying to make up for making Asher self-conscious. It was brave and smart. I was so proud of him I'd have hugged him if I hadn't thought that would make things worse again.

"I have had lovers over the centuries who preferred their lovers scarred, but you are right, you are your scars to them, not yourself."

"Exactly," Peter said.

"I knew that you had risked your life to save Anita from a shapeshifter, but I did not think what that would mean for someone who was not a shapeshifter or vampire. Again, my apologies for assuming that because you were young you did not have your own wounds."

"It's okay, most people see someone my age and assume the same thing."

"I try not to be that ordinary," Asher said.

"You could never be ordinary," I said, smiling up at him.

He finally smiled down at me just a little. I could only truly see

Asher through the lens of all the centuries he and Jean-Claude had been together first as rivals, then as lovers and best friends, then as bitter enemies, and now they/we were figuring out what the hell we all were again. They were like some star-crossed lovers who kept reincarnating lifetime after lifetime trying to get it right, except it was all one lifetime, just a really long one.

I missed Asher in the bedroom and in a few other places, and I knew that Jean-Claude missed him more, which made me say, "Now, do I finally get a hello kiss?"

Asher gave a real smile this time, the one that traveled all the way to the long curving scar that was closest to the kissable bow of his mouth. I loved that smile, because it was real, not calculated to hide his scars. It made me smile for just myself without Jean-Claude needing to interfere. I wanted to love Asher, he just made it so damn hard sometimes.

"Whatever my lady desires," he said, and bent that six feet, one inch of height down as I went up on my tiptoes to meet him partway. His lips were as soft as ever, the kiss gentle; his arms started to wrap around me, but I put a hand between us, keeping our bodies from touching completely and from him holding me too tightly.

He drew back immediately. "Will you never forgive me for that one cruel kiss?"

"If I'd been human I'd have needed stitches and weeks, or months, to be able to kiss, or eat, or so many things without hurting. Hell, I could have ended up with scars and my mouth would never look like this again."

He turned away from me then. "Did you mean to be cruel?"

"No, but brutally honest, yes."

He turned back to me, his pale blue eyes swimming in unshed tears. It hurt my heart to see him like that, but I knew part of that was Jean-Claude's emotion and we had to be firm with our beautiful man. "Unless we have certain people in the room with us, I'm not comfortable letting you wrap me in your arms until I'm out of options against your superior strength, Asher."

"I was ill, Anita. I am on meds and in therapy, what more do you want me to do to prove that I am sincere in my desire to be in your life again like I was before?"

"We'll give you some privacy," Peter said.

I moved back so I could see him and Asher at the same time; I even had a sense of Edward still standing in the doorway to the changing room. "I don't want privacy, I want witnesses."

"Anita, I would never harm you on purpose."

"You came in here tonight sounding like your old self, your old insecure jealous self. That person is not safe to be around, so I'm going to be cautious."

"Are you saying he hurt you?" Peter asked.

"I hurt everyone around me before the doctor found medication that balanced my brain chemistry. It's worse than being an addict, because at least that is something you can live without, something outside yourself, but what is wrong with me is inside me. I cannot go cold turkey as they say, because I am my own drug, my own weakness without a different drug to help me see sense."

"That sounds terrible," Peter said, and sounded like he meant it.

"It is, *mon ami*, it is."

"I'm glad they found meds that worked for you," Edward said.

Asher looked past Peter to the other man. "Thank you."

"We can shelve this conversation for privacy with Jean-Claude and the other lovers in our life," I offered.

"Do you truly feel unsafe with me holding you in my arms?"

Okay, I guess we weren't going to wait for a more intimate audience for this conversation, so be it. I looked at him and distant like a bell was Jean-Claude's love for the man in front of me, but my own heart was strangely unmoved. "We're lovers again, Asher."

"But you are not in love with me, as I am with you."

"You hurt me, Jean-Claude exiled you for months, and then you came home with Kane, who makes it impossible. The time we have together without him just enrages him more, so that it's harder and harder to be together."

"We are lovers again, but it is as if we are not together, because everything must run through Kane's jealousy and possessiveness," Asher said.

"Exactly."

"If I had married him I would divorce him, but I made him my *moitié bête*, my animal half; that is not a tie that can be broken short of death."

"Yeah, it truly is until death do you part," I said.

"I do not know what to do about Kane; if I had been healthier I would never have chosen him."

Edward said, "Maybe without Kane you might not have given therapy a real shot."

"What do you mean?" Asher asked.

"Anita had to tell me about Kane before we came to St. Louis for this trip, because she wanted Peter and me to know that he was potentially dangerous. I think Kane held up a mirror to your own obsessive jealousy. You finally saw in him what everyone else had seen in you, and you didn't want to be like that anymore."

"I knew you were a deadly foe, but I did not know that you were also a wise friend," Asher said.

"I'm not your friend, I'm Anita's friend."

"You don't like me."

"You haven't given me a reason to like you."

"That is fair." Asher turned back to me. "Perhaps your friend is correct, and I needed Kane to show me the error of my ways."

"If that's true then I'm grateful for that, but that still leaves us with Kane."

"What happens if you kill him?" Edward asked.

"His death could kill Asher."

"I thought Asher lived through the death of his human servant once."

"He did." I didn't elaborate on one of the most painful moments in Asher's or Jean-Claude's lives. The bare facts and move on.

"Then why can't he live through the death of his animal to call?"

"I am still in love with Kane," Asher said.

"I saw your reaction when Peter knocked him cold; that was not the reaction of a man in love."

"I love him," Asher insisted.

"But you're not in love with him anymore, are you?" Edward asked.

Asher hesitated and then said, "I don't know."

"Yeah you do, you just don't want to admit it."

"Just to be clear, Ted, you can't kill Kane unless he tries to kill you or Peter, or somebody else. He is not just a problem to be solved, not yet."

Edward shrugged. "If you say so."

"We can't just kill Kane because he might hurt someone, can we?" Peter asked.

"You can't," Edward said.

"No one can," I said.

"You mean that Peter cannot kill Kane in cold blood, but that you could," Asher said.

"It would be a solution."

"It could kill me."

"It would still be a solution," Edward said. I realized in that moment just how much he didn't like Asher. He hadn't even been around him that much, but he'd heard my stories and seen some of the damage Asher had caused; for Edward that would be enough.

I said, "No, it would not be a solution."

Peter said, "Ted, no."

"Then keep Kane away from me and Peter while we're here. If he hurts Anita in front of me, I will not hesitate."

"If he hurts Anita, that's different," Peter said.

Edward looked at his son, his eyes gone cold and distant like winter skies before the storm rolls down and buries you under a blizzard. "You've made Kane your enemy, Peter. He's a wereanimal; that means he's faster and stronger than you are, even now. What will you do if he attacks you?"

"I'll defend myself."

"Will you kill him?"

"If he tries to kill me."

Edward shook his head. "You can't wait that long, Peter, not with shapeshifters."

"I can't just shoot him on sight."

"I can."

"I can't," I said.

"I will do my best to see that Kane stays away from Peter," Asher said.

Edward ignored him and looked at his son. "The biggest difference between Anita and me is that I can, and she won't. It's not that she isn't capable of shooting and killing, Kane. It's that she will wait until he does something that she feels justifies it, but by then someone else will be hurt or dead. If Anita weren't here to tell me no, I would kill Kane before he hurts someone else."

"And it wouldn't bother you?" Peter asked.

"No."

"Why tell me all that, Ted?"

"I want you to start thinking now about what you will and will not do, what you are willing to do, where you draw your line."

"I am thinking about that," Peter said.

"Good, because if you go into the family business you're going to need to decide what your rules are, so that you won't waste time wondering when it's time to act. Hesitation will get you killed if you're up against vampires and shapeshifters, Peter."

Peter looked at me, maybe for confirmation or maybe for my

opinion. I nodded, and said, "If you decide ahead of time what you'll do in a given scenario, then if that happens you'll just act. You won't waste time debating your options."

"But you can't think of every scenario ahead of time," Peter said.

"No, but you can think of the ones most likely to happen next, like what will you do if Kane jumps you when you're alone?" I asked.

"Kill him if I can."

"Good," Edward and I said together.

"But surely you don't have to kill him. Could you not incapacitate him as you did just now?" Asher said.

"Not if he gets me alone," Peter said.

"Explain your answer to Asher," Edward said.

"I surprised Kane and myself with my speed, strength, and training. I won't surprise him a second time. He'll be ready for me now and he's faster and stronger than I am, plus he can shapeshift into a form that has claws and teeth." Peter turned to me. "Can Kane do just claws in human form?"

"Not to my knowledge," I said, and looked at Asher.

"No, he cannot," the vampire confirmed.

"Okay, but he's still better than me physically and he knows how good I am now, so he'll come harder, maybe hard enough to try and kill me. If he gets me alone I'll have to assume that's what he's planning."

"And if he attacks you in front of us all, as he will likely do?" Asher asked.

"If Anita and Ted are with me, or Nicky and a few others, I'll try to fight until they can subdue him, but if he catches me alone or without the people I trust with me, then I'll have to take care of it myself."

"You do not trust that I can control my own animal to call?"

Peter looked at me as if to ask, *What do I say?*

"Tell him the truth," I said.

"No, why should I when you don't seem to have any control over him at all. In fact, he bullies and manipulates you and you let him do it. Why would I trust my life to you suddenly standing up to him and saving me? I'm much safer saving myself while you stand around wringing your hands about what to do."

Asher stared at him, then turned to me. "Is this what you think of me, too?"

"Do you want the truth?" I asked.

"Yes."

"Okay, I think you'd stand there and watch Peter die at Kane's hands and do nothing, not because you want Peter dead but because you don't know what to do in emergencies, especially when Kane is involved."

"Am I that useless?"

"Where Kane is concerned, yes." In my head I thought he'd be one of the last people I'd count on in an emergency, but I kept that to myself. One hard truth at a time worked better if you wanted most people to do better, and I didn't want to hurt him that much. I still loved him, or Jean-Claude loved him enough for both of us; either way it made it hard to be completely honest in that moment.

"So, you agree that Peter should kill Kane?"

"No, I agree that Peter shouldn't let Kane kill him, and if that means he kills Kane first, then I'm okay with that."

"Even if it means my death?"

Damn it, he wasn't going to let this be easy, which was so Asher. "You are a master vampire, Asher, which means you can control your animal to call, which is hyena. I've seen you force werehyenas that hated you to attack people they liked better than you. Kane is your personal animal, your *moitié bête*, your beast half, so you should be able to control him and keep him from attacking Peter, but you won't, not can't, won't. If you want to commit suicide by letting Kane do it for you, that is your choice."

"Will you not miss me?"

I made an inarticulate sound that was somewhere between frustration and a scream of rage. "Damn it, Asher, don't be the fucking girl in this conversation. Not every damn thing is just about you! I will not let your issues with Kane get Peter killed, period, end of fucking discussion. If Kane dies and that drags you to the grave with him, I will mourn your beautiful ass, but I will not let you kill or injure anyone else I love ever again. Ever!"

"I did not know you felt that way about Peter."

"Wait, are you saying that unless I have a romantic love toward someone you think it's okay for Kane to hurt them, or kill them?"

What I could see of Asher's face looked confused. Oh my God, I was too stressed today for this shit. My phone rang and it was the ringtone for Captain Rudolph Storr of the Regional Preternatural Investigation Team.

"Answer the question, Asher, because we're going to have a lot of people in for the wedding that I'm not fucking, and you have to understand that if Kane hurts them that's still a death sentence on him."

"That is your work ringtone," he said.

"I know. I'll call back. You must understand what I just said, or Kane is going to do something unfortunate, and someone will have to kill him, and that may kill you, which will take a piece out of Jean-Claude's heart and mine, but Kane has no more free passes. None, zero, zilch. If he attacks anyone else the minimum is what Peter just did. I am about to have a lot of humans around me for fittings of dresses and shit, and Kane cannot take a swing at any of them, because if he kills any of them even by accident I will put a silver bullet between his eyes."

"He is my animal to call; he might survive even that."

I had to count slowly before saying, "You are not stupid, Asher, so you have to be deliberately missing my point here."

"I thought you might discipline him with one bullet to make your point."

I shook my head hard enough that all my own black curls flew back and forth. I was having to fight not to make my hands into fists.

"It's not my job to discipline Kane, it's yours, but if you won't do your job, you will force me to do mine. "

"You would execute him, even knowing it could destroy me, as well."

"If Kane loses his temper and hits one of my human bridesmaids or their partners, or one of my family, or hell, anyone who is in my wedding, anyone who—"

"You're making this too complicated, Anita," Edward said.

"If you can explain it to him better, be my guest."

"Your fault, our fault, no one's fault, if Kane kills anyone, we kill him. If you get in the way of that, you can die first."

I turned to stare at Edward, but his face showed no compromise. I knew he meant it. I wasn't sure I could pull the trigger on Asher; on Kane and let Asher take his chances, yes, but to actually point a gun between those beautiful blue eyes, at that face we loved . . . I wasn't sure I could do it, and because it was Edward he needed to know that.

"I don't know if I can pull the trigger on Asher, so if it comes to that I'll take Kane, but Asher has to be yours."

"Understood," Edward said.

"Anita, how can you talk about my death so coldly?"

"We are starting to plan how to take Kane and you out, Asher; do you understand now?"

"That I don't matter to you, yes."

I wanted to ask him again if he'd stopped taking his meds, but my phone rang again. It was Dolph and for him to call back that soon it was important. "If you didn't matter to me, Asher, I'd have killed Kane months ago. I have to take this call," I said as I stepped a little away from him, not so he wouldn't hear the other side of the conversation, but because I was so angry with him I didn't want to be looking directly at him while I concentrated on police work.

"Hey, Dolph, what's up?"

"We have a murder scene."

"What kind?"

"We may have a Sunshine kill."

The anger washed away on fear, my stomach clenching tight with it. "Jesus, Dolph, I was hoping it wouldn't come here."

"So was I, but we have a body at the Marriott. A maid noticed the smoke and got a fire extinguisher, so the scene is relatively preserved, but we're going to need dental to ID the victim."

"So, it's a vampire that's newly dead enough to have dental records?" I asked.

"If it's the one that signed in for the hotel room, yes."

"Is the vampire local?" My voice sounded ordinary when I asked, but my stomach wasn't fooled. I knew a lot of the local vampires now, because most of them attended the Church of Eternal Life and so did Jean-Claude and I at least once or twice a month. It was the church that Jean-Claude and I were going to be married in; I'd started to think of the congregation as mine, just like I did the Episcopal church that I went to most Sundays.

"Not if it's the vampire that checked into the hotel."

"Give me the name, I might be able to find a vampire that knows them."

"I don't want to give out the name of the victim until we notify the family."

"They're married?"

"There were photos of the victim with a family on the laptop. All the photos with the vampire in them were taken at night or inside, so it looks like it's not the family the vampire had before, but a current one."

"Okay, track the family down. What do you need from me?"

"You're still our vampire expert. I want your expertise."

"Okay, be there as soon as I can. I'm at a wedding fitting so it may take a few minutes."

"Sorry to interrupt."

"It's okay, my job doesn't change just because I'm going to be a bride."

"I'm still sorry to drag you away from something pleasant to this."

"Is it that bad?"

"We've both seen worse, but it's just that someone in our city hated vampires enough to open the drapes and let the sunlight do this to them. I was really hoping that this particular brand of hate would skip St. Louis."

"Yeah, me too."

He sighed, which he didn't do much over the phone or in person. "Get here when you can, Anita."

"Dolph, one thing. When did they open the drapes on the vampire? I mean, it's after dark, they had to be cutting it damn close to sundown."

"I'll check the timeline and have the info for you when you get here."

"Thanks."

"Don't mention it." Then he hung up, which was actually not abrupt for him.

I said, "I need to go," to no one in particular, or everyone.

"You need backup?" Edward asked.

"No, I need you to stay here and finish the fitting."

"You sure?"

"If it's a Sunshine Murder there will barely be anything for me to do," I said.

He studied my face, then said, "You'll call if you need me."

"Absolutely," I said.

"Give me ten minutes, I'll be out of these clothes, and I can go with you."

"The pants are still too long for the boots," the seamstress said as she came back into the room.

"What boots?" Edward asked suspiciously.

I didn't even try to hide my smile, but I did add, "The boots are actually the most conservative part of the outfit, you won't have a problem with them."

"You'd take Ted with you, but you don't want to leave me on my own," Peter said.

"I really do need Ted to have his fitting. I need something about this damn wedding to go right."

"If this is where you need me more, I'll stay," Edward said.

"Thank you."

The seamstress looked at me. "The makeup artist is waiting for you with the clothes that Jean-Claude picked out for tonight."

"Oh," I said, "I'll come back after the crime scene to change."

She raised an eyebrow at me over her horn-rimmed glasses. "The makeup and hair will take some time, Ms. Blake."

"Are you trying on your wedding dress today?" Edward asked.

"No, it's for the date tonight. Jean-Claude wanted me to match his outfit tonight like it's prom or something," I said, and couldn't hide my discomfort at having to get all dressed up.

"Nathaniel has been so excited about helping Jean-Claude put the new act together," Peter said.

"And they've kept it a surprise from me, I won't even know what color he's wearing until I see my dress for tonight."

"I know you have to go be a cop now, but now I want to see the date dress," Peter said, smiling.

"I'm sorry that I have the date tonight and can't be there to see you working out with everyone," I said.

"We came at the last minute," Edward said. "You can't cancel a date night this big because our schedule opened up suddenly."

"Mom would be wicked pissed if you canceled on her like that," Peter said.

Edward gave a small smile. "Donna would never forgive me if she had professional hair and makeup planned, and then I canceled for less than life and death."

"If Mom went to this much trouble for a date with you, even life and death wouldn't be an acceptable excuse," Peter said.

Edward grinned. "You're right."

"I was hoping to see you in all your finery here, since I cannot be at Guilty Pleasures tonight," Asher said.

I looked at Asher. "You're ringmaster at the Circus of the Damned, can't be in two places at once, and I need you to finish your fitting as best man today, too."

"That is why I am here," he said.

"I also need you to be okay with Ted and Peter. I need you to not take what we just discussed and be all pissy and bitter at them. I need you to get along."

Asher got this look on his face that I knew, so I added, "And you're not allowed to flirt with them or be obnoxious in that way either."

"Do you know me so well?"

"I share a lot of Jean-Claude's memories, so yeah, I do."

Then he got a look on his face that I hadn't seen much, it was more from a memory of Jean-Claude than my own. He looked lost. "What am I to do if I cannot be cruel or flirtatious?"

I realized with a start that he was serious. "Asher, there is more to you than just that."

"Is there? As the medication and therapy strip away all the broken thinking I am left unsure of who I am. I know that sounds ridiculous after almost seven hundred years, but I don't know how to behave if I'm not sick with jealousy. It's as if all of me was the obsessive negative thoughts."

"You are more than just your illness, Asher."

"Am I?"

"Is that why you don't discipline Kane, because he's the last part of your illness?" Peter asked.

Asher looked at him, careful to only let him see the perfect half of his face. "What do you mean?"

"Maybe worrying about Kane gives you something to obsess over now that your own obsessive thoughts are gone?"

"I . . . I had not thought about it like that."

Edward said, "Giving up an obsession is hard. Giving up one that is made from your own obsessive-compulsive thoughts would be even harder. You are stronger than you let us see or you wouldn't have been brave enough to do it."

"Do you truly believe that?" Asher asked, again glancing at him through a fall of hair and perfect face.

Edward nodded. "I do."

Asher ran his hands down his shirt, which was a gesture similar to one that Jean-Claude had; it was a sign of nerves. "Thank you."

"When you first give up your obsession your life loses focus. You have to decide if you're still you, or someone else, becoming someone else," Edward said.

It was all I could do not to ask him what obsession he had given up, because this was more insight into his past than I'd ever had, at least about his emotional landscape. He was my best friend and we'd known each other for ten years, but Edward knew how to keep a secret.

Asher said, "I feel empty like a seashell washed up on the shore, beautiful but hollow with whatever creature lived inside me gone."

"It will take time to fill yourself back up," Edward said.

"Yeah," Peter said, "it's sort of like being fourteen again when you don't know who you are or what you'll be when you grow up."

"I have been grown up for centuries."

"In age maybe, but you got stuck because you were sick; now you can decide what you'll be when you grow up for real."

He stared at Peter, forgetting to keep his hair in place so he gave both eyes and an edge of scars. "How can you be so wise at such a young age?"

"I've had a lot of therapy and I have a great dad, and smart friends," he said, looking from Edward to me.

"If you stop trying to be the old Asher, we'll help you figure out who the new Asher is," Edward said.

"You make it sound simple," Asher said.

Edward shook his head but stopped midmotion because his head rubbed the stand-up collar. He frowned at the clothes, I think, but said, "It's not simple. Re-creating yourself after you've given up one way of being is one of the hardest things you'll ever do, but if you pay attention to yourself you can build a life you want, instead of the life that you fell into."

I had so many questions I wanted to ask, but he'd never answer them in front of this many people, and he probably wouldn't answer them at all, but more than that I realized he'd opened himself up to Asher. Was it for my sake, for Peter's, or had Edward seen something in the vampire that made him want to reach out to him? Maybe I'd ask later when we were alone and Edward would give me the look he'd been giving me for ten years, the one that said he knew things I didn't, and he wasn't going to share.

"You would help me after I have behaved so badly?"

"Do better from this point on, and before you say it's as simple as that, I know that changing how you interact with the world is anything but simple."

"He's really good at helping you through things like this," Peter said.

I thought about it and then nodded. "He really is."

Asher spread his hands wide. "Then I will take the help, for I have no clue what to do with this new me. I am happy that I am not beset with all those compulsive thoughts, but I am afraid of the silence inside me. I do not know what to do with it."

"We'll help you figure that out," Edward said.

"But you have to control Kane so we can do that," Peter said.

I had a moment of thinking *Shouldn't the last two sentences have been the other way around*, but I saw the surety in Peter's face and the calmness in Edward's and realized that they'd be okay with the vampire, and that maybe, just maybe, he'd be okay with them.

The seamstress caught my attention at the door. "Makeup and hair will need at least two hours."

"Two hours! This is just a date, not the wedding."

"For the wedding we will need four hours, perhaps more."

My mouth fell open and I just gawked at her. I wanted to ask if she was joking, but I knew better. The seamstress had no sense of humor that I was aware of; I hoped that the makeup and hair people were better, but I doubted it. I went for the door. She called after me, "Two hours, Ms. Blake, and then you still need to go to the club."

I yelled, "I'll be back, and it's Marshal Blake."

4

I STEPPED OUT into the soft night air and could breathe a little better. It wasn't any of the people I left behind bothering me, it was the wedding clothes, my family, the wedding. I had started to associate the stress of the big day with Until Death and Beyond Bridal, so every time I walked out the door I felt better. Of course, conversely, every time I walked in I felt worse. Edward trying on clothes had made it fun again, and seeing Peter be a better adult than some of the immortals I knew, and Asher trying, and Kane getting his ass kicked by Peter. Everything fun was associated with the people, none of it with the bridal shop and clothes. It was my dress that was taking so long because I hated every design they came up with, but Jean-Claude had finally helped me pick one. I was a semi-formal-dress-on-the-beach kind of girl, or maybe a small church wedding with close friends and family that you actually liked, so how was I getting married to someone who thought a wedding started at opulent and went up from there?

"Because you love him," said a man's voice from the alley beside the shop.

I turned with a smile. "Hey, Damian."

He stepped out of the shadows into the pool of the streetlight. He was six feet of Danish Viking glory but to say he was red-haired, green-eyed, and pale didn't really cover it. He was what happens to a redhead when they can't be in the sunlight for over a thousand years. Hair the bright red of fresh blood, skin that was truly milk white, paler even than Jean-Claude's Snow White coloring, or my own pasty whiteness.

We stood there smiling at each other in that way that lovers do. Two women walked past us giggling and snapped a picture of Damian. He was dressed for his job as manager of Danse Macabre, the first supernatural dance club in the country, which meant tonight he was wearing a bolo jacket in black satin with a forest-green shirt under it that gleamed in the light so that I knew it was silk. Dating Jean-Claude had taught me what silk looked like under every kind of lighting. The skintight leather pants tucked into knee-high boots were also very Jean-Claude, but then he owned the club, so it was his taste from the decor to the dress code.

The women asked if they could have a picture with him, and he agreed, smiling. They did selfies with all three of them, then both of the women alone, while Damian smiled and looked amazing, but then that was part of his job.

I stood in the doorway of the bridal shop watching and happy to be ignored in tactical pants, an oversized zippered sweatshirt, and cross-trainers. The sweatshirt hid all my weapons easily, the Springfield EMP at my waist with my badge tucked beside it, and a Sig Sauer P238 on the other side for a cross draw along with two ammo carriers on the other side of my belt. Behind the ammo carriers was a fixed-blade Spyderco. I'd skipped the big knife in its spine sheath that I usually wore so I could slump in all the chairs like a teenage boy, or that was what my stepmother had told me when I did it. I had put on the two wrist sheaths with their matching knives. I'd worn them so many years that the feel of them around my forearms was reassuring. In most dressier women's clothes, I could never have conceal-carried all of it, or at least not easily. I was beginning to remember why I'd dressed like this for years, besides having no fashion sense. Luckily Jean-Claude had enough fashion sense for both of us.

I was debating on rescuing Damian from his fans, or just waving as I went for my car and the crime scene, when they finally moved on, giggling again. I'd never been the kind of woman who giggled much, and it was usually done in private if it had to be done at all.

I started walking toward Damian but spotted another group of women dressed for the club heading this way. I didn't have time for him to pose with a group that large, or the two couples just behind them. Damian grabbed my arm and pulled me into the alley out of sight from the sidewalk.

I was laughing by the time he had us tucked back into a well of deeper shadows. It was not a giggle, but the laugh was a little higher than normal. I wrapped my arms around his waist, my fingers caressing the silk and the body underneath as I hugged him. He put his arms higher up my back to avoid my weapons. We ended up pressed against each other as close as we could get.

He smiled down at me. "I really appreciate you carrying your guns farther back so I can hug you without risking injury."

I snuggled harder against the front of him, so that I could feel that his body wasn't happy to see me yet. "You haven't fed yet, or you'd be happier to see me."

He stroked his fingertips down the side of my face. "I'm always happy to see you," he said.

"I've got a crime scene to go to," I said.

His grip loosened around me. "Are people in danger?"

"No, the victim is already dead. I'm just giving my expertise."

He tightened his hug again, smiling. "How much time do you have?"

"Not that much, and in the alley, really?" I laughed again, and this one was definitely not a giggle, but the kind of laugh that makes men turn their heads in bars to locate the woman who made it. Boy, would they be disappointed to see me dressed like this.

"I did not mean intercourse," he said, laughing, "and it's your date night with Jean-Claude. I was thinking a kiss."

"A kiss I can do."

He leaned down and I went up on tiptoe to meet him, sliding my body up the length of his as I did it, which would have been a lot more exciting if he'd taken blood tonight. Until he did that his body couldn't react to anything.

We kissed with his body quiet against mine, at least below the waist. Above the waist his hands slid over my body, and he moved me back just enough so he could touch my breasts. It made me wish I'd worn a lower-necked T-shirt, or an untucked one. My hands roamed the silk of his shirt and searched for an opening.

He kissed his way down my throat until his lips rested just over the big pulse in my neck. He hesitated and I felt his need roll through me like it was my own. He was my vampire servant as I was Jean-Claude's human servant, but I didn't have hundreds of years of experience controlling the metaphysics. So sometimes who was in control of whom got a little fuzzy.

I spoke low and carefully, afraid if I lost control of my voice we'd lose control of more. "Why haven't you fed?"

"I'd planned to feed at the club tonight." And just the feel of his words against my throat sped my pulse.

"Like usual," I whispered.

"Yes," he said, and then licked across my pulse, just a flick of his tongue, but it drew a small involuntary sound from me.

"The police are waiting for me." I said it out loud like a competent adult who had a badge that said *U.S. Marshal* on it, but I stayed pressed to his body.

Damian drew back from my neck enough to speak without his lips brushing against my skin. "I'm supposed to be inside trying on wedding clothes," he said. His eyes were solid green; his power had spread and swallowed his pupils so his eyes glowed. If I hadn't been his master he could have bespelled me with those eyes. I could have dropped my control and let him roll me, let him take blood, let us have sex, let us . . . I pushed away from him, so I was standing rather than clinging to him.

"You need to try on clothes and get to work at Danse Macabre," I said, but I dropped my gaze so I wasn't staring into those eyes. It wasn't his magic but mine that made us want each other.

"And you need to go do police things," he said.

"We need to be grown-ups," I said.

"Yes, we do, but I love that you want me as much as I want you."

That made me look up; his eyes had faded back to as ordinary as they got, which wasn't very ordinary. He still had the greenest eyes of any person I'd ever met. True green like a cat's eyes can be, not the gray-green, or blue-green, or the hazel that most people call green. It wasn't vampire powers that made his eyes beautiful; they'd always been this color even before he died.

"We've got our date night scheduled," I said, smiling.

He smiled wide enough to flash a gleam of fang even in the dim light of the alley. "You, Nathaniel, and me."

I grinned back. "Yep, though Angel keeps asking about a foursome."

"I didn't say no, just not this date night."

"You're going to make Angel feel insecure if you keep putting it off," I said.

He laughed. "Nothing makes Angel insecure, she's beautiful and she knows it."

"You're right, but like all really secure women she won't keep sex on the table forever if you keep saying no."

"I didn't say no. I said I wanted it to be a foursome with you and Nathaniel, which means we're working around all our schedules."

"The cry of real polyamory is 'Let me check my calendar,'" I said.

We both laughed. Then we were left looking at each other.

"I would like to kiss you good-bye," he said.

"I want to kiss you good-bye, too, but I think we both need to get to work."

"No, you need to get ready for your date night with Jean-Claude."

"You're right, so I'm going now to do what I need to do, and you're going to do what you need to do," I said.

"Then go," he said, looking at me. He didn't want me to go, and I didn't want to go with the desire hanging in the air between us. If we could have shared blood or had sex, then it would have been sated, until the next time. The three of us were still working out the power dynamics. Nathaniel was my leopard to call; he shouldn't have been in charge of how things worked, but he wasn't conflicted about what he wanted from our threesome. He had helped Damian get over his conflicts, and then me, so now I had another vampire in my life that I craved. I wasn't in love with Damian, though, not yet.

"I'm going," I said.

"Go," he said, and he looked so pleased with himself, pleased that I was having such a hard time walking away from him.

I rolled my eyes at him and walked away down the alley toward the sidewalk and the growing crowd. I had to find my SUV and go to the crime scene, so I could get changed and have my date night with Jean-Claude.

"I love that you want me, Anita."

I was tempted to say *I know*, but Damian was not as secure as Angel, so I said, "I love that I want you, too, Damian." I meant it, but I was careful to keep walking forward and not look back just in case.

5

I'D STOOD BESIDE a lot of dead bodies with Dolph by my side towering over me at six foot eight. Captain Dolph Storr towered over most people, but since I was five foot three I was used to being the smallest person in the room, so it had never bothered me. His hair was still dark, cut close to his head so that it didn't touch his ears. His suits always looked fresh from the closet no matter what time of day or night it was, and he was still built bulky but trim like a football player or a wrestler. We stood with the plastic booties over our shoes, his shiny loafers and my trainers. The fancier my upcoming wedding got the more casual I was dressing, like a throwback to when Jean-Claude and I first met, when I wouldn't have known fashion if it bit me on the ass. I did realize it was a way of rebelling against the expectations of the upcoming wedding, but sometimes you gotta go with the coping mechanisms that work for you.

The body was really just black bones with the skull opened in one last soundless scream that highlighted the fangs in the middle of all the human teeth. I knew the body had been inert, dead when it burned so there'd been no screaming, but I couldn't get the idea out of my head as I stared down at the open mouth trapped in the burned remains. It lay twisted in the ruin of a nearly oval hole burned into the carpet. One side of the open drapes was barely singed at the bottom, just starting to catch fire when the fast-thinking maid had come in with a fire extinguisher and saved the rest of the room. In fact, extraordinarily little of the room was burned.

"Vampires burn too fast and hot for the room to be this untouched; the maid was very quick on the draw with the fire extinguisher," I said.

"She was, we got very lucky that so much of the room is still intact."

"I don't want to see another scene like the New York hotel," Pete McKinnon said from behind us. We glanced back as he joined us, and I was suddenly the very little middle to a very big male sandwich. McKinnon was as broad through the shoulders as Dolph, and over six feet tall, just not as over as Dolph. They'd played football together in college, but where Dolph's hair was still the nearly black it had always been, McKinnon's was gray with more white in it than when I'd met him six years ago. Dolph looked almost unchanged, but Pete looked older and more tired, just like he had when I met him. He'd put on a little more weight around the middle, but not much.

I offered him my hand before I realized we were both wearing the crime scene gloves and that meant touch nothing, not even each other. "Hello, and congratulations on the promotion to the big committee appointment," I said.

"Thanks, if I'd known the job came with a permanent move to Washington, DC, I might have hesitated. Wife isn't too pleased being that far away from the kids and grandkids."

"I'm glad for your expertise, Pete," Dolph said, "but how did you get on the ground this fast?"

"Let's just say that St. Louis is of special interest for certain DC task forces right now."

"You're going to have to elaborate on that if you want access to my crime scene," Dolph said.

I was glad Dolph had said it first.

McKinnon gave him a look, then glanced at me. "Okay, but can we clear the room?"

"We can," Dolph said, and proceeded to tell everyone to get out and give us the space. No one argued, they just moved and closed the door respectfully behind them. The smell of the burned carpet and the crisped drapes was stronger, but it didn't smell as much like burned meat as a regular human corpse would have; vampire flesh burns very differently from ours, cleaner. Less like cooking meat and more like something else. What that else was, the experts in a lot of fields are still trying to figure out.

"Why is St. Louis getting special treatment from the Oversight Committee on Supernatural Affairs?" Dolph asked.

"When the first Sunshine Murder happened, the powers that be were afraid it would spread here."

"I hate that name, by the way; 'Sunshine Murders' sounds so upbeat. It makes it seem like the vampire didn't die a gruesome death," I said.

"We can call them something else while we're alone," McKinnon said.

"Did I offend you on the phone using the phrase?" Dolph asked.

"No, Dolph, it's just . . . it seems like the press is downplaying it."

"The Sunshine Murders are starting to be the leading story on every news site," McKinnon said.

"I stay off the news," I said.

"Because of the wedding speculations?" he asked.

"Yeah."

"Why are you here, Pete? Why this fast?" Dolph asked.

"The big wedding is why."

I looked at him then; his face gave nothing away. He was a fire-fighter and arson investigator specialist, but he had always given blank face like a cop. Maybe it was specializing in arson investigations?

"You mean my wedding to Jean-Claude?"

"Yes."

"Why should my nuptials have one of the top-ranking officials from the Supernatural Oversight Committee here in St. Louis for one suspicious death?" I studied his face for a clue, but he kept looking at the remains at our feet and not meeting my eyes. Was he afraid of what I'd see in them, or was he treating me like a vampire and that was why he'd stopped looking me in the eyes? I hoped not, because it would make me sad for Pete McKinnon to believe the rumors.

"It's not just one suspicious death, Blake, it's hundreds."

"You mean the hotel fire in New York," I said.

He nodded.

"I heard the death toll was over a hundred," I said.

"One hundred and eighty-eight," he said. The fact that he knew the exact number was not a good sign. It probably meant it would haunt him. Years from now when he was closer to eighty than fifty he'd probably still be able to quote the number of dead from the New York fire.

"Has anyone claimed credit for it yet?" I asked.

"No, in fact I've never seen all the hate groups deny anything so hard and so often."

"Usually they're clamoring to take credit for killing a vampire," I said.

"That's when all that dies is the vampire, but whoever opened the drapes in New York trapped hundreds of regular people. They opened them just after dawn, almost everybody still asleep in their rooms." He stared at the slightly singed window, but his eyes had that look that let me know he was seeing the other arson scene, far away from this one.

"So, Humans First and HAV are both denying involvement with the New York case?" I asked.

"Humans Against Vampires stated that they do not condone violence to further their cause, which they usually don't," he said.

"Humans First does violence; they were the ones that firebombed the Church of Eternal Life here about six, seven years ago," I said.

"Didn't they try to shoot you, too?" McKinnon asked.

"Yeah, HAV mostly hates vampires and sees shapeshifters as victims of a disease, but Humans First hates all supernaturals including necromancers like me."

"HAV says that they would never be that careless of other human beings," Dolph said.

"Are you saying they haven't claimed responsibility for any of the other murders?" I asked.

"Not that I've heard," Dolph said.

McKinnon said, "Humans First says that just opening the drapes and letting the sunlight do the job is too passive for them. The vampire should suffer instead of sleep through it."

"They said that publicly?" I asked.

He gave a small smile that never reached his tired eyes. "No, they're better at handling the press than when they first started, but privately in interviews they think it's a coward's way of slaying vampires."

"Because the vampire doesn't suffer enough?" I asked.

"Something like that."

"So, what does Anita's impending marriage have to do with the Sunshine Murders?" Dolph asked.

"I didn't say it was connected to the murders."

"So why did St. Louis having its first of these murders bring you on the jump and mentioning my upcoming nuptials in the same breath?"

"Ah, okay, I handled this badly. My bosses back in DC would not be happy."

"You don't make mistakes like that, Pete," Dolph said.

"The first time I met you, you had brought me the files on an arson that you thought was a pyrokinetic. You risked your job to bring me on before you got permission because you didn't want people to get caught in the next fire," I said.

"I remember," he said. He gave me those tired eyes, then looked back down at the body.

"What do you need us to know now, today, that your bosses wanted you to wait to tell us?" I asked.

He smiled at me, then said, "That they're afraid that your wedding will be targeted by the hate groups."

"We're aware that the hate groups are hating us even more because of how popular Jean-Claude has become in the media. It's too much positive press for the hate groups to stomach."

He shook his head and the smile faded. "I don't mean the regular hate groups and the regular shit I'm sure you and your intended have to deal with, I mean that whoever is behind these murders is aiming at you and Jean-Claude specifically. They want to hurt people close to you." I frowned at him, then looked back at Dolph. "You said this vampire was new to town, not one of ours."

"He's never been to St. Louis as far as we know."

I looked back at McKinnon. "How is the death of a vampire new to our town a blow aimed at Jean-Claude and me?"

"I'm not sure it is, maybe it was just a convenient target, but the intel we got recently says that the group behind the"—he hesitated—"murders wants to kill Jean-Claude and anyone close to him."

"All the hate groups say that, and you can call them the Sunshine Murders if you want, I don't have a better name for it," I said.

He shook his head. "I can't give you details, but we have a credible threat against Jean-Claude and you that's connected to whoever is doing the Sunshine Murders."

"How credible?" Dolph asked.

"Credible enough that I got on a plane to visit family in St. Louis to tell you about it before this murder happened."

"You mean you came to visit family just so you could tell Dolph and me about the threats to Jean-Claude?"

"Jean-Claude and you, Blake, don't discount that. Whoever this group is, it's using the internet to connect, and some of our intel looking for other terrorist activity caught it. They want Jean-Claude and his queen dead, and they want you dead before the wedding. It seems very important to them to prevent the wedding."

"Why? Is it just the publicity being so good?" I asked.

"We're not sure, but I told my wife we'd go visit family and I told my bosses that my wife wanted to visit family here in St. Louis so I could tell you this."

"Thank you for that, Pete," Dolph said.

"I know Anita's like family to you, and yeah I know you had a falling-out a few years back, but what family doesn't fight among themselves? I didn't want to know this and have something happen and have to face you at the next reunion, and"—he looked at me—"you're a good cop, and you do your best to be one of the good guys, good people, whatever term won't offend people nowadays."

"'Good guys' is fine with me," I said.

He smiled. "Good to know, but you are one of the good guys, Blake, and no matter what the rumor mill says about you, you do your best to keep people safe on both sides of the divide between human and supernatural. You needed to know."

"We were planning to up our security around the wedding, but thanks for giving me the heads-up."

"No, Blake, you still don't get it; you need to up your security now, as in right now."

Dolph looked at the other man. "Did the online chatter mention a time frame?"

McKinnon nodded. "They're planning something this week."

I stared at him. "This week, like now this week?"

"Yes."

"Shit." I was already reaching for my phone.

"Who you going to call?" he asked.

"Jean-Claude to start with, then . . . everyone, I guess." I thought about it. "Ted Forrester is in town getting his fitting as my best man, so him, too."

"Forrester is in town this week?" Dolph asked.

"He and his son were only planning to stay for a couple of days. In fact, I left him being fitted to come here."

"U.S. Marshal Ted Forrester?" McKinnon asked.

I said, "Yes."

Dolph said, "Is there another one?"

"I know his reputation; if he could stay over for a few days that would be good."

"You could have picked up a phone and told me. I'd have told Anita," Dolph said.

"I could have, but then I wouldn't be here on the ground to help catch the bastards. The Sunshine Murders are set up online; the main part of the group doesn't have to be in the city where the murder happens, but for what they're planning to do here in St. Louis they'll need to have boots on the ground. It's our best chance to catch the leaders."

"With me and Jean-Claude as bait."

"Not just the two of you, they want to take down your whole power structure, before the wedding."

"Define power structure," I said.

"All Jean-Claude's businesses, Micah Callahan and his Coalition for Better Understanding between the Human and Lycanthrope Communities, Rafael and all the wererats, any shapeshifter seen as your ally or romantic partner."

"They can't kill shapeshifters by letting in some sunlight," I said.

"No, and they know that, Blake."

"Do you know specifics?" Dolph asked for me.

"They're being cautious even online, but they keep talking about the one thing that kills all monsters. They keep saying that sunlight isn't the only thing that burns."

"Fire kills everything," I said, and lifted my phone again.

"If you could contact everyone without using a phone or computer, that would be appreciated," McKinnon said.

"Are your analysts monitoring my phone calls?" I asked.

"That would be illegal to spy on American citizens," McKinnon said.

"But if I make this phone call your bosses will know you told me without their permission."

"Not just our people, but potentially the bad guys will know you know. They're too computer- and tech-savvy to not be trying to hack into their targets' electronic devices."

"How do you think I can contact everyone without a phone?" I asked, narrowing my eyes as I studied his face.

He spread his hands a little like, *I'm not a threat.* "Ease down, Blake, I'm on your side."

"Then stop pussyfooting around and just say shit, patience is never my best virtue, and subtle is not my skill set, talk like you know that."

He almost smiled. "I wasn't sure Dolph knew about all of your skills."

Dolph said, "It's okay, Pete, Anita and I worked out our differences about the supernatural stuff. She and Jean-Claude had dinner with Lucille and me explaining things and then another meal at the house with Darren and his wife. It's why he's still alive to donate sperm for in vitro."

"I thought vampires couldn't carry a pregnancy," McKinnon said.

I said, "They can't, but we've got a surrogate lined up. If it works it will be the first surrogate for a vampire couple in the world."

"And you're good with all this?" he asked Dolph.

He nodded. "I am. Erica is only twenty years dead, she can talk all the same memories that Lucille and I have. Would I have chosen differently, yes, but I've never seen my son happier, and that's gotta count for something."

"That's great, but last we talked in detail you said that you suspected that damn vampire had more of a hold on Anita than she let on, and if you learned he could see through her eyes at a crime scene you'd yank her badge if you could."

SMOULDER

I stared up at Dolph. "Really?" I said.

He looked embarrassed. "I wasn't rational about vampires and shapeshifters back then, you know that. I'll never be able to apologize enough for some of what I did while I was working through my grief about what I thought my son's life would be versus the reality. You could have had my badge for some of what I did to you and your werewolf friend."

"We worked it out," I said.

"We did." He looked at the other man. "I know she can contact her people mind to mind. She did it in front of me, Zerbrowski, and the SWAT people she works with most often. Not sure any of us shared that information with the other cops."

"You're all that loyal to her?"

"She's earned it."

"Even from the SWAT officers?"

"Apparently so, or more of the other cops would have talked by now," Dolph said.

"How do you know?" I asked.

McKinnon looked away from me again, hiding his eyes. He did worry I could use Jean-Claude's powers to read him or maybe even bespell him. I filed it away for another day.

"Does it matter?"

"It does, but right this second nothing matters as much as contacting my people, but put a pin in it, McKinnon, because I will ask again."

"I'd expect nothing less."

I didn't have to reach out to Jean-Claude, just focus on him more. He breathed through me, letting me know he'd heard most of it. He was incredibly careful when I was with the police, because there were a surprising number of them that had at least low-level psychic ability. It was their gut instinct that kept them from going down that dark alley, though they didn't know why, and later they'd find the bad guy waiting for them. "Magic" could make their skin creep, or it spiked through them in a rush of adrenaline like an attack. Either way, Jean-Claude had learned to work around it more than anyone else I was metaphysically connected to, but then he'd had centuries more practice except for Damian. The redheaded vampire was over five hundred years older than Jean-Claude, but he'd never be a master vampire like Jean-Claude or even like Asher. Damian had no animal to call and had never even tried to make a human servant like I was for Jean-Claude. Who's best at something isn't always about age and experience, sometimes it's about ability. Jean-Claude had it, Damian didn't.

Out loud I said, "You can be louder in my head than this, the room is all friendlies."

Jean-Claude just opened the link, and I was suddenly inside his head. It was disorienting enough that I reached out to steady myself but wasn't standing close enough to anything. I felt a hand on my arm and wasn't sure if it was Dolph or McKinnon, because my "eyes" were somewhere else. I saw the dressing table in front of him and had a sense of the mirror surrounded by lights. He was backstage at Guilty Pleasures; I'd almost forgotten he was going to do one of his rare stage appearances, which explained the array of eye shadows and other makeup scattered in front of him. He usually just introduced the acts and spoke with the crowd in between the other dancers taking the stage, but once a month he took center stage. It had been about every three to four months, but some of the older vampires had complained he was their king and kings shouldn't shake their booty onstage, but since they bitched, he did it once a month instead of four times a year. There was more than one reason we worked as a couple; a shared finger in the eye to other people's expectations was one of them.

"You okay, Blake?" McKinnon's voice.

Dolph's voice was closer. "She's okay."

Knowing it was Dolph being such a good sport about the vampire powers helped me draw back enough to let Jean-Claude know what

I'd learned in the last few minutes without being so far into his head that I couldn't tell where he and I were separate. The ability to share this deeply, almost a body swap, had been one of the things that terrified me in the beginning. It still wasn't my favorite part, but because we could do it, Jean-Claude knew the danger that he and all our people were in like magic, or maybe by magic. The line between psychic abilities and magic was thin and getting thinner, or maybe my ability to call my abilities psychic as opposed to magic was just the lady protesting too much.

My hands touched the makeup on my . . . his hands touched his makeup table, and he drew me out far enough that I was hovering like an invisible camera just above him. It was always the visual if we stayed separate from each other, like we hovered in the air and gazed down. Jean-Claude had done dramatic stage makeup around his eyes; something in all the blues, blacks, grays, and silver coaxed his eyes from a blue so dark it was almost black to something lighter, if you could call cobalt blue light. It was as if he'd taken his eyes from the blue just before the last light fades into night to twilight, when the sky hovers between cerulean and sapphire. It took me a few seconds to take in the perfect black curls that fell around his shoulders, or that he was wearing a shirt I'd never seen on him. The thought came through my head that it was a costume that went with the makeup.

"Anita, you okay?" Dolph said.

I closed my eyes for real, which didn't do a damn thing to make me not see Jean-Claude inside my head. Sweet Jesus, and I was about to marry him. I was in love with him, had cohabitated with him for years and still there were moments like this when his beauty undid me. No wonder I'd fought so long and hard not to fall under his spell.

"I'll see you at the club tonight," I said. I knew it sounded abrupt, but it was one way to fight through the reaction I was having. Hell, I had used being cranky and unimpressed as a way to fight off my reactions to Jean-Claude for years.

"Is she still talking to someone else?" McKinnon asked.

"Yes," Dolph said.

Jean-Claude whispered, "I cannot wait to see you in your new dress and shoes tonight, *ma petite*."

"I can't wait to see what you're wearing, or not wearing," I said, and just by thinking of him out of his clothes I fell into his eyes again. If Dolph hadn't been holding my arm I would have fallen for real, as if his eyes were a dark pool of water that I could drown in and I would enjoy every compromised breath until I died. That fear had been what helped me fight my attraction to Jean-Claude for so long. His own vampire marks combined with my natural ability with the dead should have kept me safer than this. What the hell was wrong?

"*Ma petite*, have I suddenly become irresistible?" I heard the smile in his voice; it helped me push back so that I could see his face and that smile most seductive. I could see all that exotic makeup again. He was breathtaking. My chest felt tight at the sight of him. I started to fall into his eyes again like I was iron and he was a magnet that I could not resist. When we'd first met I'd driven my fingernails into my hand so the pain would help me resist his charms, but I had other options now. I shoved power into that beautiful face, against that irresistible force, and Jean-Claude lashed back as if I'd tried to slice him with a blade and he'd had to use his own blade to keep me from drawing blood. I think it caught us both off guard and we just reacted. We both lashed out with near pure power. Jean-Claude cut our link so we couldn't hurt each other anymore, but the rush was so powerful I damn near convulsed with Dolph's hand on my arm. The movement was sudden enough that I jerked free of Dolph, then started to fall. Jean-Claude had tried to protect us both by shutting down the link, but it was McKinnon and Dolph who kept me from falling into the burned remains of our victim.

"What the hell was that?" McKinnon asked.

"I've never seen her like this," Dolph said.

I stayed on all fours with my gloves and booties the only thing touching the crime scene's carpet. Maybe if the men's knees hadn't been in the way I would have knelt, but part of me remembered where I was, even if most of me didn't. I'd never had a reaction to Jean-Claude like that, not just from mind-to-mind contact. I stayed down until I didn't feel shaky anymore, then pushed myself upward with my fingertips and the balls of my feet. I had a moment where I just wanted to run from the crime scene to see Jean-Claude dance. The urge was so great that I started to turn toward the door and caught myself.

"I've never seen me like this," I said.

"What did you say?" Dolph asked.

I repeated myself.

"Seriously?" McKinnon asked.

I nodded. "Very seriously. Jean-Claude and I will be having a little talk later."

"You don't sound happy," McKinnon said.

I looked at him and it must have been a good look, because he held his hands up. "Sorry, Blake, just commenting."

"Maybe you should hold the comments until later."

Jean-Claude's "voice" was in my head again. I started to slam all my shields in place, but he said, "It is not me."

I hesitated, too stressed to form a silent *what* in my head, but Jean-Claude got the point, because he said, "Whatever lowered your resistance to me is not me, or you. It is something outside of us."

"Shit," I said with real feeling and a wash of fear that left my skin cold.

"What's wrong?" Dolph asked.

"We're under attack," I said.

"Where?" Dolph said. "We'll send backup."

I promised I'd hug him later for that being his first thought. Right now, I shook my head. "Not that kind of attack, not physical, magical."

"What do you mean?" McKinnon asked.

I shook my head again. "I mean that something or someone interfered with me when I contacted Jean-Claude right now. They messed with me bad. I was like mesmerized by him. I haven't been like that in years; hell, no vampire has been able to roll me that badly in ages."

"You're sure it wasn't Jean-Claude getting carried away?" McKinnon asked.

"No, one of the reasons it took so long for him to win me over was my fear of this kind of shit. He wouldn't do it by accident, or casually, not with the wedding so close."

"Wait," McKinnon said, "are you saying this would be enough for you to call off the wedding?"

"Damn straight it would be; if he's fucking with my head like this on purpose, then I want nothing to do with him. It's like metaphysical rape, except it's a real aphrodisiac that ignites real lust, and worse, love. If he did that to me like this from a distance I'd never want to be in the same room with him again. It would be too dangerous, which means no wedding."

"Okay, but you're not really calling off the wedding, right?" McKinnon said.

"No, but if it wasn't Jean-Claude overstepping then it was another vampire or witch, something that was so freaking powerful it mind-fucked me without me knowing it, from a distance." My stomach clenched tight with the thought. I reached for the chain around my neck and drew my cross into sight, so I could hold it in my hand. Usually I let it dangle around my neck when I wanted it in sight, but tonight I needed more reassurance.

"How powerful would someone have to be to roll you like this when they aren't even in the room with you?" Dolph asked.

"Powerful, like ancient vampire powerful. Shit, my father just called. He and the rest of my family are flying in next week."

"I'm glad your father decided to walk you down the aisle after all," Dolph said.

"No, it's not like that. He's finally willing to meet Jean-Claude, but he still wants me to give him up and definitely not marry a vampire."

"Then why come at all?" he asked.

"Because if he doesn't get fitted for the bespoke clothes now, the suit will never be ready in time. I told Dad that if he didn't come for the early fitting then he'd made his choice and I'd find someone else to give me away. He's coming to be fitted, and he's agreed to meet Jean-Claude, but everything else is up in the air. I honestly don't think my very Catholic father is going to come around to attending the wedding let alone walking me down the aisle."

"Lucille and I can meet with him while he's here, tell him about how we've worked things out with Darren and Erica."

"Thanks, Dolph, if Dad gets to come to town before the wedding that would be great."

"What do you mean, if?" McKinnon asked.

"I can't let my very human, very non-cop family come to town if we are under major vampire attack. If this master vamp can roll me my family won't have a chance; hell, most of the people I love who are supernatural won't have a chance. I have more natural immunity to vampire powers than most of them."

"Don't cancel your family coming in, Blake."

"I have no choice, McKinnon."

"You do, actually."

"What are you talking about?"

"The oversight committee is experimenting with some magical protection protocols."

"Pete," Dolph said, "did you just do something to one of my officers?"

"I didn't mean to affect Blake with it. I was told to try it out in the field gently if the chance arose."

Dolph suddenly loomed over the other man, as if the extra inches had grown. He asked with each word enunciated almost painfully, as if losing control of his voice would be the precursor to losing control of other things. "What-did-you-do-to-Anita?"

McKinnon spread his hands out like he was showing himself unarmed. Neither Dolph nor I was buying it. "What the fuck did you do to me, McKinnon?"

"We have a coven of witches working with us. It's supposed to be a spell to strip a vampire of its control over us, so it can't work mind tricks. It wasn't supposed to strip you of your control and make the vampire more powerful."

"That was damn near gibberish," I said.

"Agreed," Dolph said.

"Try again, slowly and clearly," I said.

McKinnon looked from one to the other of us, his arms a little more raised as if we'd asked to see his hands; that worked for me right now. "The witches said that the charm, or spell, I'm honestly not sure which is the correct term and since Blake does more magic than I do, I just want to be clear up front that I'm not up on the latest and greatest magical vocabulary."

"Fine, the spell, or charm, is supposed to do what exactly?"

"Protect whoever is wearing it from vampires."

"So will a holy item," I said.

"Only if you're a believer; you'd be surprised how many agnostics and atheists go into government work."

"Not surprised," I said.

"Keep talking, Pete."

He looked up at one of his oldest friends as if he hadn't expected Dolph to be on my side. Pete should have double-checked that before he invited himself to Dolph's crime scene. "It was supposed to strip the vampire of their powers."

"Strip them of what powers, exactly?" I asked.

McKinnon blinked at me like the question was hard. "Mind powers."

"More specific," I said.

"How specific?"

"No single spell or charm or whatever the fuck it is could cover every vampire power possible."

"We know it won't help with super strength or hearing or anything physical," he said.

"I'm not even counting the physical stuff, so let me ask you one more time. What kind of powers is that damn thing you're wearing supposed to strip away from a vampire?"

"Mind powers, like bespelling us with their eyes."

"I damn near fell into Jean-Claude's eyes just now like a newbie, so that didn't work."

"Sorry about that, and I did not mean to throw a monkey wrench in the wedding plans."

"Thanks for telling the truth," I said.

"If you'd canceled the wedding and lost the chance to make up with your dad, I'd never be able to look myself in the mirror again, Blake."

"Good to know," I said.

"What other vampire powers is the spell supposed to stop?" Dolph asked.

"The witches said . . ."

"Don't throw the witches under the bus, McKinnon; you're the one who tricked me into contacting Jean-Claude via mind like he and I were your guinea pigs when you just admitted you don't understand the magic in the damn charm. This is on you."

"Okay, okay, you're right."

Dolph said, "So what else is the charm supposed to do?"

"Vampire gaze protection, strip a vampire of its special power abilities."

"What does that last part mean?" Dolph asked.

"Some vampires can cause panic in a crowd, or lust, or some secondary emotion, or even plant thoughts in a person's head," McKinnon said.

"Like a vampire telling a cop to shoot another cop and protect the vampire," Dolph said.

"Yes."

"We've all seen that happen," Dolph said.

I nodded. We had.

"So why did it make Jean-Claude's hold on Anita stronger?"

"I don't know."

"Why did it make me less able to fight off vampire powers?" I asked.

"I don't know, but I'd say this is a spectacular failure of a field test," McKinnon said.

"Ya think?" I said, glaring at him.

"So, you lied to Anita and me when you said if she used her phone to warn her people that your bosses would overhear it and get you in trouble?"

"No, that wasn't a lie, I swear, but it's the hate group's online presence that I'd be more worried about. They have some serious hacker skills. We've found them places we . . . I can't tell either of you but let's just say unless your phone is encrypted as well as top-secret government lines, the hate group's hackers will be able to listen in on any or all of the people in your network."

I almost told them that actually we had some of the highest security that money could buy, thanks to finding out we'd been bugged a few years back. I didn't know how it all worked, but I knew that people that Jean-Claude and Rafael paid to know this shit had assured us that within reason we were safe. The *within reason* was because hacking was a lot like torture; eventually every system and every person breaks. But the fact that we paid for that kind of specialty encryption and protection to our phones and everything else was not something to share with a government worker, especially not someone working for a committee that was spending our tax dollars on spells to use against vampires.

"Vampires are legal citizens; isn't researching how to harm them illegal somehow?"

McKinnon snorted. "You don't even want to know what our government is funding. It's not just magic to use against supernatural citizens, Blake."

"Are you admitting that the committee is researching how to use magic against all of us?" I asked.

McKinnon looked less than happy for a second, before he found a smile from somewhere to try and fake his way through. "Would our government do that?"

"Pete," Dolph said, just that, but it was enough between them.

"I'm sorry, Dolph, I've said more than I should already."

"Fine," I said, "let's go back to the spell that you used against me."

"Against vampires."

"Oh, against my fiancé and the man that I love, that makes it so much better."

He had the grace to look embarrassed. "When you say it like that, it sounds pretty rotten."

"There is no good way to say this," I said.

"Tell her what else the spell is supposed to do, Pete."

"I told you, protection against vampire gaze, being taken over and forced to fight on their side, any emotions that the vampire has the ability to raise in humans."

"Nope, that's not how the witches presented it. They didn't go into a room of government men with backgrounds in firefighting, cops, military, et cetera . . . and say it'll stop emotions."

Pete smiled. "You're right, they said the spell, or charm, would stop secondary vampire abilities, whatever they might be."

"That's pretty damn broad," I said.

"That's why they've given the prototype to a few people to test in the field under nonthreatening conditions."

"Like today with me and Jean-Claude."

"Yes."

"If you'd have told me ahead of time I'd have been glad to help you test the damn thing, but don't ever spring shit like this on me again."

"Of course," he said.

"Your word," Dolph said.

"My word," McKinnon said.

"I have to tell our security that they need to up our alert level, and I'm not risking metaphysics while you're wearing the charm."

"I can leave the room."

"What's the range on the spell?"

He looked embarrassed again. "We're not certain."

"Do you know what effects it has on normal psychics?" I asked.

"There was no impact on normal human psychics."

"It just impacts vampires?" I asked.

"We had one voodoo practitioner that had issues with it, but since he can raise the dead like you do, we discounted it."

I stared at him. Dolph asked for me like he'd read my mind. "Why discount that?"

"I'm not at liberty to share that information."

"Jesus, McKinnon, is this a charm aimed at people who deal with death magic?"

"We were looking for something that would work against all undead," he said, as if that was as much as he was allowed to share.

"I used to think you were smart, McKinnon," I said.

"She's a necromancer, Pete."

"I realize that now, I mean I knew that before, but I don't think of Blake like that. She's one of us, not one of . . ." He just stopped talking as Dolph and I stared at him. Whatever he saw in our faces made him look at the floor again like he'd been called on the carpet.

"Not one of them? Was that what you were going to say?" I asked, voice quiet because I couldn't decide if I was angry or just massively disappointed.

"I'm sorry, Blake, I came here to help, not hurt."

"I'm going to call my people now, but when I'm done I want to see this charm."

"I don't think you touching it is a good idea after what just happened," McKinnon said.

"I agree, that's why I said see it, not touch it." I started to make the call, then debated on if I wanted to do it in front of McKinnon or Dolph, but especially McKinnon. If he was telling the truth and I thought he was, he'd have tapes or whatever with the conversation on it later, but that would just be voices. If he watched me make the call he'd have body language, facial expressions, and just personal observation to put with the words.

"Let's give the room back to the rest of the crime scene crew. I'll call from down the hallway."

They agreed that giving the room back to everyone was a good idea, so Dolph opened the door and everyone who had been cooling their heels in the hallway came back inside and I went out. Though as I exited, I said, "I want to finish our talk before you leave here, McKinnon."

"I'll be here when you're ready," he said.

I wanted to say *You better be*, but out loud I just said, "Good." McKinnon had helped us with his warning; he was on our side sort of, I didn't need to threaten him. I just really wanted to because I was pissed at him about the charm. I had some ideas about what the magic in it was, but it was more important to let everyone know the security risk than to play tough guy with McKinnon. Besides, my ego was secure, so I didn't have to play.

6

I DEBATED ON whom to call but finally called Claudia. She was head of the overall security for us, but she was hands-on in charge of security at the Circus of the Damned where Jean-Claude lived and daytime-slept most of the time. It was the most secure location we had, but it was also the biggest target, because too many people knew it was Jean-Claude's daytime lair. You can't keep a secret hideout hidden if anyone but you knows about it, and a lot more than just Jean-Claude and I knew about the rooms under the Circus.

I found a relatively empty piece of hotel hallway and hit her number in my favorites. Claudia was fast becoming the best female friend I had who wasn't also a girlfriend.

"Anita, how's the best man fitting going?" Her voice was half laughing, because there was a betting pool among the guards who knew Edward. Money on him hating it and refusing to wear it, hating and wearing it for me, loving the clothes (not the safe bet), and hating them and wearing them anyway and looking good in them. That last was where I'd put my money.

"I'm just glad we didn't choose orange and black like some people thought, as if marrying a vampire has to be Halloween themed," I said. *Orange* was the code word for communications, and me saying it in a sentence that meant nothing, really, meant that I believed the communications might be compromised. It wasn't just my code word; if anyone else had called me and used *orange* in a sentence it would have meant the same thing. If it had been someone talking about groceries or ordering orange chicken from a Chinese restaurant they would have used the word *orange* twice to let me know it wasn't accidental.

Claudia's voice was a lot less happy when she said, "Someone even suggested purple and orange, remember?" *Purple* was code for physical safety, her way of asking if it was just communications or was our safety compromised, too.

"I remember, but so not happening. If you know Jean-Claude you know it has to be black and white. I thought it would look like a damn zebra crossing, but it's actually looking awesome." *Zebra* was code for *Safety is fucked, too.*

"Awesome is good, glad you talked Jean-Claude out of you both in gold at the altar," she said. *Gold* was code for her asking if someone was in immediate danger.

A couple of uniformed officers trailed past me with a glance; there was more than one reason to use codes. More and more people, mostly police, were clustering around the murder room. I eased farther down the hallway away from it all as I answered Claudia. "No way on the gold, we'd have looked like shiny Christmas ornaments under the lights." *Christmas* was code for *I'm okay currently*, or *not under duress and I don't need rescuing*. I even managed a chuckle about the thought of us all shiny for the wedding.

"Thanks for not making me be in the wedding; I'd have towered over everyone else like a giraffe." The last word was the important part; she was asking if the danger was immediate somewhere else, as in did I know where the attack was coming or was it happening like now? How high was the threat level? Was it giraffe high?

I managed to laugh again. "Trust me, Claudia, I don't want to play delicate gazelle in the damn dress." *Gazelle* meant the threat wasn't happening immediately. "We're still arguing over the last details of my dress and the flowers. He wants all white flowers, but with us in white I want more color." *Color* was code for chaos, or *I don't know*, or *I'm not a hundred percent sure that my gazelle isn't a giraffe.*

A door opened farther down the hall. I heard a woman's voice that sounded like she was crying. A second woman's voice, more soothing, said, "You saved lives today."

"You could have gone for just greenery, fewer choices," Claudia said, trying to ask me if I knew what the threat level was when it did happen. Since the wedding clothes really were black and white neither color could be a code word; we used them too often, which was why *zebra* came into the sequence. Green was the lowest threat level since white was off the board. Green, yellow, orange, red was the sequence of escalating badness.

The door to the room with the women in it was still open; I realized there was a uniformed officer propping the door open by standing in it. She was looking down the hallway like she was expecting someone. I avoided her gaze just in case she thought I was who she was expecting. I had my badge on a lanyard around my neck and was wearing my U.S. Marshal windbreaker over everything, so it wasn't like I could pretend to be a civilian.

"Orange flowers would have looked great with the black side of things, but only okay with the white and it's hard to find orange flowers that either of us likes." Claudia knew I thought the threat level was going to be bad when it happened, but not the worst. Then I realized that I didn't have enough information from McKinnon to be certain of that, so I added, "Though there are so many colors to choose from and flowers have to be fresh, so we have more time to decide on that than anything else." I'd said *color*, or *colors*, again, which meant I wasn't certain on the threat level being orange; it could be red, or yellow.

"How about yellow or red flowers?" she asked.

"Yellow would look good with the black, but not so great with the white, but red is the leading contender for the flowers in my bouquet."

"I think red roses against a white dress with your coloring would look very Snow White." Color again; how sure was I that it was going to be red? If I repeated *red* again she'd know to take maximum security measures. *Snow White* was her way of asking if the danger was aimed at only one person.

"More Rose Red than Snow White," I said, doing my best to sound casual. *Red* meant take all the precautions, all the extra security measures, and *Rose Red* meant it was aimed at all of us. Once the wedding was over I had no idea how we'd make the code words work in normal conversations; Claudia and Bobby Lee would probably make us all memorize a whole new set of words.

I heard the woman crying louder from the open door. The female uniform finally caught my eye. "Gotta get back to work, we'll talk more wedding stuff later."

"We will," she said. "Keep your head on a swivel out there."

"You know I will." I was walking slowly toward the officer with the questioning look on her face.

"I know you will." There was a moment of silence where she probably wanted to say something more, but we didn't have code words to handle it.

"Later, alligator," I said.

That made her laugh, which was the point; when your friends worry about you, the least you can do is lighten the mood. I hung up to the sound of her laughter and went to find out what the female uniform wanted from me.

7

OFFICER KAY BEECHER had been very grateful to find another woman in the hallway with a badge, because she was on her period, and she was afraid she was about to go through her uniform pants. I sympathized as only another woman can, and let her go, taking her place in the doorway. A dark-haired woman in a pink maid's dress complete with white half apron was partially collapsed on the bed crying into Kleenex from the box beside her.

Beecher had introduced us to each other. "Mona, this is Anita, she's a U.S. Marshal and she'll stay with you for just a few minutes."

I raised an eyebrow at the first names, but Beecher whispered, "She's really upset, first names help."

I nodded like that made sense to me, and I guess it did. "Thanks . . . Kay."

"Just keep her calm until Captain Storr clears her to go home."

I whispered back, "She the one who put out the fire?"

"Saved the day," Kay said, and made her power walk in the direction of a restroom that wasn't in one of the rooms connected to the crime. First-day lecture for crime scenes: you do not use a bathroom that could contain evidence unless someone tells you it's clear to use. Officer Kay was probably going to have to find a public restroom

unless she could get another room opened that didn't contain someone connected with the crime. I could be here awhile.

Mona snuffled into the Kleenex, looking at me through bleary
tear-filled eyes. "What was your name, Anna?"

"Anita," I said.

She gave a weak smile. "Anita."

I smiled encouragingly, thinking it was nice to be the comforting
presence for once instead of the threat. I rarely got to play good cop
for some reason. Oh wait, because I was bad at it, but I smiled and
really tried to look as harmless as my size and not as dangerous as all
the weapons and body armor I was wearing.

She smiled back.

"It was very brave of you to tackle the fire with just a fire extinguisher," I said.

She smiled a little more, then shivered, smile fading away. "I
didn't want what happened in New York to happen here."

"That was bad," I agreed. "Thanks again for protecting everyone
here in the hotel."

"I saw it on the news, all those poor people."

"Yeah." And then because I was never good at waiting around, I
asked, "Did you see someone leave the room ahead of you?"

She shook her head.

"Did you have to open a lot of doors before you hit the right one?"

She blinked and looked at me, frowning. "What?"

"It must have been really scary with the fire alarm going off and
everyone rushing to get out and you kept your head and looked for
the fire."

She nodded. "I was very scared, but I smelled the smoke, and I
knew we had a vampire in the one room, and all I could think of was
what happened in New York. I couldn't let that happen here."

I thought there was no way she smelled smoke, the carpet had
barely begun to burn, but maybe she thought she smelled smoke
because once she saw the flames she expected it. Memory is a funny

thing, it fills in the gaps with what you expect, not always with what happened. It's one reason eyewitness testimony is so untrustworthy.

"Did you see the light from the flames under the door?" I asked.

"No, the doors seal tight."

"I guess it was lucky the New York fire was in your head, so you went right to the vampire's room."

"What did you say?"

"The New York fire has been all over the news, so it's natural that working in a hotel, it would be in your mind."

She nodded, looking puzzled, or something. I couldn't read her expression; was she going into shock? It happened sometimes after the emergency was over even if you weren't hurt. She had been checked for injuries; surely someone had done that.

"Did you get hurt, burned?"

She shook her head, staring at a point in front of her, but I think she wasn't seeing anything in the room. It was just a direction to stare while she processed what had happened to her.

"Mona, you okay?" I glanced down the hallway, seeing if I could flag another uniform down to send Dolph this way, but everyone was too far away without me yelling. I didn't want to get Kay in trouble or have to explain why she'd had to leave the area. There might not be a sisterhood among women or even female cops, but I knew how hard it was to be one of the boys when biology meant you'd never really be one. Having a heavy period emergency could ruin whatever street cred Kay had. Or she'd find tampons and pads all over her desk, in her locker, in her squad car, and she'd have to pretend it didn't bother her, because if she let it show they'd play the joke forever. Hell, they might play it forever anyway. Nope, I would stay here on the door until she got back, or until someone who outranked me joined us, which would be Dolph. As a U.S. Marshal, I wasn't technically in the chain of command for any local law enforcement. Marshals were sort of like warrant officers in the army; you knew what our rank was, but not where we fit into your power structure, and you were never sure who could give us orders and who we'd ignore.

"I thought they weren't supposed to move while they burned," she said in a distant voice, almost like she hadn't meant to say it out loud. She was definitely going into some kind of shock or post-emergency slump. Had an EMT or some medical someone looked her over?

"Most of the time they don't move, they just burn," I said.

She blinked and looked at me with her big, brown eyes showing too much white around the edges. "It moved, it reached out all fire and black bones and it still grabbed for me."

"While you put it out with the fire extinguisher," I said.

"Before."

"Before?" I asked.

She nodded.

"The opened drapes caught the last sunlight of the day; when the sun set the vampire woke for the night," I said.

"He was all burning, flames, and he still moved, screamed. It was awful."

"You didn't put the fire out to save the hotel, you put the vampire out because he came alive while he was on fire," I said.

She nodded. "He was burning alive. I know he's dead, but he didn't seem dead when he cried out in pain. He seemed alive, but he's dead now, they told me he's really dead."

"He's really dead now," I said.

"I didn't know they felt pain like that," she said.

"Yeah, vampires feel pain just like we do."

"If it had been in the morning like in New York, would he have felt pain?"

"No, the vampire would have been dead for the day, no pain, no waking up."

"But that room doesn't get morning light, so it couldn't be then."

Something about the way she said it seemed odd, or maybe I was seeing motive where there was just a normal person dealing with a very abnormal event? I needed another officer here to help me figure out which it was before I formed the wrong conclusions. I didn't interrogate many regular humans, and I knew that vampires and shapeshifters can react very differently from human normal. The first had centuries or decades longer than most humans to control their expressions and body language. The second could smell fear and anger, and no matter how you controlled your body you couldn't control the autonomic nervous system. It betrayed you to a shapeshifter's nose, or their and a vampire's superior hearing. They both knew the second your pulse rate sped up, sometimes before you did.

I stared at the woman sitting quietly on the bed, the wad of Kleenex forgotten in her hand as she stared at the wall. She was pale, and lightly dewed with sweat; both could be signs of shock. I needed to know if anyone with more medical knowledge than I had had given her a once-over. For all I knew she could have an underlying medical condition. Shit, I just wasn't used to dealing with normal people. Cops didn't count, no first responder did; they didn't react normally to emergencies any more than vampires or shapeshifters did.

"Would the vampire have attacked me if it hadn't died first?" she asked.

"I don't know, you were putting out the fire, so you were trying to help him."

"I didn't close the drapes," she said.

"You did the best you could."

She nodded as if that made sense to her.

I got my phone out and texted Dolph without making a big deal out of it to Mona. I had a moment of trying to decide what to text, but settled for **Need you in room with the maid. Something's not right.**

"Do I know you?" Mona asked.

I shook my head. "No."

She frowned harder at me.

I eased farther into the open doorway so I could see the hallway better and still have a sense of the woman on the bed. I was relieved to see Officer Kay Beecher striding down the hallway like she had a purpose. I saw Dolph come out of the room behind her; he was so much taller that I could watch both of them at the same time without having to choose whom to look at.

Kay came up with a smile and a thank you. Dolph just behind her was blank-faced serious. The officer actually turned back toward him, as if she thought she was in trouble for leaving her post to me. I spoke before she could get herself in unnecessary trouble. "Kay, glad you're here. Mona, Officer Kay is back, you okay with her for a few minutes? I'll be right back." I even smiled when I said it.

Mona nodded, looked at Kay as if she'd never seen her, then went back to staring at the wall. It didn't look that fascinating to me, just a hotel wall with a chest of drawers and a television set and a mirror. The usual generic hotel arrangement, but then I realized I was wrong; the mirror took up more of the wall than normal. Most cheaper rooms put the mirror on the back of the bathroom door or on the closet's sliding doors. Most hotels would have put a painting there. Mona wasn't staring at the wall; she was staring at herself. She was staring as if she didn't quite recognize herself; maybe it was shock or maybe it was something else.

Dolph was waiting for me in the hallway when I stepped back out. His face was neutral, waiting. He knew I wouldn't have contacted him without a good reason. I just walked past him a little way down the hall closer to the crime scene with its huddle of people hurrying in and out. I stopped short of it so that no one would overhear us.

"Talk to me, Anita," Dolph said.

I told him what Mona had said.

"That's not much," he said.

"It's not, and she probably never saw anything this awful before, could be just shock."

"But you don't think it is," he said.

"I'd like a chance to question her and find out."

"She's a hero; the media has already gotten a hold of it," he said.
"So?"

"We need to be sure on this before we change the narrative, that's all."

"Change the narrative," I said. "Wow, Dolph, you have been reading the memos on how to handle the media."

He smiled, then went back to serious in case someone else was looking. He had a reputation to uphold and that didn't include smiling at subordinates at crime scenes. "I'm just saying we have to be careful here, Anita. We have a heroic woman, a maid, who saved this hotel from burning down with the New York hotel fire still headline news. The Sunshine Murders have been the leading news story for weeks."

"I'm aware of all that," I said.

"Can you be diplomatic in there with our hero?"

"I can be careful, not sure if I'll ever understand diplomacy."

"Fair enough," he said, "we can turn on Officer Beecher's vest cam so we'll be on record."

"Sounds good to me."

"Do you seriously think that this woman is involved in the murder?"

"I don't know, but something's off, and before we embrace her as the hero of the story I'd like to find out what that something is."

"There's a camera in the hallway," he said.

"Can we see the footage before we go back in there?"

He nodded. "We can."

"Do I need to talk to Officer Kay before we go off?"

"I'll make sure she stays where she's at, and that no one else lets her go before we're ready."

"It's good to be the boss," I said.

He gave that small smile again. "Better than not being boss."

"Amen to that," I said.

He smiled a little more, then ducked into the room to tell Officer

Kay to hold the fort, and then we went to tell everyone else what Dolph wanted them to do. I even let McKinnon trail along with us to look at the security videos; as long as I didn't use any of my psychic abilities around him we were probably good, and if that changed I'd tell him to get the hell away from me. I might do that anyway for experimenting on me and Jean-Claude with his little charm spell, but first we had a mystery to solve. I could always be cranky later.

8

I DECIDED TO be cranky when I saw how small the manager's office was; there would barely be room for Dolph's and McKinnon's shoulders, let alone the manager and me. I smiled and told him, "We'll be right back." Then I motioned Dolph and McKinnon down the hallway so we wouldn't be overheard.

"What's up, Anita?" Dolph asked.

"The room is tiny. I don't want to be in that tight a space with McKinnon's charm."

"You haven't had another reaction to it," McKinnon said.

"Because I have very carefully not used any psychic abilities since it went off on me. Some of my psychic abilities are almost automatic, which means I do them without thinking; what happens if I use them while you're accidentally brushing against me? How much worse would the effect be if you were touching me?"

"I . . . I don't know."

"Then take the charm and lock it in your glove box, and don't bring it out again while you're in St. Louis."

"Is it just too powerful for you to be around, or is it a failure as a defensive tool?" McKinnon asked.

"It's a small sample, but it stripped me of my control, my protection against vampires. What would happen if you used it on me near a cemetery and I accidentally raised zombies and I couldn't control them? What if a vampire attacked the three of us and Dolph was depending on my abilities to save our asses, but your charm made me just another victim?"

"Would it do that to a vampire?" Dolph asked.

"You mean make them lose control?" I asked.

"Yes," he said.

I thought about it before answering. "Jean-Claude doesn't tease me with his powers like he did just now. We're getting married, he doesn't have to use his vampire wiles anymore, so I think the charm used the connection between us to strip us both of some of our control."

"We were told that it would protect us from a vampire's secondary powers," McKinnon said.

"As far as I can tell, all it does is guarantee the vampire will be even more uncontrolled; maybe if it's less than a master vampire it will do what the makers of the charm advertised, but if the vampire is a master I think it will actually make them more dangerous. Hell, if you take away the gaze, that still leaves them with super strength and speed."

"No, that's the gaze, it makes people think they're faster and stronger."

"Are you kidding me?"

"Shapeshifters are faster and stronger, but vampires have to cheat by using their secondary abilities."

I looked at Dolph and made a little go-ahead gesture.

"You're the vampire expert," Dolph said.

"He's your friend."

"I thought we were at least work friends," McKinnon said.

"How would you feel if I forced you and your wife to harm each other, as an experiment just to see what would happen? Would we still be friends after that?"

Expressions chased across his face like clouds on a windy day as he tried to process, or maybe he was just buying time to frame an answer that would make him the good guy here. That's what most people do, they reframe things so that they are the hero and not the villain. I hoped McKinnon was better than that.

"If you did it without understanding that it would hurt us, I'd hope I'd listen to you explain and accept a heartfelt apology."

"I don't trust you as much as I did before, but skip it, let's get back to the fact that you are part of a government think tank committee and you all think that vampires are not faster and stronger than human normal. How the hell did the experts on your panel decide that bit of misinformation?"

"I'm not at liberty to share the names of our experts."

"If it was Gerald Mallory, he hasn't done anything but morgue stakings in decades. Maybe he doesn't remember the truth, but if you take this charm into the field and come up against someone who's not chained down with holy items for a morgue staking, you could strip the vampire's control away. This magic could turn them back into a killing machine that just slaughters everyone it sees, because you've taken their ability to control their hunger for blood away from them. Do you understand what I'm saying?"

"I'm not sure I'm following you."

"She means that even if the vampire wasn't planning to hurt anyone, the charm could force them to attack."

"We were told the charm just strips away the human mask and reveals the true monster inside."

"Whoever told you that knew exactly what the charm would do."

"You can't know that it wasn't just an honest mistake, Blake."

"I bet you a hundred bucks that they knew, and that they believe that the only good vampire is a dead vampire."

"We would never take advice from someone who thought that," McKinnon said.

"And they know that, so they'll keep the worst of their prejudice to themselves, so they can further their agenda."

"I don't believe that the people who made this charm understood what it would do."

"Most witches don't know that much about vampires, not really; their magic is all about life, so they had to turn to a vampire expert on what went into the charm, right?"

He looked away then, so we wouldn't see his eyes. I think he was out of steely cop gaze that would hide what he was thinking. That meant I'd made him doubt one or more of the experts on his oversight committee. Good.

"If it's Gerald Mallory, then he'd do anything to change the laws back to the bad old days when vampires could be killed on sight. He hates them with the kind of hate you see in hardcore white supremacists, or men who despise women at the same time that they're obsessed with them. It's that kind of obsessive hatred that I saw in Mallory the last time I worked with him."

"I'm not admitting that Gerald has ever spoken with our committee, but he's not very flattering about you either."

"He's told me to my face what he thinks of me."

"I doubt that."

"He thinks I'm sleeping with the enemy, and that Jean-Claude basically used vampire wiles to seduce me and that I'm not in love with him, I'm just mind-fucked or possessed, or I've gone completely over to the other side because he found out I'm a necromancer and that makes me as evil as a vampire."

"He did not say that to you," McKinnon said.

"No, he called me fucking coffin bait, fucking fur-banger, whore of Babylon, and an evil slut who betrayed my humanity to be in league with the devil."

"Did he call you all that in front of witnesses?" Dolph asked.

"Not unless you count the vampire that he was trying to kill, and that was so long ago that the vampire was just glad to live through it all. No way was he going to testify against a vampire hunter, and back then no one would have believed him anyway."

"How long ago was that?" McKinnon asked.

"God, eight, nine years ago now. I haven't been invited back to Washington, DC, since then, at least not to hunt vampires."

"You went to DC to speak in front of two committees. One on zombie rights and one on vampire rights," Dolph said.

"Yeah, the first one went pretty well, but by the time I was invited to speak about vampires the antivampire lobby had blackened my name so that they decided not to have me speak after all."

"You never mentioned it to me," Dolph said.

"You were still anti-supernatural-everything back then, Dolph."

"I'm sorry that you couldn't come to me back then."

"You've had me and all my sweeties over to your house. We're good," I said, and then I looked at McKinnon. "You and I are not good."

"What can I do to make this right between us?" he asked.

"Start with taking the charm to your car, and we'll go from there," I said.

He just turned on his heel and went for his car. When he was out of earshot, Dolph said, "That charm isn't just aimed at vampires, Anita."

"It's aimed at anyone who works with death magic."

"I don't think that McKinnon knew that before he brought it with him," Dolph said.

"You know him better than I do, but if that's true then his bosses sure as hell knew."

"You think they sent him to test vampires out in the field, or you?"

"Both."

"They used him to get to you," Dolph said.

"I believe they know exactly where he is and used him like a Trojan horse."

"Do you think that the Oversight Committee on Supernatural Affairs is trying to find a way past your defenses?"

"I think they're either covering their bases in case I go rogue someday, or they're actively working on ways to take Jean-Claude and me down."

"In case he goes rogue, or do you think that the committee that's supposed to be working to protect the supernatural citizens of this country is planning to do just the opposite?"

"I don't know, but you prepare for what your enemy can do, not what they will do."

"McKinnon is headed back," Dolph said.

I put a smile back on my face and watched McKinnon walk this way. Was he my enemy or my friend? The fact that I had to ask myself that question was answer enough. I would be friendly with McKinnon, but we weren't friends anymore.

9

THE THREE OF us were squished into the manager's office; there was barely room for me to squeeze myself into a corner over the manager's shoulder. He brought up the video on a small monitor. "I've got it set up to just after the alarm sounded on the floor."

"Thanks for anticipating," Dolph said.

"I'm saving the video that shows her coming out of the room with the fire extinguisher to share with the management company that runs this place. I figure if I send it up to them now, with the New York fire still in the news, Mona has a better shot at a bonus."

"That's good of you," McKinnon said.

"I saw the video from New York; Mona is a freaking hero and I want the company heads to know that."

I waited for McKinnon to say he'd been in New York in person, but he didn't, so I let it go and watched the grainy black-and-white video. Mona appeared on camera and looked at the far doors, then walked out of camera to come back with the fire extinguisher. She went straight to the door, knocked, and though there was no sound it looked like she announced herself and even waited to see if there was a reply from inside before she used her key card to enter.

"Did she knock and announce before entering the room?" McKinnon asked.

"Under stress a lot of people repeat patterns," Dolph said.

"Maybe," I said.

Dolph looked at me.

I looked back at the screen frozen with the door closed behind our heroic maid. "Can you let it play from there, please."

The manager shrugged and hit the button, so we were looking at the closed door for several minutes. Nothing happened, no one ran past in panic from the fire alarm. "Was the victim the only person staying on that floor?" I asked.

"No, we're almost full this week."

"So, if the fire alarm sounded why aren't the room doors opening and people running for safety?"

"A lot of people were at dinner, or still out for the day when the alarm sounded. We got lucky that it wasn't just after dawn like in New York."

"The rooms on that side only get afternoon sunlight," I said, repeating what Mona had said.

The manager looked at me funny, then seemed to think about it. "I suppose so, what does that matter?"

"You need direct sunlight for the vampire to catch fire."

He looked back at the video and the empty corridor. "So, we got lucky because the only vampire we have staying with us chose an afternoon room?"

"Something like that," I said.

A man ran past the camera, then two people carrying small children ran past, and a couple holding hands. Every face we could see clearly looked terrified. "Pause and check the time code," Dolph said.

The manager stopped it and checked the time. He rattled off the time on the video. "That's when the fire alarm went off," McKinnon said.

The manager frowned up at us. "But Mona went into the room because she smelled smoke; did she smell it before the smoke detector did?"

McKinnon and I both shook our heads. Dolph just started making notes in his ever-present notebook.

"Wow, even more impressive that she smelled smoke before the smoke detector," the manager said as he watched more panicked people run past the camera. The door to the room stayed shut during all of it.

"How did you know what Mona had done to put out the fire?" I asked.

"The firefighters found her in the room. She told me she was afraid it would start burning again, so she stayed until the firemen came."

"It?" I asked.

"The vampire, she was afraid it would start burning again, so she waited with the fire extinguisher. I saw what was left of the poor bastard, I couldn't have stayed in the room with the remains like that. Mona deserves a medal."

"It was dark by the time the firefighters arrived, right?" I asked.

"Yeah," he said.

"Sunlight was gone, why would the vampire catch on fire again?"

He frowned, then looked back at the video. The firefighters were on screen now. It took a few minutes, but one of them helped Mona out into the hallway and her hands were empty now; apparently one of them had taken the fire extinguisher from her in the room. She looked as dazed and blank as she had in the room when I'd seen her in person.

"Is Ms. Castel normally that calm under pressure?" Dolph asked.

"No, I mean she's not bad, but I totally underestimated her."

"She didn't have much affect in the room when I saw her, is that normal for her?" I asked.

"Affect?"

"Her face is blank, not much expression, is that her norm?"

"No, no, she's like the rest of us, I guess."

"She doesn't have any preexisting medical issues that you're aware of?" I asked.

"No, why would you ask that?"

"Captain Storr called me in late and I just wanted to know if someone had checked her out. She seems shocky to me."

"The firefighter paramedics checked her out," Dolph said.

"Okay," I said.

"Mona's all right, right?" The manager looked up at all of us from his chair. He seemed genuinely concerned; good for him.

"She's fine," Dolph said.

The manager looked at me then, and I smiled and said, "I just wanted to be a hundred percent sure she'd gotten some attention, that's all, but we're good."

"You can stop the video now," Dolph said.

"Thanks for letting us see the video," McKinnon said.

I smiled and just tried to look pleasant while we left the tiny room and looked for someplace we wouldn't be overheard while we discussed the idea that maybe our heroine was actually our murderer.

10

"THERE IS NO way that a human being smelled smoke through a closed door in an outer hallway before the room's smoke detector sounded," McKinnon said.

I leaned against the empty room's dresser and agreed. "Maybe a wererat would smell it, but I don't know enough about the sensitivity of smoke detectors to make that call."

"Why not just shapeshifters, why wererats specifically?" Dolph asked.

"Rats have one of the best noses in the animal kingdom, better than dogs," I said.

Dolph made a note.

"Well, I don't know much about shapeshifters, but a human being did not beat the smoke detector," McKinnon said.

"She got the fire extinguisher and then entered the room," I said.

"That's why she knocked and announced herself first," McKinnon said.

I nodded. "Just in case the vampire was already awake for the night. If he'd answered she'd have asked if he needed anything, or said she'd come back later."

McKinnon and I nodded. Dolph just stood there making notes and thinking. I'd begun to suspect that sometimes doodling in the notebook helped him think, but maybe he made in-depth notes. I wasn't going to arm-wrestle it away from him to check, and without a stepladder I was too short to peek.

"Are we all thinking she opened the drapes and then waited to put out the fire so there was no loss of life other than the victim?" Dolph asked.

McKinnon and I exchanged a look, then turned back to Dolph. I said, "Yes." McKinnon said, "We are."

"Let's go talk to our hero," Dolph said.

11

I'D HAVE BEEN too direct, or made it complicated, but Dolph just asked Mona Castel to come and make a formal statement. She didn't call for a lawyer or see the trap in the request. She went with him meek as a lamb, and he stayed beside her looking pleasant and hiding the wolf in his impeccably pressed suit until she was safely in the back of his unmarked car with Officer Kay Beecher beside her. Dolph told her he had to confer with his colleagues and he'd be right back, and then he motioned McKinnon and me to follow him away from the car. He started to talk to us then but noticed people with their cell phones pointed this way. It used to be that the news media had to arrive before you worried about cameras; now everyone was a potential leak about the investigation.

He started to walk back toward the hotel, and we went with him. I felt a knock at my psychic shields that made me look around. There was the crowd of people being kept back behind the police tape, most of them with phones pointed this way, and uniformed officers doing their best to keep the looky-loos contained. Whatever had caught my attention wasn't there, so I paused and looked through the more distant part of the crowd and then to the parked cars. There, somewhere there.

Dolph had backtracked to be beside me and asked, "What did you see?"

"Not see, feel." My phone sounded with my text tone, and because I wasn't sure what I was sensing I checked it.

It was Ethan texting, **We're parked waiting for you. Claudia ordered extra security.**

I texted, **Good.** Was that what I'd felt? It didn't feel like Ethan, he was tied to me metaphysically, but he was usually quieter in my head than this. Whatever this was, it was much louder in my head. **Who else is with you?** I texted.

Ru.

Ru was one of my Brides, designed to be basically cannon fodder for the master vampire that made them. They were all this calming silence in my head because they could feel my emotions, but it didn't work both ways like it could with Ethan.

I leaned into Dolph with McKinnon joining the huddle. "Ethan Flynn and Ru Erwin are here for extra security for me when I'm not surrounded by cops. That's who I texted."

"What, Murdock isn't with you today?" Dolph said.

"Nicky had something else to do," I said. If it had just been Dolph I might have explained that I'd made the mistake of kissing Nicky in public, and the image went viral. Speculation was that I was dumping Jean-Claude at the altar for my ruggedly handsome bodyguard. To calm the rumors and to keep the media from swarming me we were rotating my security for a little bit. Since Nicky had become my regular security person as well as my lover and one of the men I was in love with, it felt weird that he wasn't in the parking lot ready to back me up.

"Everything okay?" Dolph asked.

I nodded, and then there it was again. Something didn't feel right. "Something feels wrong, like I'm missing something that I should be picking up on."

"Could McKinnon's charm have messed with your abilities?"

"Since I don't know what the charm does, or is, sure."

"I didn't mean any permanent harm, Blake."

"Let's take this inside," Dolph said. We went back into the air-conditioned hush of the hotel and found an unused conference room, though the manager had informed us that he would need it for a meeting with the hotel staff to convey the concerns of his bosses and their bosses. Dolph assured him we wouldn't need the room long. I thought we were going to discuss strategies for the interrogation or the next part of the investigation. What I hadn't seen coming was Dolph telling me, "There's no active warrant of execution on this one, Anita."

"I know that."

"It doesn't fall under the preternatural marshals' jurisdiction."

"You invite me to come play and now you're kicking me out?"

"If the hate groups get her a lawyer, you being involved with the interrogation will give them ammunition to say we used supernatural influence to get a confession."

"When did I start being supernatural influence?"

He gave me a look.

"What?"

"I'll let you know what we learn."

"And that's it?"

"We'll keep you in the loop," McKinnon said.

Dolph turned to him with a look on his face that I'd seen before; it did not bode well for whoever was at the other end of that look.

McKinnon knew the look, too, because he said, "What?"

"You don't get to say to Anita that we'll keep her in the loop; I could keep you both in the loop."

"This is connected to my case," McKinnon said.

"I didn't say it wasn't, but it's still my case right now; me allowing your involvement is a professional courtesy and friendship, but you don't get to decide how much I read Anita into this case."

McKinnon looked at him for a few seconds, then nodded. "I overstepped my bounds between you and your colleague, I get it."

I wanted to say thanks to Dolph for defending me professionally, but it would have been rubbing salt in the wound for McKinnon and I didn't want to do that. He and I respected each other, even liked each other in that acquaintance/friend-with-similar-jobs-and-mutual-friends sort of way.

"Good," he said, then turned to me as we exited the conference room. "I hope you understand why I can't have you there for the interrogation."

I nodded. "I do, I don't like it, but I do."

"Okay, we'll get our hero down to make an official statement," he said as new police walked by us close enough to overhear. I might not have been able to change my words in time. The publicity with Jean-Claude had ruined me for undercover work, but honestly I'd never been that good at it.

"I guess I'll touch base with my people and get back to wedding stuff."

McKinnon laughed. "You sound more like the long-suffering groom instead of the bride."

"Trust me, McKinnon, other than getting to wear the long dress I *am* the long-suffering groom."

He chuckled and even Dolph smiled. There were new uniforms at Dolph's elbow waiting to ask questions before he left the scene, so I left them to it. I actually wanted to see Edward and Asher in their matching best man outfits just to see Edward's reaction to it. I glanced at my watch and realized that Edward would be back in street clothes by now. Damn it, I'd missed one of the few parts of all this that I'd been looking forward to; I hoped Peter had taken pictures.

I had to walk past the crowd that had gathered with their phones out, and a few real reporters, but most of them were using their phones trying to get me to comment about the case. I knew better and just kept walking quickly like I had somewhere else to be. Never make eye contact, never slow down, never make a single noise that can be interpreted as a comment, because anything and everything will be spun into something you never said.

I didn't look around for Ethan and Ru, because if security is in a separate car, then if you don't acknowledge them the reporters and any bad guys lurking around won't know that they're on your side. I didn't have to explain that to either of them, they knew their job, so I just went toward my SUV, ignoring all questions and comments. I had my keys out and was almost to the vehicle when I felt something, someone, whatever it was, and it made me do a quick glance around. I might not be good at verbal sneakiness, but I was good at looking for danger without looking obvious. The parking lot was empty except for cars and empty pools of light. The police were keeping the crowd contained, but most people were probably waiting to have permission to go to their rooms and get their stuff so they could leave. Also, most people wouldn't leave the scene of an interesting crime; they might get a video on their phones and post it first. Smartphones had raised looky-loos to a whole new level.

There was nothing to see, but the skin creeping between my shoulders and up my neck said that just because I couldn't see it didn't mean it wasn't here. I didn't call my necromancy because it was always there; all I had to do was stop blocking it and just let it out of the box. It flowed out from me like a breath of wind. I didn't need much energy to search for undead near me. I had a lot of metaphysical talents, but necromancy was the first magic that had ever come to me, the one that I couldn't refuse or hide from. Most people spent their lives trying to acquire more magic, more power; I'd spent my life just trying to control mine.

I sent that seeking power outward in a ring around me searching for anything it recognized, but whatever was out there wasn't vampire, ghoul, or zombie, or any type of undead. One area of possibilities down, lots more to choose from. Oh, and it wasn't human, or at least not wholly human. Of course, I didn't hit the radar as human anymore either, and the moment I thought that . . . I searched with a part of me that was newer and less finely tuned. I wasn't a vampire no matter how many internet rumors said otherwise, but I did have some vampire powers and they were not original to me. I felt down the metaphysical cords that tied me to Ethan and Ru, different kinds of cords, but when I concentrated I could feel the connection. There on the edge of my awareness was something, no, someone else. It wasn't like Ethan, one of my animals to call, and I'd already ruled out vampires that were connected to me, so that left Brides. I only had three of those. Nicky was helping test Edward's and Peter's skills in the workout area underneath the Circus of the Damned, and Ru was with Ethan, so that left . . . "Rodina, I know you're there."

"But where am I?" She said it out loud, but she could throw her voice really well, so I knew not to trust that for direction.

"These stupid games really piss me off, you know that."

She laughed, but the sound seemed to come from more than one place. She'd had centuries to practice her spying and assassination skills.

"As my Bride it's supposed to cause you physical pain if I'm unhappy; you shouldn't be able to go against my express wishes."

"No, I shouldn't be," she said, voice coming from an entirely new area of the circle of sound she was bouncing around me.

"Masochist much, Rodina?"

"The pain it causes me is outweighed by the pleasure I take in tormenting you."

"This isn't tormenting me, just irritating me."

"Then I will have to try harder, won't I?" There was something in her voice that sent a chill up my spine like I was actually afraid of her. I shouldn't have been; she was bound by magic so that she could not hurt me. She was even bound to give her life to save mine. Yet as I stood there in the dimness of the parking lot I really wanted to know where the fuck she was, just in case. She was a wereleopard and they were fast even for a shapeshifter. If I drew a gun I'd have to shoot her and since she was supposed to be one of my bodyguards that seemed overkill, so I went for a blade instead. If she was close enough she'd magically appear beside me before I could get it drawn and lay her finger beside my throat or something equally creepy just to let me know that she could have killed me.

I had the blade in my hand, and she still hadn't appeared. I was tired of playing with her. "This shit is making me late, Rodina."

"Then get in your vehicle and drive away," she said in that bouncing echo of a voice so that I had no idea where it was coming from, but even through the theatrics she sounded pleased with herself. I was suddenly almost sure where she was hiding.

"Get out from under my car, Rodina."

"You're only guessing."

"Let me make this simpler, I command you to come out of hiding right now."

"You don't know where I am."

"I gave you a direct order," I said.

"I'm coming," she said, no echoes this time, just a sigh. I don't know if she rolled or scooted out, but she was suddenly on the other side of my SUV. She was as slender and as five foot six as when I first saw her in Ireland. Her blond hair had grown out a little, just enough to let me know it might have waves if she let it get closer to her shoulders. The temporary dyes that she'd been trying on her naturally yellow hair were gone, leaving it silvery as she stood just out of the direct light from the tall pole above my car. I always parked in the light if I could, a holdover from when I wasn't one of the things that went bump in the night. Rodina used the shadows and her all-black clothing to hide, except her hair gave her away. Maybe she read my thought, because she pulled a hood up from her sweatshirt and it was just the pale slightly long oval of her face ruining the look.

"I miss my mask," she said, because she could read my thoughts, I just couldn't read hers. The idea was that Dracula's Brides needed to know his thoughts and feelings so they could serve him perfectly, and

Drac didn't need to know anything about them because it was all about him. But I didn't want Rodina to be all about me, so I was left staring at her across the hood of my car wondering what she was thinking, feeling, and having no idea as if we weren't bound together by magic for all eternity or until one of us died.

"I'm sorry you miss the mask," I said finally, because I was sorry that she missed being one of the masked and robed Harlequin, who had hidden their identities so completely that they never took the masks off in public and covered the rest of themselves in all black like she was doing now. If she'd had one of those blank-colored masks on, then depending on the color I'd know if she'd come to kill me (black), to hurt me (red), or just to talk (white).

"I didn't at first, I reveled in not being forced to hide. I thought I would find myself." She made a sound that was supposed to be a laugh but was so bitter I wanted a new word for it.

"I'm sorry that you don't like your new life," I said.

"I was one of the most feared assassins in the world, and one of the best interrogators among us, and now I'm a glorified babysitter who isn't allowed to hurt the reporters or the civilians with their phones taking pictures and video and posting them everywhere. No one needs spies anymore because the ordinary people have given everyone eyes and ears."

"I am sorry that you are this unhappy, Rodina."

"But you're also angry with me for being unhappy, I can feel it, hear it. Your thoughts and feelings invade me in a way that being my old master's leopard to call never did."

"I'm done apologizing."

"Good, I don't want apologies, my queen, I want purpose."

"You're stuck like everyone else trying to figure out your purpose for yourself."

"Well, it sucks. To use one of your favorite phrases."

"Yeah, existential dread and the search for identity is a bummer." My voice was casual, but I knew the look on my face and my posture wasn't. I still had the knife out, because even for Rodina she was being weird. I'd seen her in training with the other bodyguards, I knew what she was capable of.

"You have no idea what I am capable of, my white queen." *My white queen* was her newest nickname for me, I guess it beat *my dark queen* or *my evil queen*, which she'd used for most of the time I'd known her.

"Nicky can't read my thoughts as well as you can, he just gets my emotions mostly; why is that?"

"I have had eons to practice my mystical skills and he has not yet seen a century pass."

"You know that's not an answer, right?"

"It is an answer, my queen; it's not my fault if you're even younger than Nicky and understand even less."

"Why are you skulking around in the parking lot, Rodina?"

"I was making certain that no one ambushed you."

"Good, you can go back to the car, and you can all follow me to my next destination."

"I am ordered to ride in the car with you just in case someone tries to separate you from the security in the other car."

"Whose orders?"

"Why, your head of security, my queen."

"Did Claudia order *you* to ride with me or just one of you to ride back with me?"

"Me; your American press and general populace seem very heteronormative no matter how woke they talk, so she thought a woman riding with you would quiet the rumor mill that has you running away with Nicky and leaving Jean-Claude at the altar."

I knew that Claudia hadn't said anything that long-winded and explain-y. She'd have just ordered the three of them to meet me here and given the division of labor, but one of the few good things about being the "queen" was that I could change things without checking with anyone else. I was so not riding with Rodina tonight.

12

RODINA'S BROTHER, RU, was in my passenger seat looking like a carbon copy of his sister except for an inch taller and a little more muscle on his slender frame. Oh, and he'd dyed his pale blond hair a deep rich brown so that it looked black in the darkened car. I wasn't sure how I felt about the hair color, and Rodina hated it, because it made them not look alike. I guess that was weird for triplets; Rodina had requested that I not think of them as twins even in my own head because she and Ru could hear it, and their brother being dead didn't change the fact that they were triplets, not twins. Since Rodrigo had died taking a shotgun blast to the chest to save Nathaniel, Damian, and me, I could call the remaining siblings triplets.

"Where are we going?" Ru asked.

"Back to the wedding shop so I can get dressed for date night." I texted Edward and Peter, and I had missed seeing Edward and Asher dressed up together in their matching but opposite-color best man outfits, damn it. Peter assured me that he had pictures, though, which made me happier. He also asked if I needed any help at the crime scene. I was pretty sure that was Edward dictating that one. I assured them that I was done with crime for the night and off for date night. They were already at the gym with the bodyguards getting ready to work out. They would get to test themselves against real shapeshifters for the first time since they'd both been contaminated. I was sorry to miss the workout, especially after seeing what Peter had done to Kane, but like they had said, I couldn't leave the love of my life hanging on date night.

Jean-Claude was suddenly in my head saying, "I adore being the love of your life, *ma petite*, I cannot wait to see you tonight." I was in the dimness of the SUV grinning at my phone like an idiot with Ru sitting still and quiet beside me.

"So wedding shop, then Guilty Pleasures?" he asked.

"Yes, can you please text Rodina and Ethan?"

"If you lower your shields Ethan can read your mind, and Rodina and I always know when you are thinking of Jean-Claude."

I fought not to frown, because I hated that so many people were so far into my business in a way that I couldn't prevent. "Just text them, please, let's at least pretend to be normal."

"I'll text them, but why does part of you persist in wanting to be normal?"

I glanced at him, but his face was bent toward the phone typing with his thumbs. "Didn't you ever want to be normal?"

"We were trained to be part of the Harlequin from birth, this is my normal."

I started the car and reminded him to buckle his seat belt automatically but realized it was already fastened. Rodina would have made me order her to do it. "You and Rodina are the only people I know whose parents were both Harlequin; everyone else was an adult when they were inducted, or invited, or whatever."

"There were others born to Harlequin over the centuries, but it has always been rare since the female half of the couple would be unfit to serve our dark mistress's bidding during the latter stages of the pregnancy."

"So, there are other Harlequin that were born into the family business?"

"Yes," he said.

I glanced at his profile as I drove out of the parking lot and headed for the I-70. "You don't want to talk about it, or them."

"No, I do not."

I wanted to ask why so badly, but the topic obviously upset him, so I was willing to let it go, but he knew what I was feeling, and what I really wanted. "One of them was our friend, and the other was our enemy."

"You don't have to talk about this if you don't want to, Ru."

"You wish to know."

"But you don't have to tell me."

He looked at me then. "You are my master, my queen, you have but to ask and I must do it." He shivered. "You really don't like being reminded that if you give a direct order I must obey it."

"Nope," I said, and concentrated on driving.

"I do not understand your push for us to find lives of our own, but I appreciate that you mean well by it."

"I mean well by it, let me translate that for a second, that means that my good intentions are turning out not so good for you and Rodina, right?" I glanced at him in time to see him smile.

"We are having something of an identity crisis."

"Rodina said she needed for me to give her purpose."

"Yes, that is exactly what we lack. A purpose. We were literally raised from birth to serve the queen of the Vampire High Council as her bodyguards, spies, and assassins. When she fell into her deep sleep the rest of the vampire council took over as our masters, sending us out into the world to further their goals and those of all vampirekind."

"But you're not vampirekind, you're wereleopards."

"Our master was a vampire, and his interests were ours."

"I guess my interests must seem boring compared to traveling the world spying and killing people."

"We did not always travel the world, once we helped curate all the treasures that the vampire council had accumulated over the eons."

"That must have been a hell of a collection."

"It was, only the British Museum comes close in scope, but even they are missing so much of the most ancient history. They have to buy it as artifacts, but we were able to collect it in person when it was new and had people who spoke and wrote the languages on it all."

I thought about that for a few seconds as we drove through the night. There was too much light to say it was dark, but it still had that intimacy that a car gets after dark that daylight never seems to give it. "Are there members of the Harlequin who could decipher archaeological finds that no one else could?"

"Yes."

"If I ordered some of you to do it, would that be interesting to you?"

"We can safely travel to the United Kingdom, but in most of the rest of the world we would not be welcome."

"Vampires aren't, but shapeshifters can travel to more countries."

"But how would we explain that we have lived for thousands of years, Anita? Humans would know that we either had ties to a vampire or to something else that was ageless and very illegal in their country."

"I bet the British Museum would jump at a chance for you and Rodina to visit them."

"Would you come with us?"

"I don't know, the idea's too new, I'd have to talk to Jean-Claude and find out how the vamp politics are going there."

"You truly want us to be happy, I can feel that it makes you hopeful to offer us this chance to do something that interests us."

"I like my people to be happy, why is that so strange to everyone?"

"You have no idea how selfish and petty most people are, Anita."

"I'm a cop, I know people are shitty, but I try not to be."

He made a small sound that was almost a laugh. "I will talk to Rodina about your idea, perhaps that will brighten her mood."

"You seem down, and she seems depressed or dangerous. You're both in weird moods, what's up?"

"It is our birthday today."

"Why should that make you depressed?" The moment I said it, I realized why. "Shit, it's all three of your birthdays and you're missing your brother."

"Yes, and this year we have been dreaming of him."

"The same dreams?" I asked.

He shook his head. "No, but at least once a night Rodrigo is in our dreams."

"I guess with the birthday and all, that would be natural."

"It did not happen last year."

I glanced at him, then back to the road. "Maybe you've had time to process the loss?"

"Perhaps, but it is unsettling to see him when I close my eyes and then when I wake it's as if the loss is fresh again, like for a second I forget he's dead, and then I remember."

"That sounds awful, I can't imagine having to do that about any of the people I've lost."

"Thank you."

"My therapist might know a grief counselor for the two of you to see."

"This doesn't feel like grief, Anita."

"What does it feel like?" I asked.

"I feel haunted."

I looked at him, then back to the road. "Does Rodina feel the same way?"

"Her dreams make her miss Rodrigo more; mine . . . I did not always agree with the choices my siblings made, but they were my family, so I went where they went, did what they did. You give us both too many choices to be ourselves, too many decisions that we do not make together. Rodina feels like she is losing me as well as Rodrigo, and I feel disloyal to my sister. I loved Rodrigo, but I was also afraid of him. I realize now that I went along with many things because I did not want to be his victim, or Rodina's. It was much better to be their ally."

"I saw Rodrigo's cruel streak when he killed Domino."

"I am sorry for reminding you of your loss."

"No, that's not what I meant, Ru. I meant that Rodrigo was frightening."

"But he was my brother and I loved him."

I thought about my own family. "Family is so fucking hard sometimes."

"I miss Rodrigo terribly and if I could have him alive again, I would, but he hates you in my dreams, threatens you and Jean-Claude and Nathaniel and Micah and anyone that I feel an emotional closeness to, he wants to do terrible things to them, and I don't. I stand up to Rodrigo in my dreams in a way that I never did in real life."

"We work out our issues in our dreams a lot more than we think," I said.

"I suppose so," he said, voice soft. He was hunched over as if something hurt. I didn't think it was physical, though sometimes a broken heart feels that real, and no one breaks your heart like family.

I didn't know what to say that would make that level of pain better, so I didn't try. I just reached across the car and touched his leg. He was a shapeshifter and even more than for most people touch was comforting to them. I meant it to be a light pat, but his hand covered mine, pressing it against his thigh. I turned my hand under his until we were holding hands.

He held my hand and then his shoulders started to shake, and I realized he was crying. "I feel lost, Anita, so lost."

I squeezed his hand and said, "I've got you, Ru."

He wrapped both of his hands around mine and cried without looking at me. We drove like that in the dark car until we were almost at Until Death and Beyond Bridal, and then Ru just pulled himself together and stopped crying.

"I need to wipe my face, but could you please keep holding my hand after I do all that?"

"Of course, whatever you need."

He let go of me and drew Kleenex out of his jacket pocket, dried his face, blew his nose, and settled his clothes and the weapons under them back in place, and then he reached his hand out to me and I took it. We held hands on the seat beside him until I pulled off the Riverfront area where the streets were mostly cobblestone, narrow, and full of weekend pedestrians who seemed utterly confident that I wouldn't run them over. When I'd left for the murder scene the sidewalks were full of a few happy, strolling tourists taking pictures of all the vampire-run businesses and waiting for them all to open for the night. Now the streets and sidewalks were packed like sardines in a can because everything was open. Once the Riverfront had been called Blood Square and all the businesses had been very adult like Guilty Pleasures, but as vampires became more mainstream, businesses that were also more mainstream started to open up. First it was fancy restaurants where vampires might not be able to eat food, but they could cook it. People who weren't vampires would pay just to have restaurants where most of the staff were. There was even a new restaurant where vampires brought human dates, and the humans ate while the vampires played culinary voyeur. Jean-Claude was actually a silent partner in the restaurant. The chef had only become a vampire in the last two years, but unfortunately it was in a country where vampires were still illegal monsters and could be killed on sight. The chef was one of the most famous in the world, a very big deal, too famous to hide, so Jean-Claude invited him to America to open both a regular restaurant, Liberté, and Voyeur.

Ethan and Rodina were driving just behind us as I searched for parking. I needed two spaces not that far away from each other ideally. Bodyguards can't do their job unless they're with you, but on the nights that Jean-Claude was onstage the parking was even worse than usual on the Riverfront. Even though I was headed to him soon, I didn't want to reach out mind-to-mind to him in case he was interacting with the audience, even just giving his voice to introduce someone else. Hard to dance or interact with the audience when someone else tries to peek into your head. We finally found me a spot to park and let Rodina and Ru be my bodyguards to the shop while Ethan found a parking spot somewhere else.

"When Claudia said she was thinking of keeping three to four people on you until the higher alert calms down, I thought it was over-reacting, honestly, but now I'm glad she did it, because I have to leave you here while I park," Ethan said through the window of the black SUV that was part of a fleet we'd gotten for security to use on the job.

"I guess so," I said. The car behind him started honking its horn.

Ethan started to say something, but the horn sounded again. I motioned him to just go as the three of us moved closer to the parked cars to let Ethan and the impatient line of cars behind him ease past.

"So, you're going to go to the bridal store to get professional hair and makeup done, before going to Guilty Pleasures. I'd have dressed differently," Rodina said.

I looked at her hooded sweatshirt and black tac pants and boots. I was dressed almost the same except I'd opted for jogging shoes instead of the boots. Ru was wearing almost the same thing as his sister except his sweatshirt zipped up the front. I was wearing one almost identical to it. I laughed.

"If you're going to be part of my regular rotation we gotta start planning our outfits so we don't all match."

Rodina said something, but I couldn't hear her over the traffic, the groups of people on the sidewalks. I shook my head and she finally stepped closer to me. Ru started looking outward for trouble as the three of us huddled closer so Rodina could repeat herself.

"I said, we're accustomed to matching a hell of a lot more closely than this." She gave a glance toward Ru still searching our sur-roundings for bad guys, so that he didn't see the dirty look she gave him. I think she was referring to his new hair color, and not just their missing triplet.

"Are you fit for duty tonight?" Ru asked.

"What?" she asked.

"Are you fit for duty, or do you need to take the night off?" he asked, still without looking at her.

"I'm . . ." She stood a little straighter; I hadn't even noticed her shoulders were hunched until she stopped. "I'm ready for duty if you are, little brother."

"You taught me to always be ready for duty," he said.

She let out a long breath and then smiled at me. It even filled her eyes, though with black eyes you have to work hard to get them to look friendly, but she suddenly managed it. "Let's get inside so the beautification can happen in time to ogle Jean-Claude." She didn't say *get me inside in time*, but I didn't ask her if she wanted to ogle Jean-Claude, I mean, who wouldn't?

13

TWO HOURS LATER I was sitting in front of a mirror staring at someone that I didn't know. It was me, I was in there somewhere, but I'd never worn this much makeup in my entire life. My eyes looked huge and dark. I had good skin, luck of the genetic draw, but the makeup artist had smoothed me out even more, so that my skin was flawless. Once they'd made me uniformly pale, then they'd done things with blush to give back some of the color they'd covered up, and then they'd used two kinds of powder. One to contour and one to cover over everything else. I suddenly had higher cheekbones than I'd ever had before. I couldn't decide if they'd changed the bone structure of my face, or just carved out what was already there so I could see it?

My curly hair was both curlier and neater than it had ever been, because the hairdresser had used a curling iron to turn my mass of curls into perfect ringlets. I didn't even know my hair could look this good. Jean-Claude had to be using a curling iron some nights when he was going onstage. Who knew?

"It doesn't look like me," I said, voice soft. I wasn't really talking to anyone else.

"It does, you know," Ru said as he stepped out of the shadows formed by the bright lights around the makeup mirror.

I used the mirror to look at him behind me. "This so isn't me."

"Now you look like our dark, slutty queen," Rodina said, spilling from the shadows on the other side.

I turned to look at her, frowning. "Thanks for the 'slutty' comment."

"You're wearing fuck-me shoes and a dress that's barely there."

"She's wearing it for the man she loves," Ethan said, coming to stand behind me. "That's romantic, not slutty." He offered me a hand to stand. Normally I wouldn't have taken it, but I was wearing five-and-a-half-inch stilettos. They were the highest heels I'd ever attempted and some of the narrowest, spikiest heels I'd ever tried to stand up in, let alone be expected to walk in, so I not only took Ethan's hand, but I leaned into it.

I'd stood up on the heels before I sat back down for the last few touches of makeup and hair, and it was just as hard to stand up in them the second time. Two steps and I was clinging to Ethan's hand. "How am I ever going to walk even the few yards to Guilty Pleasures without falling on my face?"

"We'll help you," Ethan said.

Ru came to take my other hand, smiling. "We will happily guard your steps as we guard your body."

"They're high heels, not an enemy to defend against," Rodina said, in a voice that dripped with disdain.

"You want to try walking in heels this high?" I asked.

She looked at the shoes, then her gaze rose from them up the line of my mostly bare legs, to the shimmering, dangly edge of the beaded dress. The dress was so sparkly that every movement caught the light differently so that I felt like a blue disco ball. It had spaghetti straps, which I normally can't wear, because I'm too well-endowed not to wear a bra with a dress like this, but they'd been prepared with the best pushup bra I'd ever worn. I didn't even know that pushup bras could lift and separate like this.

"Come see yourself in the mirrors," Felix, the vampire half of the couple that owned Until Death and Beyond Bridal, said as he swept the curtains to one side so the half circle of mirrors where Edward had stood earlier was revealed. I wasn't in a dressing room, I was in the curtained area where brides would usually be getting ready, where I would be getting ready in a few months for the real deal.

"I don't want to see, just take me to Guilty Pleasures and let Jean-Claude see. This is all for him anyway."

Felix *tsk*ed at me, sighing heavily. He'd already made it clear that I was taking most of the fun out of the wedding prep. He supervised hair and makeup, so he hadn't gotten the full brunt of my disdain for all things girly and bridal, but he'd seen enough. "Barnabas has gotten to clothe you all, but this is the first time I have been able to work on your hair and makeup. I want you to see yourself in it, in front of the mirrors so that we will have a place to start when we talk about how you will want your hair and makeup for the wedding."

It was my turn to sigh. "Fine, let's get this over with, then get me to Jean-Claude. I know the shoes are revenge for me wanting to wear comfy sweats on our last in-home movie date. I swear I will never make him dress down on date night again."

"I'm surprised our king owned a pair of sweats," Rodina said.

"He didn't. He bought a designer pair just for the date," I said, as Ethan and Ru led me through the curtain that Felix was holding. I was doing pretty well until we hit the carpet around the raised mirror, and then I held desperately to their hands, because without the support I would have gone down. I leaned into their hands like they were crutches to take the step up on the little raised platform. When Ethan put his other hand on my elbow to steady me even more, I didn't protest. I thought Jean-Claude had finally taught me how to walk in heels until now; apparently I had a height limit for heels and I was past it.

I was so busy watching my feet to get up on the dais that I didn't look in the mirrors until I was standing on firm ground. Ethan let go of my elbow and when I didn't protest he let go of my hand. I didn't fall down so Ru started to let go; I held on to him for a second, then realized if I couldn't even stand in the shoes, date night was over unless one of them carried me everywhere. I took a deep breath, let it out slow, and let go of his hand. He hovered nearby in case I needed the help, but I was finally standing on my own.

I stared down at the strappy sandals, realizing that the shiny blue nail polish on my toes matched or at least complemented the bejeweled sandals. Nathaniel had talked me into the blue polish, a color I'd never worn before, which meant he'd known exactly what color everything would be tonight. I felt suddenly ganged up on by the men in my life. At least my fingers and toes matched, which wasn't always the case.

"They are lovely sandals, but please look at yourself in the mirrors, Ms. Blake," Felix said. He was trying for neutral, but I could hear the excitement in his voice; as a vampire he could have hidden it, or maybe not, maybe he just couldn't wait for me to admire the beautification he'd done.

I looked up. There was a stranger in the mirror looking back at me. The heels made me look tall, hell I was only a half inch shorter than Nathaniel now. My hair fell in perfect black ringlets nearly to my waist. They'd done something to it so that it framed my face but didn't spill forward like it usually did. It looked soft, touchable, but it stayed put at the same time. It was like hair magic.

The dress was made up of beads and crystals in shades of blue from navy to royal to sky to baby blue with a few black beads and shining clear crystals that winked and sparkled in the lights. The hem of the dress barely touched the bottom of my ass with a shimmering line of jewels, so it was like a necklace at the opposite end of the body. It really was a work of art, too bad it was on me.

"You are exquisite, Ms. Blake," Felix said.

"You are always beautiful," Ethan said, "but this is . . . you're breathtaking."

I finally looked at my body, my face, me and not just the hair and the clothes. The heels gave length to my legs that I hadn't seen before. The exercise that I did to be able to save my life and the lives of others made my legs strong and the fringe of the dress hugged my curves like a sparkling caress. There was more room around my waist, because that was always smaller than the curves on either side. I was built like an old-fashioned hourglass with more muscle on my bare arms, but no matter how hard I lifted I could never muscle up past a certain point. The body was strong, firm, and feminine. There was nothing I could do to not look like a girl. I'd spent the early part of my life dressing like I was hiding everything the dress revealed. I'd even reverted back to the old way of dressing as the wedding got closer. I loved Jean-Claude, but I still didn't see what he saw in me physically. He'd been the most beautiful man I'd ever seen, and he'd flirted with me from the beginning. I'd never understood why. Staring into the mirrors, now my face finally matched him. Admittedly he rolled out of bed looking this good and it had taken two hours of professionals to get me here, but for the first time I couldn't argue that I was beautiful. I wanted to, but I couldn't.

I remembered my grandmother telling me I was ugly, that no man would ever want me, and I better have a career and be able to take care of myself, but I'd held on to the thought that I looked like a paler version of my mother, and my father called her the most beautiful woman in the world. Then after two years of mourning her, he'd married Judith, who was everything my mother wasn't. If my short, curvy, curly-haired, Hispanic mother had been the most beautiful woman in the world like he said to her constantly until the day she died, then why was his second wife tall, thin, blond, blue-eyed, and pale like him?

My brown eyes looked almost black, large, and shining in my face, framed by the dramatic eye makeup. The red lipstick had been drawn slightly wider than my lower lip so that my mouth looked pouting and full, and . . . Rodina was right, I looked like a high-end call girl.

"I take it back," she said, and came to stand behind and to one side of me. She looked short compared to me now. She was three inches taller if we were both in flats.

"No, you were right, it's slutty, but then I'm supposed to match Jean-Claude's outfit and he'll be stripping tonight."

"Jean-Claude's outfit will be elegant, because he's always elegant," Ru said.

I smiled then, and conceded that much, but I still stared at myself and didn't know how to feel; *not good* was the closest I could come. I didn't feel good about what I saw in the mirror, and even knowing the reasons why, the damage done to me, the lessons I'd taken from my childhood, none of that fixed anything. I had entered therapy thinking it would "fix" me, heal me, make me whole. I'd been right only about the healing; therapy didn't fix you as if you'd never been broken, it couldn't do that, but as you accepted all your broken pieces, even the ones you hated most, you gradually realized you were whole. Not because you'd never been broken, but because as you discovered your pain, all the places that hurt, scared you, made you hate others, hate yourself, all the dark stuff, you needed it. You needed the scary stuff inside you as much as the happy parts, because only by accepting all of it, warts and all, could you be whole. I was working on being whole, and as I stared at this beautiful stranger in the mirror I tried to believe it was me and to be okay with the fact that not only had my grandmother been a lying bitch, but the way my family had treated me was wrong. The man I called Dad, the man I wanted to give me away at my wedding, had told me I looked just like my mother, but never that I was beautiful in my own right, and always on his arm had been Judith, whom he called beautiful, and who was everything that my mother and I would never be.

My eyes sparkled in the mirrors, shining like the jewels on the dress and sandals. I kept my eyes wide and didn't blink, because I didn't know if the mascara was waterproof. I would not cry and ruin it. I felt more myself with weapons, but I needed at least a day of practice getting the gun out of the purse before I'd been happy with my timing and body memory. I'd be better off throwing the purse at them and stabbing them with the stilettos. I felt like a fucking victim in this outfit. I widened my eyes and thought the weak thought, *I will not cry, I will not cry, I will not cry.*

14

FELIX HAD TRIED to ask me if I wanted my hair down like this for the wedding, or up, but Ethan had taken him to the side to ask something, so that Ru could get me out of the shop before I cried, or started to scream, or acted like a damn fool. I was upset enough that I forgot about the heels as we stepped out of the shop and onto the cobblestone road. I nearly twisted my ankle and fell. Only a desperate grab at Ru's arm saved me. Rodina laughed and said, "I can't believe you are our queen."

Ru turned with me in his arms, putting his body between me and his sister. I didn't feel that threatened, but he knew her better than I did, so I clung to Ru and let him work it out. I was still digging out of the avalanche of issues from seconds ago. I'd let Ru take care of Rodina while I figured out how my family issues might impact tonight's date with Jean-Claude. "She hasn't had centuries to perfect herself," he said.

"It's a spike heel on cobblestones, guys, anyone can trip," I said, but I stayed where Ru had put me with his arm around me and him between us. I let myself put most of my energy into shoveling the emotional shit that I could feel inside my head and body. Emotions didn't just live in the head, or the heart, they burrowed down into your gut, they poured over your skin, they filled up your eyes, they spilled out your fingertips and toes. Emotions were everywhere if you just let yourself feel them, and I'd worked hard to learn how to feel instead of stuff everything out of sight until it erupted in rage or made terrible choices. I was concentrating so hard on working my issues that I didn't hear what Rodina said to me.

"I'm sorry, Rodina, what did you say?"

"I said, have you ever seen us trip, any of us?" Rodina asked, peering around her brother at me.

I knew the *us* meant the Harlequin. "I've seen you all mess up in fight training."

"We can lose, but that's not the same thing as tripping on a stone. You are so damn mortal, my queen."

"Yeah, yeah, I know I disappoint you, Rodina, you aren't winning any prizes with me either."

"I feel your pain and confusion, and it hurts me that you are so unhappy, but tonight I simply don't seem to care."

"I ask you again, sister, are you fit for duty tonight?" Ru said.

"I can guard her against anyone." Ru drew me in closer but thanks to the heels I was taller than him for a change, and I could see Rodina glaring at us over his shoulder. I wrapped my arms over his shoulders and gave her very serious eye contact, as I lowered my head and drew in a deep breath of the scent of his skin. It wasn't just him, but his leopard underneath. Leopard smelled like home to me now, thanks to living with Micah and Nathaniel. Rodina's glare spread so she looked enraged. The only excuse for what I did next was that I was hurting, and she was hurting, and I'd rather have picked a fight than deal with my own emotional shit. I smiled over her brother's shoulder and settled myself around him, pressing my body so close that I'd probably compromised his ability to react if we were attacked. It was stupid, childish, but Rodina and I had that effect on each other.

He kept his head turned to see his sister, but his body reacted to the unexpected cuddling not in the usual male way, but by letting go of some tension that I hadn't even known he was holding, until he settled into my arms and my body like he'd been waiting for someone to hold him. It reminded me of holding his hand in the car, but more intimate. Not sexual, but intimate like someone you trust to hold you and not take advantage. It wiped the teasing smile from my face because I wanted to be worthy of his trust. Playing stupid games with his sister wasn't trustworthy, or even kind. Ru must have felt the change in my body because he readjusted so that he kept the close contact but moved one arm and one leg to the side so that I could still plaster myself against his right side, but his left was free to move. Both of them were ambidextrous when it came to fighting, as most of the Harlequin were. He stopped letting me hold him for real so he could defend me better.

"Can you guard her against emotional pain, sister?"

"No one can do that."

"I'm holding her, trying to soothe her, what are you doing to help?"

"I see how much she's enjoying the soothing," she said, and she sounded jealous. It wasn't usually the tone you heard from sisters. I knew she and Ru weren't a couple, and she seemed to hate me, so what the hell was she jealous of in this moment? Then I fought free of the emotional fallout in my own head and thought what she might be feeling today. Shit.

I stopped laying my head on Ru's shoulder and looked at her more directly. "I'm sorry you're hurting, Rodina."

"You can't feel my emotions. I'm drowning in yours, but you can't feel my pain at all."

"If you'd told Claudia it was your shared birthday she would have understood."

"Ru, how could you tell her? Her of all people."

"She held my hand in the car while I cried."

She stared at us sort of wildly. "You comforted him?"

"Yes," I said.

"Like I'm comforting her now," Ru said.

"An evil queen doesn't need comfort, she needs revenge, violence, not tears and handholding."

"Mommie Darkest was a sociopath. It kind of limited her emotional range," I said.

"She was a great power, and you are nothing in comparison!" She shouted it. A couple paused on the sidewalk behind her, the woman clinging harder to the man's arm. I realized there were more people across the narrow street staring at us. They'd probably been looking at us for a while, but I'd been too busy cuddling with Ru to notice.

"Sister, you are attracting attention."

She glanced back at the couple and opened her mouth, taking a deep breath as if to yell at them, and then she seemed to remember herself, or at least think better of her behavior. Ru spoke into that silence, "I ask again, Rodina, are you fit for duty tonight?"

Her spine was rigid, shoulders back like she'd come to sudden attention. Her voice was as controlled as her body. "All three of us were bred to be ready, and since our brother cannot be here to prove his worth, I will."

Rodina stepped away from her brother so I could see her clearly. She made sure that she was standing in front of me when she bowed low and graceful like she should have been wearing something swashbuckling, or at least a hat to doff as she did it. She came up smiling. "May I offer the lady an arm on the uneven pavement?"

The door opened and Ethan came through it. He looked at all of us. "What did I miss?"

"Your duty," Rodina said.

"Don't go all dark and twisted again," I said.

"He was neglectful of your safety," she said.

"What took so long inside?" I asked.

"Security called from Guilty Pleasures; they want me to bring one of the cars to park in a spot nearer the club."

"Is anything wrong?" I asked.

"I think they just found a closer parking space, that's all," he said.

"By the time I walk back to the car and let you drive me closer, I might as well walk from here," I said.

"In those shoes?" he asked.

"Yeah, Jean-Claude and I will be talking about the shoes, but I just want inside the club in a chair ASAP."

"Then allow me to escort you, my lady," Ru said.

"If someone sees her walking on any man's arm tonight, especially dressed like this, the rumors will start about you, dear brother."

"I hate to agree with Rodina, but she's right," Ethan said.

"If I escort her it will look like two girlfriends out for a night of fun; any man on her arm is the next rumor. For all the wokeness of your media now, they are still terribly heteronormative."

"Some of the women in my life are noticing that," I said.

"Then allow me to protect not only your body but your reputation." She held her arm out to me in an exaggerated manner.

I looked at Ru; he was studying his sister but finally nodded and moved me forward so I could take Rodina's arm. I took it and I swear she flexed her arm like she was a guy and wanted to impress me. I understood the moodiness now, even the hostility about their brother's death and the shared birthday, but it still didn't give me a clue to where the emotional roller coaster would end. The biggest plus was that it had helped me get a handle on my own roller coaster. Seeing her come so close to losing it while I was wearing shoes that made it impossible to fight or run had put me very solidly in the now, because that's where you survive. Past trauma is past. I'd already lived through my family's tender loving care, but if one of the Harlequin truly went apeshit on me, that might not be a survivable moment. I knew Jean-Claude had felt I'd be safe because of the bodyguards, but when one of them is the danger . . . he and I would be having a serious talk about fashion versus safety soon.

"Anita, are you okay with me getting the car and meeting you inside the club?" Ethan asked.

"I'm good, see you inside."

He looked at all of us one more time as if he was picking up more than I would have seen if the situation were reversed, but in the end he just went for the SUV.

"Since I'm dressed like a butch to your lipstick femme I might as well play the part," she said with a smile I could only describe as rakish.

"You're too femme to be butch," I said.

That earned me a better smile.

"I'll share my lipstick with you," I said.

The smile changed slightly, not less or more, just different, but her eyes held sorrow the way they usually held anger. I let go of her arm and her eyes filled back up with their usual cynicism. I got the lipstick out of the tiny designer purse and offered it to her.

There was a moment of uncertainty in her eyes before she took it. Ru handed her his phone with the video on so she could use it as her mirror. She put the scarlet lipstick on and I realized I'd never seen her in anything close to my favorite color of lipstick. I'd seen her in full Goth with black lipstick or nearly colorless lip gloss, but never red. It looked great with the black eyes and dark eyebrows and lashes. Her pale blond hair looked almost white suddenly, as if she was just doing a different Goth color scheme.

"It looks good on you," I said, and she knew I meant it because she could feel what I was feeling. Those newly red lips curled into a smile that filled her eyes with a fierce joy. I gave her a smile that was equally fierce and said, "Let's go watch one of the most beautiful men in the world take off his clothes."

She gave a little shake of her head but was still smiling as she said, "You really don't mind if other people lust after him."

"If that kind of thing bothered me, we'd have broken up years ago." I tucked the lipstick back in my purse and curled my arm through hers. "Let's go see the show."

She smiled and flexed her arm for me again. "Whatever my queen wishes, so shall it be."

I smiled and did my best to believe her and hide my doubts deep enough that she wouldn't feel them. Next year I'd see that they had their birthdays off.

15

WE WALKED PAST the line of people still hoping to get into the club until the crimson neon glow of the Guilty Pleasures sign painted everything reddish and sparkled in the beads of my dress so that it didn't look blue anymore. There were complaints behind us in the line per normal; no one likes a line cutter. I must have looked different enough in the showier makeup and dress that even the black-shirted security guards at the door stopped me with a "Sorry, miss, but you'll have to wait in line."

I looked up at the man who'd spoken. "You must be new here," I said. A woman in line called out, "It's Jean-Claude's fiancée!" Yep, not even my name, just his name and what I was to him, so damn patriarchal.

The new security guy said, "Shit," then apologized for that, too.

The crowd did remember my name, though, because they started calling out, "Anita! Anita! Look this way!" They didn't just want my attention, they wanted my picture; once I would have darted inside head down, but Jean-Claude had dressed me to be seen and we'd had enough practice this year for me to turn, smiling. Rodina smiled with me, then moved away so I stood on the steps alone for a moment, I even managed a little wave without grimacing or giving the pop of flashes from the phones the finger. My eyes were dazzled, my vision full of spots when I turned away and the security at the doors let us through. Ru took my elbow so I didn't trip in the heels with my vision ruined. If you ever wonder why celebrity security guards wear sunglasses, it's not to look tough, it's so the camera and phone flashes don't blind them. Only us celebrities get to go blind for a few seconds; okay, only those of us dating celebrities.

I was glad Ru was there to steady me through the door. Rodina's weight at my back was comforting, too, because between the shoes and the camera flashes I wasn't as able-bodied as normal. I reminded myself that I was doing this for Jean-Claude and we both knew I'd have security with me. I repeated all that to myself as I cursed at feeling helpless. It is not my favorite feeling and looking fabulous has never been worth it to me, but . . . I was safe, no one was trying to hurt me, I was safe. I was even armed, if someone jumped me I could defend myself, but I had to fight off a host of old issues not to get angry about it and aim it at Jean-Claude, or the customers with their phones, or even Rodina and Ru. Once I would have just lashed out, but I owned myself now, issues and all.

I felt something stir inside me and glimpsed bright yellow eyes set in a black velvet face. My leopard down deep inside me where my human mind visualized my inner beasts. The leopard was reacting to my anxiety, trying to protect us, but my anger was the big problem. I wasn't picking a fight with anyone thanks to therapy, but the anger was still inside me looking for a place to go and my inner beasts would help me deal with it, if by help you meant try to tear their way out of my body and ruin the night.

Ru held me close, but underneath the sweetness of his skin was something heavier, his leopard was inside there somewhere. They were both wereleopards so they couldn't help me push down my own. I needed a different kind of wereanimal to help me balance, and as if I'd called him to me, Ethan was there, pushing past Rodina, taking me from Ru. He wrapped his arms around me, and I buried my nose against his chest, but it wasn't enough. I needed bare skin.

He raised his hand with the other arm still holding me close. I pressed my nose against the back of his hand and there was his inner rainbow of tigers—blue, white, red, and gold. He alone held enough different flavors of beasts to keep me in my own skin. The leopard that was crawling up inside me growled into the darkness as the tigers showed themselves among green jungle foliage that just seemed to appear for them to give hints of their movements. The leopard's gold eyes faded into the darkness as the tigers circled inside me.

I could finally draw a deep breath and let go of the anger. Therapy helped me work out my anger issues, but nothing seemed to make them go away. I looked up at Ethan; his white hair spilled around the top of his face, still cut short enough on the sides that the top was the only volume he had. That one dark red streak that went from his forehead to the back of his skull looked like a skilled hairdresser had done it, but it was natural, the only hint of his red tiger lost in white and gray that signaled white and blue respectively. His eyes were a solid gray and if you didn't know what you were looking at you'd never guess they were tiger eyes in his human face. Nothing in his human form gave away his golden tiger heritage, but I could call the scent of it to his skin.

"Thanks," I said, and the background music was low enough he could hear me. There were strip clubs out there where the music blared so loud all night you couldn't hear yourself think, but Guilty Pleasures wasn't like that.

Ethan smiled down at me and said, "You're welcome, but it is part of my job."

I nodded and said, "Still, thanks."

Rodina turned her head and said, "They're taking pictures." She was keeping her voice low so she wouldn't be overheard by the group of people who were standing just outside the half circle that she and Ru had created around us and the wall. The women had their phones out and were filming me clinging to Ethan. They'd had to turn their flashes off because there were signs everywhere for that, so the pictures wouldn't be high quality, yay for that.

"Get security over here and remind them that they aren't allowed to take pictures of performers or their families inside the club," I said.

Ru started to go find someone, but a black-shirted figure was already there chasing them back and telling them if they broke another of the club's rules they'd be kicked out and there wouldn't be any refunds.

Buzz still had his black hair in a close crew cut and small, pale eyes. He was built like an old-fashioned weightlifter, as if with one good flex his shirt would explode off him. He was a vampire, so he could keep his muscles without lifting another weight for the rest of eternity. "Sorry, Anita, I've got new guys on the door."

"I hope they're better at the door than they were just now."

"I'll yell at them later. Allow me to escort you to your table, though I'll have to get an extra chair. I didn't expect four of you."

"I can stand," Ethan said.

"Nah, you'll block the view of the table behind you," Buzz said as he ushered us through the small tables that filled the room around the stage to our table, well, my table since now it was always reserved for me and whatever bodyguard I had with me. Last time I'd been here, Nicky had been with me. I had a sudden pang of missing him. He'd been my main bodyguard for so long that I was used to having him at my side almost everywhere, and I was in love with him, so that contributed. I hated that the rumors had stripped me of him.

Ethan knew better than to hold my chair for me, but Ru didn't yet, so we had that awkward moment of me trying to help him scoot me forward and failing to be helpful. We finally got it done but only because Ru was stronger than human normal and could finally just push the chair to the table even with me being in the way. I'd never managed to figure out how to be graceful when a man did the chair thing, and if Jean-Claude couldn't teach me how to do it, then no one could.

Ru leaned over and whispered, "I'll remember not to do the chair next time."

I whispered back, "Thank you."

Rodina started to sit down beside me, but Ethan moved forward and put his hand on the other side of the chair back. They stared at each other for a long minute while Ru took the far chair that wasn't claimed, leaving the two of them to do whatever they were doing. Ethan was usually easygoing and didn't try to dominate anyone else in my security detail, so why was he suddenly asserting himself now with Rodina?

"We all agreed on this," Ethan said, and he was as serious and unhappy as I'd heard him in a while. He spoke low so that no one could hear but us.

"I didn't agree, I was outvoted," she said, voice still soft.

Buzz came up with our extra chair. "Everything okay here?"

Ru said, "The crowd is starting to notice."

I glanced away from us to the room, and he was right, people were starting to openly stare. This was not going to quiet the rumors. "Both of you just sit down," I said.

They continued to glare at each other. What the hell was going on? "Ethan by me; Rodina, take the chair from Buzz."

Ethan took the chair and sat down beside me, and Rodina let him. Buzz scooted the chair in for Rodina and she was much better at making it look graceful instead of awkward. Maybe she could give me pointers later?

Buzz stepped back and looked at us. Ethan put his arm across the back of my chair, which I don't think he'd ever done. Rodina glared at him. "You guys okay here?" Buzz asked, but he looked at me when he said it.

I looked at my three bodyguards, but only Ru met my gaze; the other two were too busy paying attention to each other. I frowned but said, "We're good; thanks, Buzz."

"Okay, just yell if you need anything."

"Will do, Buzz." He looked at all of us one more time, then walked away. I turned to Ethan and Rodina. "Okay, what's going on?"

Ethan looked at her and Rodina looked at me. He was smiling and she wasn't. "He called rank."

"Rank? What rank?"

Ethan leaned into me so that his arm curled around my shoulders instead of resting on my chairback. I was torn between telling him to move his arm since he seemed to be doing it just to piss off Rodina, but he spoke low enough that I leaned in to hear it. "The Harlequin have been trying to dominate all of us, and we're all tired of it."

"And that explains why you're cuddling with me in public like we're dating when we're not, how?"

Rodina leaned into both of us, pressing herself against Ethan so that it looked like the three of us were having an intimate conversation. "Your guards wouldn't let the fact that we are Harlequin and thus the greatest warriors and covert agents in the world sway them to follow us."

Ethan leaned into Rodina so that his mouth was almost touching her face and thus hidden from the room as he said, "We routinely beat some of you in training, and none of you wins against us all the time. How does that make you the greatest warriors of all time?"

"The death of our dark queen has lessened many of us, but do not let that go to your head, tiger. Training is not the same as battle and if there were not referees and rules to keep us from killing you, you would not be sitting here to disparage our skills."

"Oh, so the great Harlequin only win by killing, not by being the better fighter."

"That is not what I said," she almost growled, as the first warm breath of her beast eased between us all.

Ethan drew breath to speak, but I touched his cheek, which made him look at me. "I understand that the Harlequin come in with a huge chip on their shoulders, and that hits the big chips on everyone else's shoulders. I knew that we were having some growing pains melding our security with them, but I still don't know why you're sitting beside me marking territory like we're dating."

Rodina drew back enough to give a cold, cruel look. "You're just food for her, nothing more."

I felt him flinch both physically and emotionally from her remark. "Ethan is my lover, no one in my life is just food, and I still don't know why the two of you have turned guarding me into a pissing contest."

Ru answered from across the table, voice still low. "Some of us wanted to know who outranked whom, and to save a bloodbath that would have gutted your security, someone came up with the idea that the highest rank starts with who has the privilege of sleeping with you. Ethan does, Rodina doesn't."

She turned on him with a snarl and hissed, "Neither do you, brother dear."

"That is true, but I am not trying to be top cat, and you are."

"You're drawing attention to us," Ethan said.

Rodina got control of herself before she looked around so that her face was back to pleasantly amused. Most of the Harlequin were consummate actors, but then real spies are the ultimate undercover operators. People were noticing the fight, though; not everyone in the room but enough that it would probably be at least tweeted about before the end of the night. Anita Blake, or more likely *Jean-Claude's fiancée*, having a lover's tiff with two of her bodyguards before he even goes onstage.

Ru moved his chair closer and asked again, "Are you fit for duty tonight, sister?"

"I am always ready to serve our queen, whoever she may be."

"Then control yourself."

She stiffened the anger that she'd been trying to stuff down inside her, finally welling up in a rush of rage that felt warm like she was a fire to hold my hands near in the middle of a cold night. It wasn't the heat of her inner leopard spilling closer to the surface, though I felt it dancing along my skin somewhere between heat and electricity as if it was trying to take little bites out of my skin. God she was powerful, but that wasn't the energy that made me lean closer to her. It was her rage I wanted. I was suddenly hungry, because even if you're full, having a rich dessert set in front of you is tempting, and Rodina's emotional pain had turned her into a double chocolate cupcake with sprinkles on top.

I leaned closer to her face while her energy bit along my skin like I was getting closer to a live wire. My inner leopard blinked at me with bright yellow eyes, and a throaty purr slipped from between my lips followed by a growl, so I wasn't sure if I was happy and the leopard was unhappy, or vice versa. The one thing we both agreed on was Rodina had just gone from predator to prey.

Ethan put his bare wrist between us so fast I almost smacked my face into it. I got the scent of his tigers, and the leopard sank back inside me, but it wasn't my inner leopard that wanted me to feed on the woman in front of me, it was more my inner vampire. It was emotion instead of blood, but it was still a type of vampirism. I hated that, but I was learning to accept it and starting to gain control of it.

I moved Ethan's arm down and looked into Rodina's eyes; they were like dark mirrors, black on black with the edge of white around them. There was a reflection in them, a shining flicker of light. I started to look around to find where it was coming from, but Ethan's hand slid up my back underneath my hair, grabbing my neck, keeping me from looking around.

"Let me go," I said.

"Your eyes are glowing," he said.

I looked into Rodina's eyes again and saw the dark light of my brown eyes filled with power as if I'd been a real vampire. If Ethan hadn't stopped me I'd have flashed the whole club and confirmed an entirely different set of rumors. I sat there with Ethan's hand solid against my neck and should have thanked him for reminding me, but I couldn't look away from Rodina's eyes and the shine of my power in them. Rodina leaned toward me, and I watched the reflection of my power grow in the mirrors of her eyes until just before she kissed me the reflection spilled over her eyes and for a second I saw my eyes in her face. The dark brown of them turned to cognac diamonds; then our lips met, and I drank from her lips, tasting the thick sweetness of my own lipstick along with her rage.

16

THE HAND ON my neck squeezed tighter and Ethan's voice was in my ear. "Anita, stop, people are watching."

I tried to pull away from the kiss and the spicy sweetness of Rodina's mouth, all shared lipstick and the spice of her rage, but she wrapped her arms around me, not willing to give up the kiss. I'd never had anyone that I fed rage from want to continue. It usually scared them, made them try to fight to get away, but Rodina wanted closer, and somewhere in the eagerness of her hands and mouth on mine I fell further into her mind and heart than ever before. Loneliness, she was so lonely, and lost, more lost than she'd ever been in her life, and grief, such horrible grief—her brother, her queen, the only life she'd ever known all gone. She needed something to put in its place and I hadn't given it to her. Unlike Nicky, who'd I'd accepted into my life and my heart. I'd had enough control to keep her and Ru out of my emotions. I didn't even let them be part of my main security. I didn't feed on them for energy. I was their queen now, the being that was supposed to fill a hole inside them that the Mother of All Darkness had created inside all her Harlequin. A place where they drew power from, a place that made them belong to something larger than themselves. The Harlequin were like military vets trying to adjust to civilian life, except instead of a human lifetime of service they'd had thousands of years. How do you recover from a loss that large?

I drew back and this time she let me. Her eyes were black again, my power did not fill her eyes now. Our shared lipstick was smeared across her pale face; the light gold sprinkling of freckles across her cheeks stood out like they were decoration, as if she'd put glitter across her face, but it forgot to sparkle. For that moment her face showed all the grief, the loss, everything that the magic had shown me. She was stripped bare of the toughness, the rage, the cruelty, the flirting; everything she used to shield herself and hide behind was gone. It was worse than stripping the clothes away from someone in public, this was baring their soul but only from inches away. The crowd couldn't see it, but I could, Ethan could, and as Ru stood up to put his hands on his sister's shoulders our eyes met and I knew that he didn't need to see his sister's face to know what she was feeling, because he felt the same damn way. It was there in his eyes not through magic, but just because for that moment he didn't try and hide it from me.

Rodina looked up at her brother, and then back at me. "My queen, I am not fit for duty."

I didn't know whether to hug her, or say *No shit*, so I managed not to do either. Let's hear it for maturity and not being a hugger.

17

RU TOOK RODINA back to their rooms at the Circus. Once I would have said he was taking her back home, but I'd seen too far into her heart. I knew she didn't consider it home now. The knowledge made me sad, like I couldn't shake her emotions off me completely. I was in the dancers' bathroom backstage trying to fix my smeared lipstick with Ethan standing outside the door. The trouble was I didn't usually use base makeup, so I didn't have any with me to put back on after I had the lipstick cleaned off; my skin was a slightly different color or texture or something from the bottom of my nose down to my chin and I had no idea how to fix it. I was supposed to be waiting in here until we could decide if I was safe to be around Jean-Claude or Nathaniel since I was a lot more closely connected to them metaphysically than to Rodina or even Ethan.

There was a knock on the door and Ethan said, "Nathaniel is here to be the sacrificial lamb."

"What did you call him?" I asked.

"I volunteered," Nathaniel said through the door.

"What if it gets out of hand?" I asked.

"Then we'll have sex like we've had hundreds of times. I don't have to be onstage tonight."

"You may miss seeing Jean-Claude do your choreography on-stage."

"I'll see him do it later."

"Jean-Claude wanted me to see him onstage tonight and have a date night, and now it may not be happening."

"You can have your date night another time, Anita."

I stared at myself in the mirror—the careful makeup, the curled hair, the dress, the stupid heels—and now because I couldn't control my own powers it was all for nothing, damn it.

"Anita, nothing is wasted, or ruined. Unless we rip the dress up you can wear it again for Jean-Claude."

I watched myself smile in the mirror. "I think we can keep the dress intact," I said, smiling wider.

"Aww," Nathaniel said through the door, but I knew from the tone he was smiling.

I laughed and told him to come in, and the door opened and there he was, one of the loves of my life. He'd put his hair up underneath a cap that looked like a fedora, but the brim was too small, and whatever the type of hat was called, it was giving the illusion that his hair was short. He'd meant to sit out in the audience to watch the show, so hiding his hair was a necessity. He closed the door behind him and leaned against it with his hands behind his back and looked at me from the hair and makeup all the way down to the heels.

"Wow, you look amazing."

"Thank you, I think, it doesn't feel very much like me."

He gave me that warm smile as he pushed himself away from the door and crossed the room to me. "You're always beautiful, but you're right, this is like nothing I've ever seen you wear. It's like lingerie or a costume for you, or should I say, for Jean-Claude?"

"Are you saying you didn't help pick out any of this?"

He grinned. "I saw it, and maybe the color, but except for the shoes it's not any of my kinks." He stood there and we were eye to eye with me in the heels. He wrapped his arms around my shoulders, and it was just natural that my arms went around his waist. It was weird to be face to face instead of me leaning on his shoulder and looking up. His eyes were lavender, not blue like he had to put down on any government ID. Asher had nicknamed him our flower-eyed boy. For the first time I didn't have to go up on tiptoes or have him lean down so we could kiss. Everything was exactly where it needed to be. His lips were full and pouting, made for kissing. If he'd been female he'd have been an old-fashioned centerfold, but he lifted too many weights and ran too many miles to have the curves that promised.

He drew back first from the kiss to smile at me. "Now I know you made out with Rodina, because I can taste her scent on your mouth. That is so hot."

I raised an eyebrow at him. "Really, you have some interest in Rodina that I'm not aware of?"

"You know I don't, but you also know I'm a serious voyeur. Watching you with anyone is hot but watching you with someone new is hotter."

Once I might have been mad at the remark, but now I just laughed, because truth was truth. "There's something seriously wrong with you, you know that."

"But you love me anyway," he said.

"I love you because of it, because your wrong matches my wrong."

"Are you saying two wrongs make a right?" he asked.

"Yes, that's exactly what I'm saying," I said, smiling.

He met my smile with his own, and our smiles joined together into another kiss. It grew into eager lips, tongue, teeth as he bit my lower lip just enough to make me weak in the knees, and for a second I forgot the unsteady heels. I grabbed him around the shoulders, and he grabbed me around the waist at the same time. "Wow," I said. He looked very pleased with himself.

"If I weren't wearing these shoes I'd bite you back, but I can't catch us both dressed like this," I said.

"Decorate with bite marks later in the bed, and you can keep the heels on. They're the pointiest stilettos I've ever seen you wear."

"Ah, that's why you like the shoes so much, you want to feel them pressed against your ass while you fuck me."

He shivered in my arms, his arms tightening almost convulsively around my waist. "God, yes." Then his eyes flicked behind me at the mirror. He was suddenly steadier in our embrace and the look on his face wasn't submissive anymore but sliding further to the top side of things. He'd come into my life so submissive he had been a danger to himself in the wrong hands, but together we'd learned we were switches. I watched his bottom mindset slide away and the very tippy-top slide through his eyes.

"I like the thong," he said.

I glanced back at the mirror and realized that I was tall enough that only my legs were below the mirror. I'd never been tall enough to flash my ass in the mirror before. "I'm so tall."

"Nicky would have to help me get you in the right head space for it, but I'd love to spank your ass while you wear the thong and shoes."

"One good slap and I'd fall over," I said, and I laughed a little nervously, a little eagerly. He and Nicky co-topped me sometimes, and there was something about their dynamics that turned my mostly submissive boy into a dominant head space that I hadn't even known he had inside him.

"We could chain you with your arms up, using the soft leather cuffs so you could hold on to them while we marked up your beautiful ass." One of his hands slid over my bare skin where the dress riding up had exposed me. It was a gentle caress, but the look on his face while he watched me in the mirror promised something less gentle later. It was my turn to shiver in his arms.

"I don't think I could stand that long in these heels even with the cuffs to hang on to," I said, leaning into his hand, rubbing my face against the side of his so I could lay a kiss on the warm, smooth skin of his neck.

He pressed himself tighter against me, fingers starting to dig into my ass. "We can find different shoes and matching thongs for you to wear." His voice was lower, the first rush of testosterone already pumping through his body. He used his other hand to raise the dress up all the way to my waist, then pressed the front of his body against the front of mine. For once the height was perfect for him to push the growing hardness of his body against the soft mound of mine. Usually when we stood like this he was pressed against my stomach, which felt good, but this felt better.

"Yes," I breathed.

He drew back enough so he could see my face. "Are you agreeing to spanking, or just getting distracted by this." He started rubbing himself against the front of me. He was inside jeans, and I had one layer of silky cloth between me and his efforts, which meant my nerve endings were closer to the surface.

I shuddered in his arms, eyes fluttering closed, whispering, "Both."

There was a knock on the door. "Sorry to interrupt," Ethan said, "but have you bespelled Nathaniel, or are you just having your usual effect on each other?"

That made us both laugh. "I'm fine," Nathaniel called out.

"Then Jean-Claude asked me to hurry you along, so that Anita's makeup won't delay him taking the stage."

I looked at myself in the mirror then and realized that Nathaniel had totally distracted me from the mess that Rodina and I had made of my mouth and chin. The makeup looked like what happens when a car swipes another's paint job with a little fender-bender thrown in, but the rest of the car still looks perfect. "Perfect from here up," I said, gesturing in the mirror.

"You're always perfect," Nathaniel said, "but you're lucky some of the dancers wear more makeup than I do."

"I am lucky that someone here has more makeup than you and I do." He laughed and we opened the door so Ethan could herd us to the dancers' dressing room, where they were waiting like a beauty assembly line to repair the damage and get me back to my seat. Nathaniel helped me use makeup cleaning cloths to take off all the makeup from below the line of mess. Apparently, I'd ruined it so well that they needed clean skin and to just start all over. Ethan stayed out of the way since he knew less than I did about this kind of makeup. He took up his post by the door, alert for danger, but the only danger seemed to be a fight breaking out between the dancers on exactly what color of base matched what I was wearing.

18

BUZZ CAME IN while they were adding the contouring powder to the base they'd already smoothed out. "I know this is like date night and Jean-Claude is the boss, but are you okay to be around the audience?"

I motioned the makeup brushes away so I could say, "I'm fine."

"You sure? I've never seen you lose control like that here."

I looked at him in the mirror and thought about it for a few seconds as the dancers descended with brushes and powder. When they were done and the only thing left was lipstick, I said, "I feel good now, solid in my head. I think I was picking up on Rodina and Ru."

"They're your Brides, Anita, you're not supposed to pick up on them," Ethan said from the doorway.

"I pick up on Nicky more."

"You're in love with him."

"It's their birthday, and only the second one since their brother died. I think that was too much emotion for me to be able to ignore."

"Geez," Buzz said, "they shouldn't have been working tonight."

"I'll make a note so they're off next year," I said.

"I've already texted Claudia," Ethan said.

"Thanks, Ethan."

"Part of the job, and since Buzz brought it up, are you sure you're good for being in public tonight?"

"I feel fine now. I really do think it was the twins"—I closed my eyes and let out a long sigh—"sorry, triplets, and their grief."

Nathaniel said, "You feel normal now."

"You do feel better in my head since they left," Ethan conceded.

"Then let's finish up the lipstick and get me out of here and back to my seat."

"The audience is getting kind of restless," Buzz said.

"Then no more talking," Nathaniel said with a smile.

I might have replied but the tallest dancer leaned over me with my own lipstick in his hands. He told me to hold still and started painting back the perfect lines that all the kissing had wiped away. I might have interrupted it to squirm, or even ask the dancer's name, because I couldn't remember it. He was one of our newer vampires. Not new to being a vampire, but new to the stage. Jean-Claude breathed through my mind, "His name is Hart, let him finish your makeup so I may finally see you in person tonight."

Hart shivered and drew back with the lipstick in his hand. "Our master's power is all over you."

"He's telling me to let you finish my makeup, so our date can happen."

"You are a lucky girl," he said as he leaned back in.

"I am," I said, before I had to hold still and let him finish drawing my lower lip just a bit wider than normal and color it in scarlet. The lipstick was the only thing I was wearing that was my normal shade. Again, I had that feeling of not being myself tonight. I felt Jean-Claude's eagerness down the link between us. He was excited to see me in the clothes he'd so carefully chosen, and for me to see him. I almost thought too hard at him then, which would have meant I might have gotten a peek, but he blocked me so that emotion was all I could get.

"Honey, if you keep having that much power running through you I'm going to mess up this lipstick and have to start over with the base," Hart said.

I apologized and Jean-Claude drifted farther away so that he wouldn't make the other vampire shiver again.

19

JEAN-CLAUDE HADN'T WANTED me to see him before the performance, as if he were suddenly the bride before the wedding. In our case he'd helped design the wedding dress so there wouldn't be any surprise for him on that, but for whatever reason tonight he wanted to surprise me, so who was I to argue? This was our date night, just him and me, so whatever he wanted within reason. Though the backup security person that they'd given Ethan made me want to argue with somebody. Graham was six feet and in obviously good shape in that I-lift-weights-in-the-gym kind of way. His short black hair was cut similar to Ethan's but his was baby fine and utterly straight so the haircuts looked completely different on them, which was probably not my thought, but I was metaphysically connected to several people who would notice things like that. Physically he was built like his tall, Nordic, former military dad, but the hair and the dark brown eyes with their slight uptilt at the edges was his Japanese mother. How did I know all that? His parents were still the only ones who had ever come to Guilty Pleasures to see where their son worked.

None of the above was why I was frowning at him sitting on the other side of me from Ethan. He leaned over with a smile that was too close to his usual smirk. I tensed, waiting for his usual lascivious and creepy remarks. "Thank you for trusting me with your safety tonight, Anita."

I blinked at him, and finally said, "You're welcome."

His smirk widened, and I expected one of his usual remarks and got surprised again. "Jake told me that if I would stop being such a pain in the ass he'd like to train me up as part of the new werewolf bodyguard unit." Jake was one of the Harlequin and one of the first who came over to our side; he was also one of our main instructors for combative arts, especially empty hand. He must have seen something in Graham that I never had.

"You going to start coming to Jake's classes?" Ethan asked him, putting his arm on the back of my chair so he could lean across to say it without shouting.

Graham nodded, obviously pleased that Jake had invited him personally. I just fought to keep my expression from showing how shocked I was; I seriously didn't think Graham was up to that level of training, but Jake was centuries old, so I'd bow to his opinion. He was one of the few Harlequins who had retained his superpowers, and when it came to speed, stealth, and killing it was super as in supernaturally good even compared to regular shapeshifters and vampires.

"Jean-Claude wants us to have a lot more wolves at the advanced classes," Ethan said.

"We still have the fewest former military of all the animal groups; it puts us behind on the new security training," Graham said.

"We don't have many active militaries in parts of the world where actual lycanthropy is prevalent," I said.

"Also, a lot of Muslims see wolves as a type of dog, and dogs are considered unclean, so they're less likely to accept werewolves into their military groups," Ethan said.

"Which means that fewer of our military get attacked by werewolves, so they don't get medically discharged to work in the private sector," I added.

"I'm just glad that Jean-Claude decided to let Jake look for more wolves in the local pack before they started looking out of state. If they had enough wolves with military or police backgrounds I wouldn't have had a chance."

"Why do you want to train up?" I asked.

"I don't want to still be working the door here at Guilty Pleasures when I'm fifty like Buzz, or if I am I want to know I tried for something more."

I nodded and tried not to show how surprised I was that he said something deep. I wanted to ask Graham if he'd been taking classes or reading self-help books because this was far more insightful than normal for him. I tried to remember how many years it had been since I'd really been around him and couldn't. It had been a while; I guess I was going to have to give Graham the room to have grown and changed just like I had, like the people I was in love with had. I'd just pegged Graham as one of those men who thought trying to get into women's pants was his main purpose in life and hit the gym just enough to make that more likely. He'd age badly into one of those dirty old men who forget they're not twenty-five anymore. It almost hurt to be this wrong about him.

The lights dimmed in the club, and there were squeals and excited whispers from the audience. We stopped talking and I looked at the stage. Jean-Claude and Nathaniel had been very hush-hush about the new dance routine. They wanted me to see it fresh with the audience, I wasn't sure why, but Jean-Claude had said something about wanting to still be able to surprise me. I'd told him he surprised me pretty regularly, but whatever his motivation it had been important to him, so here I sat in the dark with everyone else.

I expected someone to introduce the act like usual, but the music started with no voice-over, and no clue what was about to happen. It took me a few seconds to realize what the song was, "Send Me an Angel," because it was a version I'd never heard before. It was such an unexpected music choice that I laughed. Then a soft blue spotlight swirled over the crowd and the stage, then up to the ceiling, and there was Jean-Claude floating, levitating at the highest point of the room. My table didn't have a good view of it, so I wasn't sure why there were gasps and little screams of excitement other than it was him. I caught glimpses of pants and a sleeveless shirt, but that was about it. He slowly levitated downward and he had wings, large, feathered angel wings. They didn't flap, but the feathers moved in the soft wind that played in his long black curls, keeping them perfectly back from his face so that he hung suspended but nothing obscured his beauty as he gazed down on the women sitting below him. They were going wild, already holding up money for him to come closer.

The wings were part of his costume, but the wind was his own power pushing against gravity and keeping him suspended, enabling him to begin to fly out over the audience while they screamed and tried to touch him as he went over their heads.

"Besides," Graham said, "how's a poor werewolf supposed to compete with that."

Under other circumstances I'd have said *But it's not a competition, we're poly*, but I was too busy watching Jean-Claude fly. Holy shit.

20

A WOMAN STOOD up, grabbing at Jean-Claude, and a security guard was there to help her back to her seat as he floated higher out of reach. It took me a second to see the longish blond hair and realize the guard was Wicked, of the Wicked Truth, and as if the thought had conjured him I saw Truth among the tables. His darker hair made him almost invisible in the dimness. They were shadowing Jean-Claude through the room, making sure no one got out of hand. They were dressed in the same outfit that all the Guilty Pleasures staff wore, so I hadn't picked them out. There were at least four more regular security people circulating through the tables. Wicked seemed to be directing them while Truth just stayed close to Jean-Claude as he hovered over the mostly female audience. Seeing Truth staying so close, I realized just how vulnerable Jean-Claude was as he flew above them. I fought to keep the earlier murder scene out of my head so he wouldn't pick up on it while he was onstage. I trusted the Wicked Truth to keep him safe. I trusted them to keep anyone safe. They were just that good. I fought to let go of my fears and be here and now.

Ethan slid his arm more solidly across my shoulders, which reassured both of us since wereanimals like big puppy piles, or in this case kitten piles. I hoped he was only picking up on my emotions and not the actual memory. I tried to keep my nightmares to myself. He hugged me a little closer as if to let me know it was okay.

Graham leaned into me and asked, "What's wrong?"

I just shook my head and started to push him back from me, suddenly feeling claustrophobic with both of the men so close, but the moment I touched his bare arm a sense of calmness washed over me. Touching the werewolf steadied me in a way that touching the weretiger didn't; maybe it was because wolf was Jean-Claude's animal to call, but whatever the reason I was suddenly able to give my attention to Jean-Claude and the show.

He floated effortlessly over the excited crowd, the blue spotlights following him so that he moved in the halo of them. He was so beautiful that it made my chest tight, and over that was the thought I'd had almost from the beginning with him: *How could anyone that beautiful want me?* I cleaned up well, but who could compare to this, to him?

Then he was above me, his curls floating out from around his face. The eye makeup was almost like a domino mask across his eyes, larger than it had looked when I'd seen him in a vision earlier. The feathers on the wings moved in that small wind. I wanted to reach up and touch them to see if they were as soft as they looked. I stared into his eyes, their color lost in the blue spotlight so that they looked black like his hair. He reached down his hand toward me, and I offered him mine but let him dictate how much touching happened. It was like an even more complicated hand kiss, where if you offered your hand too forcefully you would end up smacking the man in the face.

He touched just his fingertips to mine and for a second the wind of his power played in my hair, sending it in a nimbus of curls around my face like a mirror of his. He smiled that smile that was only for me and then he was up and back over the crowd, faster this time so you could see the wings tremble as if they wanted to flap but couldn't.

The crowd was screaming and clapping, and the extra security guards had to keep making them sit down so Jean-Claude didn't hit them or they didn't grab him. Wicked and Truth stayed with Jean-Claude, using their more than human speed to keep up. They were vampires, not shapeshifters, but not all vampires have to rely on mind tricks to appear faster than human normal; like I'd explained to McKinnon earlier, some vampires are just that good.

Jean-Claude hovered over the stage, bringing his body from horizontal to vertical, one foot downward, one half bent at the knee, his arms upraised. He was pinned like a butterfly by the blue spotlight and then he slowly began to descend the few feet to the stage. One foot touched down first and then the bent leg came down behind him as if to help balance the wings on his back. The crowd went wild, standing up, applauding, and so much money appeared in the women's hands that it looked like a forest had sprung up.

The blue spotlight began to change gradually to a more natural color, and Jean-Claude's voice filled the room. I wasn't sure if he was using a small microphone or vampire powers, but did it really matter? "Welcome to Guilty Pleasures."

More screaming and shouts of "Jean-Claude! Jean-Claude!" and just high-pitched squeals, like the grown-up version of a child's delight, wordless and unselfconscious. Strip clubs are one of the few places where women are encouraged to be as uninhibited as they want to be. I knew dancers who worked both male and female crowds and they all agreed that the women got out of hand more often than the men. I'd been shocked when I'd first found out, but where else could women let down all the socialization to be nice, to be quiet, to be nurturing, and finally not have to be any of those things, sometimes for the first time in their lives. It had taken me a long time to understand why women go so wild here, because though I tried to be kind I was too blunt to be considered nice by girl standards; I always spoke my mind, and I hated being expected to nurture just because I was female, so I was controlled here because I didn't need an excuse to let go. I had had to date other women to understand my own sex better, because I was too much an outlier.

As the light changed I could finally see that his vest and pants were shiny vinyl in a rich blue, or maybe it was teal. The shininess of the fabric under the lights kept changing the color slightly as he moved. The wings were white, edged in shades of blue. "You have all tempted me down from heaven with your beauty." When he said *tempted*, the women cried out as if they were thinking of all the temptations they'd passed up or given in to, and *beauty* made them beam at him as if him merely saying the word made them feel beautiful. I sat there enjoying the audience's reaction to his voice without getting caught up in it. I was his human servant, which meant I had immunity to the kind of power that he'd spread over a crowd. His own vampire marks kept me safe, but when I'd first stepped inside Guilty Pleasures nearly ten years ago I'd used my own fingernails to draw blood so the pain would keep me free of his voice. He was a lot more powerful now than he had been then; I was happy to be free to watch but not be bespelled. There were signs at the door and all over: *Warning: Vampires, shapeshifters, and other supernatural beings are inside. By crossing this threshold you give consent for them to interact with you, and for any preternatural abilities that they may possess to be used on you.* I was still glad to be too powerful to be rolled by his voice.

Music started building again, harder music with a beat to it. "To know you better, I will give up my wings and ask you, glorious creatures, to help me earn my horns instead," he said, grabbing the front of his vest and ripping it open; the wings came with it, and two of the security people caught them carefully and were handing them back to others near the stage curtain, but the audience didn't notice they were watching Jean-Claude suddenly dance shirtless. You'd think that him with wings would have been more eye-catching, but you'd be wrong. I was in love with him, so I'd have believed I was prejudiced, but the crowd's reaction told me it wasn't just me.

The only darkness on the pale perfection of his chest was a cross-shaped burn scar. It was very similar to the cross-shaped scar I had on my left forearm. Jean-Claude's was from centuries ago when someone shoved a cross into him trying to save their life. Mine had been a vampire's daytime guardians branding me to amuse themselves until the vampires rose for the night. Jean-Claude and I had both killed the people that marked us. He'd been hunting humans and I'd been hunting vampires. He'd needed food, I'd been executing criminals—let he who is without sin cast the first stone.

Jean-Claude strutted and stalked the stage while the crowd screamed his name, and some tried to rush the stage. Security caught them, keeping them from climbing onto it. Jean-Claude teased, dancing in front of them as security fought to hold them back. Wicked and Truth stood on either side of the stage, only interceding if the shapeshifters and Buzz couldn't manage it. I was too short to see all of the dancing unless I stood up, which most of the rest of the crowd was doing at their tables. Some of the women at the stage threw money even though they were being held back by security. A pair of pink lacy panties sailed past the security to land on the stage. I hadn't seen anyone taking off their panties; did people bring clean underwear to throw at the stage? I hoped so.

The music changed and Jean-Claude grabbed the front of the pants and pulled. They came off in one piece like magic. He tossed them behind him where someone caught them and took them back behind the curtain. I had a glimpse of the thong he was wearing. He never stripped down that far, or at least not as long as I'd seen him onstage. He usually stopped with just his shirt off. I now knew why the pants had been looser than his normal for onstage: to give room for the pair of skintight leather boots that came up to at least the middle of his thighs. The boots were blue; I'd never seen him in boots that color before. From where I was sitting it looked like he was nude except for the boots, because I just wasn't tall enough and sitting in my view was mostly women from the audience holding up money, or throwing money, or a thong, or . . . were those condoms still in their wrappers?

"Buddha sitting under a tree, it's never been this bad," Graham said, almost yelling over the sounds of women screaming Jean-Claude's name.

I could only nod in agreement. There was a surge behind us almost like the ocean drawing back before it slams the shore, I couldn't describe it any better than that. I turned to look, but Ethan already had my arm and was pulling me to my feet, as I realized the crowd on this side was about to rush the stage en masse. Graham was on the other side of me, not grabbing my arm but facing the other way like he was going to block for me.

Ethan had a death grip on my left arm as he half led and half dragged me to the door beside the stage that led to the employees-only area. Graham came at our backs. I saw Truth and Wicked onstage with Jean-Claude. They were moving him toward the second exit that was literally at the back of the stage. Ethan got our door open. I must have hesitated, because he said, "Wicked Truth have him. We have you." He spilled us through the door, with Graham having to push the crowd away to get us through and close the door. Luckily they weren't trying for our door but just to rush past toward the stage.

We had a moment of silence behind the closed door, hearts pounding. I had a moment to acknowledge that it had been maybe frightening to see them go for the stage, but we hadn't been the target, just an obstacle to be trampled. Ethan and I looked toward the few steps that led up to the stage door.

"I'm counting to five," I said.

"You can't go out there, Anita," Ethan said.

"I can," I said, narrowing my eyes at him.

"You can't hurt customers, and they sure as hell will hurt us," Graham said.

He had a point because my training was mostly how to hurt or kill people. I wasn't a cop; I was an executioner.

The door opened and Truth came through with Jean-Claude and Wicked following. Someone else still onstage closed the door behind them. I got a glimpse of other black-shirted security massed in front of the door as it closed. It shook as if someone had fallen against the door.

I was trying to decide if I was really afraid of the crowd outside and did we need to rescue the rest of security when I realized that Jean-Claude was laughing. His eyes were bright, and it wasn't vampire powers. He was giddy on the energy of the performance and the crowd's reaction. He leaned against the wall in his fabulous boots and the thong, looking drunk, drunk on power.

"You enjoyed that," I said almost accusingly.

"Why did you take the pants off after they were so wild?" Truth asked.

"I did," Jean-Claude said, "it was part of the act."

"I've never seen the crowd like this," Graham said.

"What did you do to the audience?" Truth asked.

"Nothing I have not done before," Jean-Claude said, standing there so full of the energy of the crowd that I could feel it coming off him in waves.

"That can't be true, they're crazed out there," he said.

"We need to help the other security," Graham said.

"Our duty is Jean-Claude's safety," Wicked said.

The door shook again, shuddering this time under the weight and energy of the crowd still trying to get to Jean-Claude. "We need to call more security from the other clubs," Truth said.

"Or calm the crowd," I said.

All the security looked at me, and then Wicked Truth and Ethan all shook their heads. "You can't go out there," Ethan said.

"We calm the crowd, or we call the police to do it for us," I said.

Truth looked at Wicked. Wicked said, "Our duty lies here."

"If Jean-Claude caused this while we guarded him, then it is our duty to fix it if we can," Truth said.

"I did not do this," Jean-Claude said, laughing wildly, slumping a little down the wall.

"You're power drunk," I said, and I couldn't keep it from sounding accusatory.

Truth went toward the side door that we had come through, because the stage door was still shuddering as the crowd tried to push through. Wicked turned to Graham and Ethan. "Get Jean-Claude and Anita out of here."

"And Nathaniel," Truth added.

"All the principals," Wicked said, and the brothers went for the door.

Jean-Claude pushed away from the wall, trying to go after them I think, but he was too drunk and started to collapse. Graham caught him, and the moment he touched him the energy changed. I felt it like a switch turned on inside me. I felt better, clearer-headed, and I realized that it was overfeed from Jean-Claude. He straightened, keeping his arm across Graham's shoulders. "Stay by my side, Graham, there is something in the club tonight. It has tampered with us, and it does not like wolves."

"If you did not do this, then it was done to you," Wicked said.

"I fear so," Jean-Claude said.

"No vampire should be able to roll you, you're our king," Truth said.

"So I thought, and if they could attack me, it would not be here, not while I was surrounded by lust. It is the element where I command."

"You are steadier now, more in command of yourself," Wicked said.

"I felt better when Graham touched me, too, but not this much better," I said.

"Wolf is my animal to call, *ma petite*."

"Mine, too," I said.

"Wolf comes to you through your shared marks with me and the absent third of our triumvirate, but it was mine first. The first power that came to me and marked me as a master vampire." He seemed utterly sober now, as if he'd drunk a dozen cups of coffee and been dunked in ice water in the last few seconds. He was still wearing the leg-hugging blue leather boots and the thong, but the clothes didn't matter; he was suddenly every inch a king, dominant to everyone and everything he surveyed. Jean-Claude hid it most of the time; I think it was habit because playing the fop who got by on his looks and seducing the right people had been how he'd hidden in plain sight from other powerful vampires for centuries. He'd hidden just how powerful he was even from me at first, and I was good at judging ages and power levels. Standing there in an outfit that would have made most people put him in the beautiful-bimbo box, suddenly all the camouflage was gone. He stood there in a mantle of power and command that didn't need crowns or scepters. The intelligence in his face and the certainty with which he held his body said he could walk into a throne room dressed like a stripper and it wouldn't matter, they'd still curtsy as he passed and believe he had a right to sit down wherever he damn well chose.

21

THE WICKED TRUTH and Ethan went ahead of us because they wouldn't let us go through first. Buzz and the other security people were locked shoulder to shoulder trying to keep the crowd away from the door. They had their heads down or an arm raised to shield their faces. I could see fingernail marks bleeding on them. The crowd turned toward us as one, a beast with many faces, and I knew that wasn't my thought, but Jean-Claude's. He'd seen a crowd like this before, more than once. I was suddenly flooded with memories of other rooms, other crowds; the clothing was a lesson in centuries of fashion. Belle Morte, the creator of Jean-Claude's bloodline, had enjoyed the chaos of it, and what came next.

Jean-Claude gripped our hands harder to steady himself, and he reached out through both of us for help. Graham was a doorway to the werewolves, though it was an imperfect door because we weren't connected to Graham, only to his wolf. I was a doorway to the were-rats, the clan tigers, and the wereleopards, because I had my own animals to call of each; my lioness and hyena were still waiting for their special connection, so there was less for Jean-Claude to use. My wolf had chosen its other half, and because the need was great we had a moment of feeling Jason on a very different kind of stage, him hesitating because he felt us thinking at him too hard. Jean-Claude drew us back so we wouldn't make him fall, or drop a ballerina, and we were solidly back amid the overturned tables and chairs and the crowd flowing over the stage like ants over a piece of candy, so that all you can see is their bodies but not what lies underneath. I had a second of almost pure terror, as if when they stepped away from the stage there would be something underneath them, in the midst of them.

Jean-Claude didn't have to tell me he sensed it, too; I could feel what he was feeling, thinking, and I had a dizzy moment of not being sure if I was walking in the stiletto heels or the soft leather boots. Graham couldn't meld with us, he wasn't a part of us, only his wolf half belonged to Jean-Claude because all wolves belonged to him.

I wasn't sure which of us thought it wasn't enough, this wasn't enough connection to our wolves, and then I knew it was Jean-Claude, because I thought *wolf*, not plural. *It will have to do*, he thought, and I was stumbling in the stiletto heels, unable to walk in them when I wasn't sure what body I was driving.

Graham moaned. "What did you do to me?"

"My apologies, *lupe*, but you are not the big bad wolf that I need."

Graham was having trouble focusing as he said, "I can be big and bad if that's what you need."

Jean-Claude smiled at him, and Graham smiled back like he was happy to have said a smart thing that pleased him. Graham so wasn't a dominant, which meant he so wasn't a big bad anything, but he was willing to stand with us and be our wolf, and that counted for a lot. Jean-Claude stopped trying to reach for more energy and concentrated on what we had.

I knew Jean-Claude had grown in power, but I hadn't really understood what it meant until now. He filled the audience with new memories; there had been a contest for them to vote on which of the security people they'd most want to see dance onstage at Guilty Pleasures. I felt that some of the women had small scrapes and bruises and the pain made them doubt the story, but he took their pain away as his gaze could take the pain of the bite away, except he did this without meeting their eyes, or needing to; they just went back to their tables, and the security walked or limped over to put the overturned chairs back so they could sit down. Jean-Claude took their confusion of rushing the stage and trying to claw their way past the guards into them seeing the guards try to dance onstage, take their shirts off, some were awkward, and it was endearing. Some of the women laughed, as if it were happening in front of them. Some of the guards moved well onstage, and then Jean-Claude had asked them to vote on who they most wanted to see, and Graham had won.

Jean-Claude was busy implanting the memory that I had come back to guest-star tonight using the name that Nathaniel had given me the first time I'd stepped onstage with him. I was Nikki long before our Nicky came into our lives. I had a moment of missing Nicky so hard that it made my chest tight. He should have been at my side tonight. He would have helped me control things, because we'd worked our issues together, unlike Rodina and Ru.

Jean-Claude breathed through me, "Happy thoughts, *ma petite*, we will see your lion later tonight, but in this moment I need you to feel my hand in yours and be joyful of it." He squeezed my hand as he said it, and I squeezed back. I let him see that I was happy to be with him; I chased back the next thought, which was not happy with the metaphysics going wrong and having our only wolf option be Graham. He'd grown as a person, but he still wasn't one of my people, our people. The stray thought came, *But he could be.* I didn't know if it was from Graham, Jean-Claude, or one of the audience. Jean-Claude was driving the bus, because I had no idea how to do this. I was powerful, but I was a better battery than a witch, and whether you called it psychic ability or magic, what Jean-Claude was doing took training and practice that I didn't have.

I thought of running my hands over Jean-Claude in nothing but the thong and boots and that was a happy thought. It helped chase back the stray thought about Graham. Jean-Claude raised my hand

and laid a gentle kiss on the back of it to let me know he appreciated me getting into the spirit of things. I did want to run my hands over him and a lot more once we had privacy. He planted images in the audience's mind of me flirting and teasing with the men as they'd come up onstage for the first time. He made me more suave and debonair than I was capable of with strangers onstage. I'd been Nikki for Nathaniel and Jean-Claude here, but never to a bunch of people I'd never touched before.

He swung us around so that the entire audience could see us like we were being presented to them. They screamed Graham's name, or just screamed in excitement. They called out Jean-Claude's name, too, because he was showing more skin than they'd seen from him in years. A few even called my stage name and I waved and smiled like that made me happy. I could pretend to get off the stage sooner.

"Our new werewolf is overdressed, is he not?" The women screamed and called out agreement.

It was one thing to plant Graham being sexy and dancing onstage, and it was another for him to do it, so Jean-Claude thought of something simpler for all of us. Graham knelt in front of us, and the moment he stopped touching Graham the energy felt wrong. He touched the side of Graham's face, and it was as if his power got a boost. I was supposed to help Graham take his shirt off, but that left Jean-Claude not touching either of us, and that seemed like a bad idea.

Jean-Claude moved me like we were dancing so that I was in front of Graham where he knelt, and he came in at the werewolf's back. Then he let go of both of us for moment and it was as if the world contracted so fast and hard I was dizzy. I reached out and he gave me his hand, the other back on Graham. Touching made the energy expand again; it was as if Jean-Claude's area of control was expanding and contracting, which wasn't possible. He was the king of all the vampires in this country. They were blood-oathed to him, which meant he gained power from all of them.

"What was that?" Graham whispered.

I gave a bare shake of my head because I didn't know. Jean-Claude smiled and flirted with the crowd, but in his head was the thought, "The other vampire has left something behind."

What? I mouthed.

He thought, "Power."

That didn't answer the question, but before I could ask a better question, he called out to the audience, "Shall Nikki and I help our wolf strip?"

"Yes! Please! God yes!" And more enthusiastic encouragement from the crowd so that the noise was almost too much. It made me wish I'd worn ear protection like I did when I went to the gun range.

Jean-Claude helped me kneel in front of Graham and then went gracefully to his knees behind him. Graham was simultaneously excited to see me and a little apprehensive about Jean-Claude at his back. Not a lot, but a little. Jean-Claude laughed and pressed himself to the other man's back as he drew me closer, so we hugged him together. The crowd loved it, but Jean-Claude whispered to Graham, "Your virtue is safe tonight, *lupe*."

Graham was embarrassed then that he'd let his momentary fears show. He forced himself to relax between us and not be a big baby about it, his thoughts or mine, I knew they weren't Jean-Claude's. I slid my fingers underneath Graham's shirt. His skin was so warm, his body heat caught underneath his shirt, so it was like warming my hands as I caressed upward, tracing the smooth firmness of his stomach while Jean-Claude did the same to his back. I had a confused moment where I wasn't sure if I was touching the softer flesh of his stomach or the firmness of his back. Graham shuddered between us as if we'd done a lot more than just touch his stomach and back.

Jean-Claude looked at me over the other man's shoulder and we stared into each other's eyes as we ran our hands up his body, forcing his shirt to bunch around our arms, slowly exposing his upper body to the crowd. They went wild, screaming and catcalling. I sensed security moving into place around the stage just in case, but they didn't rush us because Jean-Claude was in charge of the energy this time and he didn't want violence, he wanted lust. Safe, teasing promises of lust, which is what a good strip club is, the promise but never the fulfillment of the fantasy.

Jean-Claude smiled at me over Graham's shoulder, and I smiled back; we could feel each other's hands on his body. Graham's breath came out in a long sigh, his pulse speeding from being in the middle of our power exchange. The shirt lifted, revealing his nipples; the small tips of them were hard with excitement. It made me speculate about how hard other things might be, and I got the pleasure from Jean-Claude that we had made him excited. Part pride in workmanship, part dominance; I almost never felt that way about people I wasn't emotionally connected to, but for Jean-Claude that was always a high. No wonder he enjoyed being onstage here.

I kissed Graham's bare chest carefully, leaving a perfect imprint of my red lips on his skin. He sighed again, and Jean-Claude kissed the side of his neck, oh so gently. Graham's eyes fluttered closed, and I felt the effort in his body not to shudder again. I couldn't help myself; I flicked my tongue across his nipple, and he cried out. I kept his shirt bunched up underneath his shoulders, as Jean-Claude stood over us both. There was a moment when the leather of his boots prevented him from touching Graham's back, and the power contracted again, until he touched Graham's hair, and then the power flexed outward again.

Loud enough for the crowd to hear he said, "It is time he lost his shirt, is it not?"

"Yes! Take it off! Take it off!" The crowd chanted it as Jean-Claude reached over Graham to touch my hands where they held the shirt in place. He placed his hands over mine and it felt amazing to touch each other directly, as if hands meant so much more than normal. I gazed up into his cobalt-blue eyes and I knew what he wanted me to do. He slid his fingers underneath the cloth and lifted as I leaned in to lick the other nipple. Graham's arms went up without being asked, and Jean-Claude stripped the shirt off him to fling it into the crowd. I rose up from his chest to find Graham's face inches from mine, his brown eyes wild with need. It seemed the most natural thing in the world to kiss him. It was gentle and he did not kiss me back but stayed still under my touch as if he was afraid to move, afraid I'd stop if he was too eager. I traced my hands on either side of his face and whispered, "Kiss me."

Jean-Claude stood above us stroking Graham's hair and called out to the crowd, "Has our good wolf earned a better kiss than that?" The crowd roared its approval. The chant became "Kiss, kiss, kiss, kiss!"

I kept my hands on either side of Graham's face as I tilted my head up toward him. He made a small eager sound and then he bent over me, and our lips met. He made a soft sound against my mouth, and then he kissed me. He wrapped his arms around me and lifted me off my knees so that I had to wrap my arms around his bare shoulders to help hold me in his embrace as we explored each other with lips and tongues, he was so eager. He'd wanted permission to touch me for so long. It was as if his eagerness was contagious, so that when his arm tightened around my back and his other hand slid downward to touch my ass I didn't say no. We weren't getting out of our clothes, Jean-Claude was right there, we were onstage, and I suddenly felt safe, in control of the uncontrollable. I wrapped my legs around Graham's waist too high for anything serious, but I'd forgotten how short the dress and how small the thong, and suddenly his hands were on my bare ass, holding me in place as if I needed the help to stay in place around his body, but tentatively as if he wasn't sure it was okay. I had a moment of thinking *Either grab my ass or let me go.* Jean-Claude knew what I was thinking, feeling, so he said, "Grab her ass like you mean it!" He called it out to the crowd, and they shrieked their eagerness. Graham tried to hesitate, but I kissed him harder, using just a touch of teeth against his lips, and he grabbed my ass so hard and sudden that it was my turn to make a small, surprised sound. I wrapped my arms tighter around his neck and he took that as the invitation it was to move his other hand down to dig his fingers into my ass, but my extra arm movement had raised the short skirt up so that he touched bare skin where the thong didn't cover.

He froze for a moment, breaking away from the kiss, searching my face for outrage, for a no. I said, "This may be the only chance you get, I'd take advantage of it if I were you."

He finally allowed himself the eager smile he'd been trying to hide, because he was afraid I'd back off, but not tonight. I smiled at him, willing him to be as eager as we needed him to be. He stared straight into my eyes from inches away and filled his hands with my bare ass, cupping and caressing, so that I wound my legs around his waist, pressing the front of me in the thong against the front of him in his jeans, and found him as hard and eager as I could have wanted. Jean-Claude had moved out of the way of my spiky heels, because he'd known exactly what I was going to do. He kept his hand on Graham's shoulder as he moved to the side of us. Graham's hands convulsed, digging his fingers into my ass, pressing me tighter against that hard center inside his pants. The suddenness and the force of it made me cry out and wrap my legs tighter around his waist, driving myself tighter against him. He shuddered, closing his eyes, shoulders bowing as he fought to control what he wanted to do next.

"Do it." I whispered it against his face.

"I want to fuck you."

"No," Jean-Claude and I said together.

"Then what?" he asked, and he sounded wild, trapped and too eager to think clearly.

I knew exactly what I wanted. "Grind me into the stage."

"Won't that hurt you?" That he thought to ask when his body wanted me so badly gained him points.

"I want to feel you on top of me, Graham, pushing that hard, solid piece of you against me."

He didn't ask again, just straightened his knees and took us to the ground with my legs wrapped around his waist and the dress up around mine, the thin thong all that was between me and the roughness of his jeans. In the right head space, I like the sensation, and I was in that head space. I let go of his shoulders so he could raise himself up above like he was trying to do a push-up with me in the way. It pressed him tighter against me and I loved it. The crowd's screams seemed distant as I stared up into his face above me. I stared down the bare length of his chest to his waist still safely in his pants. Jean-Claude leaned over me to whisper into Graham's ear, and just seeing them both above me sped my pulse and made me want more.

Jean-Claude leaned down to kiss me as Graham rose up higher and began to rub himself over me, dry humping is what it's called, but I was already wet. Jean-Claude kissed me, soft and eager as Graham gained rhythm against my body. I wrapped my hands in Jean-Claude's hair, crushing those thick, soft curls of his as I came eager to his mouth as my hips started rising and falling with Graham's. I felt a sharp pain like a piece of candy that you've sucked too long until it cuts your tongue, then tasted blood, sweet copper pennies. Jean-Claude drew back from the kiss, his eyes drowning in eager blue light, a dot of crimson on his lower lip. He licked my blood from his lip and whispered, *"Ma petite."*

I whispered his name back to him, and then in the power that we had raised was another power creeping like a dark thread through our nice, clean lust. Jean-Claude spoke in my mind, "It is in the crowd."

I tried to speak mind-to-mind, but with Graham's body rubbing against mine, his desire riding the air, I couldn't focus enough for it. I whispered, "What is?"

He kissed me again, but this wasn't for pleasure, it was to let me taste the power that wasn't us. It was like . . . mist clinging to each person in the audience. Some people were covered in more of it, others were a spiderweb wisp, but none of them was clean. Something, another vampire, had ridden in on Jean-Claude's power like a Trojan horse, and now unless we could cleanse the audience of this taint the vampire would possess these people, and it would be our fault. We had to save them. He rose back from the kiss to gaze into my eyes. He was thinking we needed to raise more power.

Graham had stopped moving against me as if he was sensing some of what Jean-Claude had shared, or maybe I just wasn't paying enough attention to him. No one likes to be ignored when they're doing something that sexual with you. I looked up at him not sure what to say, because the threat to the audience and the fact that any vampire could have infiltrated the crowd with us right here and not noticing had scared me. That kind of fear wasn't an aphrodisiac. I didn't know what to tell Graham or how to raise enough power to rescue all the nice people who had come to enjoy the show tonight. Jean-Claude knew just what to do. He reached down and cupped his hand over the front of my body, tracing the front of the thong where it clung to me. It felt amazing and the crowd screamed his name, urging him on.

He raised his voice, addressing the crowd. "Shall we raise the heat between Graham and our lovely Nikki?"

Screams of approval and suggestions ranged from just *yes, do it,* to pornographic. Jean-Claude gazed back at me, his hair falling around his face to hide what he said next from the room. He rubbed his hand over the thong and my body underneath. My breathing was already starting to change.

Graham started to move to all fours instead of the odd push-up position. Jean-Claude said, "Graham, we need you right where you are." He raised his voice and said, "Is that not so, ladies, we need Graham to stay, right, where, he, is." They roared their approval.

"But Nikki must say yes to being your surrogate onstage tonight." He looked down at me while his hand rested on the cloth of the thong; his hand felt heavier and more important than it should have been. The audience was chanting, *say yes, say yes.* Jean-Claude looked down at me and said, "Say yes."

I stared up into his face and felt his fear, and guilt that all these people would be victims for the vampire if we could not save them. I said the only thing I could think to say. "Yes."

He whispered, *"Je t'aime, ma petite."*

"I love you, too."

He slid his finger inside the thong, so that my eyes fluttered closed for a second, and then he slid more of his hand underneath the cloth and ripped the thong partially off me. One of my pleasure triggers was having lingerie ripped off me. It helped clear my head of doubts and put me back into the head space we needed. Graham hesitated, staring down at us, at me. Jean-Claude pulled the thong free and made sure the crowd saw him toss it to the stage.

Graham made a sound that was half pain and half growl; I liked both. He went up on his knees, which spilled my legs open so he could see that I shaved, but his body still hid me from anyone's gaze but Jean-Claude's. Graham stared down at me, and I didn't blame him for looking where he was looking. This wasn't a moment for eye contact. The look on his face was tormented, like he was in real pain. Maybe something inside his jeans had twisted on him. Jean-Claude took Graham's hand in his so he could keep contact with our wolf while he leaned down next to my face. It was the crowd's eager screams that made me realize he was flashing a very nice view to the audience behind him. He was still wearing only the blue thong and boots. He was making every move onstage as much a part of the show as he could. I knew that the more reality he could give the audience on which to hang the false memories that he needed to plant in their minds, the better. Lying in someone's mind was just like lying in real life; the best lies are the closest to the truth.

He kissed the side of my face so he could whisper, "I would not share you with another man, but his eagerness at being denied for so long is even greater than anticipated."

I nuzzled against his face and whispered back, "Enough energy to free the audience?"

"And enough to allow me to trace the taint in the audience to its source."

I hid my expression in his long hair because I knew I couldn't control my face to match the sexy tableau we were creating. I'd thought without Richard we wouldn't have enough energy to save us all once we needed wolf. I had thought our absent third was going to sink us again, and now we were saved. I was so relieved that I said a quick prayer of gratitude, and then I asked Jean-Claude, "How do we sell it to the crowd, so that they don't remember something we don't want them to remember?"

"Concentrate on the man in front of us, while I work on creating the physical illusion." I turned my face away from the blindfold of Jean-Claude's hair to the man who was waiting for us. Graham knelt above us, and I knew what the pain in his face was now: desire. He was as close as he'd ever gotten to me, but he stayed where he was, waiting for us to tell him what to do next, and maybe not trusting himself to move until he had permission. He met my gaze and the look in his eyes was frantic with need. He closed them as if afraid what I saw in his eyes would piss me off like it had in the past. If he'd been his usual lecherous self earlier tonight, then it might have, but he'd done his best to be a gentleman in circumstances that most men wouldn't have been able to manage.

I reached my free hand out for him. He glanced at Jean-Claude, who said, "Do not look to me, look to her." Graham looked at me then, his face a mix of desire and confusion; he wanted to touch me but hesitated trying to find words to ask. I helped him. "Feel how wet you've made me."

He used two fingers to stroke over my most intimate parts. He began to stroke and explore, and my breathing quickened. I wanted him to explore me, to bring me, but not onstage, and in that moment where things make sense that later might not I asked for what I wanted him to do. "Put them inside me."

He did what I asked, sliding two fingers inside me so that I writhed for him, eyes closing, because it was almost too much. He crooked his fingers inside me and found that spot that is harder to find than the one most men search for; it made me open my eyes and look up at him to find Jean-Claude's face next to his so they were both staring down at me, and I knew who was giving Graham tips and hints for how my body worked. Jean-Claude smiled down at me, and I smiled back.

"That's cheating," I said, but my voice was breathy, and my eyes were having trouble focusing.

"*Non, ma petite*, this is cheating." And he started playing over that sweet spot that was outside my body while Graham continued to flick his fingers over the deeper one. It wasn't just that their fingers seemed to know exactly what to do but them looking down at me together, the delighted heat in Jean-Claude's face and the amazement in Graham's that he was getting to touch me. We all have our kinks and one of mine was two men at once. Jean-Claude's fingers knew exactly how to touch me, and through him Graham knew exactly what to do, too. I kept thinking I'd protest but then the sensations distracted me and they brought me together, one larger orgasm chasing the deeper one so that I screamed my pleasure for them, my upper body coming up off the ground like I was reaching for something to hold on to in the air above the stage. When I lay quiet and twitching on the stage Jean-Claude's voice filled the world. "Two men giving you pleasure but taking none of their own, because this night is all for you."

Graham stayed kneeling between my legs, but Jean-Claude stood to talk to the audience, to send them home with lust and happiness and then the power, our power, contracted like it had been slapped away from them, out of them. He dropped to his knees to grab my hand and touch Graham's arm; the moment he touched us both his power, our power, flowed out and filled the audience again.

The other vampire had laid a compulsion inside the audience; that meant that if we didn't free them of it come tomorrow night the vampire would be able to call them out of their houses, out of their lives, and take them one by one.

I stared up at Jean-Claude and thought, *How do we free them?*

"You have pushed propriety as far as you are comfortable on-stage, I would not ask more but I must have at least wolf to touch, but I need enough energy of the *ardeur* to chase out the evil that has been laid inside them."

A voice came out of the darkness offstage: "You have more wolves to touch." Jake was still in his workout clothes. He was ex-Harlequin and looked like James Bond should have looked: medium skin tone, brown hair, brown eyes, medium height. He was so medium that you would never pick him out of a crowd in most of the world, he would just blend. Other figures moved in the dark, it was every wolf we had on security. Not the regular pack like Graham, but the ones who had been SEALs and had fought to the last man against a group of shapeshifters and lived to tell the tale; they'd also failed their blood tests for lycanthropy, so now they worked for us. Jean-Claude had promised not to call the werewolves without talking to Richard first, but any wolves who worked for us, that was different.

"I did not call you, so how did you know of my need?" Jean-Claude asked.

"Nathaniel called us," Jake said.

Nathaniel moved up beside the stage where I could see him. I was suddenly embarrassed and a little chilly with my dress around my waist. He opened the link between us to let me know how much he'd enjoyed the show. He was a serious voyeur and his eagerness traveled through me so that I wasn't embarrassed or cold. Graham did help me to scoot down my dress and sit up, but holding on to Jean-Claude and Graham with Nathaniel in my head was like new foreplay. It chased away any discomfort.

"Take my hand and see if it is enough," Jean-Claude said. Jake got up onstage and touched the vampire's bare shoulder, and Jean-Claude's power flexed. "Try more wolves," I said. They came to him onstage, most of them in exercise gear because they'd been helping to test Edward and Peter. I had a moment of panic that they might have come to try and help. Bad enough Edward, but I did not want Peter in the audience tonight.

Nathaniel reassured me that he'd made it clear it was an *ardeur* emergency and anyone not cleared for it needed to stay away, except for the wolves. We needed the few we had on staff too badly. As each wolf gathered around Jean-Claude, his energy grew stronger and filled the room and the alien energy inside the audience began to push back, as if it finally recognized a threat.

"I would that I could come with you, but I must stay here and control the crowd. Go, feed, and grant me all the energy you can, so we may cleanse them of the other's taint." He let me go and I was less sure, until Nathaniel took my hand and suddenly I felt solid again. Graham started to hang back, but Jean-Claude said, "One wolf must go with you, *ma petite*."

I looked out at the smiling crowd who were sitting so quietly in their seats. He had calmed their minds, would mess with some of their memories, but if he couldn't find enough power to save them from what the other vampire had done to them, they were all dead, they just didn't know it yet. He, or she, or whatever, would call to them in the middle of the night, and they would go like sleepwalkers unknowing and unresisting to be food. If they were lucky they'd survive the three times it took for the last draining bite to turn them into vampires. Unwilling vampires, which was still classed as murder, or at least manslaughter. If they were unlucky the vampire would just slaughter them, or turn them into a Renfield, a person with one or two bites that the vampire controls utterly, some with the promise of immortality eventually, and some just too weak-willed to fight the mind control. A Renfield had put the cross-shaped burn scar on my arm with a brand, so I'd look like a vampire who'd survived an attack, and because it was torture while we waited for his master to wake for the night. These people had come to Guilty Pleasures for some safe flirting, a chance to cut loose and be a little wild, not be enslaved to the newest master vampire in town, because that's what it was, a new master. One powerful enough to roll Jean-Claude and me with us surrounded by other supernatural bodyguards, and none of us had sensed what was happening until it was too late. Once we saved these people who had trusted us with their safety, then we had to find the new master in town and kill his, her, their, or its ass.

Graham was trying to control his expression and not seem eager, but the tension of it rode down his arm and into our clasped hands. Nathaniel took my other hand, and he didn't try to hide his eagerness. Voyeurism was one of his major kinks, and apparently we'd put on a really great show, because he was almost bubbling with excitement. I frowned at him, and he leaned in for a kiss, smiling. I smiled and kissed him back. "Why aren't I angry with you?"

"Because you knew I was kinky as fuck before you fell in love with me."

It made me laugh, because he was right, and because he could make me laugh in the middle of something potentially dark and horrible. Nathaniel had dragged, pushed, and just loved me into owning parts of myself that I still wasn't entirely comfortable with. He was supposed to be the most submissive of my men, but he'd been the one who pushed when the others backed off, even Jean-Claude. If Nathaniel hadn't forced me to confront certain things about myself, tonight would have sent me running for the hills and away from Jean-Claude. I was polyamorous for a lot of reasons, but one of the main ones was that without all my people in my life, I might not be with any of them.

Graham was very still as he held my hand like a rabbit freezes when the fox is near. No, he'd frozen like the fox hiding just outside the henhouse waiting for his chance to go inside and eat his fill. He was sorry for the emergency, but he wanted to go with us and help feed the *ardeur*. He'd wanted it for years. It was part of what would make him a high-energy feed for me. I squeezed Graham's hand a little tighter and let Nathaniel lead us toward the staff-only door. Looked like Graham was finally going to get his wish; he was going to be food.

22

BY THE TIME we got to the office I wasn't exactly getting cold feet, but I was unsure how to transition from not having sex to *Hey, baby.* I was good on beginnings, and great once the clothes came off and things were happening, but I had a lot of trouble with the transition between the two. No amount of experience seemed to make me better at it. If it had been one of the loves of my life, or even a regular friend with benefits, I would have just said something awkward and it would have been over and things would have progressed, but Graham wasn't either of those things.

Nathaniel raised my hand in both of his and looked longingly into my eyes. "I love you, but we don't have time for you to figure this out and be all stubborn and cute and awkward."

I fought not to frown at him. "I love you, too, and I know we don't have time to ease me through my usual issues."

"Then can I help smooth this over and get us going?"

I nodded.

He flashed me one of those smiles that lit his face up with joy. It made me smile back just to see it. "You were so incredibly hot onstage tonight."

My smile turned into a frown.

He shook my hand as if to get my attention. "You know I loved watching you with Jean-Claude and Graham tonight, and in front of an audience—I found it incredibly hot."

I closed my eyes and took deep breaths because I wanted to be angry at him. Why? Because anger was my go-to emotion. It was what I felt when I was embarrassed, uncomfortable, scared, frightened, in love when I didn't like the way it was going, or just about any damn thing I was feeling that didn't make me utterly and completely happy with the emotion and myself for feeling it. Months of therapy to figure just that out, not why I did it, or what traumas it was attached to; just that anger was my shield for everything. It's a great weapon when you need it, but it's a lousy one when what you need is something closer to compassion, or patience, or lust.

"It's okay," Graham said, "without Jean-Claude to make you want me, I know I'm not your type." He couldn't keep the disappointment out of his voice, but he gave me an out. I appreciated that and he couldn't have done anything better to help me let go of the anger.

Graham pulled his hand out of mine, and I felt Jean-Claude's energy falter. I swayed and grabbed for Graham like he was a lifeline. The moment we touched I felt Jean-Claude's power expand again. I licked my lips and then realized I couldn't taste my lipstick. Until that moment I hadn't even thought what all the kissing might have done to it, and I still didn't care.

"This should not be happening; if it was Richard here then touching him might make that much difference because he's the other third of Jean-Claude's triumvirate, but his energy shouldn't react to all wolves like this," I said.

"It doesn't matter why it's happening," Nathaniel said, "it only matters that we give Jean-Claude enough energy to free all those people."

"It does matter why it's happening," I said, "but we don't need to know why tonight. We need to fix the emergency first."

"Am I allowed to make a suggestion?" Graham asked.

"Sure," I said.

"Can't Anita just release the *ardeur* and feed on me?"

"I could."

"She could," Nathaniel said.

"Then why don't we do that?"

Nathaniel looked at me. "I don't know. Anita, why don't we just do that?"

I didn't have a good answer, except it was someone new and I didn't want to add any more lovers to my list, not even as friends with benefits, and it was Graham. I'd said no to him for years.

"I know that Anita isn't attracted to me; if she had been even a little bit I'd have been emergency food for the *ardeur* years ago." He looked down at me with a slight smile on his face, but his eyes were serious.

"Am I supposed to apologize for that?" I asked.

"No, of course not, it was an ego blow that you didn't think I was awesome," he said with something close to his usual smug grin, "but I made peace with it. I mean, not everyone likes the same thing, right?"

I frowned at him; Nathaniel jiggled my hand to get me to look at him instead of frowning at Graham. "He didn't say anything wrong, Anita."

I let out my breath slowly, trying to let go of the anger that was just there ready to come up and engulf me and everyone around me. "I know he didn't."

"Then why are you mad at me?" Graham said. "It seems like you're always mad at me. I'm sorry I get on your nerves. I thought you had a good time out there with Jean-Claude and me. I'm sorry that you didn't. I'm sorry that I misread that and you." He sighed and looked like he was trying to think hard before he said the next part. I appreciated that he was trying so hard not to piss me off more.

"You didn't misread it, Graham, but I'm fighting years of being raised to be a good girl, and what I did out there doesn't go under the good-girl code I was raised with, and the wedding is forcing me to deal with my folks more than normal, and it's bringing up a lot of old issues."

"I get that," Graham said, "family is hard. My dad wanted me to follow him into the military, and my mom hates that I work at a strip club. The only thing that would embarrass her more would be if I danced onstage, so she'd really hate tonight." He gave a half laugh that managed not to be funny at all.

"If the two of you are trying to talk me out of wanting to see you have sex together, it won't work," Nathaniel said.

I smiled, and Graham looked puzzled. "You're too big a voyeur not to enjoy it," I said.

"I'm such a big voyeur that after you feed the *ardeur* on Graham and it's my turn, it will be an amazing amount of energy, because I will find it so incredibly hot."

"It's not seeing me with Anita that will make it hot, it's watching her with someone else, right?" Graham asked.

"You're handsome, so that's a bonus," Nathaniel said. "The two of you looked good together onstage, but you're right, it's not about you, it's about watching Anita with someone."

"Then if there's a wolf in the other room that Anita likes better than me, I'll bow out."

I stared up at him. "You'd give up your only shot at me?"

"I'd love to have sex with you, you know that, but I'm your security and Jean-Claude needs you to feed the *ardeur*, so if there's another wolf here tonight that you're more willing to feed on, we need them in here now."

There was a knock on the door, but it opened before we could say anything. Another wolf stood framed in the doorway, but it wasn't a wolf I'd expected to be on the menu tonight.

23

I HADN'T SEEN Richard in so long it was a shock to see him standing there, all six feet one inch, broad-shouldered, athletic body in a
suit and tie. "You look fabulous," he said as he reached back and
undid his hair. It fell in long brown waves around his shoulders,
framing his face with those high sculpted cheekbones, the dimple
that softened the utter masculinity of his face. Nothing ever seemed
to take away from his physical beauty.

"Richard, what are you doing here?"

"You need a wolf to feed on," he said.

"We haven't seen each other in almost a year, and you just march
in here expecting sex?"

His dark brown eyes that could look so friendly narrowed.
"Would you prefer sex with Graham?"

I glanced at the man whose hand I was still holding. Graham put
his free hand up as if to show he was unarmed. "You don't want me,
Anita, I can smell that I leave you cold without Jean-Claude to help
things along."

"I don't want anyone right now," I said, and that was true. Minutes ago, it had been hot and wonderful onstage, but I now knew that
Jean-Claude had been very deliberate with me and Graham. He'd
chosen what he saw as the lesser evil when it came to sharing me

with yet another person. I couldn't even argue with the division of labor, but the choice of someone I wasn't attracted to, or an ex who had broken my heart more times than I could count? Surely there was a third option?

Jean-Claude's thoughts were suddenly loud in my head. "You must feed, *ma petite.*"

"On Richard?" I said.

"He felt our distress and came to help, and this is the help I need, *ma petite.*"

Richard stepped farther into the room. "I left a date tonight because Jean-Claude let me feel what he's sensing in the audience. No vampire could have rolled Jean-Claude and the audience like this, Anita. Jean-Claude has the energy of all the vampires in the country that are blood-oathed to him; nothing should be able to touch him, especially not when he's in his element here at Guilty Pleasures."

"They screwed with me, too, until I had a wolf to touch."

Richard took another step toward us. "Let me be the wolf that you and Jean-Claude need tonight."

Nathaniel's hand tensed in mine. It made me look at him. I realized he was shielding about as hard as he ever did from me, so that even holding his hand I couldn't feel what he was feeling or thinking. "You were encouraging me to have sex with Graham."

"I was."

"I'm Ulfric leader of our pack; by wereanimal law I don't need to get anyone's permission except for Anita's, but we aren't just animals, and before you sleep with another man's girlfriend in a poly relationship you have to have his permission, too."

Nathaniel looked startled and didn't try to hide it. "I don't know what to say, that's . . . I appreciate you treating me like Anita's partner and asking my permission."

"You're welcome, and do I have your okay for this?"

Nathaniel let out a breath I hadn't known he was holding. "I hate the way you've treated Anita and me in the past, but if tonight has proved anything it's that Jean-Claude needs his own wolf to call, so if Anita is okay with it, then so am I."

"*Ma petite*, I am close to needing you to release the *ardeur* and simply feed without all the civilized niceties." He let me feel that whatever was inside the audience was trying to spread, and where it wanted to go was back inside him. He'd been powerful enough to cast out the compulsion the first time, but that had been with me at his side. Now he had more wolves, but he didn't have my hand in his and he was the king of us all; he shouldn't have needed my hand to hold in the dark.

"We're out of time," I said.

"You have to wear a condom," Nathaniel said.

Richard started undoing his tie. "Then I need to be out of my clothes and wearing one before we release the *ardeur.*"

I didn't argue with him, but I wanted to.

24

THE CLOTHES CAME off without any preliminaries, and I got to see that Richard hadn't been hitting the weight room as much as the last time I'd seen him nude. It made his body smoother, closer to the way he'd looked when I first started dating him. When he'd left us, he'd also had to leave our gym that was set up for supernatural strength and abilities. There were other gyms in the area that had facilities for supernaturals, but they were all public gyms and Richard was still in the closet. To most of the world he was a mild-mannered college biology professor, and Clark Kent couldn't go to Superman's gym.

Graham kept touching my hand, or arm, or back while Nathaniel helped me undress, because every time I lost touch with the werewolf that other power tried to do bad things tonight. I was down to just the high heels when Jean-Claude's power pushed at us. "I need you now, *ma petite*, leave the shoes and grant me more power. Something is very wrong out here."

Nathaniel stood and offered me his arm, while Graham kept my hand. The two of them walked me toward Richard, and it reminded me of the discussion we were having about who was going to walk me down the aisle if my father bailed on me. Nathaniel and Micah were one of the ideas for escorting me. Yes, we were nude, and it was very not a wedding, and it was Richard and not Jean-Claude, but once the man in front of me had proposed and I'd said yes. We'd spent years trying to force each other to meet in the middle. Him wanting white-picket-fence monogamy, me wanting black-barbed-wire polyamory. Now here we were.

"You're beautiful," Richard said.

"You're not so bad yourself," I said; then Nathaniel squeezed my arm, and I tried again. "You're gorgeous."

Richard gave a small frown. "What just happened?"

"I'm working on being less sarcastic and more openly complimentary in the bedroom," I said.

He smiled. "Thank you, both of you," he said, nodding at Nathaniel.

"It either works with everyone, or it doesn't work with anyone," Nathaniel said, and he couldn't hide the fact that he wasn't happy to be handing me over to Richard. The Ulfric had treated Nathaniel as less than for years. The last few minutes had probably been the best interaction they'd had in a long time.

Graham held my hand out to Richard. "Since I'm not part of your poly group, I don't think it needs to work with me."

Richard took my hand, and suddenly it was . . . better. Jean-Claude's power level rose just from us holding hands. "And that's my cue to leave, because it feels like you have all the wolf energy you need," Graham said. I clung to Nathaniel's hand and stared up at Richard. I hadn't felt anything this powerful from him in years. I didn't know that Graham had left the room until I heard the door close behind him. He didn't matter anymore; I had our wolf. That last part wasn't my thought alone.

I'd had moments of hating the high heels tonight, but now I was suddenly five-eight to Richard's six-one. I might never wear them outside the bedroom again, but I'd never been able to look Richard in the eye like I could in this moment. Jean-Claude had a moment of looking through my eyes, and he loved that Richard was gazing into our eyes with unabashed desire. There was regret in Jean-Claude that Richard had never looked at him that way. The moment of sharing was cut off abruptly as Jean-Claude got back in control of his thoughts and emotions. Richard's face never changed, and I was pretty sure that if he'd just heard in his head what I had, he wouldn't still be smiling down at me with uncomplicated lust in his eyes. He was entirely too conflicted about Jean-Claude, or any man when it came to sex. For the first time I realized that it wasn't me that still wanted Richard, it was Jean-Claude. Damn.

Nathaniel leaned in and laid a kiss on my cheek. It made me turn and look at him. I had been as tall as him all night in the shoes but suddenly I was noticing how tall I was all over again. I wasn't hung up on height. I was still getting an echo from Jean-Claude. He liked tall men.

Nathaniel studied my face. He could see that I wasn't alone behind my eyes. Jean-Claude was having trouble not oversharing things he'd never shared with me or Richard before. Nathaniel leaned into me, searching my face, and I realized that he was looking for Jean-Claude in my eyes. Nathaniel had been in Jean-Claude's bed with me for a year, but Jean-Claude didn't look at him like that. I hadn't realized that it bothered him until now. What was it about this other vampire power that was screwing with us and revealing so much emotion?

Nathaniel kissed me, soft and thoroughly. It made me close my eyes and start to lean into him, but Richard's hand kept me from leaning too far, like a reminder that my attention was supposed to be elsewhere. It made me open my eyes to find Nathaniel looking back at me, our faces so close together that his lavender eyes filled my vision. We moved farther back so that I could see his smile.

"I love you," he said, and pressed a string of condoms into my hand.

"I love you more," I said, smiling at him.

"I love you most," he said, then moved to lean against the edge of the desk. He made a little motion with his hands, like *Go ahead*. It made me turn back to the man whose hand I was still holding. I stared up into the face that had once launched my heart like a thousand ships, and then we'd sunk the ships in a battle that had destroyed us both. The man that had helped put me back together more than once was sitting on the desk watching us. But the power of Richard's hand in mine was like the sun had risen to warm the earth; it would be enough to help Jean-Claude chase the other vampire out of the crowd and out of us all. As if he'd read my hesitation, he breathed through my mind, "*Ma petite*, I need you to drown your doubts in desire and feed me the energy I need to defeat this vampire. If you like, I can raise the *ardeur* for you?"

"No, don't do that." I said it out loud.

"What does Jean-Claude need?" Richard asked.

"He's offering to raise the *ardeur* for me, because I'm taking too long."

Nathaniel said, "All you need is the condom and then you can let the *ardeur* have its way with both of you."

We both glanced at him. I realized that given a choice I would have dropped Richard's hand and walked away, as in *I'm done and dusted*, but I could feel his heartbeat in the palm of his hand like it was an echo to my own. I knew that was Jean-Claude's vampire marks on both of us, but that didn't make the draw of it any less.

I held up the wrapped condoms. "We've got that covered."

"I don't think that's how condoms work," Nathaniel said. He widened his eyes with a smile.

I frowned at him because I was missing something.

"Richard," Nathaniel said, "you need to ask for what you need."

"I haven't seen Anita in almost a year, how do I come in and make demands?"

"I said need, not demand."

"Okay, one of you please explain what I'm missing," I said.

The men looked at each other. "How much do you want me to help out here?" Nathaniel asked, and I realized he was talking to Richard.

"She tends to take things like this better from you than me."

Nathaniel looked at me and smiled that smile that said he thought it was adorable that I was totally missing this. Richard was right, from Nathaniel I'd take that look, from most anyone else it would have been condescending.

"Just tell me," I said.

"Condoms only fit if a man is hard."

"I know that," I said, frowning.

"Richard isn't hard anymore."

I looked back at Richard, except this time I let myself look farther down his body. Damn. "Too much talking after the clothes came off," I said.

"Yes." Richard and Nathaniel said it together.

It made me laugh and some tension in me loosened. It would be okay; Nathaniel would be here to wingman for us. Richard had even acknowledged we needed him to do just that; if we could just keep being that honest with each other we'd be good.

25

WE STARTED WITH a hug, wrapping our arms around each other. The heels meant that I was tall enough that our hips were pressed against each other, so that the soft mound of his body lay warm and solid against me. The feel of just that made me shudder in his arms and bury my face against his shoulder. Hiding my face against the smoothness of his skin. His arms tightened around me, and I raised my face up for a kiss. His lips were as soft and full and kissable as I remembered. Sometimes you try to drown yourself in the kisses of other people, trying to forget how the one that got away tasted, but they're like that rare vintage of wine that you think you'll never drink again; the first sip reminds you why you loved it.

His body was starting to grow firmer just from kissing. I ran one hand up to touch his hair. The texture was rougher than all those foamy waves looked, but it was still soft, just not as soft as others. It filled my hand and made me go up on tiptoe to kiss him harder, pressing our bodies closer, starting to grind gently against that growing point of his body as the kiss became more. I bit gently on his lower lip, and he growled for me, pulling away, and since I knew he didn't like pain I let him. Richard bit my lower lip, tit for tat, but I didn't pull away, because I did like pain. He bit down a little harder and my eyes rolled back into my head, and then he bit more, and that was too much for there. I patted his shoulder like tapping out in the dojo, but he took it as me pretending to struggle. I hit his shoulder harder, and he let go, moving back so he could see my face. "Too much?"

"Yes," I said.

Nathaniel said, "If she can't talk she taps out."

"I didn't know," Richard said, and it was the truth.

"Now you know and just in case it comes up, my safeword is 'safeword.'"

He widened his eyes at me. "'Safeword,' really?"

I frowned at him. "Yes, really."

"Mine's 'red.'"

"Red as in stop," I said. He nodded, looking down at me, and it was both familiar and weird as hell to be gazing up at him naked. "You're a top to a dominant, since when did you ever need a safeword?"

"Recently," he said, and he was searching my face as if not sure how I'd take it.

"Are you telling me you're a switch like I am?"

"Yes, no, I'm still figuring it all out, but you should always share safewords beforehand, don't you think?"

"I do, actually," I said. His body chose that moment to do one of those involuntary twitches that can happen when a man is very eager and very hard. I had to close my eyes and concentrate on my breathing for a second. I had a second of hating that his body could still make me react this strongly, and then Jean-Claude was in both our heads.

"Release the *ardeur* now!" He'd been shielding us, because now we could feel the other vampire's power creeping into him, into us. He was the king with the power of a million vampires shared inside him; no other vampire should have been able to touch him, but the power of this vampire was like black smoke engulfing Jean-Claude. We could see him covered in it as if there was a fire between us and him.

I saw Jake beside him yelling, looking at us as if he knew exactly where our viewpoint hovered. Richard said, "Jake is yelling for us to come to our master's side."

Nathaniel opened the office door and said, "You need to touch him, Anita, like you touched Damian and me in Ireland."

"What happened in Ireland?" Richard asked.

"We called an army of ghosts to protect us from a group of evil vampires," I said, but I'd already started for the door, and since Richard's hand was still in mine he came with me.

"What?" he asked, and he pulled on my hand, which normally wouldn't be a problem, but I wouldn't normally have been wearing five-and-a-half-inch heels. Nathaniel caught my arm, so I kept my feet. Richard caught up and stopped asking questions. Nathaniel got us to the hallway and was reaching for the stage door when it opened, and Jean-Claude was standing there. He reached for me, and Nathaniel drew me forward as if it were a dance and he was passing me to the next partner. Jean-Claude's hand wrapped around mine and I could see the black smoke like a dark haze around his upper body. He drew me closer and because Richard was holding my other hand he pulled us both closer. Richard touched his arm, and the moment Jean-Claude was touching both of us the blackness thinned, and I could see two shining points hovering in that hazy darkness.

Richard whispered, "Are those eyes?"

"Yes," I said.

"We must destroy it," Jean-Claude said.

"How?" Richard asked.

"The only way I know," Jean-Claude said, his eyes filled with blue fire, as if the midnight sky could burn. The pale eyes floating in the mist seemed dimmer just in comparison, but they didn't go away, and the hazy blackness tightened around his upper body like a snake trying to squeeze his life away.

"Whatever you need to defeat that thing," Richard said, and his brown eyes filled with blue fire.

"Whatever you need," I said, and I didn't need a mirror to know that my own eyes had turned to the same burning-night-sky blue.

Jean-Claude stood there wreathed by that blackness, the eyes of the other vampire floating above him as if it could mark him the way he had marked us. No other vampire was strong enough to do that to him, but there it was like a venomous serpent clinging to him. The eyes were less clear with him touching both of us, but it wasn't gone, and it should have been gone, chased out by the power of his own triumvirate, his own human servant and beast half. We were his seat of power, the thing that had allowed him to rise to rule over every other vampire in America. There was a hiss of sound through my head, every vampire save one. That wasn't our thought.

Fear poured over us like the coldest of showers, all lust lost in the terror of that serpent body and those floating eyes. "It's a mora, a night hag, it feeds off our fear." I said it out loud as if we didn't all know, but somehow saying the words helped loosen what it was doing to us.

"Release the *ardeur*," Richard said.

"I will not have control as normal, Richard, and I would not lose you so soon again," Jean-Claude said.

"No more running," he said, "no matter what happens I swear to you both I will stay and work it out, and not abandon you."

Jean-Claude gave me a desperate look because it was too good to believe. Jean-Claude's blue eyes were as human as they ever got, but the pale eyes floating just above and beside his head gleamed like fog with headlights behind it, coming this way. The vampire was going to drive right over us unless we acted now.

"Jean-Claude, you have to raise the *ardeur* now, right now," I said.

"He feeds on nightmares and terror. He won't care about my feelings, or anyone's feelings but his own. He will take over your vampires, and then the entire country will be his," Richard said.

That hissing voice came again. "Such tender morals Jean-Claude has acquired, he will not take by force what is rightfully his, but I will."

My skin ran cold with the opposite of nameless dread because I knew exactly where the dread was coming from, no name needed. My mouth went dry, and I was so scared I could taste metal on my tongue as if I was already bleeding from wounds he hadn't made yet. I heard Richard almost moan, "I will not give the Thronnos Rokke clan over to you."

The smoke turned black and solid; it was feeding off our fears, using us to give it power. It turned a huge spade-shaped head toward me and even without the colored scales I knew that head shape.

"Viper," Richard said; I thought he'd read my mind, then realized that we both had biology degrees.

"I want to say rattlesnake but I'm not sure that it's anything natural."

"Maybe it's an ancestral viper like some of the older types of shapeshifters are extinct species," he said.

The night-dark head turned to look at each of us in turn as we spoke. Its head was as wide across as Jean-Claude's. Another wave of terror tried to travel down Jean-Claude's hands to us, but we were studying the snake, trying to classify it, not something recommended in the field with real snakes. If you think it's venomous just get away from it, figure out species later in safety, but we couldn't let go of Jean-Claude. We could not leave this snake alone, so . . . "No viper in the world was ever this big," I said.

"Not that we've found a fossil for," agreed Richard.

The more we used our brains for thinking and studying, the easier it was to slough off the fear, like a snake shedding its skin so it can grow bigger. "The eyes haven't changed color," I said.

"Still pale gray," he said.

"Shining like moonlight or rain if it could glow," I said.

"Why do you think the eyes aren't changing color with the rest of the body?" he asked.

"I don't know, maybe they're windows into his soul and all that jazz."

"You mean they're really the vampire's eye color?" Richard leaned closer and the snake's head leaned toward him. He should have been afraid to get closer to it, but he wasn't. The more we studied it, the less afraid we both were; it worked that way with real animals, too, so we'd discovered back when we were still camping, birdwatching, hiking, caving—he was the last person in my dating life who had loved the outdoors even more than I did. I saw a ghostly fringe around the top of its head, or I thought I did, but it was, like most of the body, smoke—the phrase *smoke and mirrors* came to mind.

"Is there a fringe on top of its head?" I asked.

"Yes," Richard said, "and no. It's insubstantial like smoke, and no living snake has ever had a fringe, that's only lizards."

"I am not a lizard," the hissing voice said.

Richard sniffed the air almost nose to nose with the massive head. "It doesn't smell real; it doesn't smell like snake or lizard."

The hissing voice came through our heads. "I am real enough to crawl into your souls and control you for the rest of eternity."

"Rest of eternity? Isn't that redundant?" I asked.

"Should it just be, you'll control us for all of eternity?" Richard asked.

"No," I said, "even that's too much. It should be he'll control us for eternity, because after you say that there is no more. Eternity is it."

"Are you making fun of me?" the hissing voice asked, but the snake head never opened its mouth when it spoke; it wasn't real enough to have to open its mouth. What the fuck was this thing?

Jean-Claude laughed. "I had almost forgotten that Richard shared your sense of humor once, *ma petite.*"

The snake body flexed around his chest and the laughter stopped. Jean-Claude staggered and started to fall, but Richard caught him. I tensed to see the snake hit him, too, but the coils were like mist that held its shape so that I could see Richard's body through it. I pushed my hand through it to touch Richard's arm and it felt less real than mist, there wasn't even any moisture to it. I still had Jean-Claude's hand in mine, though his grip seemed weaker. I moved my other hand to his chest, and the snake that looked so solid and black evaporated like clouds around my hand, graying out so I could see through it.

The hiss ran through us all. "You have left the door open a crack, Jean-Claude; did you think the words meant nothing? The fourth mark can only be completed two ways, by absolute force and will of the vampire involved, or by saying the spell along with the actions. Real magic is more than just rutting like beasts and thinking strongly at something, but you are so young, you don't remember when the Mother was one of us, not the queen of us. Magic was everywhere, but there were rules, there are still rules, and you don't know what they are, little would-be king. That lack of knowledge is going to be your death, and then your human servant, the greatest necromancer in over three thousand years, will be mine, and your beast, wolf king of the local werewolves. Not so powerful, but once he is mine I will fill him with such magic that none will stand before him."

"Who are you?" I asked.

"Names are old magic. I will not share mine."

"If you're going to be our new master, shouldn't we have your name?"

"You may call me Deimos."

"The personification of dread before the battle, right?"

The strangely solid snake head looked at me and something flickered in the shining gray eyes. I'd surprised him. "Most unexpected that you would know that."

"*Ma petite* is full of surprises, Deimos." The snake coils moved as if someone had walked through mist to send it swirling around my arm where I touched Jean-Claude. He sagged as Richard took more of his weight with the one arm that was free; neither of us wanted to let go of Jean-Claude's hands, as if that was more important than just touching his skin.

"Raise the *ardeur*, Jean-Claude," Richard said.

"I will not force myself upon you, I gave you my word."

This was news to me but made sense for the two of them. "You raise the *ardeur* and chase this cold-blooded bastard back to his den, or I will," I said.

"If a man's word is no longer good, then he is without honor." He sagged until Richard had to brace to hold him and withdrew the hand I was holding so he could at least partially use both arms. The stupid heels made me stumble and almost fall. Jean-Claude's skin was cool and clammy; it should have been warm and full of all the lust from the crowd. Deimos didn't have to send fear into me, I was suddenly terrified all on my own. The fear chased back my own *ardeur*. Fuck. I had to swallow hard before I could look at Richard. His eyes were solid, chocolate brown with no hint of Jean-Claude's power in them. Mine were probably just brown again, too.

I said, "I don't know what bargain you made with him, but it is not worth him dying in our arms."

"If I thought we could both survive I might have once, but that was then, and Deimos would not be an improvement."

I started to say that if he let Jean-Claude die it wouldn't matter if he survived because I'd kill him, but I'd learned enough to keep the more self-sabotaging things to myself. Somewhere in that sentence he'd agreed to help Jean-Claude.

Richard kissed Jean-Claude's cheek. I had no idea why; it wasn't something I'd ever seen them do before. Jean-Claude moved his face back to see Richard more clearly; those dark blue eyes were having trouble focusing.

"Would you really let him kill you and give Anita and me into slavery just so you didn't accidentally ravage me?"

"I gave you my word."

"That's a yes," I said.

"*Oui.*"

"Honorable men are so easily manipulated," Deimos said.

"We can be," Richard said, still staring into Jean-Claude's face like he was trying to memorize him, and then he kissed him full on the mouth. It was a chaste touch of lips, but in nearly ten years of off-again, on-again it was the first time I'd ever seen them kiss. He drew back first, and Jean-Claude's face showed the astonishment we were both feeling at our so-heterosexual Richard.

"You astonish me, *mon lupe.*"

"I'd rather not take one for the team, but if it happens in the heat of the moment, I promise no buyer's remorse from me. Now release the *ardeur* and save us."

The coils swirled, or flexed, I had no word for what they did around Jean-Claude's chest, but it staggered him so that Richard and I let go of our hands to grab him. In the fraction of a second before I was touching them both again, Deimos filled me with terror that froze my breath in my throat and damn near collapsed my chest with dread. We were going to lose, we were going to die, we were . . .

"He cannot find his lust while I ride him; your master cannot save you now, wolf."

"We just need the *ardeur* to rise," Richard said, and he looked at me.

"Lust is the balm in which men have hidden their fear before battle, their terror on the battlefield in rape and ravage, but it is too late for Jean-Claude to give you such comfort."

"I know that," Richard said, and he gave me a look that was strangely peaceful, as if he'd made peace with it, whatever it might be. I'd never thought to see a look like that on his face again, our conflicted teacher who happened to be a werewolf. He stood there, the muscles in his arms flexing, holding Jean-Claude with my arm around his waist, one arm trapped between their bodies. He nodded, and I looked up at the snake's head. I wanted to touch it to feel if it was solid enough to smash; once we'd freed Jean-Claude and ourselves, we'd test the theory. I looked at the pale gray eyes and they flickered again, maybe it was a blink without eyelids. Richard shared some of his resolute calm with me. I didn't question where that sense of peace came from, because I needed it too badly to question. It helped me regain control of myself.

"Deimos, dread or fear, is the son of Ares, god of war," I said.

"Yes, I am a god."

I smiled and I knew it was the smile most unpleasant that I got when I was about to do something violent and usually fatal for the other guy. I'd made peace with that smile and what came with it because it kept me alive. "Do you know what my nickname is, Deimos?"

"You are the Executioner, and soon you will be slaying my enemies as I bid you."

"My other nickname."

"What other name?" He sounded impatient and he tried to send fear down my skin again, but it was too late for that to stop me; I'd made my decision and there was an untouchable stillness in the choice.

"War, the other preternatural marshals call me 'War,' that's why I know Deimos is fear or dread of the battle to come: I researched it."

"That is absurd; you are a tiny, delicate woman, you cannot be War."

Jean-Claude sagged in our arms so hard we were going to have to go to our knees soon. "Hurry up," Richard said.

I called the *ardeur* from inside me, not Jean-Claude's power, but like the wolf that hid inside me, what had begun as his power alone was now mine. "What is this? What is happening?" Deimos sounded afraid, perfect.

"Who's your daddy, Deimos?" I said, and then the *ardeur* engulfed us like a wave of summer heat. I had a vague memory of Deimos screaming and then it was just the three of us with our hands and mouths on each other without Jean-Claude in enough control to save us from ourselves.

26

I DROWNED IN the taste of Richard's skin, and Jean-Claude's mouth breathed along my skin so that I shivered between the two of them like wood trapped between different flames. The feel of my hands on both their bodies at the same time with no one to tell me to stop was intoxicating. The *ardeur* gave us to each other in ways that we had always denied. It was desire so pure there were no doubts, no protests, no stopping. The next clear memory I had was being on the floor with Jean-Claude above me. Richard's face appeared above Jean-Claude's shoulder, the rich brown waves intermingling with the black curls. I was pinned under their combined weight, trapped in a way I'd never been trapped before. Richard's eyes turned wolf amber, glimpsed like a wild thing through the fall of their combined hair. Richard did something with his hips that made Jean-Claude spasm, thrusting deeper into me, which made me cry out.

"Up," Richard said, an edge of growl in his voice. Jean-Claude lifted his upper body off me in a sort of push-up. A tanned arm encircled Jean-Claude's pale waist. I loved the contrast of their skins, and then Jean-Claude did something with his hips that made my eyes roll back into my head, so I only felt his hands curve under the small of my back and hold me in place as he went up on his knees. Normally I would have wrapped my legs around his waist to help hold myself in place but there was no way for me to reach around both men. I had a moment of not knowing what to do with my legs, but I needed the leverage of the lock. It was like being in guard in Brazilian jujitsu when the person above you is massive, you just can't get a lock, but you need to find a way to get your leverage, except here I didn't want to escape, I just wanted to be able to move.

"I need to wrap my legs around someone, or a headboard to hold on to," I said, because that could make up for not being able to use my legs to help, but there was nothing within reach.

"We can come to you," Richard growled.

"What?" I asked, but Jean-Claude seemed to understand just fine because he said, "Legs up, *ma petite*, put the heels I have been dreaming of seeing you in all day on my shoulders." There was a heat, almost a hunger in his eyes that let me know he meant it about the shoes, and for that look in this moment I could wear more ridiculous shoes.

I had to move my legs wide as I lifted them up so as not to spear anyone with the stilettos. Jean-Claude held my weight in his hands, so it was easier than it would have been. I finally carefully had them on Jean-Claude's bare shoulders, framing his face. All the beading and extras on the shoes that I had hated looked like a jewel in some treasure box with his black curls touching them, his dark, deep blue eyes bluer than I'd ever seen them, and I realized the blue in the shoes brought out his eyes as if he'd planned it that way, and being Jean-Claude he probably had.

Then Richard peered around his shoulder and those feral wolf eyes didn't match the shoes at all, but their faces next to each other above me was perfect, as if I'd been waiting forever to see them like this. Jean-Claude lowered his body over mine, but with my legs over his shoulders it was the least missionary position I could imagine. I was still staring at his chest, but my own legs kept him up and off me enough that I could get glimpses of his face as he began to move inside me. Then the weight changed, and I felt Richard pressing us both to the floor. I was completely trapped under their combined weights, and I loved it.

Jean-Claude and Richard found their rhythm. In this position with Richard on top of him Jean-Claude couldn't do his usual gliding in and out of me so that I could see every inch of him going deep into me, but the angle meant he didn't need to do much to start my body building toward orgasm. I couldn't see Richard at all, but I could feel the weight of him over us, the push and pull of his body in the gentlest of movements. He normally made love like he was trying to pound his way through to the other side, but not tonight. He was as gentle and careful as I'd ever felt him. I normally liked rougher, more vigorous sex myself, but tonight gentle was enough. That warm weight began to build deep in my body as Jean-Claude pushed and pulled himself over and over inside me.

"I'm close," Richard said, and there was no growl to his voice now, just the strain of keeping his careful rhythm without pushing himself over the edge before we came.

"Yes," Jean-Claude said, and his voice held the strain of concentration as he fought to bring me before he gave himself over to pleasure.

The weight was building, but I wasn't there yet. I opened my mouth to say *Not that close* and then from one stroke to the next the orgasm rolled over me, out of me, brought me screaming underneath them.

I heard Richard say "Thank God," and then felt him thrust his weight, pinning us both. Jean-Claude shuddered above me, inside me, and that brought me again, screaming and struggling underneath them, my fingernails tearing at the carpet trying to find something to hold on to, to keep me from falling into the pleasure of it and never coming out again.

My eyes had fluttered back into my head so that I was blind and only the lighter weight above me let me know that Richard had moved. Jean-Claude rose up on his arms. I tried to look at him, but everything was white-edged and light flashes. It's a lie that you'll go blind with too much sex, but it was moments like this that I understood where the idea came from. He pulled himself out of me and that made me writhe and scream again.

I lay on my back waiting to be able to move anything. Jean-Claude collapsed beside me on his stomach, his arm flung across my waist. I turned my head and all I could see was his black curls. Richard's arm came into sight resting on Jean-Claude's shoulder, down his back so that his hand rested against the other man's body. Richard's breathing was still labored, more than I'd heard him after a lot more vigorous workout. He gave a breathless laugh.

Jean-Claude raised his head, and I still couldn't see anything but his hair. "We have won this battle, but we must make plans to win the next."

I patted his arm where it lay across me and said, "If you can move, then start that Machiavellian planning, I can't feel my legs yet."

He laughed and shook his head, long hair still hiding his face. I found that I could move my arm enough to part his curls so I could look at him. His eyes were the lightest blue I'd ever seen them, not midnight blue, but autumn skies just as the sun begins to sink. I felt what I felt most times when I looked at him: that he was too beautiful to be mine. He smiled at me, not the smile he used onstage or when he was on camera with the media, but a smile less practiced and more real and all the more precious for it.

"Can't we just lie here and enjoy the moment before we gear up for the next battle?" Richard asked, and his voice was almost sad.

Jean-Claude turned his head to look at him and I found that I could rise up on my elbows enough to see Richard's body on the other side of him, but I could not see his face. "You are right, *mon lupe*, this is a moment to be savored. Forgive me."

"Since we can't get up yet, we could cuddle," I said, because if this moment never happened again, I wanted us to hold each other.

I half expected Richard to climb back into his issues and insist on me being in the middle, but he didn't. He just turned on his side and was the big spoon for Jean-Claude, who was the big spoon for me, and I was the littlest spoon. Love it or hate it, it was the truth. Jean-Claude held me close, and then Richard's arm slipped over both of us, so that he held us. Eight, almost nine years and this was the first time we'd ever cuddled together like this, held each other like this, or if we'd ever done it before it had been so long ago I didn't remember it.

I stroked my fingers down his arm. I'd forgotten how dark his skin was, or how pale mine was against it. I liked the contrast of his warm tan to our paleness. I'd never been able to tan, I just burned. I wondered if Jean-Claude's skin had tanned when he was alive, or if all this white skin had burned like mine?

There was a knock on the office door, and we all tensed. Ethan said, "I'm sorry to interrupt, really sorry, but the audience is still waiting for you. Nathaniel is onstage trying to keep them occupied so they don't start to leave, but we need you."

I lay there in our cuddly nest of spoons and said, "Am *I* the only one that completely forgot about the audience, or should I feel stupid all on my own?"

Jean-Claude nuzzled my hair and held me tighter, pressing his nakedness against mine. It wasn't so much sexual now as comforting. "It is not stupid to fully enjoy the pleasures that you love, *ma petite*."

"Maybe not stupid, but you didn't forget them."

Richard's arm tightened around us both like he was hugging us. "I came in the back through the alley, so I didn't even see the audience. I just felt Jean-Claude call to the wolves for help, and I was close enough to answer the call."

"It is lucky indeed that you were close at hand, *mon lupe*. I do not think any other wolf could have substituted for you this night."

"Wait, did you say you were on a date and that's why you were so close?" I asked.

"Yes."

"Is she here? Please tell me your date wasn't standing outside the door while we had sex." I started to try to sit up enough to look at him, but both men held me in place.

"She isn't here. I called her an Uber and sent her home."

I tried not to struggle with their combined strength keeping me pressed in place, but suddenly being the little spoon wasn't as cozy. Richard had dumped his date to come have sex with us; it just seemed rude.

"I hope she forgives you," I said.

"It was a first date, and I was bored out of mind. I'm sorry that people are in danger, but I'm not sorry that I'm here with the two of you instead of with a stranger droning on about her divorce and how I was nothing like her ex-husband and wasn't that good."

"That sounds awful," I said.

Jean-Claude stroked his arm and said, "Why would you be on such a date?"

"Fixed up by another teacher, and my therapist has been encouraging me to date more."

"What's your therapist going to say about being here with us?"

"Nothing, she told me to either date and find someone to make me stop mooning over you and Jean-Claude or to get back with you."

I was glad that Jean-Claude was in between us because I went very still. The sex was fabulous, and we needed to repair the triumvirate to secure Jean-Claude's power base, but we weren't back together. We were not suddenly a threesome. Richard had alienated so many people in our poly group that they'd never have sex with him, and he couldn't seduce them into thinking it was a good idea. I didn't even think it was a good idea and I had the benefit of seeing him naked. Did Richard really believe that one good fuck and all was forgiven, or had I misunderstood? Please let me have misunderstood.

"I know that this doesn't make everything all right between us. I'm not expecting one good fuck, and everything is forgiven."

"Thank you for saying that out loud," I said.

He hugged us both again and then his arm moved, and I looked back over my shoulder. I caught a glimpse of his hair and upper body, so I rolled over still in Jean-Claude's arms so I could see both of their faces.

He idly stroked Jean-Claude's arm as he spoke. "I don't know how comfortable I'll be with certain things, but I finally changed therapists a few months ago, because the first one was an older man and he was more homophobic than I was, and one of my major issues was that I was totally captivated by this beautiful man that I kept trying to hate, because I didn't want to be bisexual on top of being a werewolf. It's one of the reasons I freaked out after we were together with Asher in the bedroom that first time. It felt great and then I went home and tried to be what I thought I was supposed to be instead of what I was."

We both just stared at him. "Wait, go back, did you just say you were bisexual?"

He nodded.

"Richard," Jean-Claude said, "I am astonished. I . . . you have rendered me speechless."

"Am I too late? Is there no room for me in the poly group? I've been horrible and I've vanished for months on all of you, so if it's too late then I understand. It's my own fault."

"It is never too late while life remains," Jean-Claude said. "Only true death takes away our second chances."

"I agree," I said, "but we have to talk to the rest of our people. Some of the newer ones haven't even met you or only in passing."

"I know, and I'm sorry that it took me this long to admit the truth to myself."

Jean-Claude rolled over on his back to look up at Richard, and for some reason that made me go up on one elbow so that I was mirroring Richard's pose. He got totally distracted by my breasts for a second and couldn't make eye contact with either of us.

"If that look on your face is you trying not to stare at my breasts, it's okay to stare. We just had sex, so you're allowed," I said.

Richard smiled and looked embarrassed. "Not all women feel that way, even after sex."

"That's their issue, not mine."

He looked at my face and there was a depth of feeling in his brown eyes that once would have made my heart sing but now forced me to look down so he couldn't read the uncertainty in mine.

"I'm tired of their issues," he said, then added, "and so tired of my own." He bent down and I looked in time to see him kiss Jean-Claude softly, tenderly, the way most women like to be kissed. He drew back and Jean-Claude's eyes were still closed, the black lace of his lashes making him look like Snow White in some gender-switch porn. I had sex on my mind but after what we'd just done together and gazing at the two of them nude knowing I could just reach across and touch them . . . who could blame me?

Jean-Claude opened his eyes and gazed up at Richard. "I feel like I am dreaming, and I do not wish to wake, but we must clean up enough to be presentable and use our combined energies to send the audience home safe and sound."

"Just tell me what to do," Richard said.

Jean-Claude sat up, then got to his feet like he was dancing on-stage. I was not going to be anywhere near that smooth standing up in my heels. Maybe he read my mind, or maybe he just knew me well enough, because he offered me a hand up, which I happily took, because I actually needed it. Richard stood up with us. There was a moment of awkwardness when it was like he didn't know whose hand to take.

"*Ma petite* needs the most help in those delicious shoes."

Richard moved so he could take my other hand, and we walked toward the door, and then I stopped so they had to stop. "Not everyone in the hallway gets to see me naked on a regular basis; I need my dress."

"I should put on my clothes, too," Richard said.

"And I have a robe," Jean-Claude said.

"Someone hand me my dress, so I don't have to bend down for

it." Jean-Claude bent in the boots, and I admit to admiring the view while he did it, so that I was grinning happily when he handed me my dress. He smiled back as if he knew exactly what I'd been admiring. I wrapped my arms around him with the dress in one hand so that we could kiss. We drew back at the same time to smile into each other's eyes. I suddenly felt better like everything would be all right; no matter what anyone else did, we would be good.

Richard stopped with his clothes in his hands. "If we're going to clean up, I'd rather do that before I get dressed."

"If we tend to the audience before we shower, then I might have something for you to wear onstage," Jean-Claude said.

I watched Richard hesitate. "I teach at a college, which is more forgiving than when I taught junior high, but I don't have tenure yet and stripping might make sure I never get it."

"If we hide your face and get you out of your conservative clothes I doubt any of your fellow faculty will dare admit they recognize you except in their fantasies," Jean-Claude said.

"What will you be wearing?" I asked.

"I have a robe that matches the boots."

I grinned and shook my head. "Of course you do."

"If you have clothes that will fit me and that someone is willing for me to borrow, I'm game," Richard said.

"We will find something," Jean-Claude said with a smile, and we did.

27

JEAN-CLAUDE HAD THE audience sitting in their chairs perfectly still again, eyes wide and staring at nothing, I couldn't even see them blink. I wondered how long you could keep eyes open before they began to dry out. Of course, they hadn't been sitting here like this the whole time. Nathaniel had brought Graham onstage and had an impromptu dance lesson, which the audience had loved, and then after Ethan had knocked on our door the audience had gone still like they were now. Jean-Claude had been able to concentrate on them again. Our lovemaking and the *ardeur* had given Jean-Claude back his control and power, but his attention had returned only after the door knock. Now Richard and I stood onstage holding his hands and waiting for him to wake the audience. He'd warned us not to voice our doubts or that we found the frozen, unblinking audience creepy, because like patients coming out of anesthesia they could remember what was said over them. We didn't want to go to this much trouble and then have them remember us saying things that didn't match the new memories Jean-Claude had created.

Though admittedly my greatest danger was tripping in the five-and-a-half-inch heels because I was gawking at Richard in his borrowed clothes. I wasn't sure what it was about the outfit that distracted me so; maybe it was the shiny pleather boy shorts that hugged the back of him on purpose and were having some difficulty holding all of the front of him. There were even matching shiny combat boots, but they didn't distract me like the shorts. I'd just seen him nude and had sex with him only minutes ago, so why was I having such trouble not staring at the front of the shorts? Because I hadn't gotten to go down on him or have him inside me in any way. I loved and was still totally shocked that he'd managed to cross the great divide with Jean-Claude, but it had still been a long time since I'd been with Richard. Sex had been the only area where he and I had always been good together.

He looked at me across the stage. The mask he was wearing wasn't shiny, but real black leather. It was all one piece, handmade, and the most expensive part of the outfit. It had delicate points up above his hair that could be horns, but there were two equally delicate points on the bottom of the mask, so they framed his lips and even drew attention to the dimple. Nathaniel had helped him with his hair backstage so that it was a mass of foamy waves completely hiding the string that held the mask in place. The stage lights caught hints of copper and gold in the brown of his hair, like strong sunlight could do. I stared into his brown eyes surrounded by the leather and finally realized that I liked the mask, or him in the mask. It hid the high cheekbones and all the parts of his bone structure that made him so utterly masculine and left bare the full kissable lips and the softer triangle of his lower jaw and chin with that dimple that had always been like one little extra "yes he is really that pretty" so that the thought of watching him above me in the mask just totally did it for me. Funny how you don't know something is a kink until it is.

Jean-Claude tapped our hands with his thumb to count down three, two, one, and the audience blinked to life while he led us forward, smiling in his full-length blue robe that matched the hint of boots perfectly. "Nikki and Jet are here to help me wish you a very good night!" The audience applauded and yelled our names, or just wordlessly yelled. Jean-Claude had created them seeing Jet, Richard's stage name for tonight, dancing. Apparently they were good visuals because his name got called a lot for a first-timer onstage at Guilty Pleasures.

Then Jean-Claude called power and not in the quiet way he normally did, so that most of the time I didn't notice. He was so good at subtle because he'd hidden how powerful he truly was for centuries from other vampires. He'd hidden in plain sight playing the seducer, the fob, the eye candy, so the stronger vampires would see only the lovely outside without guessing that inside he was so much more. What had started as necessity had become habit until sometimes I think even he forgot how much more he could be. If you play the dumb blond long enough you can get lost in the role, but Jean-Claude wasn't lost now; with our hands to anchor him he was found at last.

His power rose inside him and pulled mine and Richard's with it as if we were holding so much more than just hands. It was almost more intimate than sex because we were sharing our magic, which was a piece of our souls. It poured over the three of us in a skin-tingling, breath-stealing heat with that edge of cold eternity that helped Jean-Claude control us both. I couldn't remember the last time Richard had stood with us and given his power freely, but the Jean-Claude of then hadn't known what to do with all of it; he had learned and grown, and now he knew exactly what to do. He spilled it over the audience and not only had their skin running in goose bumps, their breath catching in their throats, their hands clutching eager at their chairs, their drinks, their own hands, but was inside them deep and deeper searching for a shadow that the other vampire had placed inside them. There were images, visuals of memories, hopes, dreams, fears, yes that was it, Deimos hadn't attached to their reality, he'd attached to their fears. He was dread of the future to come and everyone has something they are afraid of facing, and through that universal human dread he'd planted his shadow. He would whisper to them, *Come to me and the great, bad thing will never happen. Come to me and I will save you from it. Come to me and I will take you somewhere that death cannot find you ever again. Come with me and I will keep you safe.* Lying bastard.

Jean-Claude aimed our heat at the lie, like the sun rising to chase back the night and its terrors. He found their dread of what could happen and replaced it with joy, confidence, and memories of the evening here at Guilty Pleasures. He filled them with all the dancers they'd seen tonight, Jean-Claude flying over the crowd, Graham and the other guards having their amateur night, then Graham's win and he and I onstage with Jean-Claude, then Nathaniel as Brandon giving Graham dancing lessons onstage, then Richard/Jet dancing onstage, and then Jean-Claude stepped onstage at the end of Richard's act with me on his arm, and we were back to the present with us standing onstage.

"We have loved having you tonight at Guilty Pleasures and look forward to having you again. We love for our guests to come again, and again, until they are utterly satisfied." His voice made the words even more than they were. He said *loved* and you felt truly loved; saying *guilty pleasures* made the audience giggle and squirm; his *having you* was sexual, *again* was an echo of it, *love* was being so wanted, and *come again and again* was almost orgasmic. When he said *utterly satisfied*, he had them screaming and calling his name. His voice had always been one of his best vampiric powers, but it had never been this good, had it?

Jean-Claude pulled our hands downward, so we followed his lead and bowed for the audience. They shouted our names, they clapped, they yelled, and then he led us back behind the curtain. The door to backstage opened and we walked through it still holding hands: Richard, then Jean-Claude, then me. It was only when Ethan closed the door behind us and we let go of the tension that Jean-Claude had been holding that we both heard the thoughts of how unsure he had been that he could cleanse the audience completely of Deimos's magic.

I looked at him and realized that he thought he had enough power to never have to fight this hard against another vampire again. He had the power of the entire country of vampires most directly blood-oathed to him. There was a despair in him that I'd never heard this loud in my head, that no matter how powerful he became he would never be powerful enough literally, never be powerful enough to protect his power base.

I said, "Jean-Claude . . ." but he drew me into a hug and Richard wrapped himself around us, and then Nathaniel came and added his arms to the hug. We held the vampire king and all of us could feel that he was trying very hard not to lose his shit completely. If the larger vampire community found out that any single vampire had been able to almost take him, us, then it would be a free-for-all. St. Louis would turn into the wild, wild West with new master vampires coming to town to try their luck, because for the first time in America there was one master vampire that counted. If you took out Jean-Claude, the country was yours with one duel.

He whispered, "What have I done?" We held him closer, and tried to think happy thoughts, because he could read our minds and we were all scared.

28

I LAID A kiss on Jean-Claude's bare chest where the robe had gaped, which was enough to have him look down at me through all our interlaced arms. I stared into the dark blue of his eyes and even hearing his doubts in my head I still loved him and believed in him. I really did. He smiled and some tension went out of his face and his mind.

"If you have faith in me, *ma petite*, then that is enough."

We all drew back from the hug, and I turned to put my head against Nathaniel's, so that our faces were next to each other. "Nathaniel taught me that when you truly love someone you believe in them even when things aren't perfect."

"I have faith in you both," Nathaniel said.

Richard said, "I haven't earned anyone's faith in me yet, at least not any of you or your poly group, but I promise I will try to earn it from this point on."

Nathaniel and I looked at him and I think our looks mirrored, because Richard asked, "What did I say to earn those looks?"

"You don't mean to earn faith from me and the rest of the poly group through love, that's only for Anita and Jean-Claude, right?" Nathaniel said.

"Yes, well . . ." He looked uncertain, then added, "Maybe one or two more people in the poly group, but no, I have to earn your faith through good actions and not abandoning everyone the minute things get weird."

"Good," Nathaniel said, and smiled. "For a minute there I thought you might be reading too many enemies-to-lovers romances, because that is not how I roll."

I had a moment of wondering when Nathaniel had been reading romance novels, and he looked at me. "The foster family I was with the longest. The mom liked romance novels. It was what there was to read."

"Why didn't you stay with them?" Richard asked.

"Their own little boy got sick, really sick, and they had to concentrate on him. They were probably the nicest foster family I had while I was still in care."

Jean-Claude and I hugged him, and Richard said, "I'm sorry, I had no right to ask such a personal question."

"If I hadn't wanted to answer it, I wouldn't have."

"I'm still sorry; I'm a teacher, I should know better."

Nathaniel looked at him. "That's the first time I've ever heard you mention your profession like that."

"It was supposed to be one of the main reasons I didn't want to be outed as a werewolf, so I should mention it more if that's the truth."

Nathaniel nodded, as if that made sense to him. It didn't entirely to me, but I had learned to stop asking questions when things were working. "Showers are needed, then clothes for discussing business instead of date night," Jean-Claude said.

"I don't have anything but date clothes here," I said, and gave him a look.

"My deepest apologies, *ma petite*, but some things cannot be foreseen."

I nodded and leaned my head against his shoulder. "True, I just need out of these heels, please God."

He laughed and it was that wonderful touchable laugh he could have where it shivered down your skin as if he'd touched you with something much more solid than just his voice. Nathaniel shivered against me reacting to it, and I felt Richard's body startle as if it hadn't entirely felt good to him, but he'd felt it. I rose up to look at him and realized that he'd always felt it just like I had. He was still wearing the mask so that his face looked like a stranger's and like him, or like it was more him than it should have been behind the black leather. How hard it must have been for him to fight his attraction to Jean-Claude all these years.

"I sent for regular clothes for you," Nathaniel said.

I turned so I could offer him a kiss. "You think of everything, thank you."

He grinned and it reminded me of Jason's grin that we hadn't seen in person for so long. Again, I got a glimpse of him showering after the performance. I tried not to intrude on Jason much because the move to New York had given him a great new life with his ballerina, J.J., but tonight it was all about the wolves and I kept thinking about him, because he was my wolf. He looked up in the shower, his hair bright yellow from the water, and his blue eyes seemed bigger from the eyeliner he'd worn onstage. He stared up as if he saw me hovering above him the same way I'd have done for Jean-Claude. I don't know why the visual was always above like that, it just was. Jason said, "Anita . . ."

Nathaniel put his face next to mine, so we were both smiling down at Jason. Jason's face lit up, and we were left smiling at each other like idiots. He was one of our best friends and we both missed him fiercely.

"We're about to get in the shower here," Nathaniel said, "wish you could join us."

A look of almost real pain crossed over Jason's face, and then a stab of need so fierce went through him and into me, and through me into Nathaniel because we were too hooked up for me to protect

Nathaniel. Jason's need so was so strong it nearly doubled us over with physical need, and sorrow. How did Jason get this needy when he had J.J.? Nathaniel and I had both seen them together happy. J.J. had been one of my favorite female lovers early on, until I found some women closer to home. We still visited New York to see them, and they'd come to us, but not for a while. They were dancers in one of the best dance troupes in America and one of the best in the world, so that meant their life was dancing. They were either practicing, working out, or rehearsing for a new ballet or something more modern.

I wanted to ask what had gone wrong since we saw them last time, but Richard leaned closer to us and I realized he was sniffing the air because he'd smelled another wolf. Jason saw Richard in the mask, and he was so surprised that he broke contact. I could have forced the issue and "called" him back, but I respected his privacy. Either he didn't want to share his pain with us, or he didn't want to share it with Richard. Either way, I let it go.

"That was Jason, wasn't it?" Richard asked.

"Yes," I said. Nathaniel hugged me tight, and I knew he was wondering the same thing I was: What had happened to Jason's happily-ever-after?

29

I WAS ALL ready to pick up a phone and call Jason and just ask, but he texted both Nathaniel and me in a group chat. **Don't call. I'll call tomorrow.**

Nathaniel texted him back, **Promise.**

I texted, **Are you okay? Is there anything we can do to help?**

He texted back, **I'm okay. No, there's nothing you can do. I promise I'll call tomorrow.**

I started to text more questions, but Nathaniel touched my hand and shook his head. "Jason doesn't want to talk about it tonight."

"But . . . but he and J.J. have been so happy. What the fuck?" I said.

He laid his hand over mine on my phone. "I know, but Jason is allowed to tell us on his own schedule. Boundaries, remember."

I took a deep breath in and let it out, counting. Nathaniel had been going to therapy for years longer than I had, so he had better habits in certain areas. Boundaries were hard when you could accidentally read people's minds, emotions, and even damn near trade bodies in the middle of things. Our therapist was asking our permission to write a paper about healthy boundaries in metaphysical relationships.

"But . . ." I wanted to call him to find out what had gone wrong, to ride to the damn rescue, and that was one of the issues I was working on, because you can't save everyone, but more than that, when you rode to someone's rescue too soon and too often you stole their chance to rescue themselves, or to learn a lesson so that they wouldn't keep needing to be rescued by anyone.

"Jason is a grown-up and capable of handling his life, Anita."

I looked at Nathaniel and wanted to say something so much less adult and full of old habits. Bad ones at that. Jean-Claude joined us. "Is there anything we can do tonight to help Jason?"

I looked up at him and shook my head. I didn't bother to fill him in because if he hadn't read my mind, then he'd heard us talking.

"Then let us celebrate our own happiness tonight, *ma petite*."

"But . . ." I looked at Nathaniel and then back to Jean-Claude and then finally to Richard, who was just standing there. Anger finally flared; I guess it was actually a positive step that it took this long for me to get pissed when I was frustrated in what I wanted to do. Even as I thought, the rage boiled up like an old friend to keep me from feeling helpless about Jason's situation. I used to think therapy would fix all my flaws and issues, but that's not how it works. Therapy gives you better tools to work your issues and build yourself into a better and more complete you, but it doesn't "fix" you.

"Why are you just standing there?" I demanded of him.

"Because I'm not sure I've earned a right to be a part of the discussion yet."

"You're in or you're out, Richard, there is no in between."

"*Ma petite* . . ."

"No, let him answer." Even as I said it, I knew I was being unfair and just using Richard as a target.

"If I came in here tonight and demanded to be a full member of your poly group when I haven't earned it or talked to everyone, you'd be wicked pissed at me."

The anger was already leaking away on the ebb of Jason's sorrow. I realized I was still picking up on it. "You're right, and I'm sorry I tried to pick a fight. Jason shut off the metaphysics between us, but I'm still getting some of the emotional echo."

"Do you wish me to help you shield harder against him?" Jean-Claude asked.

I shook my head. "I can cut the noise between us; I'm just worried about him, so I forgot."

Nathaniel took my hand in his and said, "We can do something fun on our end to send back to him."

I smiled in spite of myself. "If he's not getting enough sex that seems mean, he's not much of a voyeur."

Nathaniel drew me in closer to him. "Then shield so that you're not leaking all over each other and then let's celebrate that we're happy, Anita."

I wrapped my arm around him and put my face next to his, breathed in the sweet vanilla scent of him and let go of the tightness that had started to wind me up. They were right, there was nothing I could do to help Jason tonight, and he didn't want us to interfere, so . . . "What kind of celebration did you have in mind?" I asked, but I was smiling, because I was pretty sure what his answer would be.

"We still need to shower," Nathaniel said, smiling.

30

I FINALLY GOT out of the beautiful but progressively more uncomfortable heels but was still wearing the shiny designer dress. Jean-Claude had taken off his fabulous boots, but the robe stayed on, and Richard and Nathaniel were still in their short-shorts. I had time to notice that Nathaniel was more muscular, more cut, just in fiercer shape than Richard for the first time. Richard was still taller by inches and that wasn't going to change, but the lack of access to a supernaturally rated gym meant that he'd lost some of the definition and bulk that he'd worked so hard for, at the same time that Nathaniel had increased the intensity of his workouts. We'd found workouts that helped him get cut without bulking so much that he lost the flexibility he needed to dance. It seemed wrong, like parts of them had switched places. We were ready to get in the shower, but then it got awkward. "I'm not sure all four of us will fit in one stall," Richard said.

"It will be a tight fit," Jean-Claude agreed.

"Three fits, because we've done that before," Nathaniel said.

"The three of you?" Richard made the statement a question with an uptilt in his voice.

"Yeah."

"*Oui.*"

Nathaniel slipped his arm around Jean-Claude's slender waist and laid his head on the taller man's shoulder. I realized then that while we weren't in the middle of a pissing contest, it was a who-belongs-where moment that can happen when your polyamory is as compli-cated as ours. Jean-Claude put his arm around Nathaniel, because to do anything else would have been seen as a rejection, but it upped Richard's discomfort. I reached out to him so he could at least be holding someone's hand. He took that as more invitation than I meant it to be and drew me into a one-armed hug, so we damn near mirrored the other two.

"I know it sounds weird for me to say I'm new to polyamory, because I've been on the sidelines of yours for so long, but I don't know how to navigate this without upsetting some of you, which is the last thing I want to do." He hugged me sort of nervously, and I stroked his back like you'd do to soothe someone. Touch isn't always about sex, even when you're nude and negotiating to have sex later.

"Who are you comfortable with in the shower, Richard?" Jean-Claude asked, no nickname this time, which meant he was either upset, cautious, or maybe *mon lupe* wasn't going to be his permanent nickname for the big werewolf. I'd ask Jean-Claude later in private.

"Anita and you; sorry, Nathaniel, but I'm not ready for more men."

"And I don't want to have sex with you either," Nathaniel said.

Richard startled so hard I felt it like a full-body movement. It must have showed on his face, because Nathaniel laughed, which made Richard start to get defensive and angry enough for that edge of heat to play along my skin where I touched him, his wolf waking up with his emotions. I stopped stroking his back and hugged him instead, hoping to help.

"Nathaniel, he has admitted his attraction to another man for the first time tonight, would you laugh at him for it?" Again, no nick-name, Jean-Claude was serious.

Nathaniel's face sobered. "I'm sorry, Richard, that was shitty of me, but you come in here and sweep Jean-Claude and Anita off their feet, then you reject me, and when I reject you back, you act offended like you can't believe I would turn you down. Just because I'm bisexual doesn't mean I want to sleep with everyone I meet."

Richard's anger and that hint of heat faded as he took a deep breath and let it out slowly. "I know that being bisexual doesn't mean you want to sleep with everyone, but I'm used to how women react to me, and I hadn't thought about how I'd feel if men don't react the same way."

"What way is that?" I asked, as the only woman.

He seemed embarrassed now, as if having to explain it meant something I didn't understand. "Women want to date me, or at least have sex with me. I don't think I've ever set my sights on anyone and not at least gotten a first date."

"You've been tall, dark, and handsome your whole life," I said.

He hugged me. "Yes, and I'm used to women seeing me that way. It hadn't occurred to me until Nathaniel said no that now I've got an entirely new group of people that I'll want to see me as attractive."

"But you don't want to sleep with me," Nathaniel said.

"I don't, sorry."

"That's okay, because I'm not attracted to you either."

Richard frowned. "Is it weird to say that I'm both relieved and bothered by that?"

I hugged him tighter. "It's okay to feel whatever you're feeling, Richard."

"It's not weird," Nathaniel said, "it's just how you feel. I went through something similar when Anita wouldn't sleep with me for so long. I'd never met anyone who didn't want me before and it really hurt my sense of self."

I reached my hand toward him, and he came forward to take it, his arm leaving Jean-Claude's waist. The vampire caught his hand so that they didn't stop touching, though, which made Nathaniel look back and smile at him.

"But you're together now," Richard said.

"We are. In fact, Anita being the first person who ever valued me without sex helped me see myself as a whole person. I think if we'd just fucked from the beginning I wouldn't have had all the breakthroughs that I've had."

"I valued you without sleeping with you, *mon minet*."

"But I was your mentee to be taught how to use the right fork at fancy dinners and to dance onstage at your club without cheapening the show. I never dreamed that you had any interest in me as more than that."

"You were very young when we first met and seemed even younger in so many ways. I could not have breached your trust like that even if I wished to; far too many other people had taken advantage of you, and I would not add my name to that sad list."

Nathaniel took his hand back. "You make me sound like a stray puppy."

"I do not mean to, *mon minet*. I once was also everyone's victim and thought my worth lay only in my beauty. You were like a shadow of my own past. I could not abuse you, and when we first met, you were almost incapable of saying no. When a person cannot tell you no either through your power over them or their own powerlessness, then it is rape, and that is repugnant to me."

"It took me a long time to understand how you saw our relationship. I thought you were just my boss, all business."

"I do not date my dancers; it has been a hard-and-fast rule until very recently." He said that last with a smile, holding his hand out toward Nathaniel, who came and took the offered touch.

"I had no idea that you and Nathaniel were dating," Richard said.

Nathaniel looked at Jean-Claude and I knew that he would wait for the vampire to answer the question, because it was Nathaniel who had pursued Jean-Claude, and he had said yes only recently, and now suddenly Richard was back. Someone Jean-Claude had pursued. Jean-Claude said, "Nathaniel and I are not dating, Richard; we are living together."

I felt Nathaniel let some tension go, like he'd expected Jean-Claude to dump him the moment that Richard returned. Our beautiful flower-eyed boy was secure in his beauty and sexual prowess, but not in his emotions about relationships. We all have our issues.

"Okay, I shouldn't be surprised by that but I'm not sure what it means for all of us right now," Richard said.

"What do you want it to mean, *mon lupe*?" Jean-Claude asked.

"It means I'd planned on the three of us sharing the shower, but now knowing that Jean-Claude and Anita are both living with Nathaniel I don't know what to say."

"So, if I hadn't been closer to Jean-Claude than you expected, you'd have just assumed I could be brushed aside, and you get Anita and Jean-Claude to yourself?"

"I didn't mean it like that," Richard said.

I drew away from Richard. "How did you mean it? Nathaniel is my fiancé."

Richard frowned. "You're marrying Jean-Claude, or did I miss something?"

"You missed a lot," I said.

"If it were possible to marry more than one person, there would be multiple grooms at our wedding, *mon lupe*."

Richard looked stricken. "Who else would you marry?" His emotion was so strong that I heard/saw him thinking through all the people in our lives, and he left out some important ones, ones that he knew were in our lives. We hadn't added any new people to our polycule since he vanished on us, but he had no sense of the dynamics. That was interesting and so blind that I wasn't even angry.

Jean-Claude raised Nathaniel's hand and laid a kiss on the back of it. "Nathaniel has become the heart of our home, our domestic god."

"I knew Nathaniel was Anita and Micah's like 1950s wife, but I didn't realize he'd become yours, too."

"Who do you think chose the dishes in the new kitchen at the Circus of the Damned, or helped design it in the first place?" Jean-

Claude asked. Nathaniel wasn't as close emotionally to Jean-Claude as he was to Micah and me, but in that moment Jean-Claude acknowledged the truth that Nathaniel made it all work. He planned the menus, did most of the grocery shopping, had been the go-to for the remodel of the kitchen and the extra guest rooms. Nathaniel had chosen all the new colors and pieces at the Jefferson County home and not only had Micah and I both liked what he chose, but it had been a wonderful mix of all three of us. Jean-Claude's tastes ruled at the Circus of the Damned, except for people's private rooms, which they were allowed to decorate themselves, but everything else was him except for the kitchen and the guest rooms, which were Nathaniel's—well, and the exercise areas. The last had been part mine, part Nicky, Claudia, and Fredo, because the last two oversaw our private security, including their training, but then any important guests who saw the gym area were there to work out, not to admire the decor.

"I'm sorry," Richard said, "I didn't mean to offend anyone."

"Apology accepted, *mon lupe*."

"Accepted if it doesn't keep happening," Nathaniel said.

"That's fair, thank you."

"You're welcome," Nathaniel said.

I stood there and let the men work it out. Poly had taught me patience; therapy had taught me to shut up and let other people talk and work their shit and only interject if I really had something to add. They stopped talking and we all looked at each other. I was debating on how to move the conversation forward and actually get a chance to clean up in the showers. Not for sexy reasons, but just to wash all the makeup off and get out without a fight breaking out. We were almost at a record with the four of us being together without arguing.

There was a sound in the hallway, which made us look that way. Wicked was in the doorway. Tall, broad-shouldered, with blond hair falling straight and thick to his shoulders. He was movie-star handsome with pale blue eyes, high cheekbones, a square manly jaw, and a deep dimple in his chin. He'd put his tailored suit jacket over the Guilty Pleasures staff T-shirt. He looked underdressed without his normal dress shirt.

"Is there something you needed, Wicked?" Jean-Claude asked.

"We were told to help you stay on target for tonight."

"We are fine," Jean-Claude said, and the tone alone was enough to make most people back off, but Wicked wasn't most people.

"Of course you are all fine, but either shower here, so we can move you all to a more secure location as soon as possible, or let us move you now and shower at the Circus."

"They're right," I said, "this was a serious attack tonight, Jean-Claude."

"We were victorious, *ma petite*."

"Whatever attacked us tonight, I've never felt a vampire like it, and it left its power in the audience. I didn't even know that mass hypnosis was possible without the vampire being bodily in the building."

"It was more curse than vampiric powers," Jean-Claude said.

I looked at him. "Curses don't work like that; at best you can influence one person at a time."

"You speak of modern magic, *ma petite*, but what I felt tonight was old magic."

"Older than you know," Jake said from the hallway. Wicked stepped into the room to clear the way for Jake to move into the doorway. Jake looked short compared to him, but in the exercise clothes he'd had to come to the club wearing, the muscles that he usually hid under layers were on full display. Wicked and his brother Truth, like Richard, always looked muscled in any clothes, but Jake didn't. His physicality, like everything else about him, wasn't noticeable unless he wanted it to be or didn't care if it was. Jake more than any of the other Harlequin made me remember they'd been spies as well as assassins.

"What do you mean, older than we know?" I asked.

"Not you, Anita, older than Jean-Claude would know."

Jean-Claude went very still beside us. It wasn't human stillness or even the way snakes can freeze in place, but like I was suddenly holding the hand of a marble statue, pale and perfect, but not alive. I fought the urge to shake him to make him blink, anything for him to not be standing there like he would never move again or need to breathe. The old vampires could just cease, like if I let go of his hand and blinked he'd just vanish.

His voice came distant and careful as if he was trying to move as little as possible when he spoke. "That would be very old indeed."

"You are not yet seven hundred years old, Jean-Claude, that is not so very old."

I looked at Jake's ageless face. If you'd asked me how old he was I would have said he hadn't seen fifty yet, and barely forty, but I knew he was one of the oldest of the Harlequin. I knew for certain that some of them were thousands of years old, which meant . . . "How old, Jake?" I asked.

"Millions," he said.

"You aren't that old," I said.

"I am not, but the power that I felt tonight is," he said.

"What are you hinting at?" Richard asked.

Jake's eyes flicked to him, then back to Jean-Claude and me. "How much do you want me to say in front of others, Jean-Claude?"

"I asked you to stop hinting and tell us what you know," Richard said. ·

"Technically you asked what I was hinting at," Jake said.

Richard's skin ran warm with anger. It was like my hand had just been plunged into warm, nearly hot water. "I am your Ulfric; if I tell you to do something, I expect you to do it."

"You are indeed my Ulfric; what would you have of me?" The tone was neutral, but somehow it translated to *Go fuck yourself.* I'd been accused of having my neutral tone imply the same sentiment, so I really couldn't throw stones. The thing is, I did it by accident; Jake didn't do anything by accident.

Richard's skin ran hot and trailed power up my arm in a skin-tingling rush that made the wolf inside me materialize behind my eyes. She opened golden wolf eyes surrounded by white fur and shook herself like a dog getting up from a long nap.

I pulled free of Richard, and the wolf sat down as if she were looking at us both, waiting for us to figure out what we were doing. Weren't we all? Nathaniel drew me in closer to him so that I could bury my face against the bare skin of his shoulder. Usually that was enough to make the wolf fade, but not tonight. Watching Richard glare at Jake, who looked calm and unruffled, I realized that things might have been happening among the werewolves that I didn't know, because leaving Richard alone had meant leaving the pack alone, too.

Jean-Claude remained cold and still in my other hand. What the fuck was going on? I drew my hand out of his, which made him blink and turn toward me and like magic he was "alive" again. "*Ma petite*, do not pull away, *s'il te plaît*." I knew that last part meant "please."

Nathaniel drew me closer to Jean-Claude, whom he was still touching. Richard was back for one night and I'd pulled away from Jean-Claude and him. Only Nathaniel was still holding on to us—well, two of us. He and Richard didn't hold hands.

I reached out to Jean-Claude, and he took my hand in his with a squeeze and a smile. I felt his relief that I closed the distance and didn't force him to stand there alone in the face of Richard's return. I squeezed his hand back and promised myself I wouldn't let whatever shit Richard brought with him tonight distract me from the happiness that we'd all built together without the Ulfric.

"Tell us whatever you know about the power that attacked us tonight," Richard said.

"You are here tonight, Ulfric, but unless you will be here to see this tale to its completion, I do not wish to speak in front of you."

"How dare you defy me."

"Has he defied you before?" Wicked asked.

That made Richard stop and think, and then he shook his head, saying, "No, he's stayed as neutral as pack politics allow."

"Then it must be something important for him to do so now."

Richard took a deep breath, let it out, and I felt the heat of his power begin to flow away. "Thank you for helping me think instead of just react."

"I am happy to do anything that will speed us to a safer location tonight," Wicked said.

Richard looked at Jake. "Can you tell us in the car as we drive for the Circus?"

"I will share what I know when you are all more secure," Jake said.

"Then let's go," Richard said, and just like that there wasn't going to be a fight, at least not yet.

"Showers . . ." I started to say.

"Shower at the Circus," Wicked said.

"Where's Truth?" I asked, because they were always together.

"He's outside making sure the way is clear to move you to safety."

"I only sensed one vampire during the attack," I said.

"A vampire this powerful does not travel alone, *ma petite*."

I nodded. "You're right. He'll have Renfields, and human servants, or animals to call with him. Let me get back into the sexy torture devices known as shoes and let's get out of here."

"Your clothes got dropped off," Nathaniel said smiling.

"Change clothes in the car on the drive," Wicked said.

I looked at him, and that was enough. "Okay, I'll change in the car."

"You're not going to argue with them?" Richard asked.

I shook my head. "If Wicked and Jake are both saying we gotta go, then we go."

"Put on your comfy boots to walk to the car," Nathaniel said.

"We don't have time . . ." Wicked started to say.

"She can run and walk and fight better in the boots," Nathaniel said.

Wicked and Jake said, "Change," at the same time.

I gave Nathaniel a kiss and went to find my boots.

31

THE BOOTS LOOKED terrible with the sexy designer dress, but I was so happy to be out of the high heels and back into comfortable shoes I didn't care. The fashion police could arrest me later. I was still having to carry the little purse with its thin strap because it had my gun in it, and now that I wasn't going to be onstage and the boots had ruined the outfit anyway, I could carry it cross-body without anyone bitching I was ruining the line of the dress. I realized I was relieved to not have to worry about looking perfect any more tonight.

Jean-Claude was still wearing his robe over the boots and thong. I knew he had clothes to change into, but the bodyguards we most trusted were on high alert wanting to move us, so we could all change later. Nathaniel had put all our clothes in a wheeled suitcase, like a big carry-on size. It had probably originally held just Jean-Claude's clothes; now it held his, mine, and Richard's. He was still in the booty shorts and shiny patent leather stage boots just like Nathaniel. He'd even kept the mask on in case someone got a picture of us as we left so he wouldn't be outed as "Superman" as we got in the tinted vehicles. He had thrown his dress shirt over his upper body like a jacket. It should have ruined his outfit like the boots ruined mine, but it didn't. The shirt over it looked . . . cute, or endearing, or maybe even sexy. I was so used to thinking of him as our ex that thinking of him as sexy felt bad, like a habit I'd worked hard to break.

We were waiting for Truth to knock on the outer door to the alley entrance to let us know that Ethan had the SUV in place for us to hustle from inside the club to the cars. If our enemies hadn't been able to use mystical powers it would have been super safe; as it was I just wanted to go home, and that meant the underground of the Circus of the Damned tonight.

"Why is it taking so long?" I asked.

"The traffic is heavy on the weekends, and we need to bring up at least two of the SUVs at the alley entrance," Wicked said.

Jean-Claude offered me his hand and I took it gratefully; touching him was like being able to take a deeper breath. It made me wrap my arms around his waist, luxuriating in the silkiness of the robe though I knew it wasn't real silk. Real silk is awesome, but a stain is usually forever. We'd ruined more silk sheets than I cared to think about; admittedly we'd had help doing it, but still custom-made silk sheets weren't cheap. In the flat boots I was tucked very securely under his arm because his boots made him over six feet tonight. I wondered if his feet hurt from dancing in heels? I'd ask at home when we were alone with our polycule; right now I just enjoyed the firm smoothness of his body underneath the robe.

"Why am I so tired?" I whispered it.

"Because all the energy we raised tonight had to go to defeating our enemy, not feeding us," Jean-Claude said as he hugged me and kissed the top of my head ever so gently.

"No one's fed on me tonight," Nathaniel said, wrapping his arms around both of us as he leaned in and kissed my cheek. He had let go of the suitcase handle so he could use both arms to hold us; I approved of this use of resources.

"I would urge you to feed on those not connected to you metaphysically tonight," Jake said.

We looked at him. I asked what we were all wanting to know: "Why not?"

"Because the vampire you faced tonight will try again, and you may need all your magical strength intact," Jake said.

"How do you know he didn't just give up?" I asked.

"You've faced ancient vampires before, Anita; did any of them ever give up the attack?"

Suddenly even Jean-Claude and Nathaniel holding me wasn't as comforting. "No, they attack until you destroy them, because they're too arrogant to believe they can lose."

"This one will be no different, trust me," Jake said.

"You know Deimos, don't you?"

"Not by that name, but yes, I fear so."

There was a loud knock on the outer door that led down the hallway to the alley. Wicked went forward and made sure who it was, listening through the door. "Truth says that Ethan has the SUVs at the mouth of the alley. It is time to go."

"Give us the real name of who attacked us tonight, Jake," I said.

"I will answer your questions on the ride to the Circus."

Jean-Claude started forward and since he was still holding me I had to go with him. Nathaniel came behind us with the suitcase, and Richard behind him. The rest of the bodyguards, mostly werewolves for a change, brought up the rear. Graham was with them. He'd found a fresh T-shirt to replace the one lost to the crowd. I caught a glimpse of his face and felt like I owed him an apology or a thank-you for being such a good sport about everything tonight, but there was no time. Wicked opened the door and Truth was there like a brown-haired version of his brother. The uncertain light in the alley made his eyes look gray, but I knew they were only a little less blue than his brother's. They both had blue-gray eyes that could change color depending on the color of their shirt or their moods.

He herded Jean-Claude and me out, using his body as a potential shield around us as Wicked did the same for Nathaniel behind us. Jake came with us, and the other wolves closed around Richard.

I realized as we got closer that Ethan wasn't driving my SUV but one of the larger ones that were part of the security fleet. "Please tell me my car with all my gear in it didn't drive home with Rodina and Ru."

Wicked answered, "Your car is just behind with all your U.S. Marshal and vampire-hunting gear in it."

"Okay, sorry, and I'm not on an active warrant so I don't have all the weapons I normally do, but I still need to know where my stuff is."

"You roll like SWAT, always ready." It was Graham from behind us.

I might have made a smart-ass remark, but one of the new were-wolf ex-military guys said, "What the hell do you know about SWAT, Graham?" It was Demo, short for Demolition Man because supposedly if you fought him he'd demolish you, or something like that. He was the tallest person in our group tonight, which made him six foot five at least, and the rest of him matched, but he was never a regular on my guard detail because of remarks like that. Most of the former military had made as smooth a transition as they could after surviving an attack and losing their careers. Demo was one of the exceptions. I was actually surprised he hadn't been more of a problem for Richard and the pack, but no one had come to us complaining about it.

"Graham has been doing his homework for the new werewolf training program," Jake said.

"You have former military guys now, hell you have TEAMs guys in your pack now, you don't need to train up your civilians," Demo said.

Richard said, "Leave it, Demo."

"Make me."

"You're still in your probationary period with my pack, Demo. If I say the word, you're out."

"And while I'm on probation I can't challenge anyone. Not your Freki, or Geri, or any-damn-body."

"Those are the rules for all packs in the United States and most in the rest of the world," Richard said, voice calm and a little tired as if he'd had to explain this to Demo before.

"I already know you're kicking me out once the probation is over."

I fought to keep my body and heartbeat slow and even, because I knew werewolf law, too. If someone was too dangerous to be accepted into your pack, you could send them on to another pack, but you had to warn that pack about the issues. If you couldn't find another pack to take them, then they were executed. I wonder if Demo knew that little codicil to the werewolf laws? I doubted it; even among the wolves themselves it wasn't something you talked about much. Most people would eventually find a pack structure that worked for them. The Demolition Man was going to get himself killed if someone didn't explain the facts of life and death among the werewolves to him soon.

"What is the delay?" Jean-Claude asked. The fact that he realized Wicked and Truth had stopped in front of the SUV but not opened a door for us when I hadn't noticed said I was way too distracted.

"There was a fender bender," Truth said.

"It's cleared now," Wicked said.

They usually only finished each other's sentences when they were stressed, which let me know that the fight with the crowd or some part of tonight's emergency had hit them harder than normal. The Wicked Truth didn't shake easily, but I didn't point out that I knew their tell. Until we got into the underground below the Circus we were not secure. I wasn't going to distract them until they shut the door of our bedroom tonight. Okay, maybe just the big dungeonlike door at the bottom of the mile of stairs leading down into the underground, but until that moment they were working, and I wasn't going to start psychoanalyzing them now.

They tried to herd us into the car, but there weren't enough seats for all of us protectees and our protectors. If Richard hadn't been there or had been willing to get into the second car it would have been quick, but in all the debating he touched my bare arm, and it was like a power boost, because I was still in Jean-Claude's arms. Like it, or hate it, the three of us were a triumvirate of power. Damn it.

32

ETHAN WAS DRIVING so he didn't get to play the game of musical chairs, but the rest of us did. If the bodyguards hadn't insisted on one of them sitting on each row of seats we could have shoved Jean-Claude, Richard, and me into the center seats, or even the back row. Nathaniel would have been willing, but Jake and the Wicked Truth were adamant that we needed a guard per row.

Jake leaned in to me and said, "This is an excellent spot for an ambush, please just get in the back seat with the Ulfric."

That was enough to get me in the back seat of the SUV between Wicked and Richard. Their shoulders were so wide that they had to put their arms across the back of the seats so they didn't squish me, and that was when an unexpected argument broke out.

"Can you please move your arm," Richard said.

"My arm is fine where it is," Wicked said.

"You're Anita's bodyguard, not her boyfriend."

"You're not her boyfriend either." If you didn't know Wicked, you might think he was jealous of me with other people, but I knew that wasn't it, because that wasn't our relationship, so what was going on?

"But I am her lover," Richard said.

"So am I."

"Wicked," I said, and I sounded a little surprised, because I had fed the *ardeur* on him before, so technically he was my lover, but . . .

"Is he your lover?" Richard asked.

I looked from Richard to Wicked, who looked down at me with such arrogance. He was gorgeous, but he wasn't vain like this, the arrogance was protective. In a way that I didn't understand, Wicked's ego was on the line here, or something else was.

"Yes, he is," I said, looking at Wicked as I gave the answer. He smiled, and I was glad he was happy with me, but when I turned to Richard he was scowling. I did not need this tonight.

"Is he part of your poly group now?" Richard asked.

"Not exactly."

"What does that mean?"

"It means you have not been her boyfriend in all the years I've worked for her, has that changed?"

I opened my mouth to answer, but Richard said, "You're right, I haven't been around much, and when I was around I behaved badly most of the time. I'm hoping to do better from this point on."

"Hope is cheap, Ulfric, just do better."

Anger flared through Richard like heat against my skin where we were forced to touch. "Stop it, both of you. This space is too small and you're both too powerful metaphysically to start a pissing contest with me squished between you."

Richard had to do some deep breathing to quiet his anger and his beast. While he did that, Wicked said, "I'm sorry, but as your bodyguard I've watched him hurt you and Jean-Claude over and over. I want him to know that Truth and I will do our best to protect you physically and emotionally from him."

"Wow, I mean, thanks, but this is going to be awkward enough without . . ."

"No, Anita, that's fair," Nathaniel said.

I looked up at him where he was turned around in the seat to look back at me. Jean-Claude sat beside him with Jake against the door mirroring Wicked's position on our seat. Jean-Claude wasn't turning around to join in the conversation yet.

"I thought we were getting along," Richard said.

"We are," Nathaniel said, "but it's not just me that you need to make amends to."

"I don't owe Wicked an apology."

"No, you don't," Wicked said, "but we need to get the ground rules set from the beginning so there are no misunderstandings between us."

"He is Ulfric," Jake said.

"I am not a werewolf, the only king I have is Jean-Claude."

"I didn't play the king-of-wolves card on you, that was Jake. I would never demand loyalty from any vampire based on me being Ulfric, or any other supernatural that wasn't a werewolf."

"Thank you for that," Wicked said.

"Please move your arm so that I can be the one touching Anita?"

"You are not my king, or her boyfriend, why should I move my arm out of your way?"

"Wicked," Jean-Claude said.

"Jean-Claude," Truth said from the front seat, "this isn't just Wicked and me. All the security discussed what we would do if we felt that your emotional attachments were putting you at risk."

"Richard helped me save us all tonight, he did no harm," Jean-Claude said.

"He, Asher, and Kane are the most unstable of all the people who are alone with you when you kick the security out of the room, and they've all hurt you physically and emotionally," Truth said.

"We are never alone with Kane," I said, "he's bug nuts."

"Jean-Claude will still be alone with Kane and Asher when you're traveling on business," Wicked said.

I stared at my soonish-to-be husband. "Jesus, Jean-Claude, are they . . . seriously, recently?"

He looked down, blinking those thick black lashes coyly, which meant *Yes, and recently.* "Kane is dangerous, Jean-Claude; you cannot be alone with him."

"I have no interest in being alone with Kane; Asher is always there."

"You know that Asher can't control him."

"Do you think I could not protect myself from Kane?"

"You could, but you're terrified of accidentally killing Asher by hurting Kane, just like I am."

Nathaniel gripped his shoulder. "Please, promise us that you won't be alone with just the two of them again."

Jean-Claude wouldn't look at either of us.

"Damn it, Jean-Claude," I said.

"And that is why we had a meeting about such things," Wicked said.

"That was about Kane and Asher; I did not agree with such treatment for the Ulfric," Jake said.

"You were outvoted," Wicked said.

"Putting me on the list with Asher for emotional damage is absolutely fair, but not Kane. He is unstable and dangerous."

"You have your moments, Ulfric," Wicked said.

"I don't think I deserve to be put in the same category as Kane, but I guess I have to prove that to everyone."

"We need to be able to trust you, Ulfric," Truth said.

"But until we can, all of the security will intrude more," Wicked finished.

"Fine, but what does that have to do with you refusing to move your arm so that I can put my arm around Anita's shoulders?"

"It means you have to prove yourself to get access to her."

"You didn't stop him from having sex with us tonight," I said.

"There were no other options, now there are," Wicked said.

"Are you volunteering?" Richard asked, and there was a tone in his voice that was almost threatening. He'd never seen Wicked practice with the other guards; I had. I did not want our recently re-turned Ulfric to get his ass kicked this soon.

"Stop it, both of you. I get to say who I sleep with, or feed on, and arguing about it like I'm a prize that goes to the victor is not winning points with me."

"That's not how I meant it," Richard said.

"It is not me winning you, Anita, it is making it clear that the Ulfric does not have a clear path to you or Jean-Claude without a trusted bodyguard in the room, until he proves he is trustworthy."

"I did not agree to this," Jean-Claude said.

"It is my duty to protect you, my king."

"Our duty," Truth said from the front.

"Yes, our duty," Wicked added, "and if that means protecting you from yourself then so be it."

The tiredness washed over me so that all I wanted to do was sleep. I was usually pretty good at going without rest, so it had to be the amount of energy I'd fed Jean-Claude tonight.

"Enough. I need food. Like just regular food until I can feed the *ardeur* again."

"Did you guys put the snacks into all the security vehicles like I suggested?" Nathaniel asked.

Truth just handed something back to Jake, who handed it to me. It was a protein bar. "There's a cooler in the back, Richard should be able to reach it."

He could and did, getting a Powerade for both of us, then asking if anyone else wanted one. Nathaniel took one. Richard also took a protein bar. "I'm not as drained as you are, but I still should probably shift to wolf tonight and eat more protein than just the bar."

I fought to keep my face and body neutral, because the last time I'd been around Richard he had hated changing into his wolf. I'd seen him refuse to shift when he was so injured that it was life threat-ening. To mention it so casually was shocking, a huge step forward, but still such a big change . . . I wasn't sure how to react, so I stared at the seat back in front of me and concentrated on the protein bar.

"I'm sorry that just me talking about changing form to help regain energy is such a shock to you."

"I didn't say a word."

"Your pulse rate did."

"I'm glad you're making peace with your wolf, Richard, truly, but let's hear what Jake has to say about the vampire that attacked us tonight."

"If he had not chosen to name himself after one of the followers of Ares I might not have guessed, but his arrogance in his heritage made him choose something familiar," Jake said.

"Deimos, the dread before battle, was a clue?" I asked.

"Yes, for he was the son of Ares, not merely part of his followers."

"Ares, as in the Greek god of war?" I asked.

"The very same," Jake said.

"The Greek gods are just myths, they aren't real," Richard said.

"They were very real once, Ulfric."

"Why once?" I asked.

"Why did the Christian God stop making bushes burn and sending angels down in all their terror to destroy entire cities?"

"That was Old Testament," Richard said.

"Then think something like that for the Greek and Roman gods," Jake said.

"Are you saying you met Ares?" Nathaniel asked.

"No, but I met his son, Drakon, twin of the Ismenian dragon slain by Cadmus."

"Dragons can't be the twin of a human child, I don't care how many ancient gods are involved," I said.

"Humans and dragons are totally different species," Richard said.

"The things that you call dragons now are animals, and could not produce offspring with humans, but once dragons were not just preternatural species to be studied, or cryptids to be found."

".What were they, then?" Richard asked.

"They were a different race of beings just like the djinn, or the fairy folk, or so many people who have been lost over the eons, leaving not even their myths or folklore behind."

"The fey are just another type of hominid, *Homo arcanus* to *Homo sapiens.*"

"We met them in Ireland," Nathaniel said. "Most of them looked like us, but their energy was . . . different." His face lit up with remembering, like it was a good memory. I could never smile like that about Ireland, because of what happened at the end with Domino and Ru and Rodina's brother Rodrigo. Meeting the fairy folk, real live full-blooded fairies, had been just part of searching for clues to stop a gang of rogue vampires. They'd kidnapped us, chained us up, and cut Nathaniel's nearly ankle-length hair, promising to come back and cut off things that wouldn't grow back. When I thought of Ireland what I remembered first was death, and the terror of what had almost happened.

The conversation had been going on without me: Richard thinking that meeting real, old-world fey was fascinating, Nathaniel full of the delight of it, while I was stuck in the loop of Domino's death, and then almost losing Nathaniel. Rodrigo had taken a shotgun blast to the chest to save him, to save Nathaniel and Damian, and me. Rodrigo had killed Domino in front of me, and then he'd been the one to make the big sacrifice to save us later. I'd magically rolled him, so he had to be on our side, but he'd done both— killed one lover, and then saved two more, one of them being Nathaniel.

"Anita," Nathaniel said.

I blinked and looked at him. "Sorry, I was thinking too hard."

He gave me that sad smile that he did a lot about Ireland. "I know what you were thinking, and I wish you could remember more of the happy parts of Ireland instead of just the terrible ones."

I wanted to touch his face but couldn't really reach with the seat belt on, and since I wouldn't take it off in a moving car, I settled for his hand where he offered it.

"I feel like I'm missing something here," Richard said.

"The trip to Ireland did not go as planned," Jake said.

I looked at him. His face was sorrowful and compassionate. I had to look away from it to say, "That's one way of putting it."

Richard touched my hand, meaning to comfort me, but I jerked away from him. "You weren't there. I'm sorry, you've been therapy-great tonight, but you weren't in Ireland with us when it went to hell. Domino died; Nathaniel almost died."

"They cut my hair, Anita, that's it. They didn't hurt me."

I stared at him, squeezing his hand in mine. "If my metaphysical Hail Mary hadn't worked, they would have cut you to pieces in front of me."

"But it did work, we got away. We lived, they died. We won, Anita, why can't you take the win?"

"And I want to know how you can feel like it was a win? Domino died in front of me. Rodrigo killed him in front of me, and Rodrigo's master would have done the same to you while they forced me to watch."

He shook my hand, staring into my eyes like he was trying to will me to see things differently. "Losing Domino, especially the way we did, is awful. I know what it's like to watch someone you love die in front of you. I felt guilty for years about my brother's death, but I was a little boy. There was nothing I could do to save him, and there was nothing you could do to save Domino."

"But you were a little boy and I'm a U.S. Marshal. It's my job to save people."

"Domino was there as your bodyguard. It was his job to save you."

"I put him in harm's way. I took him to Ireland, and he died there protecting me, because I couldn't protect him or myself."

"Helplessness in the face of tragedy is hard for people like us," Jake said.

I looked at him. "People like us?"

"People of action, warriors. Our weapons protect us and those we care for; when our skills fail us and we lose lives, it is hard. It erodes some of our sense of self."

I looked into his world-weary brown eyes. He'd never age like normal thanks to his own ties to his vampire master, but suddenly I could glimpse the centuries of loss in his face, especially the eyes. He let me see what the nearly immortal usually managed to hide, that even if the body endures, the spirit takes its damage.

"Yes," I said at last, "that's it, it erodes your sense of self, all the losses over the years."

"We must do our best to make sure there are no more losses," he said.

"We must," Jean-Claude said.

It made me look at him and realize that he'd slipped away again into that profound silence that the old vamps had. His face was empty, showing nothing. Like a beautiful statue, too perfect to be real. He was shielding so tight from me that I had no idea what he was thinking or feeling.

"You're shielding so tight it's like you're almost not there. What am I missing that's got you this spooked? I mean, I'm having my own PTSD mind-fuck, but that doesn't mean I'm not interested in yours."

That earned me a small smile. "I was not in Ireland either and there is guilt to that since it is such a wound to you, *ma petite*, but there is a vampiric dragon in my territory that wants to take all that I have built for his own. That would be a loss that you cannot imagine, not just of power but of lives. I have seen what the Dragon of the old vampire council could do in battle. I thought she was the last of her kind, so I did not prepare to fight a dragon to maintain my kingdom."

"Wait, the Dragon is a real dragon? I thought it was just a fearsome name to scare would-be challengers?"

"All the names of the council members are descriptive of their powers, *ma petite*, and none of the names are subtle. The Master of Beasts was the first vampire to have more than one animal to call. Amoureux de la Mort was the creator of all rotting vampires in the world. Belle Morte is beautiful death, a bloodline of seduction and lust. The Earthmover could cause literal earthquakes."

"The Mother of All Darkness was supposed to be the first vampire, and she was a scary motherfucker like the name implies," I said.

"*Oui, ma petite*," he said, smiling, "your descriptive use of language is, as always, music to my ears."

I smiled back, because I knew he meant it; he'd confessed to me years back that he fell in love with me not on sight, but the first time he heard me talking tough and realized I was armed and dangerous. When he realized the petite woman in front of him was the same person the other vampires nicknamed the Executioner. The last woman who had been the love of his life had died with his name on her lips asking him to save her. He knew I'd save myself and that meant more to him than any poetry I could have uttered.

"I love you, too," I said.

He smiled wider. "The Dragon is literally that in the shape of a woman. She led us all to believe she was the last of her kind."

"She is the last of the great dragons from ancient China," Jake said, "and they are their own people. To say 'dragon' is like saying 'human being,' they are not all the same."

"How did a dragon become a vampire in the first place?" Richard asked.

"The original strain of vampirism is contagious to everyone and everything as far as I can tell, though I guess Jake can answer the question for sure," I said.

"The Mother of All Darkness and the Father of the Day, as well as the Earthmover, could bring shapeshifters over as vampires, and any other humanoid. Modern vampirism needs three bites over a space of time and to drain the most blood on the last bite, but in the olden days one bite was enough either to contaminate you so that when you finally died you would rise as a vampire, or if enough blood was lost the first feeding for them to die, they would rise immediately."

"That's why the oldest stories have people so evil the grave couldn't hold them, and werewolves being accused of being vampires," I said.

"The dragon tonight looked like a giant serpent," Richard said.

"He had a more human form. He is called a dragon, and his name is Drakon, but he is not a true dragon like the council member. He is a dragon because that was the word the Greek and Romans used for anything snake- or lizardlike that was of unusually large size or had killed enough people. They would call your modern snakes a dragon if they were large enough."

"So, he is not a dragon, as the Dragon?" Jean-Claude said.

"No, nor is he like the old dragons of the Norse, or the more fantastic tales from other parts of what is now Europe. In serpent form he is venomous, and there will be no modern medicine that can counteract it."

"There can't be any antivenom to a venom that medicine doesn't know exists," I said.

"Precisely," Jake said.

"In human form is he just a vampire, or does he have other powers?" I asked.

"You saw some of his other powers tonight."

"When the Dragon went to battle she could cause rage in her warriors and make them stronger, faster, impervious to pain. A wise man from her old country said she was a fallen dragon because she turned her gifts to destruction. He spoke about it as if in ancient China dragons could fall like angels in Christian theology," Jean-Claude said.

"It wasn't as simple as good and evil, but the analogy is close enough," Jake said.

"So, if he can look human could he have been there tonight in the crowd?" I asked.

"No, I would have smelled him. He can look human, but he never smells human."

"The shadow serpent tonight didn't smell real," Richard said.

"It was a sending, a form of attack, but his physical form was never at risk."

"I've chased power back to its source before and been able to do harm to it," I said.

"Was he real enough to chase back to his body tonight?"

I thought about it. "I don't know, but I think it was all smoke and mirrors. That's what I thought at one point, that he was a trick, or like Richard said, he wasn't real. You mentioned djinn along with the fey earlier. The fey are real like us, solid, but the djinn are not. They're made of wind and magic, there's no way to physically hurt them."

"When did you see djinn?" Richard asked.

"Las Vegas," Wicked and Truth said together.

"I'd love to hear about it," Richard said.

I fought not to frown at him, because people had died because they couldn't physically hurt the djinn, and like Ireland I couldn't remember Vegas without starting with the losses. I could never seem to take the win. I took a deep breath and let it out slow. "They were just whirlwinds, or like heat waves in the summer, but they could wield blades and you couldn't touch them except with one spell that could disperse them. It was kind of awful."

"Awful in every way?"

"I was chasing down a serial killer that mailed me another policeman's head in a box; the killer used the djinn to decapitate him, so yeah."

"I'm sorry, Anita."

I took another deep breath, counting as I breathed out. I didn't want to be pressed against him in the seat. Richard had never understood my work, or what it cost me. He'd always been trying to force me to give up having a badge. It was hard to make the transition to this new, less cranky Richard. It was like I wasn't ready to give up being cranky at the person he'd been for so long. It made me move the minute inch I could toward Wicked, who took that as his cue to curve his hand around my shoulders.

Richard's skin ran with heat again, his anger and his beast starting to rise. I did not need his wolf to call to mine, so I said, "Wicked and Truth were in Vegas with me on that trip."

"Thank you for keeping her safe," Richard said.

And that was it. "They didn't keep me safe; I mean they did, but . . . Richard, I was there as a U.S. Marshal with an active warrant to hunt down the vampire that was behind the murders. He could control the djinn as his animal to call. Yes, Wicked and Truth were there, and they helped me, but they didn't keep me safe. I wasn't in Vegas to stay safe, or to play the victim. I was there to hunt down an ancient vampire before he killed again."

"I don't know what I said wrong, but I'm sorry it was wrong," Richard said.

Wicked said, "May I try to translate?"

"If you can, be my guest."

"You thanked us for keeping Anita safe, as if she were the maiden in distress. She is never that. Even if she gets hurt, or kidnapped as she did in Ireland, she is still never the victim to be rescued. We may someday rescue her but she will still never be the maiden in distress."

Richard looked from him to me, then to Jean-Claude. "I don't understand, aren't we all saying the same thing?"

"*Non, mon lupe,* you thanked the Wicked Truth for taking care of Anita, and that is not how it works."

"Then explain it to me."

Truth said from the front, "Anita is a fellow warrior, always."

"I know Anita can take care of herself," he said.

"Would you say it that way if she were a man?" Nathaniel asked.

"What do you mean?"

"If Anita were a male cop, a male U.S. Marshal, would you say he could take care of himself?"

Richard thought about it before answering. "Yes, I don't know, I think so."

"Anita doesn't just take care of herself, Richard, she takes care of me, of us," Nathaniel said.

"I know that."

"Then don't thank a man for taking care of me like I'm some helpless damsel in distress."

"I wasn't in Vegas, or Ireland, and you seem angry at me for not being there and helping you through it all. Wicked was there in Vegas and helped you when I couldn't; why is it wrong to thank him?"

"We weren't there to help her," Wicked said, "we were there to be her backup."

"Isn't being backup helping?"

"Yes, but not the way you made it sound."

"I don't know what I did wrong," Richard said.

"When you talk to the bodyguards or any of us about Anita, you need to remember that she is never the princess in the story waiting to be rescued."

"She's a self-rescuing princess, I know that."

Nathaniel shook his head. "No, Richard, that's not it. Anita is never the princess at all, she's the prince in shining armor who rides in with sword and shield and saves the day and the princess."

Richard frowned, trying to wrap his head around the difference. It helped me not be angry with him, because he was trying. "I know that you're comfortable being the princess to her prince." He looked at Jean-Claude. "Is that how you see yourself, too, as her princess to save?"

"*Non, mon lupe,* she is queen to my king, we are equals and take turns saving each other."

Richard nodded. "Okay, how about you, Wicked? Are you Anita's princess?"

"I see her as queen when I am her bodyguard, but in a fight she is a fellow knight who will fight beside us."

Truth added from the front, "She is our general who leads from the front lines of the battle."

"And you, Jake?" Richard asked.

"She is my queen as Jean-Claude is my king; through their power and leadership they have made a kingdom that I thought was secure."

"I get that," he said, "but I look at you, Anita, and I see . . ."

"Just say it, I promise not to get pissed."

"I see the princess that I want to hold and love and keep safe. I know you can take care of yourself, but . . ."

"*Mon lupe,* how do you see me?"

"Well, not as the princess, but a fellow prince to stand beside and fight and build a kingdom with, to keep with the metaphor."

"That is how you need to see *ma petite,* as a fellow prince to fight side by side with and save the kingdom."

"How can you say that when even your nickname for her means 'my little one'?"

"Physically, she is petite, but I do not see her as small. She is and always has been larger than life to me."

Richard frowned so hard it looked painful. "She's accomplished great things, amazing things, she's incredible at everything she does."

"But you still see me as the pretty, pretty princess to be protected and taken care of?"

"I was raised to protect the woman I loved."

"I've met your mother, she's got a temper almost as hot as mine, and she takes no prisoners when she's defending her family. Your dad, on the other hand, is this laid-back, easygoing guy."

"They balance each other," he said.

"With a mother like that, how can you still want to put me in the princess box?"

"What's wrong with the princess box?"

"You climb into it for a while and see how it feels, then get back to me."

He got that guy look, that I'm-the-big-strong-man-and-you're-being-silly look. The fact that Richard had that look in him anywhere was an issue for me, but that he directed it at me ever was the real problem.

"I don't fit into the princess box," he said, all smug at being over six feet tall and big and athletic and male.

"Neither do I," I said, "and never aim that look at me again."

"What look?"

"The guy look, the smug, big, dominant, athletic, guy look, that says with a glance that I'm just a little girl and I don't know what I'm talking about."

"I never think that about you, Anita, ever. I may not get the dynamics the way I need to between us, but I never treat you as less just because you're a woman. My mother and sister would both kick my ass if they caught me doing that."

"Shit, maybe I'm projecting, I don't know anymore."

"You're not projecting," Nathaniel said.

"But Richard is correct as well," Jean-Claude said. "He did not think as badly of her as she projected, but his attitude toward her is not what she wishes it to be."

"You could hear us both thinking," I said.

"*Oui.*"

"So, we're both right and both wrong?" Richard asked.

"*Oui.*"

And that about summed up Richard and me when we tried to date. I was just suddenly exhausted, as everything caught up with me all at once.

Wicked leaned in and said, "If you want to lean against me I would be honored to guard your rest."

"I won't sleep, I never sleep in cars."

"I'm just offering a place to rest."

"You could lean against me if you're tired," Richard said.

"No," I said, "I can't, because you see it as weakness, and I can't be weak right now. We have a dragon, a real dragon to fight. A dragon vampire, which is a new category for me. How do we fight him?"

"You defeated him tonight with the *ardeur*," Jake said.

"We chased him away with that most tender of magics," Jean-Claude said, "but we cannot slay him with it."

"His brother was killed by a large stone smashing his head."

"Like a beheading with blunt-force trauma," I said.

"Yes."

"Who was his mother?" I asked.

"What?"

"If Ares is his father, and I'll just accept that is possible and keep moving, then who was his mom?"

"Some say it was Telphusia, a lesser-known goddess, or some say a nereid, but I believe his mother was Tisiphone, one of the Erinyes."

"The Greek Furies," I said.

"Yes, attendants of Nemesis, goddess of righteous anger."

"The Furies hunted people down for punishment, didn't they?" Richard asked.

"Yes, but it was more than that. They could cause terror in any who saw them; they were nightmares given form. Tisiphone was the avenger of murder. You had to do something evil or outside the law to attract the Furies, but once that happened you were doomed, or so they say. I knew people who did terrible things but the Furies never came."

"Drakon caused fear like a night hag, so he could feed on it; maybe he gets that from his mom," I said.

"He is not the only vampire we have met that shares that power, *ma petite*."

"Yeah, but just saying, it could come from more than one source."

"I did not know he could feed upon terror. Calling himself Deimos was not an idle choice, then," Jake said.

"The dread before battle that can take a man's heart and courage," I said.

"Yes, perhaps after centuries he doesn't wish to be called simply Dragon, for that is what Drakon means in Greek."

"Vampires are allowed to name themselves," Jean-Claude said.

"Or maybe since the Dragon is still alive, he doesn't want to offend her by naming himself something so similar," Jake said.

"No one would want to challenge her by accident or on purpose," Jean-Claude said.

"Okay, then we'll call him Deimos for now," I said. "How do we kill him?"

"We find his physical body and behead it," Jake said.

"When you say 'body,' do you mean him in human form, or the original snaky dragon form?" I asked.

"His twin brother was slain in his dragon form, but he had no other form, so it may be that we would need Deimos to be in that form to slay him, but in truth I do not know. He was never heard from again so I thought him long dead along with anyone or anything that could be called dragon save for the council members and the beasts that modern science classes as dragons."

"Is there anyone else who might know more about this dragon vamp?" I asked.

"I will see if anyone else among us knows more," he said, and I knew he meant among the Harlequin.

I started to lean in against Wicked. I looked at Richard, who was fighting not to frown at us. "Why aren't you exhausted?"

"I don't know."

"*Ma petite*, may I ask the favor that you lean against Richard and see if more of your energy returns since he is more closely linked to you through me?"

I frowned at him, but I sat up and started to move away from Wicked. He didn't try and hold me in place, just moved so Richard could put his arm on the back of the seat. I gave Wicked a soft kiss before I moved away. It earned me a smile and that made it worth it. Then I moved to the other side of the seat to lean into Richard. I stayed stiff and couldn't relax, because he didn't understand me, and . . . But the minute I had enough of him touching me it was like his body was a warm blanket and a cup of hot coffee, and just what I needed. Damn it.

"May I hold you?" Richard asked.

"You *are* holding me." And even to me it sounded grumpy.

"May I wrap my arm around you?"

I took in a deep breath and let it out slow. "Yes."

His arm curved over my shoulders, and I fit under his arm better. It felt good, but I was still fighting to relax when Nathaniel said, "It's okay to touch him back, Anita; he's cute, not my cup of tea, but let yourself touch him back. Bare skin contact helps renew us."

"Thank you, Nathaniel," Richard said.

"You're welcome."

They were playing nice, so I let myself slide my hand underneath the dress shirt to touch his stomach. His skin was so warm and smooth, and . . . it felt good. I pressed my bare leg against his and that was even better. "I feel like I'm injured almost, like if I could sleep between two of the wereanimals that I carry inside me I'd heal."

"We could have one of the mystic Harlequin search you both for magical bindings," Jake said. The Harlequin had finally felt safe enough to bring the few human servants left to them. The Mother of All Darkness had killed most of them as a test to prove they were powerful enough to be one of her chosen warriors, but some had been magically gifted enough that they'd been spared as too valuable to waste. There weren't many of them, but the few left were magic with a capital *M*. They could work energy and clear a chakra so fast they'd have been the envy of any modern Reiki master or light worker.

"I do not think that is what is wrong, but it is good to have people skilled enough to look for such things," Jean-Claude said.

"What do you think is wrong?" I asked as I snuggled up against as much of Richard's bare skin as I could find and hated that it felt so good.

"All the energy we raised tonight went to me to defeat Deimos; you did not keep any for yourself."

"It's my job to be your battery."

"It is, *ma petite*, but your *ardeur* is like blood for me, without it you are empty."

Richard hugged me a little closer and said, "Will you get mad if I say I volunteer?"

"Yes," I said.

"I would feel better if Anita fed on someone not tied so closely to her and Jean-Claude metaphysically," Jake said.

"You said that before, something about us saving our energy for the next fight," I said, but my voice had that edge of almost sleep. Richard was so warm, and the hum of his energy felt like home to my wolf and me. I hated that he still felt that good in my arms; even his skin smelled good, which was usually my cue that I was still in love with someone. When I'd fallen out of love their skin smelled bitter. I'd never noticed it until I had beasts inside me, so maybe it was a shapeshifter thing.

"Rest, *ma petite*, there will be no feeding of the *ardeur* until we are safe within the walls of the Circus. There will be time enough later to decide on partners to donate to our cause." His voice was so soothing. It made me struggle to open my eyes.

"Are you making me sleep?"

"*Non*, I wished you to be able to rest and recoup your energy, for we may need it sooner than the *ardeur* can be fed."

That made sense, but somehow I felt traitorous cuddling with Richard when Nathaniel was so close. He read my mind, or guessed, because he said, "It's all right that it feels good to rest in Richard's arura. You all used a lot of wolf energy tonight."

Richard hugged me closer and said, "May I kiss the top of your head, please?"

I slid my arm tighter around the warm naked skin of his stomach and said, "Yes."

He kissed my hair and then rested his cheek against the top of my head. I settled my head against his chest, and it was suddenly the best pillow. I couldn't remember the last time I'd slept with my head against his body like this, and then I realized I really couldn't. In all the years of on-again, off-again dating we'd never cuddled like this and it seemed sad that we'd missed so much when we'd been in each other's lives for so long.

I felt his body relax around me even as he held me close, and realized we were both so tired, as if Jean-Claude had drained more energy from both of us than we'd realized. I struggled to wake enough to blink, a spurt of panic at sleeping in a moving car ever since my mother died in one when I was eight.

Nathaniel said, "You're safe, Anita, sleep."

Wicked leaned over so I could see his face. "We will keep watch, Anita; rest, Jean-Claude will need you both at full strength later."

Richard kissed my hair again, and then my forehead. "Sleep with me, Anita, please, just sleep."

Sleep with me, not *fuck me*, not *go down on me*, just sleep. It was both an innocent request and more intimate than people realized who hadn't tried polyamory. There were lovers in our group that I still hadn't figured out how to sleep with after the sex was over. It was a sweet request, romantic even, so Richard when he wasn't being a dick. That was my last thought before I drifted off to sleep in his arms with his chest as my pillow.

33

WE WERE RUNNING through the woods, so fast that the trees were just blurred shapes to fling ourselves between, around, through. The smell of the pack was everywhere around us in the trees. We ran together hunting something large that was crashing noisily ahead of us. The deer had forgotten all caution in the terror of the chase. Deer are always closer than we think, like slender brown ghosts, but this deer ran, trying to outrun us. It was no longer a ghost, but a desperate speed to escape its fate. We were fate on four legs, furred, tongues panting in the summer heat with the scent of pine everywhere so that the deer's scent was intermingled with it and the scent of the other wolves. The push of our bodies against the ground, the crashing of the deer as it made another mistake. I could feel, or smell, the far wolves circling it, cutting off its escape. It turned and came running toward us but the entire forest smelled of wolf; the deer didn't know where to run. We ran toward its panic and knew soon we would eat, but first there would be blood, death, and it would not be ours.

Then there was another smell in the forest; it wasn't us, it wasn't the deer. We ran for the deer, because whatever it was, it could not have our prey. We had worked hard for this deer, it was ours. Tiger, I smelled tiger, and the moment I thought *I*, not *us*, not *pack*, but *me*, the dream changed. Richard and I held hands on the edge of the forest, a bigger forest than still existed in Missouri. There was a grass-filled meadow decorated with wildflowers and sunlight. The grass was taller than my waist and it moved not with wind but as if something was moving in it. I thought it was one large animal moving toward us, and then it seemed to split so that the grass moved in three paths. I smelled tiger again, closer, and then it was like the wind shifted and brought the scent of . . . rat, but the stirring grass was too big for an ordinary rat.

Richard's hand tensed in mine as the grass parted and a huge golden tiger glided into view. It was bigger than any ordinary tiger, big enough to ride on like a horse. The grass parted again, and a huge rat almost as big as the tiger stepped into sight. It was black except for one paw and a spot on its chest that looked almost like a star. It wasn't just a rat, it was my rat, Astro. In real life he was the size of a normal rat, not this monster size. He didn't even live with me but stayed with the wererats in their inner sanctum, their place of power, so what was he doing in my dream? He looked at me with his black, button eyes, showing brown in the strong sunlight.

The grass stirred again, and a monster-size hyena stepped out into the sunlight. It looked made of gold and bronze in the bright light, because the sun was sinking downward. I reached out my hand toward the hyena and it came to me like it was a pet. Its short fur was rougher than I'd expected, but the moment I touched it I felt better, safer. The gold tiger came to Richard's hand; he rubbed it behind one ear, and it chuffed for him in a rolling, friendly sound. I scratched the side of the hyena's face, and it made a low almost mooing sound, if a cow could growl in a friendly way . . . I'd never heard any sound like it before, but it was a good sound.

The giant rat that looked like the one that had chosen me sat up on its hind legs to look out over the grass, and then it was suddenly smaller and vanished into the grass. That was all the warning we got, and then the lion leapt onto the hyena. The growling moos turned to high-pitched chittering screams, the lion's roar like a deep bass death drum.

Richard grabbed me and tried to pull me back from the fight. The gold tiger tried to stand between me and them, but it was too late, the monstrous beasts rolled over me. A massive claw caught my outer thigh; the hyena's teeth missed lion and caught my shoulder in a crushing bite.

I woke screaming in the back of the car to find that the nightmare wasn't gone, it was inside me. My inner lion and hyena were having a fight to the death inside my body where they couldn't escape, and neither could I.

34

RICHARD AND WICKED tried to hold me still, but it wasn't my arms and legs that needed to be pinned. I was just the cage for the fight. Huge claws raked the hyena's body, but I was the hyena. It was my throat that screamed in high-pitched sounds that were not human. The hyena darted in and tried to tear open the lion's belly, but the big cat rolled away, and my body rocked with the force of that weight falling against my side. Wicked was thrown against the far wall of the car, as if the lion had rolled into him. He'd lost his grip on my arm and thigh. The hyena didn't leap after the staggered lion, it stood there legs braced as if it had won something, but I knew the lion wasn't finished. I wouldn't have been finished and I was the lion. The hyena started running up that impossible path inside me. It wanted to be real, and the only way to do that was to get out of me.

Richard wrapped himself around me; the scent of wolf was everywhere. It should have called my own wolf and slowed the hyena down, but it didn't. Instead, the hyena ran faster in that loping, rolling run that looked awkward but could eat up the miles.

Nathaniel was suddenly kneeling on the floorboard at my feet. He pressed his bare arm against my face, but the scent of leopard meant food to the hyena, either to steal their kill before they could hide it or to eat the leopard, either worked for the hyena rushing toward the surface of my body. Always before when my beast ran for the exit my body reacted like it had with the lion rolling into me and Wicked, but there was something different tonight. It was like the hyena knew something I didn't. It ran toward me giving that high excited giggling, gibbering cry that would raise the hair on your neck if you heard it in the dark, or, hell, in the light.

Then I felt something bigger running. The hyena looked behind it, and the lion rose like a semi truck coming up too fast behind you on the highway, dwarfing your car like a giant about to crush you. The hyena gave a squealing cry as the lion grabbed its rear leg and threw it around like it wasn't one of the top predators in the world. If you think hyenas are scavengers you've watched too many cartoons. I screamed as if my own thigh had been grabbed, and I expected to see the blood, like something had bitten me for real.

Wicked was at my side again, not holding me down, but just holding my hand. He exchanged a look with Richard and Nathaniel; it was not a good look. I managed to say, "The lion is coming." My voice was already hoarse from screaming.

"I know, *ma petite*, I know." Jean-Claude was on his knees in the middle seat, reaching back toward me. I reached out, and the moment our fingers touched, the lion slowed; it didn't stop, but it wasn't running full out now. It came at a fast walk, as if it was less sure of what would happen when it got to the end of me. Certain victory was gone with the touch of my lover's hand, no, my master's hand. I had three lovers in the back seat with me, but only Jean-Claude's touch had slowed the inevitable.

I didn't realize the SUV had stopped moving until Jake opened his door and moved the seat forward so that Nathaniel could get out. Jean-Claude held my hand, and that one touch held the lion to a walk. Wicked cradled me in his arms and lifted me closer to Jean-Claude as Richard slid out of the car. Then Nicky's shoulders filled the opening; he almost didn't fit through, his muscles gleaming in a tank top cut so wide through the neck and shoulders it was more flirtation than a real shirt. I saw his short blond hair and one blue eye above me. He'd worn an eye patch tonight where the scars had stolen his other eye.

He took me in his arms, smiling, and growled. The sound went through me like my spine was a tuning fork and he'd found just the right note. It made me shiver. He leaned in and sniffed above my face, and the next growl was deeper, more menacing. "That's not your lioness I'm smelling," he said in a voice that was more growl than speech.

"You're my Rex," I said in a voice ragged with screams.

He gave a fierce snarling smile. "You bet your ass, I am."

That made me smile, but the huge lion was still walking up the path inside me. Nicky was right, it wasn't my lioness, and it should have been. I couldn't have a male lion inside me, because I wasn't that, and yet there it was, with a huge dark, almost black mane encircling a rich gold face. The contrast made him look almost like a Valentine card, all dark lace and velvet lion. I thought, *What a weird way to think of it*, and then I felt my lioness behind him. It was how she thought of him. She'd shown me once before that she wanted a mate, but never this forcefully, or this painfully.

"Damn it," I said, "I'll look for a lion to call, just stop doing shit like this." The big male sat down, and the lioness came up to rub her body along his like she was scent-marking him.

"I feel your lions, *ma petite*, Nicky. I feel them as I can feel wolves."

We looked at him. "Wolves are your animal to call, lions aren't," I said.

"I am aware, *ma petite*." He squeezed my hand, then reached toward Nicky, hesitating just short of touching him, playing his long, slender fingers above Nicky's aura. The lions inside me looked up, the lioness sniffing the air as if Jean-Claude's almost touching him had changed something.

Nicky rubbed his cheek against my hair. "That's much more fun," he said, voice already deepening with testosterone.

"What has changed, *mon lionne*?"

I put my face against Nicky's and it was like something tight and angry inside me loosened and just floated away. God, it felt good to have him near me.

The male lion inside me faded away, and the lioness flopped down on her side on the path and gazed at me with big amber eyes. The expression in those eyes had completely changed. She rolled over, exposing her snowy white belly like a cat trying to lure you in for a belly rub so they could sink claws into you. She looked utterly relaxed as she flopped onto her other side and blinked those big golden eyes at me again. Her eyes were soft, and I'd never noticed before how thick and black her eyelashes were, framing the rich amber of her eyes. If she'd been human I'd have said she was batting her eyes at me. No, not at me.

"Anita's lioness is in heat," Nicky said. His face still pressed against mine, so it was the most natural thing in the world for him to kiss the side of my neck. I turned my head, exposing more of my neck to his kisses. I remembered that Nicky and his old Rex had told me my lioness was in heat when we met, but it had never happened again.

Jean-Claude's lips brushed the knuckles of the hand he was holding. "Make love, not war," he said, and his voice glided over my body so that I shivered more from his words than any touch. Wicked poked his head back in the car. "We must get you inside in a secure location before you do anything else."

Nicky drew back from nuzzling my neck and said, "Wicked is right, safety has to come first." He drew back again enough for me to see his face. His one eye changed from yellow to blue as I watched, and I realized that I couldn't see my lioness in my head anymore. I was alone for the moment.

"Let's get inside while the getting is good," I said.

Jean-Claude's hand was more solid on mine. "*Oui*, there is much to be done before dawn."

Somehow I didn't think he was talking about romance, more's the pity, but if we could figure out what the hell was up with my lion so she didn't try to tear me apart again, the romance could wait.

35

I LOOKED FOR Nathaniel in the mass of bodyguards as we crammed through the back door of the Circus of the Damned. Jean-Claude and I ended up shoved against the stacked boxes on the far side of the room. Jean-Claude squeezed my hand, which made me look up at him. "Nathaniel is not here."

"Was I thinking that loudly?"

"Yes," Richard and Nicky both answered from closer to the outer door. I looked toward them, but it was just a sea of bodyguards with Ethan's back my closest view. Wicked and Truth were on either side of Jean-Claude. I realized it was Jake still in his exercise clothes standing beside him. I'd expected him to stay near Richard, being a werewolf and all. I wasn't complaining, just noticing.

Jean-Claude put his arm over my shoulder, drawing me into the circle of his body and making us take up less room in the crush of people. "*Oui, ma petite,* but I believe he has gone ahead to prepare food for you and Richard, since I have taken so much energy from you both."

I wrapped my arms around him, enjoying the feel of him underneath the silk of the robe. I laid my head against his chest, and his heart beat against me. It was slower than any human could survive, slow and thick like it had to wake up to beat, but it was there. I'd gotten so used to his heart not beating that this was startling, the way it had been at the beginning when I realized I missed the beat of his heart.

Wicked yelled, "Whoever is nearer the door, open it so we can move our principals downstairs."

"We don't take orders from any vampire but Jean-Claude." It was the Demolition Man again, sounding sullen and unhelpful.

"Do as you are told," Jean-Claude said.

"I'll do what you tell me to do, not Wicked."

"Are you seriously going to make Jean-Claude repeat what Wicked said, because you have some kind of beef with him?" I asked.

"Who's next to the door besides Demo?" Jake didn't yell, but his voice had that tone that didn't need to yell to tell someone they were in trouble. I didn't recognize the man's voice that said, "I am, sir."

"Then open the door so we can move to a more secure location," Jake said, still in that unfriendly, not-yelling voice.

"I can open it," Demo said.

"You had your chance," Jake said.

The door opened and the nearest guards began to filter through while Demo tried to argue with someone near him. Jean-Claude and I kept our arms around each other as we moved with Wicked in front of us, Ethan beside us, and Jake and Truth behind us. The only thing that would have made me feel safer was if Nicky could have been beside us. I took one arm from around Jean-Claude's waist, so I'd have one empty hand as we passed through the door. As we got closer I could see Demo beside the door. He was waiting to cause more trouble, like I'd half expected. I moved my arms so I wasn't hugging Jean-Claude and he didn't argue. He could read my thoughts, so he knew. I was being overly cautious since Demo would have to get through Wicked and Ethan to get to us, which wasn't happening, but I never like to rely entirely on anyone else when it comes to personal safety. It was part of what I'd hated about the shoes tonight; they'd practically crippled me from running or fighting. It was part of the argument we'd been having about my wedding dress, and if you say *But it's your wedding day, there will be plenty of security*, you've missed the point.

"I am sorry that tonight's shoes were such a problem for you, *ma petite*."

The whole mind-reading thing used to creep me out, but now I thought it just saved so much time. "They can be bedroom shoes, but I won't wear them out again."

"Agreed, *ma petite*."

My stomach was tight, my shoulders bunching for a fight as we got closer to Demo, and that was when I knew he could no longer bodyguard anyone, because you absolutely must trust anyone who is supposed to take a bullet for you. I didn't trust Demo not to take a swing at Wicked as we tried to go through the door.

Wicked was almost even with the bigger man when I suddenly wasn't tense anymore. I was strangely relaxed. The inside of my head had gone to that quiet place. I unsnapped the purse and slipped my hand inside it until it wrapped around the little Sig Sauer so all I had to do was flip the safety off, get closer, and pull the trigger. Normally I wouldn't have been caressing the trigger this soon, but he wasn't just a wereanimal, he was former military, which meant he was superhuman fast and trained. It was why I kept the gun inside the little bag so he wouldn't see it coming. I hoped the purse wasn't as expensive as I feared, because I wasn't taking the gun out of it to fire it. When seconds count, just shoot through your damn purse. You only need to take it out if you have to aim at a distance, and ladies, if you need to do that then just freaking run.

Was I overreacting, and if I was, why? Demo hadn't threatened me, or Jean-Claude, so why was my finger on the trigger? Because I'd felt helpless. Jean-Claude had dressed me like the princess in the story and . . . it wasn't me. It would never be me. That wasn't a good enough reason to shoot someone, though. I took my finger off the trigger. Wicked could handle himself if Demo tried anything. I didn't need to protect my protectors.

Jean-Claude leaned close to my face and whispered, "I am so sorry, *ma petite*."

"I know," I said, but I didn't look at him. I kept my attention on Demo and getting through the door. The gun was still in my hand; I'd just gotten off the trigger because I didn't trust myself not to overreact, which wasn't like me. Did I want to prove that I could protect myself? Was I having a macho moment? I didn't know, and if you carry a gun, you need to know. Shit.

I used my thumb to slide the safety on, then took my hand out of my purse and accepted that the inside of my head was too snarled to be trusted to make the right decision. If Demo managed to get past all our security, which was incredibly unlikely, I could go for his knee, dislocate it, then try for an elbow to his head or dislocating his shoulder depending on what openings he gave me. I had a plan now, and I was calmer. It would be okay, but part of me didn't believe it.

"May I put my arm around you, *ma petite*?" Jean-Claude asked, and because he asked, I said yes. If he'd just wrapped himself around me in that moment without asking, I'd have been pissed. It wasn't just the wedding prep, or the clothes for tonight, it was talking to my dad. It was raising old ghosts that no amount of psychic ability would chase away.

Demo went through the door with two other werewolf guards who had been special teams like he'd wanted to be. He'd washed out, left the military and become a civilian contractor, read *mercenary*. He'd been the only contractor to survive the shapeshifter attack that had ended the SEALs' military careers. If he could manage not to get himself killed for two years, some of the contracting firms would hire him again, the idea being that two years of control meant he was safe to hire. Some firms demanded five years of shapeshifter experience, but most only two. If someone could convince Demo to behave himself, in two years he could be someone else's problem. If only it worked that way with family.

I slid my arm inside Jean-Claude's robe so I could touch all that smooth skin and let myself lean against him. He wrapped me into a hug and started murmuring comforting things in French. I even understood some of them, but it was the sound of his voice, not what he said. Jean-Claude's voice had become the white noise that let me know I was safe and loved.

There was a moment of longing and sorrow that was almost pain. It rang through us and made us turn toward the source. Richard's brown eyes shone in the overhead lights with unshed tears. I realized that until that moment he hadn't understood just how much Jean-Claude and I loved each other. His thoughts were too close to the surface, they just came tumbling out. He'd known we were in love, that hot lustful can't-keep-your-hands-off-each-other falling in love, but he'd never realized that we'd moved on, gone deeper while he'd been away fixing himself. We'd been building a life to-gether. One that didn't include him, and for the first time he wondered if he'd come back too late.

Jean-Claude was able to hide his thoughts and emotions like he'd flipped a switch, but I hadn't had centuries of practice. So Richard heard that I'd been afraid of him expecting too much, that I didn't love him, that I worried that I was already stretched too thin with all the people in our poly group now. It was like the harder I tried to not overshare, the more I shared.

"I'm sorry," I said out loud, because I didn't know what else to say.

A lone tear trailed from each eye, down those perfect cheekbones of his. "I've come back too late."

"*Non, mon lupe*, while there is breath in our bodies it is never too late." He held his hand out to the other man, but Richard hesitated, looking at me. He'd already read my mind; what could I do?

"Either you're here to take both their hands," Ethan said, "or you just came back for the girl."

I expected him to get angry, but he just said, "You're right." He took Jean-Claude's offered hand and smiled at him, a smile that was warm and couple-y. Then he looked at me, the smile fading around the edges. "I know how you feel about me now. You're afraid I'll demand too much, destroy your poly group, your happiness. You don't trust me because of what I did before, and why should you?"

"But if the Ulfric hadn't come back tonight, could you have defeated Deimos?" Jake asked.

Jean-Claude said, "No."

I shook my head.

"Then take his hand, Anita."

"Anita doesn't have to do anything she doesn't want to do," Nicky said.

"No, Jake is right, Nicky. If we hadn't had Richard tonight . . ." I realized I didn't want to admit how close a call it had been in front of everyone in the room. They were good to be security for the clubs, but none of them were on our personal details. The fewer people who realized that Deimos had almost possessed Jean-Claude tonight, the better.

I held my hand out to Richard, and he took it with a smile. It wasn't as warm as the one he'd given Jean-Claude. In fact, the smile left his eyes uncertain, but that was okay. I'd earned his doubt, hell I was more comfortable with it. It made me feel better about my own doubts. But none of that mattered to the power that thrilled through the three of us.

"You are almost complete," Jake said.

The hair on my arms was standing up, and my voice was breathless as I said, "What do you mean, almost?"

"This power is a small thing compared to what you could have if you were a true triumvirate," he said.

"How much truer can we be?" Richard said; his voice sounded as strained as mine. His eyes were full of blue fire. I looked at Jean-Claude; his eyes were glowing with power, too. I didn't have a mirror, but I knew mine were glowing as well.

"We are a triumvirate of power," Jean-Claude said, and his voice echoed around the room.

"You will not be a true triumvirate until you share the fourth mark," Jake said.

"No," I said, and I pulled my hand away from both of them.

"We must solidify my power base, *ma petite*."

"You don't understand how intimate the connection will be," I said, "you've never given anyone the fourth mark before."

Richard said, "Wait, how do you know more about this than Jean-Claude?"

"I have a triumvirate with Damian and Nathaniel, you know that."

"I know how you feel about Nathaniel, but you're not that close to Damian. Sharing the fourth mark with them didn't change that," Richard said.

Nicky gave a deep chuckle. "You haven't seen her with Damian in a while."

"What's that mean?" Richard asked.

"It means you need to see me with Nathaniel and Damian together, before you agree to letting Jean-Claude share the fourth mark with us."

"Can we do that before dawn?" he asked.

I stared at him, he looked so calm. I didn't bother to look at Jean-Claude as his face wouldn't give away anything unless he wanted it to. "Damian should be home by now, so yeah, we can do show-and-tell tonight."

"If we are to do that on top of everything else, we must make haste, or the sunrise will find us before we have secured our power base," Jean-Claude said.

"I haven't agreed to do the fourth mark with the three of us," I said.

"Night will fall again, and Deimos will still be out there."

"I know that."

"We must have enough power to destroy him once and for all," Jean-Claude said.

"We won tonight without the fourth mark."

"Did I mention that Deimos is a fire breather?" Jake asked.

We all looked at him then. "No, you left that part out," I said.

"I will tell you everything I know about him once all of you are securely downstairs and Jean-Claude has done what he must do before dawn."

"Fire breathing," Richard said.

"A real fire-breathing dragon?" I said.

"I'm afraid so," Jake said.

"I guess it's lucky he doesn't just want us dead, then," I said.

"He can only make fire when he is in full dragon form. He would not fit in the alley or side streets. He would have to march up the main road in front of Guilty Pleasures. He will not want to show himself where humans could see him, not like that," Jake said.

"Good to know," I said.

"I have so many questions," Richard said.

"Be a biologist later, *mon lupe*, in this moment I need you to be my beast half. Dawn must not find me unprepared."

"Is Edward still here?" I asked.

"He wouldn't leave until he saw you in person and made sure you were okay," Nicky said.

"Good, because if we're going to plan how to take out a fire-breathing dragon I want him in on it."

"Didn't he burn a house down once with you and him still inside it?" Richard asked.

"Yeah, no one knows fire like Edward does."

Richard looked at me like I'd lost my mind, but thanks to the vampire marks I felt the fear behind the arrogant, angry look. He was afraid of Edward; he saw him as careless and danger-seeking. He was afraid he'd get me killed someday.

"He saved me that night, Richard, I wouldn't have had the guts to use a flamethrower inside a house with us in it, but it was the only way for us to kill the vampires and save ourselves."

"I know you believe that, Anita."

"And there we go, Richard, right back to the arguments we started having almost from the moment we started dating. You hate my job. You hate my best friend."

"I don't hate Edward, I just know when he's involved it's a case so dangerous you needed his help, or something so dangerous he needed yours," Richard said.

I was all set to argue, then realized he was right. I thought about it for a few seconds, then said, "I see it as when either of us gets in over our head, we have each other to call for backup."

"*Ma petite, mon lupe,* we do not have time for squabbling tonight."

"You're right, I'm sorry," I said.

"I won't let old habits ruin this second chance," Richard said.

Jean-Claude held his hand out to us with a smile. "Then let us go downstairs."

We took his hands and the moment we did I didn't want to argue anymore. I was suddenly thinking sex and remembering the smell and feel of Richard's body. It was so strong it made me trip on a step. Shit.

"*Ma petite,* are you well?"

"Was that your thought in my head?"

"This one I am not to blame for, *ma petite.*"

"What thought?" Richard asked.

"Never mind," I said, and I sounded grumpy because I was being defensive, "just get us down the damn stairs, Jean-Claude. We're running out of night."

No one argued, and we started moving like we had a purpose on the uneven stone steps. I had to concentrate to keep up with their longer strides, even wearing combat boots. I was glad I had to concentrate on the physical, I welcomed it, because it made it harder for my mind to wander. The best part of my old relationship with Richard had been the sex; it had been the only part that always worked between us. Of course that would be what I thought about and wanted more than anything else from him. It was logical in a way, but it didn't make it any less embarrassing. I sure as hell didn't want him to read my mind while I was thinking about him like that, so I concentrated on the steps by staring at my feet, tuning into my body in the now, letting the physical act carry me with no thought, a moving meditation. I held Jean-Claude's hand, his longer stride forcing me to move faster and in a rhythm that wasn't best for me, but that was okay. I'd found that moving meditations needed to be hard in order for me to keep an empty mind. I upped my speed until Jean-Claude had to protest, because he was still in the high-heel boots. I loved so much that he was the one in heels who asked to go slower. Maybe it wasn't being the girl that made me feel helpless, maybe it was just whoever had to wear high heels?

36

RICHARD WAS BREATHING hard by the time we got down the stairs and in front of the huge dungeonlike door that was part of the defenses at the Circus. "I thought I'd kept up with my cardio, but I'd forgotten the StairMaster of doom." He had his hands on his hips, leaning a little backward against the stitch in his side. People always bend forward over the stitch, which just makes it worse; if you bend backward it hurts more for a few seconds, but it goes away quicker.

Nicky came down the steps to stand near me. I wasn't sure if he was feeling my unease, or if he needed a little reassurance. Nah, it was probably me. Either way I reached my free hand out to Nicky. The moment we touched I felt a little steadier, more myself. I leaned my head against Nicky's chest, and it was like I was breathing in the warm solidity of him.

Jean-Claude squeezed my hand. I turned my head with my forehead still on Nicky's chest. It put me looking at our clasped hands rather than his face.

"You are so weak," Demolition Man said.

I raised my head with a sarcastic remark ready but realized he was looking past us at Richard. I felt Jean-Claude move like he was going to go to Richard's side, but I pulled him back toward us. Demo wasn't the only one who saw a civilian Ulfric as a weak link; Richard had to handle this himself or it would just make it worse. If Richard needed our help, we'd help, but until then we had to let him lead.

The other werewolves tried to push Demo through the open door, but Richard stood up straight and said, "Let him stay." The werewolves looked at each other and clearly thought it was a bad idea. Hell, I thought it was a bad idea. Jean-Claude made another small movement toward him. I pulled him in against me, which put him touching Nicky, but neither man minded. They were both secure in their different flavors of masculinity.

"If you could have stayed with your contract firm, would you have?" Richard asked.

"You know I would."

"On condition that you never let anyone outside your firm know you were a werewolf?"

"A lot of countries won't let shifters in, so sure, we'd have a secret weapon," Demo said.

"How would you work out?"

Demo frowned. "If there's a gym, I use that. If not, run, push-ups, pull-ups, you know, whatever I can to stay in shape."

"How would you know how to fast to move, or how many reps to do and still come off as human?"

"What?"

"I have to work out with humans. I can never run fast enough, or do enough push-ups, or pull-ups, or lift heavy enough to really get a good workout, because if I do, then I'll lose the job I love."

I wanted to say *You teach college now, not junior high like when we met, maybe you wouldn't,* but I didn't say anything, because Demo seemed to be listening and that didn't happen often. "So, you can never push yourself?"

"Never," Richard said. "It's impossible to get away from everyone's phones. They're always there waiting to film anything interesting or weird and putting it online instantly."

Demo looked thoughtful, honestly more thoughtful than I'd thought he was capable of, but maybe his bad attitude made me underestimate him? I'd try to keep an open mind if Demo would just stop doing stupid, mean-spirited things.

"I get it, fucking phones are everywhere, and the fuckers put everything online," Demo said.

"We're having to watch out for them in really remote areas where you'd think no one would have a smartphone," one of the tall, dark werewolves said. What was his name? Jones, Jim, J-something.

"Got that right," Demo said, and the others agreed.

Crisis averted; Demo went through the door without a complaint. The other werewolves went with him as if afraid he would do something they'd regret. They seemed to feel responsible for him since they'd all survived the same attack, but I wasn't sure they liked him much. I wasn't sure anyone here in St. Louis liked him much. What were we going to do with him?

Richard walked toward us, then looked at how the three of us were standing. I watched doubts and questions go through his eyes, while he fought to keep them off his face. Only knowing him so well once upon a time let me see the confusion.

"Is there something I need to know about Nicky and Jean-Claude?" he asked.

I reached out to him delicately, using some of the new skills I'd learned at last, but his own confused emotions were blinding him. He couldn't feel anything outside himself. Strong emotions could fuel your magic or cripple it. I realized that Jean-Claude had narrowed the marks between us, so that we weren't getting every damn emotion back and forth. Great by me, but I wondered what Jean-Claude wanted to hide enough to do it. Weren't we supposed to keep the marks open for power right now?

"I'm not his type, not pretty enough," Nicky said, smiling wide enough to make his face crinkle all the way to the scars where his eye should have been. I loved that he was willing to smile like that now. I went up on tiptoe to kiss his cheek; to reach his lips he had to meet me partway, but he didn't. He kept staring at Richard, only changing from holding my hand to wrapping his arm around me. It forced me to wrap my arm around his waist, or just stand there awkwardly, but I didn't like that he had passed up a chance to kiss me to play dominance games with Richard.

Nicky said, "Sorry, babe," and he started to lean down for a kiss. I raised an eyebrow at him. "Babe?"

"We're supposed to be trying out endearments," he said.

"Not 'babe,' or 'baby,'" I said.

He grinned at me. "I'd let you call me 'baby.'"

"Would you, really? Baby?" I said, smiling.

He grinned. "Let us confound societal expectations, Big Daddy."

I laughed out loud, and everyone left with us joined in, even Richard. Ethan said, "If you're actually going to call each other 'baby' and 'Big Daddy,' please do it where I can watch people's faces."

"I tried to be jealous, I mean I am jealous, but you are fun together. It's like this couple dynamic I've never seen Anita do before," Richard said.

"You will find *ma petite* much more comfortable and much lighter with many things, and many people," Jean-Claude said.

"I can't wait," Richard said.

"Then let's get you all through the door and secure it behind us," Jake said.

"You really think Deimos could attack us here in the Circus?" I asked.

"He is a powerful foe who has surprised us once tonight, it would be foolish to underestimate him again."

Suddenly I didn't feel cheerful, I felt scared. Nicky hugged me, then stepped back so Jean-Claude could lead me forward. He started to, then stopped and reached his other hand out to Richard. I didn't complain, I didn't even feel weird about it. Richard had been a really good sport tonight and there would be a lot more chances for him to keep being a good sport tonight. We followed Jake and Wicked through the door hand in hand in hand.

37

THERE WAS A wall of gauzy curtains almost immediately through the door. They were the "walls" for the living room because it was really just one big cave. Wicked held the gauzy curtains aside for us to enter. Jake went ahead of us just a little, but if something jumped us in the living room that would mean they'd gotten past all the other guards, which would mean we'd already lost. Luckily the scariest thing waiting for us was the anxiety radiating off Damian. He stood at the edge of the antique Persian rug that looked like brilliant stained glass, but we'd put a thicker cushioning underneath it, so you'd never know it sat on bare stone.

Damian's red hair was the closest to true red, like a Crayola crayon, than any other natural redhead I'd ever met. I guess a thousand years of no sunlight on your hair will change the color. It fell past his shoulders, so red that it brought out the red in the rug. He was wearing his favorite robe. A dark, rich, blue velvet a little frayed at the cuffs and hem, and though I couldn't see it from this angle I knew that the elbows were starting to come out. It was a Victorian dressing gown that he'd gotten when they were all the rage. Now it was one of his comfort objects. He must have been ready for bed, which meant there'd be silky pajama pants on under the robe.

Damian's anxiety rode my body so that my heartbeat sped in

sympathy. He wanted to run to me, kiss me, but he wasn't sure if it would be welcome with the three of us standing hand in hand. I might have used our metaphysical connection to find out what was wrong, but I wasn't sure if what I learned would translate directly to Jean-Claude and Richard. I could open up and hear everyone, but I wasn't so good at keeping the individual parts from intermingling. So I said, "Damian, what's wrong?"

"I don't want to overstep," he said, and his voice had a note of tormented uncertainty that I hadn't heard in it for a year.

"You have greeted *ma petite* when she is on my arm many times, why do you hesitate now?"

"Rumor has it that the three of you are back together. The last time that was true you did not share well."

"There is no need to be so formal, *mon ami*," Jean-Claude said.

Damian didn't look convinced that he didn't need all the vampire formality that we usually did without among ourselves. "I thank you for your words, Jean-Claude, and I feel what Anita wants, but what does the Ulfric say?"

"Richard isn't the boss of you," I said, and that first snap of anger was there in my voice and tightening through my shoulders. I knew I had unresolved anger from our breakup, but now was not the time. I would not be the one who lost my shit first. If Richard behaved, so would I.

"Anita's right," Richard said, "and I don't know what rumors you've heard, but I didn't come back expecting anything, except a chance to try again. You're part of their poly group, and I respect that."

"Thank you for saying that, Ulfric."

I frowned, studying Damian, realizing that he was shielding from me enough that I could only get the strong emotions that he couldn't hide. "I'm glad Richard came back in time to help save the day, we might not be standing here if he hadn't, but our poly group doesn't suddenly get an overhaul for him that we wouldn't make for any other new member."

Damian gave a tentative smile. "I'm glad to hear that."

"Then go give her a kiss," Wicked said, "I've already made it clear that I'm not giving up my place in Anita's life, and I'm barely in the poly group compared to you."

I looked at him again; it was so unlike him to speak out like that.

"You did?" Damian asked, and didn't quite hide his surprise.

"He did," Ethan said.

"All of us did," Truth said.

"I missed it," Nicky said.

"I'll fill you in later," Ethan said.

Damian looked at all of them, then back at Richard, Jean-Claude, and finally me. "I guess the rumors are wrong."

"They are," Richard and I said together, then glanced at each other and smiled. I looked away, because all I could think was, *How could anyone change this much and stay changed?* People can change with a lot of effort and therapy, but they hardly ever do the work to stay with the new version of themselves. They do just enough to fix their marriage, or reconcile with their family, but once they're back in their old life it's incredibly hard not to fall back into old familiar patterns, even destructive ones.

"I'm committed to my therapy, Anita."

It startled me, and Jean-Claude squeezed my hand; so much for my ability to shield my thoughts. "I'm sorry, I didn't mean to think that loud."

"No, it's good, I need to know your doubts and fears about this."

"I know that you're worried how you'll fit into the larger poly group."

"I know if I had been able to work all my issues sooner that it would have been the three of us and maybe that would have been it, or who knows"—he added that part because I couldn't hide the flash of anger at his presumption—"but at least I'd have been in the poly group from the beginning instead of trying to fit myself in when it's established."

"That's fair," I said.

"I want my kiss of reassurance, but I feel like I'm watching a therapy session, and that should be private," Damian said.

"We don't have time for this tonight," Truth said.

We looked at him.

"Damian is right, the personal issues should be private. We were attacked tonight and barely won. Why are we not talking about strategy for the next battle?"

Wicked stepped forward and added, "What darkness remains to us needs to be about securing our power base and planning for Deimos's next attack, not doing couples therapy."

"You're not usually this chatty, but especially when you're on duty," I said.

"Bodyguards are meant to be seen and not heard," Jake said.

"Have you ever been a guard for one of the bloodlines descended from Belle Morte?" Truth asked.

"I have not."

"Then trust us when we say that silent observation hasn't been working."

"We're going to help keep you all on target," Wicked said.

"And if we do not wish for such help? If I wish to spend the rest of this night rejoicing in the people I love instead of planning for war, what then?" Jean-Claude said with that tone in his voice that master vampires just seem to have somewhere inside them. It wasn't yelling, but the threat was still in there somewhere.

"You are our king, Jean-Claude," Wicked said, "do you not understand that as powerful as you were tonight it was still sex magic, and that will not save us from this new enemy. He is a dragon, an intelligent, undead, fire-breathing dragon. We caught him off guard, but the next attack will use other weapons in his arsenal that sex magic will not prevail against. Do you not see the danger we are all in, Jean-Claude?"

Jean-Claude took his hands back from both of us and strode into the room, whirling so that his robe spilled around him like a cape. "Yes, I know how much danger we are in, and yes I know that sex magic will not save us, and that is all the magic I have to offer. I was convinced by my hubris and others that I was the best choice to lead vampirekind into a modern world, but modern sensibilities, modern rules, only work if everyone plays by them. I felt the mind of Deimos deep inside mine tonight. He is playing by very old rules, the ones that say if you want to rule a kingdom and are strong enough to take it, then it is yours by right."

He turned toward Jake, hands clutching and unclutching as if he was fighting not to make fists. "I would not have allowed myself to blood-oath all the other American masters to me if I had not been assured that there were no ancient vampires to challenge me. You and the other Harlequin promised me that there were no vampires left like Deimos."

"I believed what I said to you, my word of honor on that," Jake said.

"But now here we are with him out there, and he will attack again. Wicked is correct, Deimos will choose something else for his next foray, something that I have no defense against, that we have no defense against."

"Tonight caught us off guard," I said, "but sex magic isn't the only type of magic we have."

"It is all that I have, *ma petite*, and it will be I who is challenged. It is my defeat that will give him my crown, or my body to drain of power and possess."

"It's too late for him to challenge you to a formal duel now," I said.

"Better that than attacking us with his full strength and no rules forcing him to restrain the worst of his damage against us, the city, and all the people in it."

"I remember the rules from when the Earthmover came to town, Jean-Claude. If he had just caused mayhem in general then he could challenge you to a duel, but attacking you directly without a formal challenge first means that there are no rules," I said.

"Without rules, he will destroy us," Jean-Claude said, and I felt his fear full bore. It tightened my throat and made my stomach so tight I thought I might be sick.

I took a deep breath in and out to get control of the fear, because I didn't believe it. That belief helped steady me. "Not if we find him first," I said.

"It is a dragon, *ma petite*, if you have never seen a real dragon then you do not understand."

I couldn't help myself, I asked, "When did you see a real dragon?"

"I've seen dragons in the wild," Richard said.

"*Non, non*, you have seen mindless lizards, some with wings, but none with the abilities of true dragons."

"They aren't lizards, or any reptiles, they're warm-blooded," Richard said. He was right, but it didn't matter right now. We could talk nonessential biology later.

"How could anything breathe fire without burning itself up?" I asked.

Edward came through the far curtain wall with Peter at his back. They didn't look alike physically at all, but how they moved echoed each other as if Peter had absorbed parts of Edward just from close proximity, no genetics needed.

Edward said, "Did I hear the words 'dragon' and 'fire-breathing'?"

"You did," I said.

"A for-real fire-breathing dragon. I thought they were just legends," Peter said.

"Deimos is very real," Jake said.

"You said he couldn't fit in the alley behind the club, so how big is he in full dragon form?" I asked.

"I do not know in inches or centimeters, but taller than the roof of a modern house."

"A ranch-style one-story house, or a two-story?" Nicky asked.

"One story."

"So, he's sixteen to twenty feet tall in dragon form," Nicky said.

"Can he fly?" Edward asked. No *Holy cow, a dragon*, just practical questions.

"No," Jake said.

"If we can isolate him somewhere away from civilians, a LAW might do it," he said.

"Law enforcement?" Richard asked.

"Light antitank weapon," I said, "LAW."

"How do you have an antitank weapon?" Richard asked.

"Never ask questions you don't want the answers to," I said.

He frowned at me.

"Save questions that won't help us kill Deimos until later."

Richard held up his hands like he was giving up, but he nodded.

I turned back to Edward to ask, "I thought we used the last one you had on that case in Washington State?"

"That was years ago, did you really think I wouldn't have more by now?"

I grinned, almost laughed, and said, "Silly me, okay, but if we blow him up, will the fire-breathing part make the explosion something we can't plan for?"

"It depends on what type of fire breathing it is." Edward put his fingers up in quote marks around *fire breathing*.

"Okay, Jake, explain the fire breathing to us?" I asked.

"Have any of you heard the term 'Greek fire'?"

"It's like ancient Greek napalm," Peter said.

I looked at him. "How do you know that?"

He pointed at Edward, who offered him a fist bump, which he took grinning. "It was supposed to be worse than modern napalm, or even the Greek fire that survived into later Greek history."

"So, there are two types of Greek fire?" I asked.

Edward answered, "The first was supposed to be so deadly that nothing could stand against it. It clung to things like modern napalm, or a phosphorus grenade, and like phosphorus, getting it wet made it burn harder, but it was supposed to be worse than anything we have now."

"It was, or I suppose is," Jake said.

"I hadn't thought about one of you being old enough to know the lost recipe for original Greek fire," Edward said.

"History does say the recipe for it was lost, but they also say that the Greek heroes didn't use poison in battle, and neither is true," Jake said.

"What are you saying, or rather, say it more clearly," Jean-Claude said.

"The original Greek fire was not lost; we, the Harlequin, killed all the demigods that could spew it from their bodies. The Greeks had to re-create it from ingredients they could find, because our dark queen declared that beings that could create a substance that burned through armor, flesh, anything it touched and could not be extinguished were too dangerous to vampirekind to be allowed to exist."

"Didn't you say that Mommie Darkest turned him into a vampire? Why would she do that if she wanted him dead?" I asked.

"She thought she would be able to control him and create a living weapon that all vampires and shapeshifters would fear."

"What went wrong?" I asked.

"He was too alien from the rest of us, even from her."

"She couldn't control him," Damian said.

"She could not."

"Can we kill him by blowing him up?" Edward asked.

"And can we blow him up without turning him into pure spirit like what happened to the Mother of All Darkness when she got assassinated? It was so much harder to kill her once she could jump into and out of the vampires and shapeshifters connected to her," I said.

"He never had the ability to leave his body," Jake said.

"That is good to know," I said, "but wait, if he can't take over Jean-Claude's body, then how was he going to possess his power as king?"

"By plugging himself into the vampire marks I have with you, through the marks you share with others, to the blood oaths I have given to every master vampire in America. He does not need to possess my body, only hook himself into my mystical connections like a . . . what is the term for someone who steals power that they do not pay for?"

"You mean like someone piggybacking onto your internet service, or cable, or whatever?" I asked.

"*Oui.*"

"But that's done in secret, you don't want people to find out you're stealing from them. Tonight was the magical equivalent of a frontal assault," I said.

"Deimos has never been subtle," Jake said.

"Then he won't be patient either," I said, "so now answer the question. How do we kill him?"

"Deimos's brother was killed by a large boulder crushing his head, so a bomb should work, but I do not know what will happen to the Greek fire inside him," Jake said.

"If we accept that Deimos can spit Greek fire, then the chemical or whatever he uses internally to create it have to be separate until the moment he uses it, or he would injure himself," Richard said.

I nodded. "True, if we accept that fire breathing of any kind is possible, then the substances the animal uses to create the heat or ignition of the fire would have to be kept very carefully separate in the body until it's time to use it, or they'll burn themselves."

"If the substances have to come together in a specific order and timing, then blowing him up shouldn't activate the Greek fire," Richard said.

"But if it's not just about a specific order and timing, then blowing him up could spread Greek fire over a large area." I looked at

Edward. "Do you have any ballpark on how much of an area could be affected?"

"I'd need to know more than just height for Deimos to make even an educated guess, plus what kind of building he will be in when it happens, there are just too many variables."

"What if he's out in the open?" Richard asked.

"The outside range on a LAW is seven hundred twenty feet; if Greek fire adds to the potential of the explosion, then any of us close to ground zero are dead, or wish we were."

"And if the Greek fire dies when he blows up, instead of adding to it?" I asked.

"Then we should be fine."

"Could the Greek fire set off a wildfire in a wooded area?" Richard asked.

"It burned through wooden ships," Jake said.

"Damn," Richard said.

"Why?" I asked.

"If we could lure something the size of a house into a heavily wooded area it wouldn't be as maneuverable as we are, so we'd have some advantage."

"Until it set the forest on fire around us," Edward said. "I know you think I'm careless with fire, but I have a healthy respect for it as a weapon against the supernatural."

"I didn't say or even think anything about you being careless with fire just now," Richard said.

"Forest or grass fires have a lot more variables to consider: wind direction and speed, dryness, and amount of underbrush. I've only ever used a flamethrower outside against ghouls or zombies in cemeteries with short, well-watered grass, or caught them in the middle of paved areas, or near a water source."

"Don't explosives have some of the same issues?" Richard asked.

"It's still an interesting idea that in dragon form he doesn't fit in small spaces," I said.

"How fast can he change from dragon to human or vice versa?" Truth asked.

"I saw him in both his forms, but never saw him change," Jake said.

"We did," Ru said as he came through the curtains from the hallway beyond. Rodina was at his side. Nathaniel came behind them. I thought Nathaniel had gone to find any Harlequin that knew Deimos, which was smart and helpful, then realized that couldn't be it. There were other Harlequin as old or older than the twins, but they were the only other wereleopards here currently. Why had Nathaniel brought every wereleopard that was in the underground tonight? I'd ask him later in private. Right now, we needed to stay on target, and learning more about dragons topped leopard on the to-do list.

38

RODINA WENT DOWN on her knees in front of me. "My weakness stripped you of our strength when you needed us most. I have failed my duty." It would have been more warrior-falling-on-their-sword if she hadn't been dressed in the button-up top of a pair of silky pajamas. Ru dropped on his knees beside her wearing the long bottoms of the pajamas. It would never have occurred to me that siblings could split pajamas the same way a couple could. It made perfect sense, it just threw me for a second, like a lot of things about them. Of course, maybe me thinking about romantic couples had something to do with how nice Ru looked out of his shirt. I stopped the thought train right there, dead in its tracks, done, because they could hear me.

"It's okay, Rodina, you're allowed to grieve for your brother."

"Grief is for the weak. We are Harlequin, nothing should distract us from serving our dark queen." She seemed so earnest that I didn't have the heart to correct her about calling me their dark queen.

"It was wolves I needed tonight, *mes petits chatons*," Jean-Claude said, coming to stand beside me. He seemed utterly calm now. I wasn't sure if talking about a real plan to kill Deimos had helped him feel better, or if he'd just regained control of himself. I'd ask later.

Rodina looked up at him; her face looked as open and vulnerable as I'd ever seen it. Grief and her supposed failure tonight had left her emotionally raw. I liked her better for the glimpse behind the curtain of her usual grumpy exterior. "We are better than any wolves."

"Of course, you are," he said, but not like he believed it or expected anyone else to either.

She didn't take offense, just seemed more earnest as she looked at me. "We are better than wolves, because we have seen the enemy in person more than once."

"We will tell you what we can of him," Ru said. He didn't look open and vulnerable, he looked worried. He glanced at his sister, and I agreed, she still wasn't okay. Hell, neither of them was okay. They were grieving the loss of their brother, a triplet brother, and I had been so tied up in my own issues with Ireland that I hadn't been able to allow them to grieve. I realized suddenly that I didn't know if that was literally true. As their master, how much did my emotions and issues impact them?

"Stand up and tell us how he shapeshifted," I said.

They stood in unison like it was part of a practiced dance. I'd seen them do it before, but it sort of creeped me out, so they tried not to do it often. "One moment he was a dragon, the next a man," Ru said.

"A human would say a moment and mean that they'd watched one of us split open and change, which is never as quick as they think," Jake said.

"We are not human," Rodina said, and she gave him a look that said how much she hated him. Since he'd been one of the major people behind the plot that had ended with me killing her dark queen, she had reason.

"It is faster than any shapeshifter I have ever seen," Ru said.

"So, no time to kill him as he changes shape?" I asked.

"You seek to use the moment in between when we are trapped by the shifting of our bodies, helpless for just those few minutes," Rodina said.

"That was the idea, I mean it's got to take longer to go from man to dragon size than even a regular shapeshifter."

"One moment he is a dragon, then a man walks out from where the dragon stood," Ru said.

"There's got to be a transition between the two shapes," I said.

"There was none," he said.

"I had hoped since he was only a demigod that he had not inherited the Greek pantheon's ease of shape-changing," Jake said.

"Did you see one of the Greek gods change form?" I asked.

"I did, and if Deimos changes as his father could, then there will be no weakness to exploit there." I felt Richard want to ask details about the Greek gods and what Jake had witnessed, but he resisted. Brownie points to him because I wanted to ask, too.

"His scent is always dragon, even in human form," Ru said.

"It is a unique scent, and I did not smell it in the club tonight," Jake said.

"I thought we'd already decided Deimos wasn't physically in the club," I said.

"We did, but since the three of us may be the only ones who know his scent, I thought I would share that with Ru and Rodina."

"Our dark queen wanted only her most trusted Harlequin to deal with him," Rodina said, and she looked at Jake. "How did you hide your treachery from her, from us?"

"I helped teach you how to spot a lie, what scent to search for, and like all who train warriors that may one day be sent against them, I did not teach you everything I knew, Rodina."

"But she made your master, who made you, how did you hide from her?"

"It makes Anita uncomfortable when we confront the traitors," Ru said.

"She says she wants us happy; well, I want to know how they

deceived our dark queen, perhaps that would bring me some peace that they destroyed our entire way of existence." She sounded almost enraged, each word thick with it.

"We do not have time for such games tonight, Rodina," Jean-Claude said. "I am sorry for your grief, though I do not share it, but we have an enemy here and now, that must come first."

She frowned, rubbed her forehead. "I do not feel myself tonight. I am sorry that I keep failing in my duty."

"Neither of us is ourself tonight," Ru said, putting his arms around her shoulders to hug her from the side.

"Next year you get your birthday off," I said.

"Thank you," Ru said.

Rodina said nothing, just clung to her brother's arm where it crossed the front of her body. Her eyes were closed, and I was betting she was hiding tears. *Enough*, I thought. "Is there anything else the two of you can tell us that will help us defeat Deimos?" I asked.

She clung tighter to her brother, eyes clenched so tight that her forehead wrinkled, like she thought if she could just keep her eyes closed the bad thing wouldn't get her. I'd always pictured Rodina more like me, look the monster in the eye and if all else failed, spit in it. She buried her face in Ru's arm like she was breathing in his scent. I wouldn't have done it with my own brother, but then he wasn't a wereanimal and wouldn't understand how scent and touch were just for comfort, not for sex. I was a little fuzzy on that myself, but I understood that was my human hang-up.

Nicky came up to me and leaned in against my hair to whisper, "She can hear everything you're thinking."

"I'm sorry, Rodina, I don't mean to make you feel worse by what I'm thinking, you know I'm not great at controlling my thoughts sometimes."

"You should be disappointed in me," she said, "I am not serving you as I should." She opened her eyes and let me see a slit of leopard yellow before I felt the warmth of her beast like a faint breeze. If I hadn't been standing this close to her I either wouldn't have felt it or I wouldn't have known who it was in the room. Ru's eyes were leopard yellow, too. God, they had so much control.

"We are Harlequin," she said in a low voice.

"I know you are," I said.

"She did not answer your question, *ma petite*."

"Neither of them did," Nicky said. He moved up beside us.

"They're my Brides, it's impossible for them to hurt me," I said, but I admit that it was hard not to have the teeniest, tiniest bit of doubt when I said it.

Nicky moved me back from them. The Wicked Truth were doing the same for Jean-Claude. Richard moved with him, so it was a twofer. Jake stayed close to the twins.

"We are not twins," Rodina yelled through clenched teeth, "we are triplets! Rodrigo's death does not change that."

"I'm sorry, you're right, but I just thought it, I wouldn't have said it out loud."

"First you destroyed our evil queen, then you took our brother from us. I hate you, Anita Blake," she said.

"We can't hate Anita, we're her Brides," Ru said.

She glared at her brother, and suddenly his arms around her didn't seem just for comfort. He was only a few moves away from a choke hold. I saw the tension as she realized it, and the peace in Ru. It wasn't accidental. This wasn't just their birthday and grieving their lost brother, so what the hell was it?

"Anita didn't screw you like she screwed me," Nicky said.

"Belle Morte and Jean-Claude are the only bloodlines that use sex to create Brides, and yet all the other bloodlines have them," Jake said.

"But Anita is not a vampire, not a real one," Jake said. "We know that fact has changed things in how she uses power and how Jean-Claude's power works. Perhaps Brides are different, as well."

"Wait a minute, how does my being human change Jean-Claude's power? I'm his human servant so I make him more powerful, period."

"You have stolen his power as you stole our queen's," Rodina said. She hadn't tried to get free of Ru. They were still standing somewhere between comfort and danger. I tried very hard not to think beyond that, because I couldn't seem to shield my thoughts from them.

"We're your Brides, we're supposed to know what you're thinking and feeling so we can serve you better," Ru said.

"I don't think Rodina sees it that way right now," I said.

"If you had been the evil queen we sought I would have served you forever," she said, and then she moved her head just enough to look at Jean-Claude. "You are supposed to be king above us all, but you are so afraid that you will become what you fear most that you let her, your human servant, take the burden and the prize that should be yours."

"I have claimed the prize, I am king."

"I do not agree with everything that Rodina said, but the spirit of it, I fear, is true," Jake said.

"What are you talking about?" I asked.

"Yes, Jake, enlighten us," Jean-Claude said. The Wicked Truth had moved him back so that they were between him and everyone.

"You should have more power by now. The blood oaths from the other masters alone should have made you godlike, but though your abilities with seduction and sex have grown exponentially, the other powers that we all expected to come to you have not."

"Did I not just tell you that all I have to offer is sex magic, and that it is useless for defeating Deimos, or any other challenger?"

"You did, and then Anita and her friend began to plan how to kill Deimos in a way that did not require your powers."

"You were one of the loudest voices convincing me to take their oaths, to accumulate the power of all the master vampires in America inside me." Jean-Claude slapped his chest hard enough that it sounded like someone had hit him.

"It never occurred to me that you would not become as the old council members, a god among vampires. Had it ever crossed my mind that you would accumulate so much power and control over the supernatural in this country without the ability to protect yourself and them from any would-be challenger, I would have urged something else."

Jean-Claude said, "If it is not too late we will build an American council and I will share the power among them all; that way if they kill one of us, the others may band together and protect our country from the truly ancient ones who would not be able to cope with modern rule."

There were cries of protest and I joined in with, "When did you decide all this?"

"Tonight, when I realized that perhaps the vampire council existed exactly to keep this from happening. That the death of one vampire is the ruin of all."

"That is not why we had a council," Jake said. "The Mother of All Darkness could never envision herself losing to any challenger. The council was created for love. She would not let the Father of the Day be equal ruler with her, but she cared for him, so she conceded that he would be part of the ruling council. He would be equal among them, or higher, but only she would be highest."

"I knew that the Day Father was once a council member, but I did not know the rest," Jean-Claude said.

"You lie, wolf; our dark queen never cared for the Day Father like that," Rodina said.

"Do not take my word for it, ask the other Harlequin, some of them are far older than me. I only heard about the start of the council from my master, I was not there for it," Jake said.

"Our dark mother and shining father were almost gods themselves before they tore themselves apart fighting each other, but I am no god," Jean-Claude said. "I am not even a demigod like Deimos. Whatever power the Mother of us all had did not pass to me."

"It was supposed to pass to her," Rodina said, pointing at me.

"It was," Jake said.

"I'm good, but godlike I'm not," I said.

"It is not a god we need, but powerful rulership, but you are both deeply conflicted about power. Having it, using it, all of it."

"They fear it will turn them evil," Rodina said, like it was a huge character fault.

"And if they were conflicted, then I was worse," Richard said.

"Yes, Ulfric, you were the most conflicted of all. We did not realize how much your inner conflicts crippled all of you until Nathaniel became the master of Anita's triumvirate with Damian."

"I didn't even know I could be in charge of it. I'm just her leopard to call. I wasn't even psychic when I was human. I still don't understand how I ended up being able to control the power of it," Nathaniel said.

"You weren't conflicted. You didn't crave power, but you wanted the triumvirate between the three of you to work. You had expressed to several people, including Anita, that you missed Damian, felt the pull of him."

"Yes, but I thought Anita had to fix it, she was our master."

"But Anita hates taking freedom of choice away from anyone. She and Nicky are in love with each other, but she still feels guilty for mind-rolling him even to save you all; that is why she didn't roll Rodina and Ru as completely as she did Nicky."

"It creeps her out that I can't say no to her," Nicky said.

"I can say no now," Damian said.

"You can say no to Anita, but can you say no to Nathaniel?" Jake asked.

Damian started to say of course he could, but then he thought about it. "I don't want to say no."

"I didn't realize what was happening until it was too late, because I'm not supposed to be able to do the vampire and magic stuff," Nathaniel said.

"If you had not taken control of Anita's triumvirate with Damian you would have all died in Ireland. It was only your combined strength that allowed Anita to turn Rodrigo and both his siblings into her Brides with her gaze and allowed Anita to raise an army of ghosts to defeat your enemies."

"Are you saying if I'd still been stumbling around afraid to take over my triumvirate and Nathaniel hadn't accidentally stepped up before that . . ." I just stopped, not wanting to say it.

"That is exactly what I am saying, and that is why I fear that even with the fourth mark, Jean-Claude's triumvirate will not be all it could be."

"Because all three of us are conflicted about power and turning into the monster for real," Richard said.

"I fear so."

"Anita has stepped up and accepted more of the power than either of you two, but she's still too afraid of it," Rodina said, pushing at her brother. "Either choke me into submission, kill me, or let me go."

He looked at Jake, and when the werewolf nodded, Ru let his sister go. She pushed him away. "I cannot believe that you want to stay here with their fears and limitations."

"I like having a master who cares what I think and feel. I like that Anita wants us to be happy."

"I was happy! I was happy as instruments of her vengeance and judgment. I want to be able to hurt people again, and neither Jean-Claude, nor Anita, or even our Nimir-Raj will allow it. I had the world to travel and now I am trapped in the middle of America in a city that isn't even half as old as I am. How can you possibly be happy here?"

"I am learning what makes me happy for the very first time, Dina; before this you and Roddy took up all the space and left none for me. I love you, and I loved him, but there was no space for me between you. You were both so strong, it was like I was erased."

"It's your fears in our dreams of Rodrigo," she said. The anger seemed to leave her for a moment.

"Perhaps it is, I hadn't thought of it being me, because I am not important enough to fill our sleep with nightmares."

"You are important to me, brother."

"Brother can be either of us. Tell me that I am important to you, Rodina, just me."

"Of course you are important to me, Ru. We only have each other now."

I tried not to think what I wanted to think, but it was like being told not to think of an elephant, all you can think of is elephants. Big ones, small ones, elephants wearing ballerina tutus, roller skating, until trying not to think it made the thought so loud that I knew everyone connected to me heard it like I was yelling in their heads. Maybe Ru and Rodina should have taken us up on that offer of therapy.

Rodina turned and looked at me. "If Ru is turning himself into Rodrigo every night in our dreams, saying over and over that he is being . . . erased, consumed, then yes, I am willing to see your therapist. If Ru is willing to come with me?" She held her hand out to her brother.

He stared at her hand but made no move to take it. He looked up so he could meet her eyes. "You will go to the therapist and talk about all of it? You said you didn't need therapy, that there was nothing wrong with you."

"If it will help you, Ru, then yes, I will go." She started to lower her hand, looking down at the floor and away from him. He grabbed her hand and she looked up at him with a smile that made me happy to see it. The smile faded a little as she looked at me. "I do not understand why you are happy for us, but I can feel that you are. Perhaps I will ask the therapist to explain it to me."

"They're good about explaining emotional stuff that you don't understand," I said.

Ru came to stand closer to her, their hands still clasped. They were all grown-up, and achingly old, but there was still an echo of two lost children holding hands in the woods when they'd lost their trail of bread crumbs.

"Then help me find my way out, Anita," Ru said.

I frowned and said, "I can shower you with bread crumbs if you give me a minute."

He smiled, then turned to his sister. He kissed her on the cheek, ever so gently. "You know what I want."

"I do," she said.

"But it will impact you as Rodrigo being enchanted in Ireland."

"More." And she frowned as she said it. She started swinging their hands a little between them like an old habit from real childhood come back to haunt or remind.

"You forbade me to ask her for it."

"I did"—she looked at the ground again, swinging their hands idly between them—"but if you are in our dreams as Rodrigo, then you must believe that I would rather have him here than you, or that he is you, or some complicated emotional . . . confusion." She looked up at him suddenly, her face very serious. "I did not mean to make you feel like that. Rodrigo did not mean to make you feel less than we are."

"He thought I was weak and told me often."

She shook his hand in hers harder. "Rodrigo said what he believed, but he loved you, Ru. He loved you dearly, as I do."

He smiled, and I was beginning feel like we were voyeurs at their first therapy session. Like we should all just quietly go take showers and leave them to it.

"Please don't go without me," Ru said.

"Go where without you?" I asked.

"The shower, or the bedroom, I feel how hungry you are for the *ardeur* and I would ask to be your food tonight."

"Um . . . since you can't tell me no, that's a little too close to nonconsensual sex, so no. It's a lovely offer, but I will not take advantage of someone who cannot tell me no."

"Gods and goddesses of the ages, you are so sincere, so earnest, like some holy knight of old who actually meant his vows. You aren't approaching him for sex, Anita, he's approaching you. He wants to have sex with you, he's wanted to since the trip to Florida," Rodina said, rolling her eyes and sounding like every disgusted mean girl you'd ever heard.

"I don't know what to say."

"I can feel your confusion. Somehow you feel responsible for me—sorry, for us—even though our brother did so many terrible things to you and yours."

"I don't blame you for your brother," I said.

"Thank you, but I want a home, Anita. I want to truly belong someplace that is for me, not because Dina or Roddy chose it, but because I want it."

"Sex doesn't make you belong, not on its own," I said.

"Not having sex doesn't make you belong either," he said.

I couldn't argue with his logic, but I really wanted to. Since they could read my thoughts I said it out loud. "I don't know what to say right now, so hold that thought." I turned to the rest of the group and caught Edward at the edge of the crowd. I realized that he hadn't moved in to protect us when all the supernatural bodyguards had been nervous. He'd known somehow that it wouldn't come to that. How was it that one of the few people in the room with no ability to hear anyone's thoughts, or feel anyone else's feelings, was the one person who had read the situation right? He gave me a little smile and then raised his eyebrows at me and just like that he brought me back to myself, to the now. Everything else could wait.

"We need a plan for Deimos before we do anything else," I said.

"He will want to sleep in dragon form," Ru said.

Rodina nodded. "Ru is right, he changes shape, and each shape is real, but he is not as comfortable in human form."

"So, he'll need someplace big enough for him to sleep comfortably in," I said.

"Warehouses," Nicky suggested.

Jean-Claude said, "Does he prefer creature comforts, or will sleeping rough on a warehouse floor be enough for him?"

"Why does that matter?" I asked.

"If he is staying in a warehouse, but cushions and bedding are being delivered to it, that would raise a flag, would it not?"

"Some warehouses sell bedding, or at least store it and ship it out to stores," Nicky said.

"But I am not saying we look for mass purchases of bedding, Nicky. I mean soft pillows, velvet cushions, expensive coverlets in small, personal purchases delivered to warehouses or semiabandoned buildings."

"If you do not want to be found, then you live without luxuries until your mission is over," Rodina said.

"I have known more than one master vampire who was found because they could not live without their comforts," Jean-Claude said.

"He slept on bare floor in a cave back in ancient Greece," Ru said.

"If he has been active in the modern world he will be accustomed to softer care than that," Jean-Claude said.

"If he hasn't changed, then his needs will be minimal," Jake said.

"So, luxuries will not be the way to find him," Jean-Claude said.

"Where has he been for the last few thousand years?" I asked.

"I would like to know that, as well, *ma petite*."

"What difference would that make?" Ru asked.

"Has he learned to read modern Greek, or any other language? Can he read at all?" Jean-Claude asked.

"You want to know if he would have books or other reading material delivered to where he's staying," Edward said.

"*Oui.*"

"Can he see in the dark?" Peter asked. We all looked at him, and suddenly the fourteen-year-old him peeked out from the six-foot-plus twenty-year-old as he fought not to look embarrassed. He ended up glaring at everyone; at fourteen he had looked sullen when he did, at twenty he looked a little menacing. I was strangely proud.

"You're wondering if he would need light to read by," Richard said.

We looked at him, but he kept his attention on Peter, and Richard didn't give a damn if anyone stared at him. "I know he's supposed to be a different sort of dragon, but some of the dragons we have today can see in the dark and they only hunt at night."

"Yes," Richard said, "the prevailing theory is that all the big dragons that were day hunters got killed off by humans."

"And the night hunters spread into that ecological niche, which is why the fossil record has the ones we know today as smaller," Peter said.

Richard nodded. "But seeing in the dark to hunt is different than seeing in the dark to read." He looked around the room. "Leopards see in the dark better than wolves; can you read a book in the dark?"

All the wereleopards in the room looked at each other, and then Rodina said, "We don't read books to each other in leopard form, Ulfric."

"But if you tried to, would you be able to see the print at full dark?"

There was another round of looks, and then Ru said, "I've read a printed book by near full moon, but it was before electricity spoiled the night so it's never truly dark."

"So that's a yes," Peter said.

"Good point, Peter, just because we'd need a lamp to read by doesn't mean that Deimos will."

"He never came out at night much," Ru said.

"He didn't have good night vision," Rodina said.

"How do you know?" I asked.

"We attacked him at night as leopards, because we do have excellent night vision," she said.

"You weren't the Harlequin sent to kill Deimos," Jake said.

"Officially, no."

"Then why would you attack him?"

That look passed over their faces that I'd come to realize was their version of exchanging a look without having to actually do it. It was part of their physical shorthand that they used when they didn't want me to figure something out. It was one of their few tells.

"Tell me why you attacked Deimos at night in wereleopard form?" I asked.

"We were ordered to do it," Rodina said.

"By whom?" I asked.

"We only ever had one master before you," she said.

"Why would the Mother of All Darkness want you to attack Deimos at night in wereleopard form?"

"She wanted to know if he was more vulnerable at night," Rodina said.

"So, you're letting us brainstorm and plan and you know what will work and won't work, already," Richard said.

Ru just shook his head.

"Answer him," I said.

"It doesn't work that way," Ru said.

Nicky said, "Repeat what Richard said, but make it a question."

I did. "We don't know what you're planning so we have no idea if it will work," Rodina said.

"I order you to tell me if you won the fight that night against Deimos."

Rodina said, "No," as Ru said, "Almost."

"You are Anita's Brides; you have to tell her the truth if she asks it. We can't lie to her," Nicky said.

"You are her Bride completely, but she never finished the ritual with us," Ru said, "It's why Rodina can do so many things that make Anita unhappy."

Jake said, "Ask them if they know how to kill Deimos?"

I did, and they both said no.

"Ask them if they know how to defeat him?" Edward suggested.

"Define 'defeat,'" Rodina said. Ru just said maybe.

I was catching on to the game. "Do you know how to defeat Deimos in such a way that he can no longer harm us or challenge us for rule of the vampires in America?"

"Yes," Ru said, and Rodina nodded.

"Why didn't you just lead with that?"

"Because the last time we tried to kill him was when Greece was the leading world power in what is now Europe. We didn't have the technology you do now; if we have to go up against him I'd rather do it from a distance with your LAW or some other device," Rodina said.

"Okay, that makes sense, but tell us how you did it back in the day, and we'll combine that with modern tech and see what we come up with," I said.

"Also, Brides are traditionally sacrificed in battle to save their master, and I'm afraid once you hear what we did you'll do exactly that with Ru and me."

"I'm proof that Anita doesn't do that kind of shit," Nicky said.

"She's in love with you, and we're a source of guilt and remembered trauma for her."

"I won't sacrifice anyone on purpose to take Deimos down," I said.

"She means it, sister."

"I can feel her sincerity vibrating like some kind of devoted puppy." Rodina sounded disgusted.

"If you want Anita to value you more, comments like that aren't the way to go," Nathaniel said.

"And what happened to you down on your knees contrite that you left me when I needed you most?" I asked.

Rodina made a harsh sound deep in her throat like she couldn't decide if she was going to spit on me or scream. "I feel the pull to be your Bride, but you have left us half done like you and Jean-Claude have left everything else."

"*Ma petite*, the sun will rise, and I would like to have a plan before that happens."

"Okay, do we have to worry about Deimos once the sun comes up, or does he die at dawn like most vampires?" I asked.

"He did."

"It was one reason that he would not serve our dark queen," Jake said. "He hadn't expected to lose the ability to move around during daylight."

"Does he burn in sunlight?" I asked.

"We never saw him in burn in sunlight, because he would go to the back of his cave when he felt dawn coming," Ru said.

"Sunlight doesn't help us if he explodes into Greek fire," Edward said.

"Good point," I said. I looked at Rodina and Ru. "Okay, you're up. Tell us how you attacked him back in ye olden days."

"It's not pronounced 'yee,' the *y* sounds like a *th*, like in *the*," Rodina said.

"I was making a joke, but okay, thanks for clearing that up. Now tell us about you going up against Deimos."

"Our dark queen put pieces of herself inside the three of us," Ru said.

"What does that mean?" I asked.

He looked at his sister, and she said, "How do we explain her to you as she was then?"

"She was at the height of her powers then," Jake said. "As frightening as you found her, Anita, it was nothing to what she was then."

I tried to process that; my stomach went tight at the thought of facing her when she'd been even more terrifying. "Well, that's fucking scary."

"You would not have prevailed against her if she had not been diminished by the traitors among us." She glared at Jake.

"Yes, I betrayed her, and I would do it again."

"If I was not bound by Anita's emotions I would kill you where you stand."

"You would try; remember I helped train you."

"I hate you for what you did."

"I understand."

"Enough," Jean-Claude said. "We do not need to understand how the Mother of All Darkness put a piece of herself inside the three of you since no vampire alive today can duplicate it. Just tell us what happened."

"Seven of us were sent to kill him," Ru said.

"I knew of only four, why were three not listed with them?" Jake asked.

"We did many things off the books, as they say," Rodina said.

Jean-Claude said, "No more interruptions, please, Jake; I want at least the beginnings of a plan before dawn."

Jake just nodded, not bothering with any reply. Smart, I'd at least have apologized.

"The four were sent to approach him from the front of his cave, but we came over the hill at his back," Rodina said.

"We were in half-human form," Ru added.

"We could not see the battle, but we heard him make the noise that was always a precursor to him spewing his deadly fire. The four in front were outfitted with hardened leather to drape over them. We know that they hid under them, because Drakon spit fire, then bragged that their puny shelters would not save them from his wrath. We leapt on him while he watched them burn, I to the right, Rodrigo to the left, and Ru at the monster's back."

"Forgive me, but I must ask if the placement was important to the spell?" Jake said.

"It was," Ru said.

Rodina continued, "We needed to surround him as much as safely possible so that his larger form was enveloped in the magic. The four in front threw off the burning leather sheets and scattered, because he thought they had used up their shield against his greatest weapon and that his next spout would destroy them, but our claws scored his flesh from three sides simultaneously and for that night they were her claws, filled with her power and magic. He screamed and whirled toward me as I landed on the ground at his feet. I heard the rumble as his body formed the Greek fire, but I was not there when we heard the click and he spewed the fire. It burned and melted the small trees on that side of the cave mouth, but I was safely behind him with Ru."

"He turned around toward us," Ru said. "If he'd looked to the other side first he might have caught a glimpse of us running into the forest on the other side."

"If he didn't have his fire we could have had him chasing his tail," Rodina said, "but he was too dangerous to play such games with."

"The others were shooting arrows into him, to cover our escape," Ru said.

Rodina added, "If it were possible to fill him full of enough arrows all at once it might kill him, but the number of archers needed to do that when they had to shoot one arrow at a time . . ." She shook her head. "The first archers would hit their mark, but he would use his fire on the rest, those not horribly injured or dead would run, and no one would blame them."

"I can still hear the sound he made just before he breathed fire as we ran through the trees. I thought he would burn us before we could race clear of him," Ru said.

"We would have lost one, or all of us, but one of the other Harlequin must have moved and drawn his attention. If it was done to save us, I wish I knew whose name to praise, but I think it was carelessness, or simple bad luck that turned his attention to them and away from us. It gave us enough time to be out of the range for his fire," Rodina said.

Edward said, "So you could tell us how far away we need to be for safety?"

"Not down to the inch, but yes," she said.

"Sorry, Jean-Claude, but that was important to ask," Edward.

"Questions that help us plan are fine," Jean-Claude said, with no nicknames, no French, just a bare sentence. It almost didn't sound like him, but Edward was my friend, not his, I guess.

"Before we circled around to the planned vantage point we heard the screaming," Ru said.

"When we turned, there was a burning figure on the ground at Drakon's haunches," Rodina said.

"We saw no other movement even with leopard eyes, so we assumed the others were in hiding, or had run, like we had, far enough to be out of range," Ru said.

"He bellowed for us to come out and face him, called us cowards and worse," Rodina said. "I admit to a moment of doubt, and then we saw him shudder from the top of his head, down that snakelike neck, to the heaviness of his body. It made his tail shake among the leaves and small trees with a great, dry sound like some enormous rattlesnake."

I wanted to ask when she'd seen rattlesnakes since they were a New World snake, but I let it go. It was an idle question and wouldn't help us defeat Deimos.

"Then he began to fall," Rodina said, "to shrink until he was human-sized. The magic that our evil queen had put inside us had worked. We started to run toward him, because as long as it lasted he would be unable to become his dragon. We could kill him."

"But you didn't kill him," I said.

"We never got the chance. The three Harlequin who had survived his fire appeared out of the darkness and attacked him. We raced toward them, afraid they would finish him before we could arrive, but we never got close enough to join them. There was a sound like a modern gun, though then we had no idea what it could be. We could not have guessed that it was the shell of the earth itself breaking open."

"An earthquake, are you saying an earthquake saved Deimos?"

"It didn't save him, the earth split open underneath him and the three Harlequin." She shook her head, as if the memory were weighing on her.

Ru said, "We watched our fellow Harlequin try to run to safety, but when the very ground underneath your feet is not to be trusted there is no safety. We watched the first one fall into a great tear in the earth. Deimos didn't run, he reached his arms toward the heavens and was calling out. We could not hear his words. Then the ground collapsed underneath his feet and he fell into darkness."

"We think he was calling for Ares to save him," Rodina said, "but we thought we would never know for certain. I will ask him when we find him."

"How about we just kill him," Edward said.

She gave him one of the most disdainful looks I'd ever seen aimed at him. "If that is all we can do, of course, but if we have the opportunity to question him I want to know where he has been all these long years. How he escaped. How he put together the plan to come here to challenge Jean-Claude. He was not a deep thinker, and no amount of time will change that."

"You think he has an accomplice?" I asked.

"At least one, maybe more."

"You think he's found a human servant?" Jake asked.

"I do not know, but if he is here completely on his own, I would be much surprised."

"Can we ask questions now?" Peter asked.

"If they help us find and destroy our enemy," Jean-Claude said.

"You talked about a noise that Deimos made before he breathed fire, did he make it every time?"

"Yes," she said.

Richard said, "You mentioned a rumble in the body when you

were right beside him, that was his body getting ready to breathe fire."

"We did," she said.

"Did you see anything in his mouth that coincided with the clicking noise?"

"It has been thousands of years since that night, Ulfric."

"I know it's asking a lot for you to remember such small details, but I wouldn't ask you to try if it wasn't important, Rodina."

"What are you hoping we will remember?" Ru asked.

I answered, "We're trying to figure out if we can hit Deimos with modern weapons if the Greek fire will blow all over us and maybe innocent bystanders."

"How does the clicking noise help you decide that?" Ru asked.

"You also mentioned the body rumbling before he breathed fire," Richard said.

"I still don't understand how that will help us decide if modern weapons will be safe against Deimos," Ru said.

"Antitank weapons especially," I said.

"If arrows hurt him but didn't make him leak fire, then how about just modern bullets?" Edward asked.

"Could a sniper take him out from a nice, safe distance?" I asked.

"As long as the head exploding didn't spew Greek fire all over everything near him," Edward said.

I looked at Richard. "What do you think?"

"If Deimos's brother was killed by a boulder smashing his head, then it should work for a sibling who is the same species."

"His brother was not a fire breather," Jake said.

We looked at him. "It would have been good to know that up front," I said.

"That may change his biology so completely that information from the first death doesn't help us," Richard said.

"You are right," he said, "I did not realize how practical your approach would be to the problem of Deimos."

I frowned at him. "You've known me for a few years now, when have I ever not been practical about hunting down and killing monsters? It is one of my jobs."

"Forgive me for not understanding that we would be using science and modern weapons to solve this problem. When dealing with kings and queens among vampires, it usually devolves to vampiric magic."

I shook my head. "No reason to use magic if bullets will work."

"But if we had more information about how he forms the Greek fire internally so that his own body doesn't get damaged by it, then we might know when best to use the guns, or whatever weapon," Richard said.

"Deimos breathes fire, it does not harm him," Rodina said.

"But Greek fire isn't exactly fire, is it?" Peter asked.

"It burns whatever it touches," Rodina said, "that is the definition of fire."

"But it covers things like a thick liquid, right?"

"He's right," Ru said.

"It is still fire," she said.

"What are you trying to get at, Peter?" I asked.

"Does it look like a movie dragon where fire comes out of the mouth like turning on a sink and instead of water it's fire that pours out?"

"I'm not sure," Ru said; he looked at Rodina. "Sister?"

"It doesn't look like a child's fantasy-story dragon if that's what you mean," she said.

I nodded. "I see what you're getting at, Deimos either has to spit the different components of the Greek fire away from his body so it mixes after it leaves his body, or . . ."

"It's more spitting, than breathing out," Ru said.

"Does the fire ever touch him when he's spitting, or breathing out the fire?" I asked.

"It has to touch him," Rodina said.

"What does it matter if it touches as he spews it?" Jake asked.

"If the components of Greek fire are inert inside Deimos's body and only dangerous when they come together just before he spits it out, then I think we can blow him up without triggering the Greek fire," Richard said.

"How about shooting him?" Edward asked.

"We'd have to shoot him fast and a lot to make sure he dies before he can spit out the Greek fire," Peter said.

"He's right," I said.

"What about a head shot?"

"If you can guarantee that it's enough damage to qualify as a beheading, it should do it," I said.

"If he is in human form, then there are those among the Harlequin or among the wererats who could make such a shot, but if he is in dragon form the head is . . ." She seemed to be doing a size comparison in her own head, then spread her hands in front of her like she was measuring a fish she'd caught.

"That's three or four times longer than a human head," Jake said.

"The head size doesn't matter," Edward said, "the brain size does. Most living animals have a smaller brain per body size than humans do, so the target is either the same or slightly smaller. I don't have to take the whole head out, just the brain."

"I'm not as proficient with a long gun as you are, so would you have enough time for a second shot to the base of the skull, or the upper spine, because beheading means the job is done. Shooting the brain is trickier because we won't know exactly where the brain is sitting in the skull," I said.

Edward looked at me, Richard, and then Peter. "If you biologists can help me make an educated guess, then we should be able to take him out from a nice, safe distance."

"I'd rather take his heart, too," I said.

"We'll need the best protective suits we can find if we try carving him up like that," Richard said. He didn't even call me bloodthirsty or a lover of violence or whatever he used to call me, he was just helping me think it through, that was nice.

"In case we hit pockets of toxic or caustic substances when we're trying for his heart," I said.

"Yes."

"Good thinking."

"And if you're wrong and hitting him with a sniper bullet causes him to explode or just spew out Greek fire?" Rodina asked.

"Then we'll be glad we're all far enough away that it doesn't matter," I said.

"So have we abandoned the LAW for sure?" Edward asked.

"I think so, I just don't think we can guarantee that it won't set off some bigger explosion and we're just not sure what real, original Greek fire does," I said.

"Good," he said.

"Because you don't have any with you," I said.

He smiled. "Even a federal marshal can't bring an antitank rocket on board a commercial aircraft."

"Well, if anyone could figure out how to do it, I was betting on you," I said.

He gave a nod like a bow of acknowledgment.

"So now we just have to find him, right?" Peter asked.

I nodded, and everyone else agreed.

"We can begin with searching for warehouses that have been rented recently," Jake said.

"We have no way of knowing how long he's been in town," Rodina said. "He could have been scouting for weeks, or months."

"He had to be here long enough to know that Jean-Claude was at his most vulnerable at Guilty Pleasures tonight," Wicked said.

"I opened my power up to capture the audience, I did not think that it opened me up to being magically challenged," Jean-Claude said. I felt the sorrow in his voice; the loss of performing would cost him, because he loved it so much.

"We will find a way that you can perform onstage again," I said.

"Perhaps the other master vampires are correct, and it is beneath my dignity, and our safety."

I put my hand on his thigh, feeling the solidness of it underneath the silky robe. I felt his anxiety ease a little just from that. "They're old fuddy-duddies who wouldn't know a modern idea if it bit them on the ass."

He smiled. "Fuddy-duddies?"

"Yes, damn it," I said, and laughed. "They've lived so long apart from the rest of the world that they don't know what's possible."

Richard wrapped his arm more tightly across Jean-Claude's shoulders. "You love being onstage, you shouldn't have to give that up."

"Until Deimos is found and dealt with, perhaps leave the stage to others," Jake said.

"Of course," Jean-Claude said.

"That goes without saying," I said, "we can't give him any more openings into Jean-Claude's power like that."

"And that brings us to you giving your human servant and your *moitié bête* the fourth mark before dawn," Jake said.

"You're pushy, you know that?" I said.

"Only when everything I have worked toward for thousands of years is at stake."

"Touché, Jake, a fine hit that," Jean-Claude said. He got to his feet in one of those smooth movements that was all grace and centuries of practice. He turned and held his hands out to Richard and me. "Come, *ma petite, mon lupe,* we cannot leave it undone, for our enemy will use it as a breach in our castle walls."

Richard took the offered hand and let the vampire help him to his feet. I stared at the offered hand, then raised my gaze up to the two men. It was still Jean-Claude, but Richard was smiling beside him, smiling like he knew I'd take the hand, like . . . like we were all starting over, and . . . panic, I started to panic. I didn't try and shield it. Richard's smile slipped. He said, "I'm sorry, I don't know what else I can say."

"*Ma petite*, we are shoring up our defenses tonight, and I would like Richard to sleep on the other side of me in the bed tonight, but that is all until we have time to adjust to the changes."

I turned to Nathaniel beside me on the couch and stared into his amazing lavender eyes. I felt calmer. Damian leaned over him to take my hand, and I felt icy calm like the world was solid and always would be.

"Wow," I said, "you're good." I stared into his green eyes and felt that pull that vampires have like I could fall forward and be safe and steady forever. It was so tempting in that moment.

"*Ma petite.*"

I leaned toward Damian, but then Nathaniel was in the way. Once I couldn't see Damian's eyes, his hand in mine wasn't enough to make me lean into it. Damian said, "I'm sorry, that was wrong."

Nathaniel put his arm around me and put his hand over our clasped hands. "Nothing is going to change except that we add another person to our poly group."

"How can you say that?" Damian asked. "Jean-Claude and Anita both loved him once. He is the missing piece to their triumvirate. I know how much our triumvirate has meant to me, how much I love you both, and that is all from the vampire marks that bind us together. I am still not attracted to any man but you, and all other women seem frivolous and too soft compared to Anita. I am never happier than when the three of us are together. My favorite nights at work are those when Anita comes to partner me for the dances, or you come to teach modern dances to me and the customers."

"You are so good at learning the dances, so sexy," Nathaniel said, smiling and leaning toward the green-eyed vampire. Damian leaned in toward him and their lips met, soft and tender. It filled me up with that happy warmth of knowing they were mine and I was theirs. Nathaniel pulled back from the kiss, and I moved in to take his place, so that Damian startled, eyes flickering open, and then he leaned into the kiss and so did I.

I kissed him long and deep, sliding my tongue between the hard tips of his fangs as he opened his mouth wider for me. Our free arms wrapped around each other, and Nathaniel's arms held us tighter, so we drew back from the kiss to turn to him. I found his mouth, and Damian found his neck.

Jean-Claude yelled, "Enough!" and thrust his power at us. There was a moment of confusion as I wasn't sure where I was, or who, or even when Nathaniel whispered through us, *Enough*. I wrapped myself around Nathaniel, a leg over his thigh; part of me knew I might be flashing the room, but it didn't bother me enough to shift position. Damian was wrapped on his other side, though he was too tall to have his head on Nathaniel's shoulder like I did. I looked up at Jean-Claude standing over us and could feel how upset he was, but it slipped away on Nathaniel's pleasure and Damian's centuries-old control, though he'd given that up to Nathaniel in that moment. I realized that part of Nathaniel's strength was that he used the icy control that Damian had built for centuries but was afraid to use now. Nathaniel wasn't afraid of using anything in that moment.

"Are you challenging me?" Jean-Claude asked, and his voice was more astonished than angry. Richard was at his side, but his face said clearly that he didn't know what to do in this moment; he was out of his depth already.

"No," Nathaniel said, and his voice was so certain, there were none of the near-overwhelming sensations that Damian and I were experiencing.

"Then what is this?"

"This is the fourth mark when one of the people isn't afraid of the power. If I weren't already engaged to marry Micah, if the three of us weren't already a happy threesome, this could be it. If I were less moral, I could overwhelm them both."

"It looks like you already have," Richard said.

"I let it get out of control to show the two of you what it's like. I didn't understand what had happened when I first got control of Anita's triumvirate. The animal to call isn't supposed to be able to do this shit. Once I realized what I'd done, I did my best to learn control and not take over Damian especially." The vampire kissed his cheek, but Nathaniel ignored it and kept talking as if it hadn't happened. "Anita has you, and her own power as my master, so I probably couldn't overwhelm her completely, and even now I'm not sure what I did to Damian before I realized that it was me doing it."

"Richard has come back to me as a lover on his own," Jean-Claude said.

"That's good, because if he hadn't and you were in control of the three of you, he would have given it up to you. By the time I realized that Damian's consent for a lot of things wasn't voluntary, it was too late."

"But it feels so good," Damian murmured against his face. I was beginning to come out of it, and had moved my one leg off his thigh, but I still wanted to be wrapped to his side with Damian on the other.

"It feels good not to fight or worry or push at it, but just to let go," I said.

Nathaniel kissed the top of my head, then turned to rub his face against Damian's cheek. The vampire turned it into a kiss and Nathaniel had to flex power like the sharp tug on a leash. "Not yet, handsome," he said, and the vampire moved back so that he could talk to them again. I was sitting up a little straighter because I hadn't liked that tug-on-the-leash feeling.

"Who is going to be in charge of your triumvirate, Jean-Claude?" Nathaniel asked.

"Jean-Claude will be in charge of it," Jake said.

"Will he? Will you?" Nathaniel asked, looking from him and back to the raven-haired vampire standing over us.

"They don't want to be evil, and they all see controlling the others as evil," Rodina said.

Nathaniel glanced at her and nodded.

I sat up a little straighter, pushing so that I wasn't glued to his side. "If I can't be in charge of the three of us, I'm not going to work with Jean-Claude any better. I'm so conflicted about Richard showing up like this after so long."

"But don't you remember that Richard had his own version of the *ardeur* briefly in the hotel room in Asheville?" Nathaniel asked.

I nodded. "He wanted me to be in love with just him, monogamous with just him, and if I hadn't had Jason to do an emergency metaphysical shout-out, Richard might have succeeded."

"I didn't know that's what I was doing, Anita."

"Just like I didn't know," Nathaniel said.

"It's never happened again, not with anyone," Richard said.

"But if Jean-Claude gives you both the fourth mark and he's too conflicted to take charge and so is Anita, wouldn't it be tempting to roll them both? I think it would have to be both, I don't think you could do just one, but you might be able to roll them so that it was just the three of you again. You might be able to erase everyone else they love but the three of you."

"I am more powerful than Damian, by far," I said.

"You are, but you also have a near phobia of forcing yourself on anyone unless safety and lives are at stake."

"And might I be tempted to roll over both Richard and Anita and make them mine in a way that *ma petite* is never quite mine." Jean-Claude nodded, thinking it over, as I fought to escape whatever Nathaniel had done to me.

"I can tell you it's fucking tempting to make yourself the adored one," Nathaniel said.

"I already adored you," I said as I moved a little away from him on the couch, hoping that would help me clear my head.

"Lucky for me, because if I'd made you love me when you didn't, you'd have probably killed me to be free of it."

I wanted to argue, because I loved Nathaniel and had for years, but I thought of all the vampires that had tried to control me over the years, and . . . "If you'd been just someone I knew and had no place in my life, yeah, I would have risked death for all of us rather than stay enslaved."

"And if I wasn't a nicer person, a better person, it could be enslavement," Nathaniel said, and he looked up at them.

"Master vampires are not nice, or the better person," Rodina said.

"We try to be," Jean-Claude said.

"Anita is still too conflicted to be in charge; that leaves you or Richard, and you don't want it to be the Ulfric."

"You don't trust me to do what's best for everyone?" Richard asked.

"I'm happy for your personal growth, and embracing that you're bisexual for Jean-Claude is a big deal. Congratulations, but breakthroughs aren't permanent unless you keep doing the work. The fourth mark could give you so much of what you've wanted for so long, it's going to be tempting, like apple-in-the-Garden-of-Eden-level temptation," Nathaniel said.

"I don't want to take people over, and especially not Anita when I can feel that she's not in love with me anymore, in fact she's pissed at me. If she wakes up tomorrow thinking I'm great, then I'll know I'm to blame."

"Maybe not, Jean-Claude's life would be a lot easier if you and she were in love again."

"I would never betray us all, and it would be a betrayal," Jean-Claude said.

I scooted farther toward the end of the couch away from all of them, but mainly Nathaniel. "Don't ever roll me like that again."

"I shouldn't be able to roll you at all," he said.

"I don't care, just don't."

"Even when we have date night with Damian?"

I closed my eyes and took a deep breath and let it out while I counted slowly, but I had to breathe again, before I counted enough to not be pissed. "Damn it, Nathaniel, I love you, but this is pushing it."

"Our triumvirate works because I'm in charge of it; I'm careful, but I make it work so that all three of us are happy with it."

"Nathaniel embracing the power saved your lives in Ireland," Jake said.

"But it was my necromancy that let us raise an army of ghosts," I said.

"But it was Nathaniel who bridged the gap between your power and the battery of energy that he and Damian offered you."

I sat there for a few seconds, sighed, then said, "No, I don't want you to stop making the triumvirate work with Damian. Part of me hates saying that, but I may never be ready to take charge of it, and I know Damian won't be."

"Good, and thank you. I'm sorry this scared you, but I had to make sure Jean-Claude and Richard understood what could go wrong with the fourth mark."

"Thank you, *mon minet*, though perhaps I should stop calling you my kitten, for it seems you have become a very grown-up cat."

"I love it when you call me your kitten, you know that. I don't want to be one of the big cats, I'm happy being a little one."

"With the power you have over Anita and Damian, you could be a major player," Nicky said.

"I don't want to be a major player; I just want the people I love to be happy and safe."

"If you wanted to make me refuse to do the fourth mark tonight with them, then you succeeded," I said.

"No, Anita, the point is you have to do it." He turned toward me with Damian draping his arms across his shoulders, still drunk on power. "And you have to do it now, before sunrise, because you cannot leave Jean-Claude that vulnerable."

I shook my head.

"I love you, so much, but if you don't do the fourth mark then it's like having a house with an alarm system but you leave the door wide open. All the metaphysical power in the world won't save us if Deimos or some other vampire gets in through that open door."

"We would have gone happy to do the fourth mark if you hadn't done this," Richard said.

"Anita wouldn't have."

I looked down, not wanting to meet anyone's gaze, but my emotions were so raw it didn't really matter. I looked up into Richard's handsome face, but I was strangely alone in my head, and I did not want him. Pretty was as pretty does, and we'd hurt each other too much, too often. I was happy now; my life worked, damn it, and it had never really worked with Richard.

"The fourth mark won't work if she's still fighting it," Nathaniel said.

I looked at him. "You think I'd have said no at the last minute."

"I'm sorry, but yes."

I rolled that around in my head, and couldn't argue with it. "Damn it."

"Dawn is coming, *ma petite*, what would you have of me, of us?"

I looked up at one of the loves of my life, my fiancé, and didn't have a good answer. I looked at Richard standing solemnly at his side, because he didn't know what to do anymore either. *Jesus, Nathaniel, did you have to do it this way?*

"If I could have done it differently in time for you to still do the fourth mark tonight before dawn I would have, but you're a rip-the-bandage-off type of person, you always have been, nothing else works with you."

I nodded because he was absolutely right on that. I took another deep breath, stood up, and reached my hand out to Jean-Claude, and the other a little slower to Richard. Jean-Claude took my hand immediately with a relieved smile; Richard hesitated, then took the other one. That rush of power as we all touched each other felt like it should blow my hair back from my face.

"Let's do this."

"Are you sure, *ma petite*?"

"That it's a good idea, no; that we can't leave the door open for Deimos to walk through tomorrow night, absolutely fucking yes." I led them toward the far curtains. Ethan and Nicky got ahead to open them for the three of us to go through. Truth, Wicked, Rodina, Ru, and Jake fell into step behind us. They came to protect us in case there were more enemies hidden somewhere, but there was no one in the underground of the Circus for them to fight. There was just the three of us, the two men that I'd loved first, longest, hated, feared, too many emotions to list. Jean-Claude's hand was cool in mine, as if even the blood he'd taken from Richard earlier had gone to defend us. The fourth mark required him to take blood, so that was fine. Richard's hand was warm in mine, and he was still gorgeous, and he'd really tried tonight in that beyond-perfect-apology sort of way, but it still felt wrong to be about to get in the shower and bind ourselves even deeper to him. One night of good behavior didn't fix years of bad. I believed he had changed, but such drastic changes weren't usually sustainable over time. People gradually reverted back to their "normal." I had to fight against myself not to revert back to the patterns that left me isolated and miserable. I understood how hard it was to fight the good fight, when old habits, comfortable habits, whispered sweet nothings and tried to destroy your happiness all over again. Could Richard sustain it? Was he strong enough to live his truth outside the Circus, or had he come back only partway? Would he stay closeted both as human and as straight, and would that be enough for Jean-Claude?

"*Ma petite*, we can hear you."

"Shit," I said.

"I understand your doubts, Anita," Richard said. "You've earned them, or I've given them to you. I've already informed the head of my department that I'm a werewolf."

I stumbled, because I tried to stop but Jean-Claude kept leading us onward. "*Ma petite*, questions can be answered as we move toward the showers."

I kept walking while I said, "What did the head of your department say?"

"He was surprised, but so far I've still got a job. I have my doctorate now, so if I get fired I'm more employable somewhere else. I told him how American citizens are signing themselves into government safe houses with promises of being let out once they have control of their Therianthropy, but because they're never taught any control they never get out, and people have signed their children in without realizing they'd never see them again."

"If he's head of your department I'm assuming he's a biologist and a teacher; how could he not know all this?"

"He believed the government lies that they let out shapeshifters once they can control their beasts. He did know about the children signed in by parents and then they disappear. That's been all over the news since the school here has been so successful. I told him I wanted to help more with kids in other states both as a teacher and to show them that they can have a good life, that testing hot for Therianthropy wasn't the end for them. He understood that, even agreed with it."

"You helped us come up with some of the plans for the school here in Missouri," a woman's voice said from farther down the hallway. I turned to find Angel stalking down the hallway dressed in a red nightie that just emphasized all her luscious curves. She was one of the few shapeshifters I knew who preferred to sleep in nightclothes—the fact that her choices ran very high to lingerie was just a bonus.

With her hair finally gone back to its natural pale blond she looked more like a 1950s sex symbol than the next victim in a 1970s vampire movie.

"You look good enough to eat," I said.

"Delectable," Jean-Claude said.

"I was going to say something polite and businessy, but I can't remember what it was now," Richard said.

Angel gave us the smile that went with the outfit. She liked attention paid to her when she was dressed in her daytime rockabilly Goth, or lingerie like now. If she was wearing business attire as a social worker she dressed so conservatively that it was like she was in hiding. "Congratulations on your doctorate, Richard."

He looked startled, as if he hadn't expected her to talk to him first. "Um, thank you."

"You hadn't gotten it the last time we spoke," she added, and though her smile and body language said *sexy as hell*, her voice could have been in a business meeting. She did that at will, and seemingly without effort, so she could be doing God knew what on the other end of the phone, but you'd never know it by her voice.

"No, I hadn't."

"I don't blame you for waiting to come out until you got it," she said, one hand on her hip. "It was hard enough to get my master's in social work. I wouldn't have wanted to get kicked out of the program just before I finally got a doctorate."

"That's one reason I waited," he said, "but 'Doctor' in front of your name impresses people, even if it's not medical. I think if more of us who are professional come out as shapeshifters it will help people realize that we can live normal lives, good lives."

We'd stopped moving as we got closer to her, and Jean-Claude said, "Let us greet our delectable Angel and then we must move with purpose to shower and finish the fourth mark before I am lost for the day."

I let go of their hands to move toward her, but the moment I let go it was like all the stress and strain of the night caught up with me and all I wanted to do was sleep. I reached back for them, and they were already reaching for me. "What was that?" I asked.

"It is as if our enemy knows that we are about to close the door he used to enter us," Jean-Claude said.

"You mean he's trying to drain us now? How is he getting through to here?" I asked.

"I do not know, *ma petite*."

"Then kiss us quick and do the fourth mark," Angel said.

It took me a second to parse the *us* and then I felt Mephistophe-les, my Devil, Dev, before I heard his voice say, "I was going to be sexy or pouty about you bringing another man into our bed without talking to me first, but I felt that drain on your power." Then I saw all blond, golden-tanned, six-foot-three of him coming down the hallway toward us. The only thing that marred the usual view was a pair of silky brown jammie shorts that clung to his groin so that I wasn't sure it actually hid anything, so much as emphasized it like good lingerie is supposed to. It made me wonder if he'd had a date with Asher interrupted, since the vampire had a thing for brown silks and satins. His thought in my head was no, they were just the only pajamas he owned. He said out loud, "You must finish the marks tonight, as much as I hate it." That model-perfect face was as serious and unhappy as I'd seen it in a while. It almost didn't sound like him.

I looked at Angel for an explanation, because she wasn't just an-other gold tiger, she was his sister. She gave me a look like I should have known exactly what was wrong; since we'd started dating I had had that look aimed at me more than once, but like all people who date beautiful women I had no clue what it meant most of the time.

I tried to read his thoughts again, but he thought loudly and clearly, "Please don't push, I'm shielding for a reason." I backed off, because that was our agreement with anyone we were psychically tied to; reading minds, like touching bodies, was by consent only.

Sometimes strong emotions or thoughts would leak by accident like hearing a fight in another room, but short of that, consent was everything.

Angel rolled her eyes at me but came closer for a kiss. "Keep touching the men, I'll do all the work," she said with a smile that was flirtatious, with that touch of evil in the corner of her lips where she could quirk the smile up and show a small dimple like a period at the end of some sexy comment, except this comment curved with her full lower lip. Without the lipstick she normally wore her upper lip looked thinner, but her bottom lip was lush with or without lipstick.

I tightened my handholds on Jean-Claude and Richard as I moved toward Angel. She leaned down to meet me; her hands caressed my cheeks until she cupped my face between her hands. She kissed me softly but thoroughly, until my eyes closed, and I leaned into her. She wrapped herself around me and I tried to free my arms to hold her, but Jean-Claude and Richard held my hands tighter, which was just enough bondage to make me kiss her harder with tongue and teeth, pressing my body against hers. She returned the favor, and we must have gotten a little vigorous, because the men's hands tightened around mine, so that I pulled against them not because I wanted them to let go, but because I couldn't not struggle at least a little. It fed into the kiss, until when Angel pulled away she was breathless and so was I.

She was half laughing as she said, "If we had time I'd make you suck my breasts."

I laughed back, still pulling at the men's arms, but in that moment my attention was all for the woman in front of me. "You don't have to make me do it."

"I want to be the wicked lesbian forcing the straight girl to experiment while the men hold you down so they can watch."

"No, our tigress, you know that watching alone does not please me," Jean-Claude said.

She grinned at him, mouth wide enough to show teeth, her eyes sparkling and eager. "Watch until it's time for you to join us, maybe."

"Much better, my tigress."

"Wouldn't that make you the wicked bisexual?" I asked.

"True, but in porn the fantasy is always the lesbian gets carried away and one good fuck makes her at least bi. It's not true, but for building fantasies it works," she said.

"You do enjoy role-play," I said.

"I do," she said, looking very pleased with herself.

I felt Richard's thoughts scramble as he tried to decide what to ask, or if he should say anything. Was he allowed, was he invited, was he just supposed to shut up and let it play out? How did he get consent without seeming pushy? How would I feel about it? How would Jean-Claude? He'd been so controlled, but now his emotions opened him up. I didn't blame him on this one.

I looked back over my shoulder and found that his face showed almost nothing of his confusion; good for him, it would have shown on my face. "It's okay, Richard," I said, then looked back to Angel. "Richard doesn't want to take anything for granted, but he's wondering if he's included in this scenario?"

She looked at him, up and down like she was considering every inch that she could see, and some she couldn't. She met my eyes with a very serious face. "You know my taste in men, what do you think?"

"I think you'll like each other, and this scenario will work for all of us."

She smiled and it filled her eyes with that joyous mischief that she had so often when she wasn't working. "Then yes, he's invited."

I heard Richard swallow behind me, either clearing his throat or just figuring out what to say. He settled for "Thank you, I look forward to accepting the invitation another night."

"You're welcome," she said, and winked at me before she sashayed to Jean-Claude. "Your turn."

"Let me officially introduce you to our third," he said, and I would have watched Angel and Richard meet, but Dev was in front of me, handsome face so serious.

"Is it my turn?" he asked. The need in his eyes was raw, but it wasn't lust, it was something more complicated than that. "Don't try and read me right now, Anita, please."

"Okay, then kiss me, you handsome devil."

He smiled and leaned down to put his lips against mine.

39

DEV KISSED ME gently, his fingers tracing my bare shoulder in delicate, skin-tingling lines while his other hand cupped the side of my face until his fingers slid into my thick curls. He let out a sigh of contentment against my lips and as if that had been a key to the door; my mouth opened to him in invitation and he stepped gently through, teasing and exploring with his tongue, instead of the forced thrust he could have had. I was open to either, but a part of me relaxed into his kiss and into his hands as they caressed across my bare back until the dress's rough beads got in the way and I wished it gone so I could feel his hands all over my bare skin.

He knew what I wanted, because without pausing the kiss, his hands slid to the hem of my dress and pulled it up and over my right arm, but he couldn't finish without breaking the kiss or moving Jean-Claude's hand from mine. Then I realized that Richard wasn't touching me but the energy hadn't gone down, and nothing was trying to intrude on our energy. I was so startled that I pulled back from the kiss and the energy fell like a bird whose wings had been clipped.

Dev touched my face and our energy soared again. Richard grabbed my arm but the energy had already stabilized. Dev stared down at me, his eyes a little wide. I realized that I was standing naked in the hallway with the dress bunched on the one arm that Jean-Claude was still holding, in my work boots. I had totally forgotten that there were people in the hallway who weren't my lovers, or hell, that there were people in the hallway besides the five of us.

"What just happened?" Richard asked.

"Let go of *ma petite*, for a moment."

"Which one?" I asked.

"Richard," Jean-Claude said.

"You want me to let go of her?"

"*Oui.*"

"But . . ."

"*Mon lupe*, the night will fade, please do not make me ask twice."

Richard looked from him to me. He widened his eyes and I knew the look meant was I okay with this. Not from our metaphysical connection, but because once upon a time I'd memorized most of his expressions, because we were in love and I'd thought he was the one.

I nodded.

He let go of my arm, and the energy just kept humming without him; interesting. I glanced over and realized that Angel and Jean-Claude were holding hands. "Did I miss you kissing each other?"

"*Non, ma petite*, the moment you touched our Devil the energy drew both Angel and me to pay attention to it."

"Can you sense her golden tiger as you sensed lion earlier?" Jake asked.

"I can."

"Let go and see what happens," I said; Jean-Claude knew what I meant and simply dropped my hand. My energy stayed the same, but his didn't. His legs buckled and Angel and Richard had to catch him to keep him standing. He reached his hand for me, and I took it. He stood and blinked at me.

"I do not understand," he said.

"Anita has the fourth mark with Mephistopheles," Jake said.

"Dev is a werelion and a weretiger, maybe you need both," Nicky said.

"Come to me, my Devil, let us embrace."

Dev kept one hand in mine but went to Jean-Claude. Angel moved so that Dev could wrap an arm around the vampire. Jean-Claude leaned his face toward him. "Richard, let go, please."

Richard hesitated, but then stepped back so it was just the two of us with Dev. The energy did not fall. Jean-Claude asked the tall weretiger to kiss him. He leaned in and the moment of the kiss the power washed around us, playing in our hair. Dev was my gold tiger so it should have been my power, but it was Jean-Claude's.

"Is it lion or tiger that calls to you, my king?" Jake asked.

Jean-Claude pulled back and said, "Gold, it is gold tiger."

"I've given him the fourth mark, how is there any room for Jean-Claude?" I asked.

"You are not a vampire," Jake said.

"It is as if Mephistopheles is waiting for me to finish . . . it," Jean-Claude said, but not like he was sure.

"Nothing personal, but if we only have time to finish one fourth mark tonight, it's me, us," Richard said.

Dev looked at him and growled. I'd gotten used to hearing animal sounds coming out of human throats, but Dev was one of the least likely to fight for dominance. He was very much go along to get along, but I guess everyone has their line in the sand.

"There is a way to finish both marks before dawn," Jake said.

Jean-Claude shook his head. "We cannot use the *ardeur* to speed things up, Jake. I must be in control, and using the *ardeur* will strip me of that, along with *ma petite* and Richard."

"The fourth mark doesn't have to be sex," Jake said.

"For Belle's bloodline it must be."

"But you are your own bloodline now, Jean-Claude, you do not have to do things as your old mistress taught you."

"I . . . I do not know how to do it without. Belle said that a sexual exchange was the fourth mark because blood was done at the third mark."

"It doesn't even have to be blood, you only need to exchange body fluid while the master vampire says the words; if the words were not needed, a kiss and an exchange of saliva would be enough," Jake said.

"When I marked Damian and Nathaniel it was sex and blood, because it's hard to take blood from two people at once."

"True, it is traditionally done one at a time, either beast or servant first," Jake said.

I remembered a vampire who had done the fourth mark with me, it hadn't been sexual at all. I'd killed that vampire knowing I'd probably die with him rather than letting him control me forever. Now here I was volunteering for it, but I was in love with this vampire. The other one years ago had taken by force what I was offering freely. Sex and magic is like that; force and free will make all the difference. "It won't be as fun sharing just blood, but if Jean-Claude cuts himself twice, then Richard and I can both take his blood into us while he says the words over us."

Jean-Claude looked up at the ceiling, but I knew he was looking further than that, he was sensing all the way up to the sky. Night was losing its strength. Whatever we were going to do, we needed to do it now.

Dev looked from one to the other of us. "We're all out of time for anything but a quickie."

"I just got back to them, I won't give up my place to you, or anyone else," Richard said.

"Then you shall be first," Jean-Claude said.

Dev growled again, but Jean-Claude turned to Dev and put a gentle kiss on the side of his cheek. "I will mark you this night, my Devil, have no fear that I will leave such bounty untouched."

Angel pulled his arm and drew him away from Jean-Claude so

that Richard and I were left standing with him. I heard her murmur "You're next."

He said, "I'm tired of being everyone's second and no one's first."

I might have gotten distracted, but Jean-Claude let go of me to spill the dress down my arm. I would have rather gotten dressed again, but dawn was trembling close. Modesty could wait—they were all shapeshifters and nudity didn't mean to them what it meant in human society. Jean-Claude took us to the wall so he could sit down. "You will have to kneel or lie on the floor to reach the traditional cuts. I would have done this in our bed in comfort if there were more time."

"I thought you didn't know where the traditional cuts for the fourth mark were supposed to be," Rodina said.

"I have seen other bloodlines do it; I still do not know if it will work for us, but there is no time. I need a blade."

"I don't have one on me for once," I said.

"We can see you are unarmed," Rodina said, and made it disdainful. I ignored her, because arguing with her would take too much precious time.

Ethan drew the Emerson folding blade from his pocket, the quick release hooking on the edge of the cloth like it was supposed to, so that it was straight and locked in place when he offered it handle first to Jean-Claude. I'd given him the knife one of the first Christmases he'd been with us because he'd admired the one I had. I vowed to not be the one without a blade next time.

Jean-Claude settled his back against the wall, then took the offered knife. He set the tip near the burn scar on his chest where some human long ago had tried their best to save their life and failed. Once I'd been in sympathy with them; now I was just glad he hadn't died centuries before I could have met him. "Does it have to be on the left side?" he asked, looking past us kneeling to Jake.

"No, anywhere on the chest, or even the wrist."

Jean-Claude moved the knife higher on his chest to leave the burn scar untouched. He drew the tip of the blade high on his left pectoral, leaving a thin red line behind on his pale, white skin. He raised the knife, then moved to the right side and mirrored the cut. The left side had started to bleed down his chest by the time he was finished with the right. He handed the bloody knife back to Ethan with a thank-you. Ethan wiped it clean on the side of his pants, then put it back in his pocket. "It's my honor to serve."

"Come, my loves, take of my blood while I say the words over us," Jean-Claude said, reaching his arms out to us.

I hesitated for a second, watching the bright blood flow down his chest; I wasn't really a fan of drinking blood unless one of the supernatural hungers had gotten triggered. "I will not force this upon you, *ma petite*, it must be willing or not at all."

"I'm willing," Richard said, and moved forward, lowering himself over the wound on his side. I couldn't let him be braver than I was about something we'd both fought against for years, so I put my hand against Jean-Claude's stomach to steady myself, then licked the wound.

Jean-Claude made a small pleasure sound and I realized that Richard was licking the wound on his side, too. I glanced at Richard—we were so close that our hair had intermingled, black curls to brown waves. He leaned slightly to me and I met his lips for a kiss, sharing the blood between us, and got a hint of his eagerness and how differently a werewolf looked at blood than I did. It helped me turn back to the wound on Jean-Claude's chest, eager to latch my mouth over the wound and suck, sweet copper pennies on my tongue.

Jean-Claude stroked our hair and said the words. "Blood of my blood," and the air tightened around us, thick with power; "flesh of my flesh," and magic danced down our bodies; "the three shall be as one," and it was almost too much, as if someone was trailing electricity down us with a violet wand set a little high so that I wasn't sure if it felt wonderful or hurt. He put his hands in our hair and pulled

us back from his chest. "Breath," he said, kissing me, "to breath," he
said, kissing Richard. He cuddled us in his arms, our heads on his
chest, and said, "My heart to yours."

The power ruffled around us, playing in our hair, tugging at
Richard's shirt and Jean-Claude's robe. It rose around us and moved
through the hallway like invisible hands stirring anything that
would move on anyone. "There will be other nights for sex, but only
one night for this, my loves, a triumvirate in truth at last."

40

WE WERE STILL basking in the afterglow of the magic. Dev knelt beside me. "Just being near it feels amazing."

Richard pushed himself to sit up taller and kissed Jean-Claude lightly, then moved to sit farther down the wall. He motioned wordlessly for Dev to take his place. I understood why he was being so generous; the power was . . . complete. A key had been turned inside the three of us, nothing could unlock us short of death. It made the vows at a wedding seem like whistling in the dark. This was truly until death do us part. We could be generous because nothing could part us; I wasn't even upset at thinking it about Richard, because it wasn't about Richard. It was about Richard and Jean-Claude, and that was perfect.

Dev kissed Jean-Claude, licking the blood off his mouth. "Make me yours, Jean-Claude."

I pushed away enough to start to ask, but Jean-Claude read my thought and answered, "I do not know if I need to say the words again with you and our Devil, or only over him. You are the only human servant to ever have their own animal to call, so there are no certainties."

"Excuse me, and I apologize ahead of time, just know it's not our idea." It was Custer and one of the newer werehyenas walking toward us. Custer's dark brown hair had grown out enough that he had curls, and they were sleep tousled liked he'd just thrown on his T-shirt and pants and hadn't looked in a mirror. The second man, whose name I couldn't remember—it was something short and began with a *J*, or was it a *G*?—whatever his name was, he'd just put on pants and hadn't bothered with the shirt.

"We're busy, Custer," I said.

"Dev doesn't smell enough of you or Jean-Claude; tell me we got here before Jean-Claude made gold tiger his next animal to call."

"It is none of your business what I do, or with whom," Jean-Claude said.

Custer ran his hands through his hair and looked even less happy. "You're right, it's not, but when the Oba of your werehyena clan calls you up and tells you to move your ass, you move."

"This is not Narcissus's business either," Jean-Claude said.

"Has there been another attack?" Jake asked, and it was a great question; the fact that I hadn't thought that Deimos might have attacked Narcissus's club across the river made me realize I was drunk on the magic.

"What do you mean, another attack?" Custer asked, and both men suddenly looked wide awake. The new guy even glanced back to where they had been sleeping and the majority of their weapons would still be. I didn't have to search them to know they'd have at least one gun, maybe a gun and a knife on them, but an attack made them want things that couldn't be hidden under a shirt or tucked down a pair of pants.

"We're safe currently, Jake can fill you in, but we're running out of night to finish this," I said.

"Our Oba told us to stay close to Jean-Claude until he gets here," the new guy said.

"Wait, do you mean Narcissus is coming here tonight?" Richard asked.

"Who's this guy?" New Guy asked. He jerked his thumb at Richard.

"Ulfric," Custer said.

"Nice to meet you, Ulfric, I'm Geoff."

Now I remembered his name was Jeff, but he spelled it *Geoff*, that's why I kept forgetting if his name started with a *J* or a *G*.

"He's *the* Ulfric," Custer said. "I told you all the titles of the local kings. Don't make me look bad in front of three of them."

"I forgot one, sorry."

"Focus, Custer, answer the question—is Narcissus coming here tonight?" I asked.

"Yeah."

"Why?"

"Because Narcissus felt Jean-Claude's power spike earlier tonight. Narcissus is convinced that he's going to pick a second animal to call," Custer said.

"I have already chosen gold tiger for my next *moitié bête*," Jean-Claude said.

"Narcissus told us to stop you from choosing anyone else before he gets here," Geoff said.

"You aren't the boss of any of us," I said.

"I know," Custer said, "hell, we're both your security so it's really awkward that Narcissus told us if we don't interfere he'll take a pound of flesh or two, and it's not a metaphor, Anita."

"Narcissus wants to be sure that the hyenas do not get left out this time," a voice down the hallway added. We turned to find Kane walking toward us.

41

KANE WAS DRESSED in a brown silk robe. It was a nice robe, I knew just how nice, because I'd bought it for Asher one Christmas when we were closer. The color looked warm and just right with Asher's golden hair and the autumn undertones of his pale skin, but the color was all wrong for Kane. His black hair and tanned skin needed something in bright jewel tones like royal blue, or red. If it was possible to make him less attractive to me the color did, and he was wearing a present I'd bought Asher. I tried to think it was an accident, that he'd just grabbed it to cover himself, but the sneer on his face as he stroked his hands down the front of the robe let me know he'd done it on purpose. God, was there anything he ever did that wasn't for spite, or jealousy?

The energy of his beast swirled through the hallway. It hit Custer and he let it flow over and away from him, but Geoff was too inexperienced to resist. His hyena swirled to life, changing Geoff's dark eyes to a paler shade of brown. Their combined energy danced over my skin. The hyena inside me blinked awake, pale brown eyes in the dark. She stepped out into the light so I could admire her spotted coat. Her long face with the slightly floppy ears looked almost comical, but the expression on her face in her eyes was . . . thoughtful, but she wasn't thinking at me, she was thinking about me, or about something. I waited for her energy to rise up and change my own eyes to that shade of pale caramel brown, but it didn't. She sat there patient, waiting, but for what?

It wasn't words, but I still knew that she was waiting for someone worthy. *Worthy of what?* I asked. "Us," she said, or thought, or something I still didn't have a word for. Unlike the lioness that was progressively more frantic to find a male to keep us safe from other lions, the hyena waited for no one to protect her. Female hyenas are bigger than the males; they don't wait for anything bigger to come protect them, they do it themselves.

Geoff dropped to his knees.

"Shut it down, Kane," Custer said.

"You're going to bring his beast," Ethan said.

"I don't care if his beast comes or not."

I looked into the eyes of my hyena. I swore she smiled at me. "My hyena isn't going to rise for you, Kane, never for you." He was weak, too weak to have in our clan. In the wild we'd chase him off or kill him.

"I don't give a shit about your inner bitch." Killing him sounded good.

"He is seeking me, *ma petite*," Jean-Claude said.

I didn't understand at first, and then my hyena sniffed the air. I thought at first she was smelling the other hyenas, but then she "looked" toward Jean-Claude. "You can sense the hyenas, just like you can lion and gold tiger," I said.

"*Oui*, Narcissus seeks to force my choice."

"You've called gold tiger, I'm here," Dev said.

"He still calls hyena, because I can feel it," Kane said.

"It is an embarrassment of riches," Jean-Claude said.

I looked at him. "You can still sense hyena."

"The choice is not finished," he said.

"No," Dev said, "this is mine."

Custer was kneeling by Geoff, telling him to fucking hold on, to not lose his shit. The energy went up a notch as Custer looked at me with hyena eyes in his human face. I waited for my hyena to join the fun, but she just sat there, calm. She really meant it, Kane didn't have enough juice to interest her, not even with Asher's vampire marks upping his energy.

"Enough," Richard said, and his energy filled the air like sunlight flickering through the forest, warm and welcoming. I felt him try to calm the energy in the hallway, but a warm spring walk in the woods wasn't enough to go up against Kane and Asher's power.

Richard's power faded until the only thing in the hallway was hyena. Geoff fell facedown on the floor, the skin of his back rippling and starting to push upward. Custer fell to all fours beside him. His voice was strained so that each syllable came out like he was fighting to still be able to speak. "Can't-hold-it-to-gether." Custer was stronger than this, so why was he losing control? Then I felt it, another vampire's power, and if it was Kane it could only be . . .

Jean-Claude yelled, "Asher, stop this!"

Asher walked down the hallway with his golden hair floating back on either side of his face like from a wind machine in a photo shoot, so that every scar on his face was exposed, but more, he was shirtless, wearing nothing but silk pajama pants. He'd never willingly appear in public showing that much skin, because the scars on the right side of his chest and stomach were so deep they looked like his skin had partially melted in deep runnels, rough waves of flesh frozen forever to remind him of the worst moment of his life. It was as rough to touch as it looked, because I'd explored every inch of it. If he was self-conscious about his face, that was nothing compared to how he felt about the rest of his scars. I'd never seen him expose himself like this willingly. Jean-Claude's thoughts backed me up; centuries and he'd never done this, so what in the fuck was going on?

"If hyena is your new *moitié bête* we will still have something in common after you abandon me for the perfection of your wolf king."

"I would never leave you, *mon chardonneret*."

"Lies!" Asher shouted, and the energy was skin-tingling heat, but it was all coming out of Kane like he was a speaker playing Asher's power over us. Geoff screamed as his face elongated and the ridge of his spine thrust up through his back like a small ridge of skin-covered mountains, and gray and black fur poured over the skin. Custer crab-walked away from him until he hit the wall. "Boss, Geoff is new, not sure how forced change is going to work for him, especially if I can't control him while he shifts."

I yelled, "Asher, one of the werehyenas is too new, he's dangerous when he shifts."

"Let your wolf king protect you!"

Rodina and Ru moved between us and the werehyenas. Truth joined them; the rest of the security stayed around us.

The power changed slightly; now a different kind of energy was trickling through it like a small stream of safety in an ocean of crazy. Something stirred inside me, blinking blue eyes in the dark. The hyena glanced back but stayed sitting. There was none of the usual hostility to the other beasts, just that continued calmness in the face of Asher's energy. The blue eyes stepped out into the light and it was my gold tiger, cream with stripes of rich yellow. She looked at the hyena, and it was like they acknowledged each other, but there was no hostility, just *I see you, I see you, too, and we are not here to hurt each other today*. The gold energy grew from a trickle to a fast-moving stream, but it was still trying to pour itself into the ocean. Dev took my hand in his, and I knew where the stream was coming from. Ethan came to kneel beside me; I thought he was getting between me and the hyenas struggling to hold their human form, but he touched my hand and it was as if he gave his power over to Dev, and I was just the conduit between them, and the power that flowed from him to me matched the new power that was trying to chase back what Asher and Kane were doing. I looked up and found that Ethan's eyes had changed to hazel blue, his gold tiger looking out at me. My tigress started walking up the path; she looked back at the hyena as if waiting for her to protest, but the hyena just sat there with the almost-grin on her face. Asher had no energy she wanted; it wasn't that he lacked power in this moment, but that she chose not to accept it. Female hyenas choose their mates always; there is no force possible for spotted hyenas, only shared pleasure. Kane would never be a pleasure and as far as she was concerned neither would Asher.

Jean-Claude said, *"Ma petite,"* and stroked his hand just above my skin and Ethan's, and Dev's. My gold tigress rubbed up against some invisible point as if she were trying to rub up against something I couldn't see. Then I realized she was reacting to Jean-Claude's stroking just above our skin. Ethan started to rest his head on the vampire's shoulder, then caught himself.

Jean-Claude curved his hand around the side of Ethan's face and the moment he touched him there the stream of new energy got bigger. Jean-Claude helped the weretiger to lay his head on his shoulder. Ethan took that as an invitation and rubbed his face against Jean-Claude's like a cat scent-marking. Richard came closer, but it was too late for wolf. Jean-Claude touched my shoulder and there was another leap in the energy. My tigress flopped on her side the way that real-world female cats do when they're in the mood. She rolled around on the ground in invitation, but only I could see it.

I traced my hand up Jean-Claude's chest where the blood was starting to dry; the blade hadn't been silver and the wounds had closed. Jean-Claude reached for Dev, and the moment they touched directly, the tiger energy was stronger, the stream overrunning its banks, but the ocean of hyena energy still filled the hallway, because Kane was a full *moitié bête* of a master vampire and Dev was not. He was mine, but in this moment I understood why my tie to Nathaniel was stronger than any of my other animals to call, because Damian was with us, had been with us from the beginning. To truly make this work you needed a real vampire, not the in between that I had become.

"But I'm part of a real triumvirate now," Richard said, "why is my power less than Dev's even before Jean-Claude marks him?"

"I've been trained to work energy since I was small," Dev said.

"Dev was the best magic worker of his generation," Jake said.

"Then why hasn't he shown this level of power before?" Richard asked.

"Because Anita didn't have the fourth mark from Jean-Claude before; as your master grows in power, so do you," Jake said.

"Think what I'll be able to do once Jean-Claude marks me himself."

"You will be nothing!" Kane shouted.

"I am sorry that you are the one who will suffer here, Dev, but I will not lose Jean-Claude to Richard, not if I can hold him to me with shared power," Asher said, coming closer down the hallway until he stood just behind Kane.

Dev kissed the healed wound on Jean-Claude's chest like a promise for later, touched Ethan's hair, and kissed me on the mouth, before he stood up and faced them. "You talk about losing Jean-Claude to Richard's perfection, but I'm as beautiful as he is, and as unscarred. Why do you never fear losing Jean-Claude to me? Why do you never see me as a threat for Anita, or for Nathaniel? You call him your flower-eyed boy, but he is with me more than you. I sleep in Jean-Claude's bed almost every day. I sleep on the other side of your flower-eyed boy from Anita, or beside Jean-Claude himself day after day. Richard has not been in that bed to sleep or for anything else in years, but yet you still think that Jean-Claude would leave you for him."

"I think he would leave us all for him, except Anita."

Jean-Claude pushed away from the wall and stood with my hand still in his. Ethan stayed close to us. I realized I didn't know where Angel was; she must have left sometime during the fourth mark when the only thing I could see was Jean-Claude's chest and Richard beside me. Richard came to stand behind us, putting his hand on Jean-Claude's shoulder.

"See, see, already they are a threesome again; if the rumors are true and the Ulfric fucked him at last, then they will be complete without the rest of us," Asher said.

Jean-Claude made an exasperated sound and said, "Asher, we are polyamorous, we add to our poly group, we do not have to give up anyone."

"Yet there you stand, just the three of you as of old."

Jean-Claude reached his hand out to Dev, who took it, and Dev's power deepened like a river that could threaten an ocean. "Mephistopheles is our handsome devil, we could not do without him in our lives and in our bed."

"Where will he sleep now that the Ulfric is back?"

"Tonight he will sleep on the other side of the bed at Nathaniel's back with Anita between us."

"And when Micah Callahan returns from his business trip and takes his spot at Nathaniel's back, where will Dev be then? The Ulfric will be at your back, Jean-Claude, in the place that Dev sleeps when Micah is in your bed."

I felt Dev's power falter, the doubts hitting home. Kane cackled that hyena sound that raised the hair on the back of my neck. Richard saved it by saying, "I came back to fit into Anita and Jean-Claude's life with no expectations. I'm not going to demand that they kick anyone out of their place for me."

Dev looked back at him. "You mean that?"

"If you sleep with them every night, then you're important to them. What's the word, you and I are *metamours*, because you're the lover of my lovers. You were here for them when I was off getting my doctorate and working on my issues. I want a place in their life, but that doesn't supplant your place, or anyone else's place in their lives." Dev smiled at him, and the tiger energy pulsed back to life.

"Where will you sleep when Micah comes back?" Dev asked.

"I don't know, I don't even know if Micah would be okay with me sleeping in the same bed with him even if we slept as far away from each other as we could get."

"When we go to bed tonight, Dev, you will be on the other side of Anita with your arm tucked over both of us," Nathaniel said.

Jean-Claude raised Dev's hand and kissed it. "We could not do without our devil."

"You will be cast out, and after defying Asher like this, you will not be welcome in our bed again," Kane yelled.

"That is not for you to say, Kane. I am your master and I say who joins us, not you."

Kane looked back at him, and it was their energy that faltered now. "You don't need him when you have me. He fills no needs that I cannot fill."

"He is Dev and you are not, that is need enough. I do not have to justify it to you," Asher said.

"As I do not have to justify my actions as ruler here," Jean-Claude said. "You cannot hold me hostage for Narcissus, or for yourself, Asher." He drew Dev into him, so they faced each other. "I have made my choice for my next animal to call and it is not hyena."

"No!" Kane yelled; the hyena power spiked and then began to bleed away as if the entire ocean was drying up in the sunlight. Asher was crying, the tears tinted pink with blood, shining like pale rubies in the hallway lights. He was done fighting and had moved on to sorrow. I guess it was an improvement.

"I missed you, too, Asher," Richard said.

The vampire blinked and stared at him. "What did you say?"

"I missed topping you in the dungeon, so much."

"No, no, Asher doesn't need that anymore, not from you, he has Narcissus and Anita and Nathaniel," Kane said.

"I top all of them, I do not bottom to him."

"What does it matter? It's still bondage, you still get the need met," Kane said.

"Topping and bottoming are very different needs," I said.

"Shut up! I'm not talking to you!"

"You will keep a civil tongue in your head toward my queen, or I will tear it from your head and let you wait in silence for it to grow back," Jean-Claude said.

I looked at the love of my life and thought, *Damn, that was a very specific and disturbing threat.* "We have tried kindness for Asher's sake, *ma petite*, but no more."

"If I can have some security to make sure we don't hurt each other too badly, I'll handle this end of the hallway; you mark Dev before sunrise," Richard said.

"I will go with him," Jake said.

"I wish I could," Custer said, "but Asher controls hyena in a way that you don't control wolves, Jean-Claude."

"You and Geoff stay away from Asher until we fix this," I said.

"You're a great boss," he said, smiling and looking at me as if I wasn't still standing buck naked. When he first arrived he'd stared at the female shapeshifters, but he'd acclimated. Geoff was just looking at the ceiling as he added his thanks. That was okay, it had taken years for me to get used to all the nudity.

"We'll go," Rodina said, and she and Ru followed Jake and Richard down the hallway.

Richard said, "I want to flog you while you're tied up and I want to feel you lust after me and deny you."

"See, he will only fuck Jean-Claude, no other man, or even you," Kane said.

"I want to fuck you, Asher, but I want to come up with a bondage scene that will be everything you and I want it to be."

"No!" Kane yelled, and there was movement, but Jake was there and Kane was just suddenly face first against the wall with his arm twisted up behind him. "I will break it," Jake said in a voice that carried.

Kane yelled for Asher to help him, but his vampire master was talking with Richard and I knew now why Asher feared Richard stealing Jean-Claude away from him and no one else, because Asher wanted Richard, too.

I felt the sun start to rise like a blow through my heart. Jean-Claude clutched my hand. "Moments only," he said.

"Make me yours," Dev said, leaning over to put his mouth on one of the healing wounds.

"Do it," I said.

"I will collapse unwashed and dead if I can finish it at all."

"We'll go to bed smelling like great sex, and we'll carry you to bed, do it now."

Dev sucked hard enough that it brought a gasp from Jean-Claude, but it wasn't a bad sound. He touched his free hand to Dev's blond hair and said the words with my hand in his, so that it was the same as he'd said over Richard and me, down to the *three shall be as one*. And with each sentence the power grew until the last of the hyena energy was blown away in a warm rush of gold tiger energy that seemed to greet the sunrise that I could feel spreading above us.

Truth and Wicked dropped in the hallway. I heard a sound and glanced to see Richard catch Asher before he hit the floor. I still had Jean-Claude's hand in mine, and he was still holding me tight.

Dev rose up with Jean-Claude's blood smeared on his mouth. "You're still awake," Dev said.

"The energy buoys me up, but it will not last, I think, so kiss me, my devil, with my blood across your lips." He didn't have to ask twice. They wrapped their arms around each other and kissed like they meant it, until Dev came back with fresh blood on his lower lip from getting nicked on a fang.

"Forgive me, I was carried away," Jean-Claude said.

Dev's tongue slid over the blood, and he smiled fierce and so happy, maybe happier than I'd ever felt him. "I'm not sorry, I love that you lost control with me the way you can with Anita."

Jean-Claude smiled at Dev and took his hand as he still had mine. "Take me to bed before the magic leaves and I die again."

Richard turned toward us with Asher insensible in his arms. "Does he sleep in his coffin, or in a bed now?"

"He sleeps with me!" Kane yelled, still up against the wall with Jake holding him in place.

"Take Kane to a cell tonight and guard him well. No harm shall befall him tonight, but if a night imprisoned teaches him nothing there will be time for punishment," Jean-Claude said.

Jake turned Kane around and marched him deeper into the underground. We didn't exactly have cells, but we had guest rooms that were more easily guarded than others. Kane ranted and raved that Asher would hear about this, but we ignored him. It was pretty much the only logical thing to do with him.

Angel came down the hallway as Jake was leading them away. She'd brought the other gold tigers with her. They were all tall and golden- to brown-skinned with varying shades of blond hair and eyes ranging from blue to hazel blue to pale brown. "I thought we'd need help; I guess I was wrong."

"Your help is much appreciated, our angel," Jean-Claude said.

"We can at least take Wicked and Truth to their room," she said.

"Thanks," I said. She smiled at me, then both of us. Her smile melted a little around the edges when she got to Richard, but she said, "Tucking two gorgeous vampires into bed, no problem."

"Where do I take Asher?" Richard asked again.

"I want you with me, *mon lupe*. When I finally die for the day I want to feel you at my back."

Richard handed Asher to Custer to carry. I sent Geoff with him to tuck Asher into his coffin for the day. That was where he preferred to sleep when he would wake up alone. Nathaniel came up the hallway in the wrong direction. Apparently he and Damian had gone through while I was otherwise occupied, just like Angel leaving. "Why didn't you help?"

"Damian likes to be in his room before dawn, and you didn't need your leopard and another vampire you were connected to, this had to be all about you and Jean-Claude and other animals to call." I couldn't argue with him, but I did ask if I'd missed anything else while I was pressed to Jean-Claude's chest. Everyone assured me that was it.

We got to our bedroom with its orgy-sized custom-made bed. We did the cleanup that washrags and toothbrushes could manage, and then we all crawled into bed. I was in the middle, Jean-Claude beside me, though usually Micah or Nathaniel slept between Jean-Claude and me. I still didn't like that he truly died and then his body would cool during the hours we slept, but tonight I wanted to feel him pressed against me as his life slipped away, so he'd feel me holding him as the last thing. I curled up in the circle of his naked body, still warm and alive as he wrapped his arms around me. Nathaniel spooned on the other side of me and Jean-Claude's arms went across me to him, and then Dev spooned on the other side of Nathaniel so that our arms overlapped and held each other. Jean-Claude's arms were long enough that his hand touched Dev.

Nathaniel was already asleep by the time Richard came out of the bathroom. He hadn't brought any pajamas, so he was as nude as the rest of us as he left the bathroom door slightly ajar like a nightlight. He'd remembered, that was nice.

Dev tensed watching him walk around the room. The bed moved as he climbed in bed behind Jean-Claude. I heard my vampire fiancé make a small contented sound and then Richard's arm was over him and touching me. Richard's hand tensed, started to move, but I moved my hand so I could press his hand back on my side. I patted his hand and felt the tension leave his hand and arm. I put my arm back over Nathaniel and Dev, who reached up to touch my hand as if for reassurance. I wasn't sure I could keep everyone out of my head, but I thought at him how happy I was to feel him on the other side of Nathaniel and how proud I was to call him my golden tiger, and my lover. He raised my hand and kissed my fingertips, which were about all he could reach without moving everyone.

Jean-Claude stroked his hand along Dev's side under the silky sheets. Nathaniel snuggled lower in his sleep, and then Jean-Claude died. I felt him leave, heard the pained sound he usually made when it happened. Richard moved closer on the other side of him, holding him in place. I did the same on my side, so we held him as close as we could. We would hold him that way all day as we slept, and when he woke we were both there to see him smile up at us. Nathaniel and Dev kissed him, kissed me, then gave us the room, because the first time waking up together after such a long time apart needed to be just us. We started by cleaning up in Jean-Claude's huge tub with its mirrored walls, but we didn't end there. We ended on the bed in the silk sheets with our hair still wet, which is very bad for silk, but there would be other sheets to buy, and there would never be another first time for the three of us to wake up together and remind ourselves why we'd tried to love each other ten years ago, and why we'd failed, and why this time we just might succeed.

The wedding of the century is imminent for Anita Blake but first she must overcome the biggest obstacle of all: her family.
Read more for an exclusive sneak peek at

SLAY

the next Anita Blake novel.

I WAS STANDING at the arrival area for the A gates at St. Louis Lambert International Airport trying to see through the continuing crowds of people that kept spilling out past the TSA agent sitting at the little lectern. Arriving passengers had been streaming past the roped-off lines of other passengers waiting in line to go through security and depart. None of them had been my family, either coming or going. I was nervous, which made me want to touch the gun at my waist, but since I was carrying concealed and people tend to panic if you flash in the airport these days, I resisted the urge. Flashing the gun would have flashed my U.S. Marshal badge, too, but I'd found that people who wanted to freak about the gun never seemed to see the badge clipped next to it. I really didn't want my dad and stepmom's first glimpse of me in eight years to be kneeling on the floor with my fingers laced behind my head while some newbie from Metro police was yelling at me to comply. I was also really beginning to regret the high, spiked heels. They took me from five-three to five-seven and made my legs look long and shapely, and looked amazing with my short swishy skirt, but the heels weren't made for standing around in the airport on hard tile floors. Walking was fine in them, I'd even been learning to dance in heels this high as we

looked at possible footwear for the wedding, but standing was beginning to hurt.

"You're actually scared," Nicky said beside me. He stood like a
friendly, blond mountain, so muscled that he'd had to get his leather
jacket custom tailored to fit over his upper body. The jeans he had
gotten from a bodybuilder site, but he'd wanted a jacket that could
cover carrying concealed and for that he'd had to buy from a site that
catered to athletic men and even then he'd had to find an in-town
tailor. He wasn't nervous and reaching for his gun like a dangerous
comfort object. He was standing cool and calm, keeping an eye on
the crowd and the customers who went into the little store against
the opposite wall. I caught a glimpse of a slender figure picking up a
magazine from the rack near the entrance to the store. They were
wearing an oversized hoodie, nondescript jeans, and jogging shoes.
They looked like a dozen teens to twenties that had passed by us, so
why had they caught my attention? I tensed, trying to feel if it was a
vampire, or something else supernatural that wasn't on our side, and
then Ru turned around so I could see his face and a bit of his short
blond hair. His bored why-did-my-parents-make-me-come-here expression never changed, but his startling dark eyes looked into mine.
He was part of my security tonight. He and his sister, Rodina. I
hadn't even caught a glimpse of her yet; then I realized that Ru had
done something small on purpose so I'd look at him. He was still
undercover, but he wanted me to see him, so I'd feel better. Seeing
him helped me feel better about Deimos, the ancient vampire who
had come to town recently and attacked us. We'd almost canceled
my family's visit, but after the one attempt Deimos had left us alone.
We were hoping he'd found us too powerful and just gone back into
hiding. We'd delayed my family's visit for weeks, but when we
couldn't find him, and he didn't try to find us again, we finally had
to move forward with fitting my dad for his outfit if he was giving
me away. Since he was very Catholic and I was marrying a vampire,
that was still up for debate. Hell, my family was only now agreeing

to meet Jean-Claude. They might not even be coming to our wedding.

Ru turned away, putting the magazine back and sighing so heavily that his body language said just how bored he was with the magazine, being in the airport, waiting for some stupid relative, or . . . I had no idea how he and all the Harlequin did it, but they were some of the best covert operatives in the world, maybe the best, I hadn't met enough covert-ops people to judge.

I looked at Nicky. "I was going to say, I was not scared-scared, maybe nervous enough that it's a type of fear, but if Ru broke cover to try and reassure me, he's picking up on more than just nerves."

"The three of us can feel it, Anita, it's more than just nerves."

I frowned up at him and in the five-inch heels I was five-eight, only a few inches shorter than him, so I didn't have to strain my neck. I almost said what most of us say: *Aren't you scared of your family?* Most people say it as an offhand remark, a joke almost, but Nicky looked down at me with his one blue eye, and an eye patch where the other eye should have been. I wouldn't joke with Nicky about scary families because his mom was still in prison for what she'd done to him and his siblings. My family had its problems, and some of them had screwed me up pretty bad, but compared to Nicky's childhood mine had been a cakewalk on *Sesame Street.*

"I don't think I'm afraid of my family," I said, shifting my weight again in the heels; they'd been a mistake, but I looked fabulous in them, and my family made me insecure enough to want to look fabulous. Nicky gave me a look that said plainly he didn't believe me, but I believed me, so it was okay.

Was I really afraid of my very Catholic family meeting Jean-Claude for the first time? I ran my fingers down the pleats of my skirt. I was regretting it like the heels. The skirt was short, which made my legs look long and beautiful, according to the loves of my life. I wasn't usually a pleat kind of girl, but it made the skirt swing as I moved, and it was the nicest skirt I had that wasn't skintight.

Somehow skintight and short wasn't a meet-the-family outfit. So, pleats with a royal-blue silk shell blouse that matched the blue in the plaid of the skirt. The short bolero jacket was black, which matched the rest of the color in the plaid. The jacket didn't quite hide the badge clipped to my waistband but did hide the gun that was in an inner "pants" holster just behind the badge, and the extra magazine/ammo holders on the other side of the skirt. I had a tailor who reinforced all the waistbands on my girlier clothes, otherwise the skirt would never have held up to this much equipment.

I was even in full makeup, which I almost never wore. I looked like I was ready for a hot date instead of seeing my family for the first time in years. I knew why I had dressed up and thanks to being metaphysically connected to Nicky and other people in my life, they knew, too. I'd been prepared to see my dad and stepmother, Judith, to discuss if he was walking me down the aisle or if they were even coming to my wedding, but I hadn't expected that my stepsister Andria would be coming with them. She and I were both over thirty. She was a lawyer, and I was what I was; she was even engaged to another lawyer. Of course she'd get engaged if I was engaged. I couldn't beat Andria at anything that mattered to my family.

Andria was the girly one. The perfect blond, blue-eyed, straight-A student. She was even tall like her mother. I got good grades, but not as good. People told me I was pretty when I cleaned up or wore makeup or dressed nice. She was always dressed up, always perfect. She had a sense of style and what clothes matched and flattered her that only dating Jean-Claude had taught me. Fashion was neither natural nor a strength for me and I found the fact that Jean-Claude didn't have any comfy clothes disturbing. What kind of person didn't have any sweats, or lounging jammies? He had pajamas, but they were all silk and he never slept in them. I wasn't complaining about sleeping in the nude, and silk looked great on him and felt even better next to my skin, but I had old jeans and sweatshirts I'd had since college. I had clothes to do yard work in, or paint something. He didn't. Centuries of being judged constantly by the other vampires so that any sign of weakness was used against him and using his beauty to survive had made him always be on, always aware, like some wandering photographer would come by at any second. To me it would have been a terrible pressure; to Jean-Claude it was normal. Dressing up made him feel better. It had taken me a long time to realize that fashion was part of what made him feel comfortable. Dressing up was his comfy clothes somehow. I knew that now and accepted it, but it would never be my version of comfy. I wanted my clothes to cover me and to serve a purpose. Today's purpose was to be the beautiful swan instead of the ugly duckling. Sad but true that my family's opinion of me still mattered that much to me. I'd really hoped I'd grown past the need for their approval since I was almost certainly not going to get it. I was marrying a vampire; to them I might as well be marrying a demon straight out of hell. If they'd ever met a real demon they'd understand the difference, but they hadn't seen real evil with a capital *E*. They lived in ignorant bliss while people like me risked everything to fight against the forces of evil, so they could come here and be self-righteous and tell me I was corrupt and going to hell.

I caught a glimpse through the crowd of people coming our way. Did I recognize that blond head? Was that them? My stomach clenched tight, my pulse racing into my throat so it was hard to breathe. Was Nicky right, was I actually afraid of my family? That was ridiculous, they'd never laid a hand on me in violence, well no one who was coming on this visit. It wasn't like Nicky's past, or Nathaniel's. Nothing that violent or monstrous. The relief when I realized the people were strangers was huge. Damn it, my dad wasn't that bad.

There was a lull in the passengers going past us, I guess they were between planes or something. Only a handful of people were in line to go through security. Ru had vanished again, though I don't know how. I didn't look around for him because like concealed carry, if you mess with undercover people you draw attention to them. The long hallway that my family would be coming down sometime soon stretched empty until you got to the bored TSA security person at their small lectern. They were the one who would tell people you've crossed the line and can't go back.

Nicky leaned over me and spoke low for just me as people rushed past to make their planes, "It's not a game of who had the suckiest childhood, Anita. It's okay to be afraid and to feel fucking traumatized if that's how you feel."

I stared up at him, his face so close to mine. "But I wasn't traumatized," I said.

"Your lips say that, but your pulse rate and the sweat on your palms and down your spine say different."

"Can't hide anything from a shapeshifter," I whispered.

He grinned and said, "Therianthrope, or didn't you get the new vocabulary memo about using a more inclusive term for lycanthropes and other shapeshifters?"

It made me smile like he knew it would. "You don't give a damn about politically correct vocabulary."

He smiled down at me, his face so close it filled my vision. "Not a damn bit."

"You're always telling me you can't bodyguard and kiss in public," I said.

"I think we're safe unless someone runs into us with a roller bag," he said, and moved in for a kiss, and I helped him lay his lips against mine. I was wearing bright red lipstick and full-on base makeup, so we had to behave ourselves, because if we smeared it I didn't have the makeup with me to fix it. Usually I don't do base, so I just clean off the lipstick and then reapply. No muss, no fuss, but I didn't have the products or the skill to fix clown makeup lipstick if we got carried away today. It was one of the most careful kisses Nicky and I had ever shared. He pulled back with a line of red down the middle of his lips. Some of the men in my life had coined the phrase *the go-faster stripe*. Couldn't really argue, so I hadn't.

Nicky smiled and whispered, "Zoom, zoom."

I giggled, which I almost never did. "You read my thoughts."

"Part of my job," he said. He wasn't wrong. He whispered, "I'm your Bride, you're supposed to fuck us, throw us at your enemies so we delay them and allow you to escape. You're not supposed to keep us around this long, and you're definitely not supposed to fall in love with us."

"I guess if I'd been a vampire I'd have known the rules," I said.

"Necromancers, all the vampire powers, none of the downsides," he said, smiling.

"Not all the powers," I said, smiling up at him, and somehow we were holding hands while I gazed up at him, far too romantic for public when my face had been plastered all over the place in connection to Jean-Claude. Not long ago the internet rumors had me dumping Jean-Claude and running away with Nicky. It had gotten so bad he'd had to stop being my main bodyguard, but then Deimos attacked and I'd wished for Nicky that night, so screw it, safety first. The public and the press knew we were all polyamorous and in a larger-than-normal poly group, but knowing Jean-Claude and I both had other lovers, some shared, some not, didn't stop outsiders from defaulting to monogamy rules and trying to apply them to us. One gossip site had posted pictures of Jean-Claude with Angel, one of our shared girlfriends, on his arm for a public event. I'd been serving a warrant of execution in a different state, and the rumor mill had him dumping me for her.

We broke the kiss and turned to see a group of younger women either high school or early college age texting busily on their phones. Shit. They'd post it to social media before I could collect my family from the plane and flee. It wasn't Deimos I was afraid of finding us but various hate groups or media. The first-ever vampire king of America was getting married to one of the U.S. Marshals with the Preternatural Branch, which meant he was marrying someone who hunted down and executed rogue vampires and shapeshifters, or any other supernatural citizen that started piling up a body count. But I wasn't any preternatural marshal, I was the Executioner, I was War. The first was a nickname the vampires had given me back when I still believed sincerely that I would never, ever date a vampire, but the second nickname the other marshals had given me. It was a play on the Four Horsemen of the Apocalypse; I was War because I had the highest legal kill count of any marshal. If they'd only known that my best man, Marshal Ted Forrester, aka Death, had a much higher count if all his kills were counted, but Edward wouldn't tell and neither would I. Marshals Bernardo Spotted-Horse and Otto Jeffries were Hunger and Plague respectively. They knew Edward's background, too, but since they had secrets of their own they weren't talking either.

Nicky took a Kleenex out of his pocket and started wiping at his mouth to get off the go-faster stripe. "Let's not confuse your family."

"They know I'm poly," I said.

"Knowing it and being able to deal with it aren't the same thing," he said.

He had a point, so I let him wipe my lipstick away and reassure me my lipstick still looked perfect. Another big group of people started down the hallway's slight curve toward the TSA check desk. I caught a glimpse of very blond hair again, but this time when the crowd parted it was my dad. He hadn't seen me yet. His face was neutral just walking. He was five-eight, still trim, and looked, well . . . like my father. He was wearing khaki slacks with a blue polo shirt, and some sort of jacket unzipped. Even his wardrobe was the same. He looked like he always did, always had; part of me was relieved and part of me resented it. I don't know why that last part. We hadn't seen each other in eight years. He turned his head to speak with someone and I caught a flash of pink. The crowd thinned as people passed us with their bags. My stepmother, Judith, was with him, tall, slender, smiling. It wasn't unexpected. I'd known she'd be here, but my stomach knotted anyway. What I could see of her bright blond hair was fastened back with a bright pink scarf or head-band. The hair was smooth and styled and perfect. Her makeup would be the same. She was wearing a pink designer sweatshirt, I couldn't see what else, and then I realized she had a pink shadow with her. It was Andria in a matching outfit, with her own straight blond hair tied back with a pink band. They'd done matching outfits a lot when we were younger. Mother-daughter outfits in pastels, which I looked terrible in but made both of them look great. I'd protested the outfits until Judith stopped including me in the mix; I was about eleven. I hadn't wanted to be excluded since Judith was now the only chance for a mother that I had, I just hadn't wanted to wear pink.

Nicky moved me behind him automatically as some other passengers almost bumped me. It hadn't been on purpose, but he was officially my bodyguard, so I let him do his job. The hate groups had gotten worse as the wedding got closer; they didn't want us to have a happily-ever-after ending, monogamous or otherwise.

My father's face lit up when he saw me; he looked genuinely happy to see me, which was great, because that hadn't been a given. It made me smile back and wave. He waved and then they were there with us. He hugged me with enthusiasm, and I did the same, and then his hand found the gun at my belt, and he tensed, unsure where to put his hands, so he pulled away awkwardly. He hadn't been a fan of his little girl working with the police, let alone becoming one, too dangerous.

Judith hugged me next, and it had enthusiasm to it, too, which caught me completely off guard since she stopped hugging me about the time I turned twelve. She kept her arms around my shoulders so there were no gun issues. "Anita, it's so good to see you again. You look great!"

Andria said, "Seriously perfect outfit." She didn't seem upset that I was better dressed than she was, which spoiled it for me a little. I'd wanted to be the best-dressed for once, but I'd wanted her to feel bad

about it even more. Yes, it was petty, but at least I acknowledged my
motives instead of hiding from them now.

"Thanks, you both look cute and comfy for the plane."

They put their arms around each other, heads together like they
were posing for a camera. "It's been so long since we did mother-
daughter outfits I couldn't resist," Judith said. They then both
showed their white athletic shoes with bright white and pink spar-
kles on them like they'd been bedazzled, but I knew they'd come that
way. I also knew they'd paid around three to four hundred dollars
for each pair. I'd seen them at one of the stores where I'd done emergency shopping for my outfit. I'd paid that much for shoes, or Jean-
Claude had paid that much for shoes he wanted to see me in, but
nothing quite like these.

Dad held his hand out to Nicky and said, "Are you Micah or Nathaniel?" Neither of them look anything like Nicky, which meant
my dad hadn't even bothered to google me.

"Fredrick," Judith said, "Micah Callahan is on the news all the
time and he looks nothing like this gentleman." She offered her
hand. After the slightest hesitation Nicky took the offered hand. Her
hand was big enough to match his, and she'd always given firm hand-
shakes.

"Then this must be Nathaniel Graison?" my father said, smiling
and looking relieved like he was getting his feet under him in the
conversation.

Judith and Andria laughed together. It was a very we've-got-a-
secret-you-don't-know laugh. It was usually a laugh that women
make when they've just said something dirty about a man in the
room but they don't want to tell him, but somehow they want people to know they're bad girls. I'd never liked that attitude of "safe"
naughtiness that so many American women seemed to adopt. I
started adding the *American* when too many women I knew who
weren't raised here pointed out that it wasn't the same in every country. Either way, I didn't like the laugh or the attitude that went with

it, but maybe I'd spent too many years being on the outside of their girl secrets and I was projecting? I'd keep that as a backup thought. I'd try to be fair.

"Fredrick, darling." She said his name a lot like that, first name and *darling* as if that was his real last name. Sometimes it was an endearment that I'd hoped to feel for someone myself someday, but sometimes it was that sly, condescending tone that seemed to say *Poor men, they just don't understand.*

He looked at her waiting for her to add to the sentence. If he didn't like the unpleasant look on her face, then he hid it, but again maybe I was projecting on the unpleasant part. My therapist and I had talked a lot about this visit and how it was going to be difficult for me to see Judith and Andria, but especially Judith, in a fair light. So fucking true.

"Didn't you look at any of the links Mom sent you about Anita's boyfriends?" Andria asked in that condescending voice that only women and catty gay men seem to have, oh and one other group. Mean girls from about junior high when they start practicing the attitude and running into their twenties to the grave for some women. I had a moment to realize that Judith and Andria were mean girls; the revelation suddenly made my childhood make so much more sense.

Dad looked flustered and then he blushed, so that's where I got it from. "I . . . they weren't links I was comfortable with looking at."

"You sent him the link to Guilty Pleasures, where Brandon dances," I said, trying to keep my face blank as I pictured my incredibly conservative and very straight father looking at a website full of male strippers.

"Such a cute . . . stage name," Judith said with just enough hesitation to let me know she meant something else.

"Oh, Dad," Andria said, rolling her eyes.

My dad blushed harder and didn't make eye contact with anyone. Judith laughed and hugged his arm to her and leaned her perfectly straight hairdo on his shoulder like they were still honey-mooners. It made him smile and lean into her. He loved her still, and maybe she really loved him. I wanted Dad happy after Mom died, and he was once he fell in love with Judith. The fact that his happiness added to my sorrow never seemed to compute for him.

Nicky's hand found my right one and for once I didn't argue with him compromising my gun hand. I needed the handholding more than I needed my gun. If violence broke out around us we'd react, but right now the touch of his hand was the best protection I had to what was happening inside my head and my heart.

"I'm sorry," he said, "for assuming who you would bring to the airport to meet us, Anita. I understand that you are polyamorous as your lifestyle. I just . . . it's hard for me to think about my little girl living like that."

"Living like what, Dad?" I said, and realized that I sounded angry, mean. I didn't want to be like that to him or anyone else. I could be angry, but I didn't want to be a mean anything.

He looked up, giving me the full stare of his perfectly blue eyes. "I'm sorry, Anita."

I wanted to ask sorry about what, but I took a deep breath, squeezed Nicky's hand, and tried not to be childish and still stand up for myself. "Let's start over, Dad. I had planned on easing you into how big our poly group is, but it didn't occur to me that you wouldn't look online and google Micah, Nathaniel, and Jean-Claude. This is Nicky Murdock, he lives with me, and he is part of our poly group."

He offered his hand to Nicky again, as he said, "I know what the vampire looks like. Judith made me watch some of his interviews online."

Nicky took the handshake and very carefully didn't look at me. He knew how I'd feel about Jean-Claude being called *the vampire*.

"His name is Jean-Claude, Dad, not 'the vampire.'"

My father shook his head. "He is a vampire, Anita."

"I'm aware of that," I said.

"I just don't understand how you can want . . . to be with . . . him."

Andria said, "Did you see what he looks like, Dad?"

"He's fabulous, Anita," Judith said, and seemed to mean it. She even wasted a smile on me like we were friends.

I nodded but had to fight to manage a smile, because Judith being friendly was just too weird. "He is fabulous."

"Not that this one isn't a ruggedly handsome hunk," she said, wasting a smile on Nicky. He didn't smile back either. Let's all be sociopaths together; it was the only sane reaction to my family dynamics.

"I never thought you had it in you, Anita," Andria said.

"Had what?" I asked, finally looking at her again.

"Dating such hunky men, you were so terrible with boys when we were growing up."

"You mean I wasn't popular, and you were."

She shrugged her pink-clad shoulders. "You were always so gloomy when we were growing up. No man likes someone with that kind of attitude."

Nicky said, "Anita's bad attitude is what brought us together."

The women looked up at him together like a choreographed movement. They had a lot of body movements that were mirrored; the matching outfits weren't necessary to let you know they were mother and daughter. "Really?" Andria said it like she didn't believe him.

Nicky smiled and it looked like a real smile; it even filled his one blue eye. "Really," he said, voice soft. I didn't need to read his mind to know he was already beginning to think of ways to at least hurt her for real. He was reacting to my dislike of her and that she was being snide to me. I played at being a sociopath, but he was the real deal. Only me having a conscience and sharing mine with him metaphysically had tamed some of his . . . issues.

I wanted to say *No killing my family on this visit*, but didn't think saying it out loud would help smooth things over. He knew it, because he could literally read at least my feelings and a lot of my thoughts and then I realized that it caused all my Brides literal pain for me to be unhappy sometimes. Damn it, I shouldn't have brought Nicky today. He leaned over and whispered into my hair, "I'm supposed to keep you safe, I needed to be here."

I smiled up at him, then heard my name called in a happier tone, "Anita!"

I looked past my family to find a very tall, young blond man that it took me a second to realize was my baby brother. He was in college now and a foot taller than the last time I'd seen him. "Josh!" I said, and went to greet him through the crowd, leaving Nicky behind with the others. He wouldn't hurt them in front of this many witnesses. They couldn't hurt him emotionally because his emotions didn't work that way. Everyone was safe, or so I thought as Josh bent down so we could hug.

Then a voice with a thick accent said, "Anita Katerine, God has sent us to save your immortal soul from damnation."

Josh stiffened and whispered, "I'm sorry."

I turned from him to see an elderly woman who was even shorter than me walking up behind us. I said the only thing I could say. "Hi, Grandma."